CW00506311

Dedicated to my family.

To Rashell
One of the joys in this adventure is the discovery of new friends. Thank you for walking The Paths

PARADOX

Wish You Were(n't) Here?

MAR '19

ANDY SMITHYMAN

BOZ publications

Boz Publications Ltd.
71-75 Shelton Street
Covent Garden
London WC2H 9JQ
United Kingdom

office@bozpublications.com
www.bozpublications.com

First published 2019 by Boz Publications Ltd.

ISBN: 978-1-9164216-0-8

Printed and bound by CPI Group (UK) Ltd, Croydon, CR0 4YY

CONTENTS

Acknowledgements 7
Preface: Memories 9

Stave 1 – Setting The Scene 13
Chapter 1 – The Confession 15
Chapter 2 – Change Agent 21
Chapter 3 – Welcome 27
Chapter 4 – Bah, Humbug 33
Chapter 5 – Them 39
Chapter 6 – Follow 45
Chapter 7 – Aisle 6P. Shelf 7S 51
Chapter 8 – Extracts 57
Chapter 9 – To See Or Not To See 61
Chapter 10 – A Tale Of Two Lives 67
Chapter 11 – Eki 73
Chapter 12 – A Paper Dance 79
Chapter 13 – How It Starts 85

Stave 2 – Before The Decision 91
Chapter 14 – Nowhere 93
Chapter 15 – Trott's Wonderland 97
Chapter 16 – Plastic Bell 103
Chapter 17 – Fancy A Play? 109
Chapter 18 – The Sound Of The Bell 115
Chapter 19 – Scream 119
Chapter 20 – Rumours 125
Chapter 21 – A Dream Within A Dream 131
Chapter 22 – When Seven Is Not Seven 141
Chapter 23 – War, What Is It Good For? 145
Chapter 24 – The Market 149
Chapter 25 – Meet Santiago 155
Chapter 26 – Meet Peccadillo 159
Chapter 27 – Time Is Up 163
Chapter 28 – Now Run 169

Stave 3 – During The Decision 175
Chapter 29 – How The Pillar Came To Be 177
Chapter 30 – Things Have Changed 183
Chapter 31 – The Paths 187

Chapter 32 – Tshilaba 193
Chapter 33 – Mystery Box 199
Chapter 34 – A Strange Path 203
Chapter 35 – Meet The Kids 209
Chapter 36 –Dot-To-Dot 215
Chapter 37 – The Pictures 221
Chapter 38 – Knock. Knock. Who Is There? 225
Chapter 39 – The Boy 231
Chapter 40 – The Whole Board 237
Chapter 41 – Time For Church 243
Chapter 42 – Surprise 247
Chapter 43 – The Magical Mundane 253
Chapter 44 – Game Changer 259
Chapter 45 – The Fourth Path 265
Chapter 46 – The Abandoned Place 271
Chapter 47 – Number Sixteen 277
Chapter 48 – The Magician 283
Chapter 49 – Time For Godot 289
Chapter 50 – And The Story Goes On 295
Chapter 51 – Micawber's Shop 301
Chapter 52 – Order In Chaos 305
Chapter 53 – Pounding The Streets 309
Chapter 54 – Court In Session 315
Chapter 55 – The Cabin 321
Chapter 56 – She 327
Chapter 57 – Many Sides Of The Story 333
Chapter 58 – The Show 339
Chapter 59 – Tristan 345
Chapter 60 – The Two Seats 349
Chapter 61 – Echoes 355
Chapter 62 – The Trick 361
Chapter 63 – The Setup 365
Chapter 64 – It All Comes Tumbling Down 371

Stave 4 – After The Decision 379
Chapter 65 – One Year Later 381
Chapter 66 – The Apple Seed 387
Chapter 67 – All Good Plans 393
Chapter 68 –Witness 397
Chapter 69 – Final Act 401
Chapter 70 –Another Confession 407
Epilogue 409

ACKNOWLEDGEMENTS

To my family who have heard this story many times and shaped its words. I adore the life you are revealing to me.

To the band of dreamers who have helped put this book together. Thank you. The adventure isn't over. That's the beauty of friendship. You can't get rid of me.

To every reader who has stumbled upon this book. Invisible connections but fellow travellers. Maybe one day we will meet. Until then, my gratitude and thanks from afar.

And to The Twins. I finally see you.

I have endeavoured in this Ghostly little book, to raise the Ghost of an Idea, which shall not put my readers out of humour with themselves, with each other, with the season, or with me. May it haunt their houses pleasantly, and no one wish to lay it. Their faithful Friend and Servant,

(Charles Dickens: A Christmas Carol. December, 1843)

PREFACE: MEMORIES

"I almost wish I hadn't gone down that rabbit-hole — and yet — and yet — it's rather curious, you know, this sort of life! I do wonder what can have happened to me! When I used to read fairy-tales, I fancied that kind of thing never happened, and now here I am in the middle of one!"
(Lewis Carroll, Alice's Adventures in Wonderland)

16th October 1843. 7:06pm

MEMORIES.

Kill.

With a twisted smile and a rusty blade.

The cold steel of regret cut into Dickens as he edged closer to the empty grave. He was only thirty-one years old, yet his eyes revealed the abyss of a haunted life. Lurking behind his bloodshot gaze were tales of a childhood that had a front row seat to society's hatred for the poor. He knew what it was like to feel the loving hands of child labour tightly grip his young throat. Lives were disposable. Countless deaths on the factory floor bore witness to the shocking truth. The traffickers always hung around the back door. A child often left those places in a coffin. The only question was which type: one in the ground or one in the heart.

Dickens peered into the dirt-walled abyss.

Memories kill.

But there was one that demanded more than just death.

*****

The old lady kept in the shadows.

Watching the grave. Keeping safe. It took a courageous soul to walk out at night with a skin tone other than white. The recent law against slavery hadn't stopped the violence. Vigilante groups were everywhere.

Her wrinkled hands gripped a bundle of tatty paper. Carefully, she placed it on the ground, positioning it 'just so' to catch Dickens' eye when he turned around. His journey hadn't finished, no matter what he believed.

That memory had a few more tricks to play out.

*****

18th December 1843. 11:32pm

"More time."

Was there such a thing?

Dickens scrambled down the midnight streets. In the distance he could hear the faint rumble of applause. It was quieter this time. A chill ran down his spine. It couldn't end like this. He turned around and checked no one was following. The lanes looked empty, but he knew he wasn't alone.

They were out there.

Watching. Searching. For him? No. Dickens' grip tightened around the bundle of papers. He needed to get to the one place that would keep *them* safe.

*****

11:59pm

The old lady pulled up the collar of her coat.

It was cold tonight.

A shadow caught her eye, moving closer to the library. Another one lingered by the door. *They* were here. Just as she expected. She moved back a few steps, pressing her body against the trunk of a tree. Dickens had been a long time in there. No doubt he was still struggling to work out the best place to hide his journal. She let out a prolonged sigh, but not too loud to spark attention. How many times had she seen people do that over the years? The journals never remain hidden.

That was the beauty of stories.

When one chapter ends, another one begins.

One hundred and seventy years. Then a few more.

That tatty bundle of paper stayed within the London Library.

Always hidden. Always found.

Always watched from the shadows by the old lady.

STAVE 1
SETTING THE SCENE

CHAPTER 1
THE CONFESSION

"Eventually we all have to accept full and total responsibility for our actions, everything we have done, and have not done."
(Hubert Selby Jr., Requiem for a Dream)

16th October. Present Day. 7:54am

MY NAME is Samuel Abrahams and this is my confession.

I am a fake. A well-seasoned imitation who's forgotten the signal to walk away from the con. To the onlooker, I am a champion for social justice. A writer who gives voice to the downtrodden and forgotten. In reality, I am the nightmare to any author's dream with my words up for sale to the pimp of my selfish greed.

I shamefully live off the spoils from telling tales about poverty and pain, while the heroes in my books struggle to find enough food to get through the day. But to think my words are just about the money does this living curse an injustice. The book covers that hang on my wall reveal the devastating truth: I want my life to mean something.

In my early thirties, I tried my hand at writing. The first novel did what any virgin author would dream of achieving. It became a bestseller. Against all the odds, the manuscript landed in the right hands at the right time. I swore blind I would keep true to myself, but the party of self-importance was too hard to pass up. The indulgent celebration lasted a year before the public turned off the lights.

My next two books flopped. Agents passed me around like a hand-me-down jumper. The failure had an upside though. Reality check. The wilderness years gave me a chance to find my moral roots again. A writer for the people, not for selfish gain. What I didn't count on was how much I hated the dusty landscape. There was only one thing on my mind.

A comeback.

The fourth book outshone my virgin work. Reviewers loved how the desert plains of rejection strengthened my voice. I never corrected them. Why should I? In a way they were right. It brought out the real 'me', but I hated the person who had shown up. If the secret behind how I landed the story ever came out, my world would come crashing down like a house of cards. To ease the conscience, my mind constructed a room down the long dark corridor of forgotten shame. I locked up the memory. Threw away the key. I never wanted to face the temptation to step inside that God-forsaken place. Within those shadows lived a darkness that could never see the light.

The plan worked.

For a time.

Until someone found the key and opened the door.

All it took was an envelope, delivered during breakfast.

I recognised the handwriting straight away. It should have gone into the bin, just like all the other times. But the untamed beast of curiosity opened its blood-stained mouth as I pulled out the two items. The stench of rotting memories gushed from the beast's stomach as I pushed the unread letter to one side. It was the second item that seized me in its teeth. Every part of me was held transfixed to the postcard's facsimile illustration.

That image had a backstory.

My secret.

I touched the card, checking it was real. My finger traced the outline of the picture. It was a scene from *A Christmas Carol*. Harmless on the surface, but looks can be deceiving. The dark lines within that image painted a scene of something I had worked hard to forget. Already I could feel its ink weaving its way down the corridor of my mind. The thick, sludgy liquid of guilt seeped into every crack and crevice of my defensive wall. It was looking for an opening, relishing the opportunity to expose the darkest part of my illegitimate success. I watched in horror as liquid fingers, holding a key, slowly emerged from the pool of ink. My mind screamed out for mercy, but the pitiful cry served only as enjoyment for the dripping, torturous hand. It paused for a few seconds, letting the realisation of the moment sink in.

There was no such thing as a secret.

Just a delay of the truth.

And now it was time to face its judgement call.

*****

The door opened.

Inside the room, only darkness.

This place had been off limits for me, decorated from floor to ceiling in tormenting shame. But I still felt the tug to step inside. *'Curiouser and curiouser.'* Was this how Alice fell down the rabbit hole?

One step. Two. Pause. Indecision.

My left hand rubbed up against the wall. The velvet touch was familiar. I lingered in the darkness, trying to recall why I had such a strong sense of *déjà vu*. A nervous chill ran across my skin. Something lingered within the shadows. Calling me, urging me to step further inside. Under my tentative steps I could feel the sodden carpet of ink. Small bubbles of air popped with every move. There was a damp smell lingering in the air. My secret room had fallen upon hard times. Through squinted eyes I tried to get my bearings. At first I thought I was in a hall, but then felt the gentle incline of the floor. In the shadows I could see the outlines of chairs, row upon row. Next to them, a walkway, leading to a stage.

"A theatre?"

The words left my lips quieter than a whisper. Confusion stopped me shouting. Fear softened my voice. This place was sacred – a perverted form of holiness that would kill anyone who dared go up against it. Whatever curiosity dragged me in had now drained away. I wanted to leave. But where was the door?

I spun around.

"Who's there?"

The deafening silence held my feet to the floor, but I knew I wasn't alone. Out of nowhere, from everywhere, a slow, wheezing breath echoed around the room. In. Out. In. Out. I could feel unseen eyes staring right back at me from the shadows. Its hidden gaze was scrutinising every part of my body. Checking, double checking that it was really me. The wheezing breath intensified as an invisible hand pushed me into a chair. The worn-out fabric welcomed me with a loving embrace. There was a part of me that wanted to

fall deeper
into its arms. An-
other part feared what
would come next.

“What are you doing here?”

The drawn out male voice brought back every childhood nightmare of the shadow in the closet. It was neither friend nor foe, gentle nor angry. An unknown tone, waiting to show its teeth.

“Answer me! Why are you here?”

Like some twisted version of Dorothy wishing there was no

place like home, I clicked the heels of my mind, begging this horror show to end. All I wanted was to be back at my kitchen table holding a coffee cup of safety. I closed my eyes as tight as I could, picturing everything I had considered mundane. The fridge. A chair. The temperamental kettle and overpriced toaster. Everything around, slowed down. The wheezing faded away. I was alone.

Silence.

My nose twitched with the aroma of fresh ground beans. I was back home, but nothing felt normal. In front of me was the postcard, my fingers still touching the outline of *That* image. It had taken me somewhere. Somewhere dark.

I needed answers. But from where?

One place.

The coffee cup remained untouched. Before turning the handle of the front door, I looked back towards the kitchen table. Next to the card was the unread letter from a woman I'd worked hard to forget. I knew it was tempting fate to leave it there. Moments later, the kitchen bin welcomed a new tenant.

There are some memories that should never be unlocked.

CHAPTER 2
CHANGE AGENT

"Plot is no more than footprints left in the snow after your characters have run by on their way to incredible destinations."
(Ray Bradbury, Zen in the Art of Writing)

ARRIVED.

Thank God.

It had taken me forty minutes longer than usual to get to the London Library. Rush hour. I took a deep breath of relief as I opened the door.

From the outside, this converted house on the northwest corner of St. James's Square, London, gave nothing away. It looked an odd building, squashed between two larger siblings. That's why the place was magical. Once inside, everything would change. The labyrinth of chronicled literature could make even the hardest heart crave an adventure into an imaginative world. I would often lose myself inside these four walls, but not today. I needed one thing from its corridors. An answer, and I knew where to find it.

Except.

It wasn't there. I scanned the shelf again, hoping that my quick search had missed the prize. Nothing. Panic set in. Someone must have taken out the book. But the records were clear: *available*. I headed to the nearby shelves, dragging my fingers across each spine and cover. It had to be here.

It needed to be here.

My body tensed. Why was I being so silly? It was just a book. The local store down the road would have plenty of copies. No. This wasn't just any old book. I was looking for *A Christmas Carol* – the 1843 edition – the birthplace of the famous story.

My frequent visits to the library had often sought it out. There was something spiritual about staring upon the origins of a tale that meant so much to me. It became a strange form of pilgrimage. More so after those precious memories became overshadowed by what I had done for the sake of my comeback. Today's pilgrimage had taken on a haunting edge. My journey to touch the book came out of a desperate plea for solace. I knew it was a crazy idea, but there was no other option. If only I could look at the original drawing of *That* image again, then maybe I would understand what had happened in the kitchen.

Understand? How could I? I didn't need to close my eyes to see the shadowy lines of a theatre fill my mind. With every passing second, I lived out that terrifying scene. The damp smell. The velvet touch. That whispering voice. They wouldn't leave me. The horrifying climax was the sense of *déjà vu.* The theatre was familiar. And I didn't know why. My knuckles turned white as I gripped the shelf. I had to get hold of the book.

Find *That* image. Find the answer.

I looked down at my watch. 11:33am. My grip loosened, followed by a shot of pain that ran through both arms. The wooden edge of the shelf had pressed deeper into my palms than first thought. Why was I so anxious? I took a deep breath. Then another. I needed to calm down.

"Find the book. End the nightmare."

The whispered mantra focused my mind. The world around me became small as I continued the search. Nothing else mattered. That's why I didn't recognise the figure sitting in the corner of the room, watching my every move.

Life is like a movie script.

The main cast are those close to our hearts. Casual acquaintances take up the supporting roles. The non-credited extras are strangers we pass by every single day. But there is one member of the cast we all dread. This character has one purpose only. It doesn't matter if they have a starring role or just a small part. One simple scene can smash the frame through which we see the world.

The Change Agent.

Every story needs them. Mine was about to make their appearance.

"Looking for this?"

I looked up as though caught in the middle of a guilty act. The first thing I noticed was the book that the elderly man was holding. An instant wave of relief crashed over me. It never crossed my mind to think how he knew I was searching for it. All that mattered was that I had found what I was looking for.

My Change Agent was in his late seventies. The quintessential image of an eccentric professor. His wild greying hair had no sense of order. The bushy eyebrows continued the disordered trend, reaching out towards the hairs camped out in his nose. His dress sense had one foot in the sensible world of Marks and Spencer's, the other in the anarchic fashion of Carnaby Street. The crowning piece to his bizarre outfit was a chained pocket watch. Outdated, but historically vogue.

His staggered walk towards me brought with it the smell of alcohol. The stale odour of a drunkard's natural aftershave. He carefully tried to lift a finger to his dry, cracked lips. There was a little detour towards his cheek before the shaking finger reached its goal.

"Shhhh. *They* could be watching. Even in here."

They?

His slurred words would have been comical if not for his eyes. Those windows into his drunken soul told me he was serious. Whatever this odd man was talking about, he had an unshakeable belief. It felt dangerous. Whenever there is that level of passionate faith, extreme measures are often near. This man had that look. Worse still, his drunken performance felt like an act.

I didn't have time to think about why. His staggered walk came to a sudden stop as he played back a private memory. Whatever scenes were being lived out in his head, I had a starring role. It was the way he was looking me up and down that gave it away. The old man was trying to find answers too. A look of disappointment flashed across his face. The search had come up short, draining the last bit of energy. I pulled up a chair just in time. He slumped down, his alcohol soaked body breathing heavily.

Another act?

Out of the corner of my eye I noticed an open wallet next to the chair leg. It must have fallen out of his pocket. I bent down and picked it up. The embossed name on the front read MR. S. PEVENSIE. I hadn't come across that name in a long time.

As a child, the magical stories of Narnia had captivated me. Of all the characters in those tales, Susan Pevensie was my favourite. I even had a schoolboy crush on her, but not for the obvious reasons. After she had returned from the wardrobe adventure, she sold her soul to the pleasures of the world. In the eyes of C.S. Lewis, Pevensie was a rebel because she wore the lipstick of adulthood that gave a killer kiss to the childlike heart. By the final book, her fame was that she was *'no friend of Narnia'*. I could relate to that, exchanging childhood imagination for the pursuit of an adult mind.

Since dumping those books in a charity shop, I had never come across the name Pevensie. Until now. It wasn't serendipity.

I didn't believe in coincidence.

*****

Alarm bells were ringing inside me.

Partly, Pevensie looked harmless. He was an oddly dressed fool whose love of conspiracy made him walk too close to the edge of madness. Haven't we all? It was the other part that was bothering me – his drunken act and the book he was holding. I wanted to grab *A Christmas Carol* and run. Find the book. *End this nightmare*. But my heart held my feet to the ground. However strange it sounded, the rush of blood pumping around my veins told me this moment was important. That's the horrible thing about living in a scene with a Change Agent. Every word and action mean something. The mundane suddenly becomes extraordinary; even silently waiting in front of a drunken old man.

Pevensie looked up. He still had that questioning expression layered across his face. Softer this time. I wondered if my decision to stay had given him hope.

“You went there again, didn’t you?”

There was a hint of uncertainty in his whispered voice. He didn’t wait for a reply. He handed over the book but didn’t let go. We shared one of those awkward moments where neither of us had sole ownership. Pevensie was having second thoughts.

“But I’m still not sure.”

“About what?” I asked.

“About finding you.”

CHAPTER 3
WELCOME

"We are all subject to the fates. But we must act as if we are not, or die of despair."
(Philip Pullman, The Golden Compass)

IT'S *all in the planning.*

That's how Pevensie approached his introduction to Abrahams. He had carefully thought out every detail, including the smell of alcohol on his clothes and breath. The wallet was a nice touch too. He was proud of how he had positioned it in his pocket to fall out when he arched his back. The finishing touch was the name on the card. It would always seal the deal.

Pevensie and Abrahams had a history; not that Abrahams would remember.

It had been a while since they had last met. Pevensie couldn't get over how different Abrahams looked. Life had enjoyed beating up his skin – evident from the punch marks of regret. Sleepless nights had given the bags under his bloodshot eyes a matching set of tormented luggage. He knew of the rumours about Abrahams' memory. That's why he was here. It was the only way to gauge whether the whispers were true. Pevensie wanted to believe, but he still couldn't get past the last time they had met. According to the rules, there were no more chances. Abrahams had sealed his fate. And yet. The tormented look was telling him that things weren't that simple. Against all the odds, the rumours were in fact, true.

Abrahams had another chance.

CHIME.

The clock on the wall rang out its midday call. Pevensie looked over Abrahams' shoulder and gazed at the two vertical hands. Time had marched on. It wouldn't be long before they would have visitors.

If he was going to act, it had to be now.

"*They* will be here soon."

It took a moment for me to register Pevensie's cryptic whisper. The way he had emphasised the first word carried a messy backstory of hatred and fear. Sensing my chance, I pulled the book towards me. It felt good pressing the cover against my chest, clinging to it as though I was a junkie relishing the next hit. I was desperate for it to soothe the crave of knowing what had happened this morning.

Pevensie let out a muffled grunt. He reached into his waistcoat, pulling out a silver pocket watch. As he opened the clasp, I noticed that the timepiece was slow. Not just minutes. Hours. The defective watch didn't bother him. Pevensie's schedule was operating on a different timeline to mine.

CLICK.

The dull metallic sound of the closed clasp would have made any antique dealer dribble with delight. It carried the rare tone of quality that was caught up within the ripples of history. Pevensie took a moment as his thoughtful pause miraculously sobered him up. I hated that I was right, it was all an act.

"So I guess this leaves us with one question."

Neither of us blinked. Pevensie dragged out the locked stare before drawing his breath to continue.

"Are you going to turn to *That* page, or shall I?"

*****

My grip tightened around the book, pushing it harder into my chest.

He knew about *That* page? Impossible. What else did he know? Questions. Confusion. Pevensie reached over. A tingling sensation ran through my arms as he gently guided my fingers to open the book. With each turn of the page, the conflicting battle of wanting him to stop and continue played out in my head. My eyes followed his every move. Soon Pevensie would reach That tormenting image. Then what?

I had no answer.

My short intakes of breath made the last few page turns, torturous. He was close. I recognised the scene. Three pages to go. Two. Please God, Stop. But I wanted him to continue. I needed answers. One page to go. I felt lightheaded. My vision blurred as everything around me merged into a sprawling mess of colour. An invisible hand poured water over my painted world. I closed my eyes, a silent act of prayer for normality to return. But God wasn't listening. It only got worse.

My senses went into overload. I could smell the rotting odour of a damp building. Then came the whispers; mumbling voices all around. A taste of panic filled my mouth, its acidic flavour stinging my throat. My stomach twisted with pain as the liquid crashed back and forth. Breathing was becoming hard. The last thing I wanted to do was to pass out. Fear told me to open my eyes; logic begged that I keep them shut. If I didn't see what was out there, then the nightmare didn't exist. But nothing in life is that simple.

Through squinted eyes, I knew I was no longer in the library.

*****

Familiar.

Strange.

I was back in the coffee table theatre, but it was no longer derelict. The velvet walls silently conveyed the touch of wealth. Sodden, broken boards were replaced with the soft bounce of a pure wool carpet. Above me, the crystal chandelier shone brightly, casting a ray of wonder across the red velvet seats. I instinctively turned down ROW 6. My hand rubbed against the cushions as I made my way towards the middle. And there it was. My seat.

My seat?

I questioned the certainty of conviction, reminding myself that it was just a dream. But it didn't feel like one as I gazed longingly at the seat. Unlike the rest of the building and chairs, this one looked old and well-used. The frayed black piping had seen better days. There was a haphazard collection of stains on the fabric. Even in its tatty state, I felt drawn to sit down. But something inside warned me off. A sense of 'home' wrapped around me; I was coming back to an old, trusted friend. My hand reached out and touched the back cushion. The feel of its worn-out fabric brought back a surprising memory. Wasn't there a rip under the right armrest? I kept moving down the side of the chair until I reached the hidden tear. It was bigger than I remembered.

"Sit down. For a minute. Just like the old days."

My hand jerked backwards. I spun around. Whispers.

"Who's there? Pevensie?"

My high-pitched tone sounded like a teenager struggling with a broken voice. Around me, I could hear people coughing, clearing their throats. Some were mumbling in hushed voices with the occasional 'excuse me' and 'sorry' breaking up their inaudible conversations. Without warning, everything fell quiet all at once. A silly thought came to mind. It was just like being in a theatre when the show is about to start.

'Sit down. For a minute...'

I edged closer to the seat.

"…Just like the old days."

But there was something about the old days I didn't like, even though I didn't know what the old days were. I remained standing, feeling like the odd one out in a room of invisible onlookers. Behind me, I could hear someone moving towards me. Soundless footsteps, coming closer. Full of nothingness. And then. Breathing. Wheezing. In. Out. In. Out.

A croaky voice, filled with the odour of cigarette lungs, tickled my ear.

"You never answered my question. Why are you back? And more to the point, why aren't you taking your seat?"

*****

Gone.

Back.

Just like being yanked from a terrifying dream, I was struggling to figure out what was real. My body was in the library, but my head was still picturing the red velvet chair. Controlling the endless onslaught of questions was impossible, as cold silence met every pitiful plea. I wanted Pevensie to give me some hope – anything to assure me that I wasn't going mad. All he gave me was an invitation back into my nightmare. He was looking down at my feet. I followed his gaze. In front of me was the dropped copy of *A Christmas Carol*. It lay open on the one page I dreaded most of all. A drawing. *That* image. The one from the postcard.

It was welcoming me back to a past I didn't want to remember.

CHAPTER 4
BAH, HUMBUG

"Then the Grinch thought of something he hadn't before. What if Christmas, he thought, doesn't come from a store. What if Christmas, perhaps, means a little bit more."
(Dr. Seuss, How the Grinch Stole Christmas!)

A CHRISTMAS CAROL has always been a part of my life.

I was eight years old when my mother introduced me to the ghostly tale. Bedtime stories were never the same. This fascination carried on at school. My teacher, a fan of the Victorian author, ditched the tried and tested nativity for the Dickens masterpiece. I was the first in class to raise my hand for a part.

My role in the play was Tiny Tim, the disabled boy who delivered the heart-warming line, '*God bless us, everyone!*' On the opening performance, I stumbled my lines in front of a packed school hall. Five words, that's all I needed to remember! I only made it to *'God'* before freezing. The room fell silent. Embarrassed, I ran off, leaving a bemused eight-year-old Scrooge called Kevin to learn the art of improvisation.

He survived his ordeal.

So did I. My mum bought me a chocolate bar and my friends thought I was cool because I swore on stage.

I found *A Christmas Carol* magical. Even dangerous. I loved how the story centred around the ghost of Marley. His warning to Scrooge was terrifying. Eternity is shaped in the present by personal decisions. Each action can liberate or forge heavy chains around the soul. Three other ghosts then visited Scrooge. Their mission was to teach the cruel businessman the error of his ways. The Ghost of Christmas Past revealed how history had shaped his evil heart. The Ghost of Christmas Present encouraged Scrooge to look outside his small, self-focused world. As for the Ghost of Christmas Future – that's the visit nobody wants, but everyone wishes they could hear just a few words. Scrooge's future was horrifying. Fearful of what was to come, he begged for another chance. The ghost gave him one.

As a child, I thought the ending sucked. Who wanted a fairy-tale last scene? At least it had ghosts, so I wasn't too harsh on the acclaimed author.

A Christmas Carol meant something different during my teenage years.

Acne changed everything. One day I was the rebel who swore on stage, the next, the butt end of jokes about skin care. Secondary school was tough. Friends were hard to come by, dates even harder. I became a loner, discovering the safety of a cubicle and a world full of books.

Dickens was my coping mechanism. He too struggled as a kid and somehow survived to tell the tale. With only printed pages to bear witness to my pledge, I committed that I would do the same. And that included becoming a writer. My career choice wasn't to do with a love of stories. I was a hurting soul with too many scars. Writing was my way of proving to everyone I was someone of worth.

With no great fanfare, I ditched my playful games of youthful imagination. It was time to grow up, fast. By the time I turned twenty, the beauty of childhood had long gone. No doubt C.S. Lewis would have labelled me *'no friend to Narnia'*.

Random writings about society turned into paid articles. Paid articles turned into a book deal. The book deal turned into a loudhailer for my pain.

Then came Terri.

We met in a community library, there for different reasons. I noticed her from across the floor. It wasn't 'love at first sight', but damn close. There was nothing fake about her. No overpriced fashion trends or vain attempts to impress onlookers. She drew upon an inner beauty that made her the most captivating person in the room. Nerves almost stopped me from speaking to her. My shaking hand spilt a drink. She came over to see if I was alright. The world stopped for my heartbeat to catch up.

Terri's clothes were practical, but worn in a way that carried an elegant style. Her long brown hair, tied up for efficiency, had a few dangling strands that teased her curls. She signed off the look with a canvas rucksack and a pair of beaten-up trainers. Distinctive, with an air of adventure. That was a rare combination. But it was her eyes that made me want to stay. Her emerald pupils almost masked the sleepless shade of red that covered the white of her eyes. She enjoyed life, but it also had a dark side. I knew that look.

Our small talk revealed that she was thirty-eight and had a love for stories. Terri ran a book club. I couldn't resist dropping the line about being an author, quickly followed up with a joke. I didn't want to sound pompous while trying to impress her. It took a lot of convincing for Terri to exchange numbers. I waited a few days before texting. She waited a week before replying. It was after our fourth coffee get-together that she lowered her guard around her painful backstory.

She was a single mother. Her ex-husband left after the first year of sleepless nights and the endless chore of nappy changing. The separation was messy. Arguments around finance could have gone on for years if it hadn't been for Terri giving into most of his demands. He was after the apartment. She was after the hope of her daughter not growing up hearing that money was more important than a young life. Terri worked hard to create a safe space for the two of them to live. It made sense why she controlled my request to get close. This safeguarding of relationships was her version of my teenage Dickensian book corner.

We started a new reading club, just the two of us. Terri made it very clear that these weren't date nights. I agreed, in public. Internally, I was playing the long game, hoping she would change her mind. Terri suggested the first book to launch our club: *A Christmas Carol*. She wanted to understand my fascination for the ghostly tale. Revisiting the story became a healing balm for me. It was good to find the heartbeat of my first love again. I told her how Dickens had broken all the rules with that Christmas story, sticking two fingers up to the illusion that Victorian Britain was living in a golden era of success. Nothing could have been further from the truth during the 19th century. The rich were getting richer; the poor were getting poorer. And middle-England happily lived in the middle of the road. The themes of the day were *Ignorance* and *Selfish Want*. It was rare people wanted to know the impact that their lives had upon others.

Dickens said 'screw that'. He held up a mirror to the injustice and pain that lingered within society. And the reflection staring back at every reader was Scrooge himself. The ruthless businessman represented the Poor Law – a controversial piece of legislation that declared that the needy were a commodity for the rich and successful. Its ideology was fearful. God's blessing was visible through prosperity. Poverty indicated bad morals. It was the duty of the blessed ones to teach the sinful souls the error of their ways. The solution was repentance through work and the Poor Law was its legal mechanism. If the needy wanted any bread to eat, then they first had to earn it.

Dickens hated the life and soul of the workhouse system. When he was a young boy, he too fell victim to that cruel system. Something had to change and his prophetic cry for society to repent came in the most surprising of ways.

Tiny Tim.

The Poor Law machine hated the physically and mentally impaired. Through the eyes of this evil ideology, disability was the evidence of the worst kind of sinner. But with the final stroke of his pen, Dickens delivered one of the best endings of all time. He gave the last word to the voiceless.

'God bless us, everyone!'

Dickens even referenced the Divine in that scandalous sign-off. By doing something like that, he not only rocked the boat of accepted thought, but attempted to sink the whole damned machine. Scrooge, the once hero of the Poor Law, was now a transformed man. He became a second father to a child that society had rejected.

Love your neighbour as you would yourself. It was the mother of all endings.

I also had a kicker of an ending with Terri; one that screwed everything up.

I took a different slant to the love your neighbour idea. My adaptation focused upon just loving myself. It gave me my comeback fourth book, but lost me the girl that could have saved my heart.

A Christmas Carol has always been a part of my life.

Especially *That* image inside.

CHAPTER 5
THEM

"We always have a tendency to see those things that do not exist and to be blind to the great lessons that are right there before our eyes."
(Paulo Coelho, The Pilgrimage)

I COULDN'T STOP looking down at the open book.

There were so many memories attached to that Christmas tale. Happy ones. Painful ones. Shameful ones. And they all led back to Terri. I had never meant to hurt her – that was the last thing on my mind. All I wanted to do was to make her life a little bit easier. Even when I betrayed her trust.

She had recognised the change in me long before I screwed everything up. Her quietness was Terri's way of hoping I would find my way back home. What she didn't factor in was that I had travelled too far off course to see any redemptive lighthouse. That's the difference between making a mistake and living with shame – one is an action, the other is who you are. I knew she would find out every ugly detail. Not just of what I had done, but my free will in doing it. And when that day happened, I didn't want to bear witness to the pain I had caused her. The shame of who I was made me walk away during her sleep. I ignored the intercom buzz on my apartment door and stopped answering her calls. It was that simple to turn my back on someone I loved. Still loved. Then one day it all went quiet. I knew then she had found out.

The story should have ended in that pathetic scene of personal regret. But there was a damn sequel. An envelope came through my door a year later. I recognised the handwriting. Terri had a way of curling her vowels. The letter was a plea for help. Every word was soaked with a tangible sense of fear.

It was a conscious decision not to read past the third line. If I'd continued, I knew I would have run straight back into her arms. Then what? Time hadn't erased what I had done. My shameful actions would always hang over us like a haunting shadow. I couldn't inflict that painful reminder onto Terri. The letter went in the bin. So did the next one that arrived a week later. Three more envelopes came through the door over the next five months. Each one of them disappeared, unopened. Until this morning. I don't know why I broke my own rules. Destiny?

The postcard was from Terri's ten-year-old daughter, Natasha. There was a little note on the back.

'Saw this picture and thought you would like it. I miss you.

Mummy says you have gone on a long trip. I hope you come back soon.'

Natasha was right about the picture. She knew I loved all things Dickens. It was a scene from *A Christmas Carol* – the famous John Leech illustration depicting the Ghost of Christmas Present standing next to two children. Twins. A boy and girl. Both are malnourished with sunken eyes and pained expressions. The boy is short for his age, his hair cut in a way that told a painful history of medical care. It was the type of treatment performed in dark alleyways and mental institutions hidden in shadows. Next to the boy is his sister, with matted wild hair and torn clothes. She had taken on the role of parent, her eyes never once leaving her brother. The illustration caused quite a stir in the 19th century, but it wasn't because of how they looked. These kids had a story.

That image.

There was something haunting about the way Pevensie carefully picked up the book like a new born child or a sick loved one.

He ran his finger over the illustration, caressing the image of the two children. I could see in his loving stare that he longed to pull them off the page into his outstretched arms. He gently stroked the young girl's hair. I remembered back to when Natasha first let me hug her. It had taken a while for that fragile life to trust another man. The memory of her absent dad had buried itself deep in her heart. The three of us had just been watching a cartoon. It was bedtime. She kissed her mother, wished me goodnight, then walked off to her bedroom. Seconds later she came running back and hugged me. It was one of the most precious things I had ever experienced; a child's trust.

"Were they there?"

His question surprised me.

"Who?"

Pevensie looked up. Behind his disappointed expression at my answer, was an anger yearning to be set free. How dare I not know who he was referring to! His finger resumed the comforting caress.

"You mean that kid on the page?"

"THAT KID?"

In one violent motion, Pevensie stood up and rushed towards me. His hands momentarily grabbed hold of my shirt before the horrifying reality sank in. The book! Anger made way for the turbulent cocktail of shock and panic. Collapsing to the floor, his hands picked up the book, cradling it against his chest.

"I'm sorry. I'm so sorry."

Pevensie was in a world of his own. Rocking back and forth, repeating his heartfelt apology to the book. To the kids. He too was haunted by *That* image. The only difference was that we were living in different nightmares. I bent down and helped him back to the seat. He took a minute to come back out of his sorrowful world. One more gentle caress, followed by a pretend ruffle of the boy's short hair. He put his fingers to his lips, kissed them, then transferred his affection to each child. Not wanting to drag out his departure, he shut the book and looked away. I waited a few seconds before offering some generalised words of comfort. His look said it all.

"What do you care? You only came here because of the postcard. I doubt you even remember what you did. They trusted you!"

The level of hostility in Pevensie's voice took me by surprise. He was blaming me for something linked to the kids. In the swirl of confusion, I registered the rest of his words. The postcard.

"How did you know about that?"

His face went a ghostly white. Pevensie stumbled for a few words but found nothing. The flustered expression on his face told me he was beating himself up for having a loose tongue. There was a long intake of breath. He was buying time.

Pevensie counted down the seconds in his head.

He needed to be patient and not rush the moment. And yet. Time was short. They would be here soon, checking up on his movements.

7. 6. 5.

Every second felt like a minute. He wanted to move on to the next scene, but it was critical to make Abrahams think he was angry about his loose tongue. It's all in the detail. He needed every move to spark curiosity. It was the only way.

4. 3.

Nearly there. Not everything was an act. His affection for The Twins was real. So too was his anger towards Abrahams for not remembering who they were.

2. 1.

Pevensie knew his next move. It would set everything up perfectly.

Details.

"And the man, was he in the theatre too?"

I didn't respond. I couldn't respond. My mouth was sealed with confusion and fear.

"The wheezing always gives him away. But you know that already."

Pevensie rechecked his pocket watch. A look of concern flashed across his face.

“I need to go.”

“Wait!”

Desperation broke the seal on my lips. Pevensie ignored the plea and made his way to the door. He took hold of the handle then stopped. Without turning around, he replied to my cry.

“I’m sorry that it has to be this way. It’s not what you think. If I could do things differently, I would.”

There was a pause. He leaned his head against the door, checking if anyone was around.

“Do me a favour. There’s a copy of *The Chimes* on the shelf over there. Read it. Join-the-dots. Dickens did it on purpose, connecting all his books.”

With that, he opened the door and stepped into the hallway. I hesitated before running after him. A voice inside told me it was a waste of time chasing him down, but I did it anyway. By the time I got into the hallway, my Change Agent had gone. I wasn’t surprised. There was an odd feeling lingering in the pit of my stomach that he had left like this before.

Déjà vu.

CHAPTER 6
FOLLOW

"My advice is, never do tomorrow what you can do today. Procrastination is the thief of time. Collar him!"
(Charles Dickens, David Copperfield)

THE CHIMES was waiting for me.

It lay on the shelf, teasing me to fall deeper into whatever mysterious rabbit hole this nightmare had become. Unlike Alice, this wasn't an accidental trip into a twisted wonderland. I was choosing to throw myself into its dark embrace. *'Curiouser and curiouser.'*

The front cover was one of the strangest book jackets I had ever seen. Ghost-like fairies and stern looking goblins filled the page. They weaved themselves in and out of the mismatched fonts. It was an artistic mess, and yet the whole disordered scene tempted me to come closer. To see. To hear.

The Chimes.

I had read this book once before. The scene came back as though it was yesterday. I was in Terri's kitchen. She was putting Natasha to bed while I poured another glass of wine. It was our book club night. A quick reckoning told me I had about five minutes before she would be back. I looked over towards my bag. Pandora's box was inside. This was the seventh time I had almost come clean to Terri about what I had done. I had high hopes for this time. Except. No matter how hard I tried to convince myself it would work out fine, I was having doubts about the truth. My shoulders felt heavy as I took a large mouthful of wine. I was sweating again. A familiar feeling. Tonight was going to end like the other six times: with regret. I kicked the bag under the chair. Out of sight; out of conscience.

On the table, the copy of *The Chimes.*

Pevensie pushed the fire escape door open.

He looked to his left, right, then left again. The alleyway was strangely empty. Something wasn't right. They never made things this simple. He would have expected at least one of them covering the back entrance.

Pevensie scanned the bags of rubbish scattered along the edge of the path. He was trying to find a shadow, a dark outline, anything that would give their presence away. None of this made sense. Shaking hands and beads of sweat made it difficult for him to open the clasp of the pocket watch. They should have been here by now, checking up on him. Abrahams wasn't the only one who had rumours following him around.

The rhythmic fan of *The Chimes* was hypnotic as my fingers flicked through the book.

Blurred letters flashed across my eyes. I wasn't reading a single page. All I could think about was the departing words from Pevensie. *'Read it. Join-the-dots. Dickens did it on purpose, connecting all his books.'* Helpful guide or the ramblings of a mad mind overdosed on conspiracy pills? I continued to flick through the book. The need for answers. That was the only thing driving me forward.

My hand froze. A three inch by two inch library ticket lay between the pages. Scrawled on the top right corner of the card were the words *'AISLE 6p. SHELF 7s.'* I had been a member of the London Library long enough to know they didn't operate a system like that. Yet the card looked official. Maybe. There was no logo, only the name of the building typed on a typewriter whose plates were living on borrowed time. I shut the book with a determined thud, only to open it up again two seconds later.

'Curiouser and curiouser.'

I tentatively turned over the library ticket.

*****

Pevensie stepped into the alleyway.

The fire escape door locked behind him with a dull clank. There was no turning back now. He still couldn't get rid of the uncomfortable feeling he was missing something. His whole plan hinged upon him being one step ahead. All he had now was the sense of playing catch up. He tentatively reached the main street. He looked to his right, then towards the park benches in the middle of St. James's Square. Strange. Everything else was in place.

A horrible thought formed in the darkest corner of his mind. Pevensie watched in slow-motion as it crept out of the shadows and made its way into the light. He wanted to push it back, hoping that he could forget that it ever existed. But it was too late. The thought made perfect sense.

They were still here.

They were not after him.

They had their sights on someone else.

*****

There was handwriting on the other side of the card.

I had to strain to make out some of the words. Whoever had written the note had little time to get out their thoughts.

The Twins

They made me hear it

The Applause

Beware

They are not what they seem

I beg of you

NEVER FORGET

The quivering lines of ink told the author's tale of sheer panic. They feared for their life, begging that whoever read the note wouldn't make the same mistake. What mistake – forgetting? My finger ran across each word. I could tell my mind was already joining the dots that shouldn't join together.

The Twins – the two children in *That* image.

The Applause – something to do with the theatre?

Questions laid upon questions. I desperately scrambled around in my mind, trying to find the smallest amount of logic to bring me back from the edge of madness. But every time I thought I discovered a glimmer of hope, the feeling of *déjà vu* dragged me back into the insanity. A distant memory. Unclear.

Forgotten.

NEVER FORGET.

CLANK.

What was that? I looked around. No one was there. My mind was playing tricks on me. I took a deep breath before focusing back on the note, but I couldn't shake off the feeling that someone was watching me. My shaking finger hovered over the words. *'NEVER FORGET.'*

Had I?

CLANK. The noise again. I spun around.

*****

Pevensie hated indecision. Carry on with the plan, or go back?

His next stop was waiting for him at the end of the street. But he couldn't leave now. They were still in the library. Running back into the building would help Abrahams, and yet it could put everything else at risk.

Indecision.

Think about the primary goal. Except. Abrahams. Didn't everything hinge on Abrahams? Pevensie didn't know. He was only following orders. Or was he?

Damn it.

Pevensie clenched his fists and slowed down his breathing. He needed to pull himself together. His mind pictured a chessboard as he played out all of his options. Every move and subsequent response, carefully observed. It was all about the end game, not the odd piece. The last move played out. He got his answer. Pevensie turned his back on the library and walked down the street.

Abrahams was on his own. A gamble. But a calculated one.

I wasn't alone in the empty room.

Invisible eyes analysed my every move. I needed to get out of here. Taking the mysterious note, I headed towards the door. I was tempted to run down the stairs, through the corridor, into the foyer and finally onto the street. But it quickly passed. I couldn't live without knowing where this rabbit hole was taking me. Answers. I needed answers.

I needed peace.

And the only way to end this nightmare was to do what the message said.

'Follow the aisles until you reach the dial.'

CHAPTER 7

AISLE 6P. SHELF 7S

"All shall be done, but it may be harder than you think."
(C.S. Lewis, The Lion, the Witch, and the Wardrobe)

THE PROBLEM with searching for the unknown is that the destination could be anything.

For an hour I had been walking up and down the library aisles. I had no idea what I was looking for and it showed on my face. Frustration and disappointment had ripped apart the hope of finding anything other than a dead end. I couldn't believe I had let myself fall for such a stupid idea as a mysterious note of redemption. The small rectangular sign hanging above the door told me I was on the sixth floor. Only another ten minutes of self-inflicted mockery and then I could return to normality.

Normality?

Pulling down on the light cord ordered a row of fluorescent bulbs to burst into life. The solitary tunnel of flickering white welcomed me into the unknown of the first aisle. Anticipation turned to disappointment as I reached the opposite wall. Just like every other tunnel of books, the only thing that greeted me was another dead end. I pulled down on the light cord next to the second passageway. Then the third. The familiar pattern mocked my fragile belief. I paused in front of the fourth aisle. As the lights flickered down the narrow passage, the heart-breaking pattern broke.

At the end of the aisle was a wooden door with a stained glass window arched over the top. The lead framed image depicted a large pillar with seven clock dials. Standing next to the column were two small silhouetted figures. Children. Another character, larger, was standing behind them. I inched forward, torn between the certainty of what I had found and the mystery of what lay beyond the door. My gaze didn't leave the image of the two children. A question rested on the edge of my lips. I pretended it didn't exist. Goosebumps danced across my skin as I tried the handle. Unlocked. A sudden sense of danger hit me. It was as if I had touched the future for a fleeting moment and it was warning me to turn back. My hand remained on the handle. A locked door would have made my decision easier. Now I faced the choice of walking away or stepping into the unknown.

Into danger.

I pushed the door. It opened with no great fanfare or gust of magical wind. But it was anything but a normal door into a normal room. That lingering touch of the future was telling me I had made the greatest mistake of my life.

They were getting worried.

Things hadn't gone to plan. Following Abrahams to the library should have been a formality. Everything was running like clockwork until Pevensie appeared. That was a surprise. The drunken fool wasn't supposed to be there, and certainly not around Abrahams. The two of them had history. And there was no such thing as coincidence. The tapestry of life had many weaving hands. So that left them with a disturbing question. Whose hand was messing up their plan?

It certainly wasn't Abrahams. He had already sealed his fate during his last visit. Tracking his movements here was just a matter of routine, making sure everything had slotted back as usual. They knew of the rumours, but that wasn't out of the ordinary. Lots of people came back with tales. It was rare any of them turned out to be true. Abrahams was just another person whose subconscious was clinging onto a fading dream.

As for Pevensie, his motive for being there was harder to read. Yes, his job permitted the travel between worlds, but never without permission. The only reason everything remained civilised between the two places was due to the strict guidelines. No one broke the rules. No one. And yet Pevensie had rumours of his own following him around. It hadn't gone unnoticed, the unauthorised trips. But the drunken fool was harmless. He wouldn't dare mess things up. That's why They stayed in the library when the old man left. Someone had yet to reveal themselves.

Follow Abrahams, find the hidden weaving hand. Except. Things hadn't gone to plan. THEY had lost Abrahams.

And He would not be pleased.

******

The room behind the door was a store cupboard.

Limited shelving meant that books and bundles of paper had spilt out onto the floor. One wrong move and these dusty skyscrapers of precariously balanced literature would fall like dominos. Dancing particles of dust, illuminated by the glow of a swinging light bulb, sparked my imagination. I had just walked into a treasure trove of tales.

My hand rubbed along the nearest tower of words. All the manuscripts were different. Some were recent additions with their crisp, clean paper. Others had an aged look. Fragile. Dusty. Held together with string. I moved to another tower, old and new stacked together like bricks. Unknown authors. Unpublished works. This place was a storyteller's dream hideaway, full of tales away from public sight. I untied a bundle of paper and read. In that spellbinding moment I forgot about the lingering sense of danger, urging me to leave.

The manuscript was less of a book and more a journal written by multiple authors. Some typed, others handwritten, a few sketched out. The whole thing reminded me of the childhood game where I would draw a face, before folding the piece of paper over for the next kid to carry on with the picture. None of us would know, until the end, what creative, disjointed image lay under those folds. The final reveal would always bring laughter. But the reveal from the manuscript had a chilling edge. Different stories. Diverse characters. Yet every author ended up in the same place.

The Theatre

I grabbed another manuscript from the nearest paper tower. This time there was no careful untying of thc string. The store cupboard walls closed in on me as I raced towards each story's final scene. It couldn't be just a coincidence. Try again. Another tower. Another book. Different adventure but same destination. My shaking hands couldn't hold the paper any longer. Watching the sheets fall to the floor sent a wave of panic crashing over me. Someone would know I had been here.

I bent down, gathering up the mess into an ordered pile. The dust covering the floor was thick from days, months, maybe years of loneliness. As I picked up the last remaining stragglers I noticed the outline of some letters scrapped into the floorboard. I tentatively rubbed away the layer of dust.

AISLE 2p.

I pulled out the note, joining the dots. This room wasn't magical at all, but a monstrous lair that was drawing me into its dark embrace. I could still run away; the door was just to my right. But a tentacle of curiosity wrapped itself around my neck, turning my head back towards the floor. If I ran, I would never find AISLE 6p. I had no option.

Crawling on my knees, I found another mark. AISLE 3p. I was getting close. Splinters from the wooden floor were now burrowing themselves into my flesh. The irritating pain was just a distraction. I didn't want to stop. Couldn't stop. 4p. 5p. And there it was.

AISLE 6p.

I looked around for SHELF 7s. Nothing. The only thing by the aisle was a teetering tower of manuscripts. My rainbow had been nothing but a pot of fool's gold. The cocktail of stupidity and failure brought with it a hangover of pain. My hands were raw from searching the splintered floor. In some prayerful act, I reached out, rubbing my finger upwards along the pile of books. I paused. What if? One bundle, 7a. The next bundle, 7b. 7c. 7d. As I reached the nineteenth book, a tingle. 7s

Found it.

******

It?

I didn't know what I was holding in my sore hands. A thick layer of dust and cobwebs covered the book, giving it a sense of being sacred. It felt like an act of literary worship just rubbing my skin along the top half of the title page. The dust drew back like a holy veil during sacraments. Written in faded ink was only one word.

'PATHS.'

Slowly, reverently, I moved my hand down the remaining half. A picture emerged through the dust. My act of worship transformed itself into a judging finger, pointing without redemption towards my fearful soul. My nightmare had returned.

That image.

CHAPTER 8
EXTRACTS

"There is no greater agony than bearing an untold story inside you."
(Maya Angelou, I Know Why the Caged Bird Sings)

THE CALLIGRAPHY inside the book was from a bygone age.

Each page of the preface carried the imprint of the author's heart. Thick lines of concentration. Thin strokes of speed. Staggered character spacing from a tired hand. The writer had laboured over every sentence, sweated blood crafting each paragraph. This was more than just another story to them.

It was their confession.

The author was refusing to go easy on themselves. Line after line of verbal punishment tore into an already broken heart. Their painful admission of an unspoken mistake was full of regret. The only solace was a faint hope that there was still time to make amends.

Their handwriting got messy by the third page. Emotions were running high. Whole sentences scribbled out. Words underlined. Circled. Then replaced. Memories of a troubled past weighed heavy upon their soul. The fourth page was the hardest to read. Their confession was coming to an end. Four words were at the top of the page. Underlined. Three times.

'The Red Velvet Chair.'

It was amazing that the paper had survived the pressure of the writer's hand. Hatred lined every indentation as it tore into the fibres. A torrent of scribbled words followed. Sentences were all over the place, written at angles and up the sides of the page. The author was on the verge of an emotional breakdown. The confession was straying close to being their last-will-and-testament.

These rushed lines of ink were familiar. This writer wanted their confession found, and the only way they could do it in time was to scribble down a few mysterious words on... I looked at the small note resting on my leg.

A library ticket.

Join the dots.

I tried to link the erratic paragraphs of the confession together. The pained writer, male, kept talking about a sound in their head. The applause led them to a building with red velvet chairs. This gold and crimson theatre had a chandelier hanging from the middle of its decorated ceiling. The candle wax dripped like a magical waterfall onto the carpeted floor.

It couldn't be. My body tensed up.

The writer knew it wasn't their first visit, even though the memories told them to forget. They had clung onto a fading hope that things would be different this time – they knew the punchline. But nothing had changed. The show kicked off. *He* stepped on stage. And the betrayal happened in the Third Act. Even though the writer saw it coming, they still fell for the same damn trick.

But there was a subtle change.

This would be their last visit. They had failed. Failure meant death and death meant fear. This wasn't the kind of terror of losing the ticket to the sweet by-and-by. It was the fear of death about living.

Living after The Applause fell silent.

I stopped reading for a moment. It had taken every ounce of emotional strength to read through this confession and I feared how it would end. I wanted the mysterious writer to come out fighting, kicking and punching for every last second of life. It would be their ultimate send-off. A hero's death. But their ink-stained middle finger to destiny didn't read like that. They had sold their final battle for some magical beans of delusion. Their plan to change this nightmare was to tell stories. *'Stories change the world',* they wrote. Circled. Underlined

What a let down. Stories don't change the world; self-preservation does.

The writer's final lines were more like scribbled ideas than complete sentences. They had begun to flesh out their rescue plan, thinking through plot lines and character names. I froze. The room closed in around me. Some of the names were familiar. I had grown up on these storylines.

And the writer was the reason I had first picked up a pen.

Dickens looked at his confession.

He had never intended to write such a note. The manuscript was enough. But everything changed when he had stepped into the library storeroom. Dickens had found the place by accident. It was the perfect spot to hide his journal; the room was full of manuscripts piled up high. If only he had walked away, but curiosity got the better of him. He had only looked through a handful of the papers, but it was enough to know he needed to do something more than just leave his story in the room.

He wasn't the only one who had seen the red chair.

Writing the confession was his way of navigating through the storm of confusion raging in his head. There was the distant memory of a conversation. In a cabin. With a lady. About a plan. And he needed to get it out of his head. He knew mentioning about the Third Act was bending the rules. That was OK. Just one line, but it would be enough to make the reader question what would inevitably happen. It wasn't easy revisiting the scenes of The Theatre; he hoped the pain would be worth it.

Dickens placed the manuscript under a pile of books, then scribbled out a note on the library ticket. It wasn't supposed to be like this. A Christmas Carol should have been the answer. He had underestimated the power of the show. His lack of strength was pitiful, but it was too late to dwell upon the past. He needed to concentrate on the present.

The first part of the plan was simple. Hide the library ticket. People often used those pieces of card as markers. Leaving it on the counter would mean

the card would travel around the library unseen, finding a home in numerous books. As for the second part, there lay the problem. Dickens didn't need a crystal ball to realise that as soon as he stepped out of the library, They would be watching him. He needed to use that to his advantage. Play the game. See the whole board. Wasn't that the lesson he had learnt in PARADOX?

He took one final glance around the room, taking in the towers of manuscripts. How old was The Theatre? Some of these tales looked ancient. A familiar sensation rushed through his body. The longing for the next show hadn't left him yet. In this room was a testament to the countless lives who had walked through those doors and taken their place on a red velvet seat. Could he finally end this nightmare once and for all?

Dickens hoped so, but the world's greatest show had run for a long time.

Time had raced ahead of me.

The library was closing, but I wanted to stay. Since I was a kid, I had dreamed of holding a piece of paper touched by the famous author himself. Now, I had a whole manuscript in my hand that I hadn't even read; just his strange confession as a preface. I couldn't leave it behind now.

But I needed to. It was the safest way of keeping what I had found a secret. There was no way I could smuggle out the book, and if I owned up, then I would be letting the staff know of my unauthorised entry to the room. My only option was to leave it here, come back the next day. It seemed a good plan. Except.

It never occurred to me that I couldn't guarantee seeing tomorrow's dawn.

CHAPTER 9
TO SEE OR NOT TO SEE

"But what did Scrooge care? It was the very thing he liked. To edge his way along the crowded paths of life, warning all human sympathy to keep its distance."
(Charles Dickens, A Christmas Carol)

STEPPING outside the library was surreal.

St. James's Square hadn't changed and yet, everything had. I couldn't silence what was echoing around my head. Everything I had read in the storeroom spoke of a strange sound that led people to a red velvet chair. Every writer, including Dickens, said The Applause was everywhere; within earshot but rarely heard. My mind didn't need to ask permission to play its cruel trick.

I could hear the sound of people clapping all around me. In the square, an old lady was sitting on a park bench. She was eating a baguette, wrapped in a brown paper bag. My imagination amplified every crunch and rustle into two hands coming together. A few yards down the street, someone had left a water pipe on. The narrow trail of liquid weaved itself into the gutter before dropping into the grated abyss. Drip. Drip. Clap. Clap. The deep rumble of a car engine. A clanking bike chain and the rhythmic buzz of a mobile phone on mute.

The Applause was everywhere, waiting for the perfect moment to drag me kicking and screaming into its velvet madness.

*****

The old lady watched from a distance.

She was a living jumble sale of mismatched, hand-me-down clothes. Her face continued that well-worn look. The deep brown eyes, framed with wrinkles, were vibrant with life. Those windows into the soul had stared into the universe, and now its enchanted glow blanketed her dark skin. The etched lines on her face were deep, but not from worry. They were caverns of mystical adventure, holding secrets that defied the restrictions of age.

Age? What a strange concept. She looked down at her baguette. It didn't taste like the old days. The new owners of her once favourite café had changed the recipe. Cost cutting and rent increases had brought about the altered flavouring. And now a lost customer. That was a shame. She had fond memories of the place.

Memories were important. It was her way of staying connected as months turned into years into... That's why she loved the park bench, even though that had changed too. The new metal frame was OK, but she preferred the wooden one it had replaced. Yes, the old splintered structure was a lawsuit waiting to happen, but it had character.

And history.

Years of life had soaked itself into its wood grain. She had seen the bench built, placed in the square, then sadly removed just before Christmas. The one saving grace was that the replacement occupied the same spot. That was a blessing. It was the perfect place to rest, watch and talk. Being old had its bonuses. People made time to speak to the elderly. She knew the manipulation. No doubt people thought she was lonely. It wasn't too far from the truth. Just not in the way they expected.

She took another bite of the baguette. A wince of disappointment flashed across her face as she looked towards the library. The building was an improvement on the old location on Pall Mall. Her mind flicked through the index card of memories, trying to recall when the library moved to St. James's Square. 1845.

It took the conversational recipe of 'the old and lonely lady trick' to make sure that the storeroom found a home in the new building. Her efforts paid off. She couldn't have asked for a safer place. Those stories were valuable, and they deserved a sacred space to work out their final chapters. The London

Library wasn't the only building that kept such stories, but she had a soft spot for the place. Memories. Some great moves had been played out there.

And some were still unfinished.

The old lady was about to take another bite of her baguette, but then threw it into a nearby bin. She hated throwing food away, but this sad excuse for a sandwich was leaving a bad taste in her mouth. Or was it because of Abrahams? Most times she could see the next chapter. Today was different.

Abrahams had changed since the last time they had met.

I needed a drink.

Five steps into my pilgrimage to the nearest bar, I caught sight of a homeless woman making her bed for the night. Her cardboard mattress rested against the iron railings of a converted townhouse-cum-private office. Two overflowing supermarket bags of collected rubbish were her pillows. These lay next to a makeshift tarpaulin blanket. It was a pitiful sight, but normal. The commonality of rough sleepers had lost all its shock value. Even my books had to spice it up for the audience.

The only unusual thing was the location. Homeless people didn't get to camp out around St. James's Square. It was a 'no go' area for ragamuffins. There wasn't any official law, but high society had a way of making the rules up with private security firms. I felt sorry for the woman. She must have been new around here. It would only be a matter of time before a minimum wage guard turned up. The residents preferred a heavier hand than the local police.

I considered crossing to the other side. That felt too obvious. Even I wasn't that harsh. The woman would see enough cruelty when the security van turned up. She didn't need any appetiser from me. My compromise would be a brisk walk past her bed. It was important not to make any eye-contact. That would be easier on my conscience. I couldn't feel guilty if I didn't see a human life.

Ignorance is a beautiful thing

"Spare change?"

Her outstretched hand tapped my left leg, catching me off guard. She had broken the unspoken rule. The homeless could look, even speak, but never touch. It was the way both camps of society could deal with the raw injustice of the situation. My leg moved. Her tap turned into a grip.

"If not spare change, then spare time?"

*****

The old lady watched the scene intently.

She had waited a long time for this moment. It had taken subtle moves and a few distractions to arrange their meeting. Although she couldn't guarantee the outcome, her careful planning was paying off. For now.

Her hand reached into her coat pocket, feeling around for the two chess pieces resting in their fabric home. She often carried them around on her travels. Of all the pieces on the board, these two were the ones usually forgotten. But not by her. And not by Dickens. Memories.

What a move that had been.

She gingerly pushed herself up. The cold evening air was playing havoc with her knees. Eating the tasteless baguette had made her thirsty. She needed a drink. Fresh lemonade and lime. It reminded her of home, but sadly few places around here made anything fresh like that anymore. Except one. A five-minute walk from the square. It was one of the benefits of living without the constraints of time; you get to know all the back alleyways hidden from sight.

The old lady took one final look towards the orchestrated meeting. The two of them were talking now. That might be a good sign, but then again. She still had questions about the both of them. The homeless woman was a gamble; her backstory had an edge to it that could cut through any prepared script. Abrahams was unreadable. So much had changed since his last visit to PARADOX.

Her hand went back into the coat pocket. Next to the chess pieces was a small rectangular sheet of paper. A theatre ticket. She pulled it out and examined the writing advertising the next show. So many things had changed over the years, but not The Theatre. It played the same show as when she first stepped through its ostentatious doors.

But looks can be deceiving.

She folded the ticket and pushed it back into her pocket. Her cold fingers danced around the chess pieces again. See the whole board. The old lady was counting on others to disregard that foundational principle of the game. Her mind played through her next move on the board. First, a ten-minute walk to the café, there and back. Next, add another ten, maybe fifteen minutes to finish the lemonade and lime. Finally, by the time she got back to the park bench, Abrahams would have long gone. So to speak.

There was a faint smile. She was never good at keeping a poker face. It was an impressive series of moves which had enough surprises to grab the necessary attention. That was the reason after all. Distractions. Her smile widened, then a whisper.

"The show must go on. For now."

CHAPTER 10
A TALE OF TWO LIVES

"Sometimes it's moments like that, real complicated moments, absorbing moments, that make you realise that even hard times have things in them that make you feel alive. And then there's... homeless people who've read Pauline Kael."
(Nick Hornby, A Long Way Down)

SHE DIDN'T SMELL.

That was the first thing I noticed. All homeless people should have 'that' smell. It was the paradox of living on the streets. Only the lingering odour of stale urine and damp clothes found a permanent home.

Apart from the ill-fitting clothes around her thin frame, there was nothing stereotypical about the homeless woman. Her skin had a lived-in glow to it, giving enough hints within its contours that her life had seen its fair share of adventure. The travelled look continued with a thick crop of matt hair; windswept and sprinkled with distinguished silver streaks. I would have expected to see the lethal combination of cold nights and the constant display of human rejection, drain the life out of her eyes. But it was the opposite. Creation and its wild plains had imprinted its majesty deep within those soul-shaped windows. Glorious perfection was shining brightly for all to see.

If anyone bothered to stop and stare.

Sadly, whatever wonders this woman had seen, it lived within the closest thing London had to a modern day plague. Homelessness. The ringing bell of the unclean.

"Ekitaldia. That's my name. But folk at the shelter call me Eki. You too, if you want."

The last sentence was more of a heartfelt plea. Eki's voice was rough. The vocal chords had gone through a lot of self-inflicted abuse. It wasn't alcohol or drugs. This damage was something worse. Harder to cure. Eki had a debt that she could never clear. Personal retribution. She was judge, prosecutor and defendant, all wrapped up in one neat, twisted little package. She loosened her grip, then reached out her hand.

Crap. What now? I had never shaken the hand of someone homeless before. Physical touch was something I didn't do with people like 'them'. Loose change. Cup of tea. And if I was feeling generous, a sandwich. But never my name and certainly not an outstretched hand. I never quite knew what they had touched. 'They'. What a horrible phrase to use. 'They' had done a lot for me. 'They' had landed me a book deal. 'They' were the main characters that kept the money pages turning. And yet I couldn't even shake their hands.

I looked over towards the townhouse opposite. The street always had twitchy curtains. True to form, there was already activity. Rolex and diamond-clad hands were making phone calls. It would only be a matter of time before a van arrived, acting out its human version of a dog catcher. It was compassion that made me stretch out my hand. I wanted to make sure Eki didn't get hurt.

No spare change, but I did have time.

Our opening conversation took me by surprise.

It was honest. Even though Eki and I belonged to the same human race, our worlds were different. It was society's version of *A Tale of Two Cities.*

Best of times. Worst of times.

Within minutes a security van would turn up. I would get their ticker-tape parade to stay. Eki would get their harsh words. If resisted, the words would turn into fists dragging her away with minimal but necessary force. Down the street, restaurants would roll out the red carpet of welcome for me, while Eki would face their closed door of rejection. If my wallet had no change, credit cards would come to the rescue. There was no such luxury for Eki. Asking for spare change was never just casual words. It came with a high price tag.

Humiliation.

If she were lucky, Eki would get a room for the night, giving her food and a warm bed. Except, it often required more than luck during these days of charitable cutbacks. She had better odds of winning the lottery with no ticket than finding a space in this metropolis. Middle-aged women were near the bottom of the handout list. Eki was OK with that. She never thought for one minute that her comfort should come before that of a teenager or mother and child.

No hostel meant that Eki would need to fend for herself. The first task was to find cardboard that was dry. It would take the chill off the concrete floor. That job was always harder than it sounded, thanks to the damp night air. She also had to fend off the desire to find the softer mattress of a grass verge. The morning dew loved to bring back childhood memories of wetting the bed.

Choosing a location was more than just a dry spot of land. The homeless had territories. Sometimes, there was a turf war. Eki noticed the ironic nature of the homeless fighting over a piece of land. But she understood. Stealing someone's spot was a slur upon whatever ounce of dignity a person had left within their beaten up heart. If someone took that away, what else did they have left to fight for?

Eki kept the rawest part of her story until the end.

What she feared the most wasn't the wet cardboard or damp air. It was the public. They knew how to hurt a life like nothing else. She could handle the mindless acts from drunken partygoers by playing along as the star attraction in the freak show. But the ones who didn't need alcohol to fuel their hatred, that brought the worst kind of hurt. Broken glass in the bed, spit in the face, or their favourite, a puddle of piss by her head. Eki had experienced it all.

Sleep was, and would always be, temporary.

She told me that the people who had it worst were families, unaccompanied minors and young women. Not a day would go by without the street grapevine telling another tale of someone being hurt, taken or being missing-presumed-dead. The list of culprits never changed. Traffickers. Labourers. Pimps. There was a long queue of people waiting to pick up the low hanging fruit off the streets. And when that harvest was running short, the focus would turn towards the fields called 'the hidden homeless'. Hostels. Bedsits. Couch surfing. The tactics were the same. So were the results. A number on the back of a business card worked wonders. The hook was the offer of cash, food and dignity. Payback was something no one would wish upon their worst enemy.

I nodded one of those knowing nods, but what did I know? Every Christmas I would tweet out a message about how many children would be without a home over the season of goodwill and cheer. But did I really know what that meant? Hell no. I knew nothing. The homeless were just numbers.

Page numbers that brought in the quarterly royalty cheque.

And, of course, I didn't offer any solution with all those empty words I had written. The problem was too complicated. There was no magical solution. So I would ignore it. Pretend it wasn't there and walk on the other side of the street. Until.

Eki.

Our conversation came to a pause. I could tell most of those stories had names attached to them. Friends. Acquaintances. People she had met between shop fronts and back alleyways. She spoke from experience. It put my weak words to shame.

"What brought you... made you... err..."

"Homeless?"

Eki finished my question. I nodded, thankful she was taking the lead.

"You really want to know?"

I did. My question wasn't some voyeuristic plea. Surprisingly, a deep well of compassion was rising inside me. Maybe it was because I was out of my comfort zone, or the memories of The Theatre were screwing with my head, but I felt a connection to Eki I didn't understand. It was real. Authentic. She looked over towards the square. Her eyes focused on the empty park bench.

"Nightmares. The damn things wouldn't go away. I thought I could live with them. There were always pills to deal with the sleepless nights, right? But that just made it worse. Soon I was having those dreams throughout the day. That's when I realised I couldn't see my family anymore. Nothing would erase what I had done. There was only one thing left for me … I had to run."

Eki fixed her eyes upon mine.

“But then again, I’m preaching to the converted. You’ve had the same nightmares. I’m not the only one who has seen that damn red velvet chair.”

CHAPTER 11
EKI

"Uncontradicting solitude supports me on its giant palm; And like a sea-anemone or simple snail, there cautiously unfolds, emerges, what I am."
(Philip Larkin, Collected Poems)

EKI KNEW *what she was doing.*

Mentioning the red velvet chair wasn't a mistake. She had to be sure. Someone's life depended upon it. For the last three hours Eki's world had turned inside out with her worst fear coming true. Now, there was only one option left. She had to get back to The Theatre. The problem was, the door was bolted from the inside. Her history with that place meant denied access. There wasn't even a chance for a day pass.

Eki continued to examine the stranger's response. She was looking for clues, hints, anything that would give her the next step. Somehow this man had a connection to what had just happened to her. He was a piece of the puzzle. But how? She needed to tread carefully. There was too much at stake to make any mistake. Eki took a deep breath and started to playback the last three hours. Somewhere within that disturbing timeline would be her answer.

Hour one.

It started with an unsuccessful hunt through the bins between Agar Street and Piccadilly Circus. The failed early dinner hadn't been down to the lack of menu choice – the food was plentiful – but there was a distracting tug inside her that refused to go away.

Living on the streets had taught Eki to pay attention to such feelings. Hunches were like a sixth sense for navigating through the ever-changing landscape of people. Police presence, angry pedestrians, private security firms... the list of things that could change her world in a single moment was endless.

The tug led her to St. James's Square, a twenty-minute walk between bins. It wasn't a place Eki would usually visit, even though she loved being around libraries. She heard the street grapevine, recounting horror stories about The square's treatment of the poor. If you were homeless, you had to be naïve or mad to head over there. Eki was neither, yet she had done the crazy thing of sitting down. Waiting. For what? She hadn't the slightest idea. The only thing she had was faith.

Something was coming. Eki could feel it in her bones.

Hour two.

The sound of a church bell in the distance sent a chill down her already cold body. She had heard those chimes before. Even though Eki tried hard not to join the dots, her eyes were already scanning the square. Faith. Evidence of things not seen.

Seen.

The old lady on the park bench wasn't a surprise, but it still caught her off guard. She assumed they would never set eyes on each other again. The toxic concoction of pride and hurt kept Eki from walking over to her. There was a traumatic history between the two of them that was still unresolved, and she was content leaving that part of her life untouched. The old lady hadn't changed. Even from across the road Eki could tell she was still choosing to look like a kind and wise grandmother that had travelled the world. That image was just an illusion; a way of making whoever was around drop their guard. Eki had fallen for it before. Not any more. She had learnt her lesson.

Or had she? The old lady had been eating a sandwich and, by default, Eki looked for the lemonade and lime. That brought an inner smile that made her annoyed. She desperately wanted to hate the old lady and everything she symbolised, and now a stupid drink was bringing back warm memories. She remembered how fussy the old lady was. There had been one day when they had walked for miles to find the perfect lemonade drink. Even then, she complained it was nothing like her recipe back home.

Home was in a place called PARADOX. Eki had visited that world many times, sat on her porch outside the cabin and drunk the old lady's sugary drink. They would chat for hours about life, dreams and family. It was a special time, full of hope. Then everything changed. All it took was one day. Eki finally saw what PARADOX was all about and by then it was too late.

Hour three.

Pevensie. That oddly dressed man was the messenger for PARADOX. He was the go-between, the broker of good and bad news. Pevensie had the vital role of delivering communication across opposing camps. Some even called him a peacekeeper, noting how he could keep people talking at the worst of times. It was true. He was someone both sides trusted because he refused to take sides. But Eki knew of the rumours.

The peacekeeper preferred one side more than the other.

Seeing him walk from the library had filled Eki with dread. After what had happened on her last visit, any message from PARADOX would be distressing. The meeting was short and to the point. Pevensie handed over the antique pocket watch; Eki's watch. He had found it under the red velvet chair. Pevensie thought she would have wanted it back. That simple message was the reason her world was now turned inside out.

The pocket watch had been a fortieth birthday present from her family. Her oldest daughter, Louisa, had chosen it. Eki never had favourites, but Louisa was the one she looked out for the most. The girl was good with numbers, and even at fourteen, could tear through data like a pro. If she played her cards right, Louisa would be the natural successor to the family business. Follow in her mother's footsteps. That was Eki's dream. But her daughter hadn't been a fan.

The two of them never had arguments, only heated debates. That was OK. She always wanted her daughters to hold their own. But she never understood why Louisa was so passionately against her line of work. Especially her latest client. The job was paying her triple. On completion, it would have set the family up for life. Louisa had seen it differently. Eki was 'selling her soul', the client was 'dangerous'. She ignored her daughter's plea until the dreadful day she discovered what her work was all about.

Eki's family was in danger. For weeks she tried everything to change the outcome. Against her professional pride, she even attempted to cook the books. But the books were already cooked by her client. Every Path she took, it always led to the same failed destination: The Theatre. The only option left for her was to run, and that broke her heart.

Saying goodbye to her family was the toughest thing she had ever done. Eki managed the pain by assuring them that this would only be temporary. She would find a way to put things right; walk The Paths again. As a sign, she had given her watch to Louisa, promising her that she would be back to wind up the hands.

That had been fifteen years ago.

And now Eki's worst nightmare had come true. The Theatre had finally found her family.

Eki's mind came back to the present.

Reaching out, grabbing hold of a stranger's leg wasn't something she would typically do. But desperation makes people act irrationally. The stranger had 'that' look. Only one thing could leave an image like that on a person's face.

The red velvet chair.

She opened the clasp of the pocket watch. The hands hadn't moved. That was a good sign. Eki had played the game enough times to know that the stranger wouldn't understand what was going on. That didn't matter. It was all about following the hints now. She never understood why she still remembered the visits to PARADOX and The Theatre at the centre of that strange land. Most people forgot as soon as they left. For the stubborn ones, it might take them a week, maybe a month. But for Eki, the memories had never let up. She had always thought it was a curse; punishment from the old lady for what had happened. But right now she was considering it a blessing. It was good that she remembered. Those memories were telling her what to do next.

She needed to wait. The Applause was her way back. It would find them. It always did.

They just had to look.

CHAPTER 12
A PAPER DANCE

"You see, but you do not observe."
(Arthur Conan Doyle, A Scandal in Bohemia)

I COULDN'T STOP looking at the pocket watch in Eki's hand.

Frantically, I searched for an explanation other than the one foremost in my mind. She stole it. Found it. A coincidence. None of them stuck. I couldn't silence the inner knowing that Pevensie had given it to her. I just wished I knew why. CLICK. Eki closed the antique clamshell.

"Everything's an illusion, you know. So many people pass by me, and they don't see The Paths."

I recognised her stare. Flashbacks and regrets. I had tasted the same lethal cocktail many times. Her facial twitches gave away the struggle to keep the tears at bay. Without thinking, my hand reached over to hers. Compassion. A few seconds later I pulled it back, aware that I had broken the golden rule of not touching. She gave me a warm smile, before carrying on.

"I thought I had figured it out, the various Paths. But I hadn't learnt a thing. Even though I knew what was coming up, I still made the same decision. That's the power of the place. It makes you see what you want to see."

Eki was now looking all over the place, darting from the street to the square. Her rambling speech wasn't making any sense, but I had the uncomfortable feeling she was doing it on purpose. She wanted me curious, willing to fall deeper into a mystery yet to be revealed. But this wasn't about me. That's why she never asked for my name. I was just her tool.

She was buying time.

*****

Keep a distance.

Eki didn't want to ask for the stranger's name. Knowing something like that would complicate things. It was best not to know too many details. He was being played, just like her. Getting involved in his journey would risk messing up her way back. Anyway, it could turn out they were enemies. That's how PARADOX worked sometimes. It turned people against each other.

PARADOX.

She hated that place, and now its claws were around her family. For fifteen years she had kept silent about its secrets, never once overstepping the mark. The reason for her sealed mouth was the hope that this unspoken bargain would keep her family safe. That was before Pevensie had given her the watch. Screw the silence. This was now war.

It didn't matter that the stranger looked confused at what she was saying. What she needed to do was to buy time. The entrance would be around here somewhere.

She always intended to get back to PARADOX. One final time, to end it. End the whole damn thing. But the thought of being this close made her stomach wrench with intense hatred. Destroying the place wasn't good enough for her. She wanted to inflict pain on everyone there, just like they had hurt her. And Eki's final act of judgement would be The Theatre. She would lock the doors during a full house and light a match. Watching it burn down would be the perfect send off.

But she was jumping ahead of herself. Judgement needed to wait. To save her family, she needed to find the entrance. And for that, she had to keep the stranger distracted. The Applause would come.

Give it time.

*****

"Look at that."

I followed Eki's finger. She was pointing to a discarded newspaper caught in the breeze. I tried to look impressed, but it was just a piece of rubbish.

"Don't just see it. Observe it."

I played along with her overdramatic plea. The newspaper gracefully danced around the street. It soared to a silent rhythm. Dipping. Turning. Twisting. The invisible wind transformed something considered trash into an item of beauty. My body tingled with a childlike wonder.

"Beautiful, eh? It's amazing what wonders you see from this concrete stage. Louisa taught me that. She's one of my daughters. Did I tell you that already? I have three children. Whenever I used to work too hard, Louisa would come into my study and tell me to take a break. Mummy, walk outside. Mummy, sit on the grass. Mummy, watch creation's show.

I would protest at first. There were always jobs to do. But deep inside, I enjoyed having the excuse to leave work behind. We watched countless performances together. Sometimes she would join in with the show. A duet with a butterfly or a synchronised dance with a leaf caught up in the breeze. It was beautiful. Creative."

Eki stopped talking, her outstretched finger shaking. She was holding back the tears again. Her memories of those performances weren't so beautiful after all.

"One afternoon during one of these shows, she told me about her morning. A travelling funfair had turned up in town. Louisa met someone in a tent. A storyteller. They recounted to her tales of mystical lands that lay beyond the horizon of mere data and results, where imagination walked hand in hand with creation. I could tell it was a con. Most people could. But Louisa, such a creative girl who loved to dream, she fell for it, hook line and sinker. Then came her bombshell: she wanted to join the funfair."

Eki never moved her gaze from the dancing newspaper as she continued with her tale.

"I stopped her. Don't judge me. That's what parents are supposed to do – be the guardians of a fragile life. But you must understand, it wasn't because I was stubborn. I would never stand in the way of my daughter finding happiness."

She cleared her throat. This was hard for her.

"I refused because I knew things. My high-paying client was working on a new project. It was horrible. They had this crazy idea about how to measure human worth. For those who didn't match up to the expected grade, my client would raise such hatred against those poor souls that there would be nowhere safe for them to go. The funfair, and everything it stood for, was high on their list.

If Louisa joined, I couldn't imagine what would have happened to her. I had seen how my client had worked in the past. It wasn't just their rage that made me scared. No. It was their gleeful vengeance. They got a kick from seeing the undesirables suffer. Even though I hated it all, I turned a blind eye to the cleansing. It was in the distance, never impacting my family. Until Louisa. That's why I had to stop her from joining; to save her. You understand, don't you?"

I didn't. But I nodded. Eki needed reassurance that she had done the right thing. It was clear from her drained expression that she was fighting an uphill battle. She didn't even believe the reasons herself.

Suddenly, the wind died down. We both watched the newspaper float into the wet gutter. Within seconds the dirty water became a sodden chain around any future dance. Eki sighed.

"We all get a chance to fly. And we all get our wings clipped by the weight of the world. I saw my daughter fly. And I saw her crash down in tears."

*****

Eki didn't want to move her gaze from the motionless paper.

The scars from her past hadn't healed. Everything she had done – running away and trying to change PARADOX – was all for her family. The pain of being away from them had been manageable by believing that they were soaring high. But the message from Pevensie had been clear. She had failed.

But there was hope.

Something caught her eye. In the distance. Eki gave it a quick glance, not wanting to make it obvious. She didn't want to scare the stranger away. Not now. The sense of anticipation grew as it slowly moved around the square. In a few minutes, she would be back in PARADOX. Then what? Old friends would be waiting for her, so would... She stopped herself. The wind was picking up again, so why wasn't the paper moving? It should be. That was the sign, part of Pevensie's message to her. A chance to fly again.

Unless.

A horrible feeling started to weigh heavy upon her once hopeful heart.

CHAPTER 13
HOW IT STARTS

"The moment you doubt whether you can fly, you cease forever to be able to do it."
(J.M. Barrie, Peter Pan)

"ARE YOU OK?"

I was concerned for Eki. Her hunched-over form was shaking, willing with all her might for the water-soaked paper to fly again. All around us, small twigs and fallen leaves had taken over the dance. For someone who minutes earlier had encouraged me to watch the wonders of creation, she was now ignoring this impressive show.

"Please God, move."

Her broken voice attempted to make itself heard over the increasing sound of the wind. When the paper didn't respond, she opened the clasp of the pocket watch and stared into its mechanical heart. The time hadn't changed. A look of confusion etched itself onto her face. She turned the clock towards the motionless paper.

"Look! The hands. They're not moving. Why aren't you flying?"

I tried touching her shoulder to offer comfort. The sudden turn of her head told me to back off. Behind those red, tear-filled eyes was a fear verging on insanity. I didn't understand, but somehow her life depended upon that sodden paper lifting off the ground.

*****

Pevensie noticed the change in the wind.

It was beginning. Right on schedule. There was a fleeting desire to be back in the square, watching the scene unfold. He entertained the thought long enough to bring a smile to his face, then he moved onto more pressing matters. His checklist of jobs still wasn't complete.

Leave PARADOX unnoticed. Done.

Contact Abrahams. Done.

Misdirect Them. Done, sort of.

It still troubled Pevensie as to why They weren't waiting for him outside the library. His moves were designed to be a sleight-of-hand; a subtle misdirection to keep spying eyes off his next task. Thankfully, it didn't matter that things hadn't gone to plan, he was still able to tick off the next item on his checklist.

Deliver the message to Eki. Done.

But why had his misdirection failed? He had the uncomfortable feeling that someone was playing him. They knew something he didn't. Maybe that was why the old lady was watching from the park bench. He pulled himself back from going too far down the rabbit hole of conjecture. These questions were not going to be answered quickly. Whatever was in the shadows would eventually come into the light, he just needed to be patient. And prepared. He continued to go through the checklist.

Deliver the second message to Eki. In progress.

It wasn't his idea to use the dancing paper. He knew it would be a cruel touch, but understood why it was an effective tool to push things forward. Sometimes he hated his job. This was one of those days.

The last job was to find The Twins. That task would be the hardest to complete. They were hiding for a reason. And even if he did find them, there was no guarantee they would believe any of his words.

Pevensie had his doubts about all these moves. Just like any grandmaster, his employer had thought through every position on the board. But that didn't mean the outcome was inevitable. These moves were designed to bring chaos. And with chaos, came uncertainty. That was his employer's greatest weakness. For some unknown reason, they never liked to interfere in the game as much as they could. That left the board open for surprising moves. Pevensie wished he could pull off a surprising move of his own. Someone would be waiting for him after this job. The rumours were true. He had chosen sides, and would now have to face the consequences.

And something more.

I felt powerless to help Eki.

And scared.

The wind was turning into a gale. There was a haunting atmosphere in the air that only amplified Eki's strange behaviour. A storm was coming and it wasn't just from the sky. Sensing that I was about to leave, she spun around and pressed her hand into mine. A shot of pain ran up my arm. Something cold and sharp dug into my skin. Her watch.

"Take it. I beg of you. Take it."

I tried pulling away to relieve the pain. Eki wouldn't let go. Her hand pressed harder against mine, creating a protective cocoon.

"*She*."

Eki didn't want to accept the premise of what was about to come out of her mouth. Verbalising it would seal her fate. But what choice did she have?

"*She. She* still remembers."

In amongst the wind and dancing twigs, her defeated eyes were trying to tell me something. I opened my mouth to ask, but the strengthening gale had given her hope again. Eki threw herself onto the floor. Her face lit up as one edge of the newspaper fluttered. She let out an encouraging laugh tinged with relief.

"Yes. I knew it! You can do it."

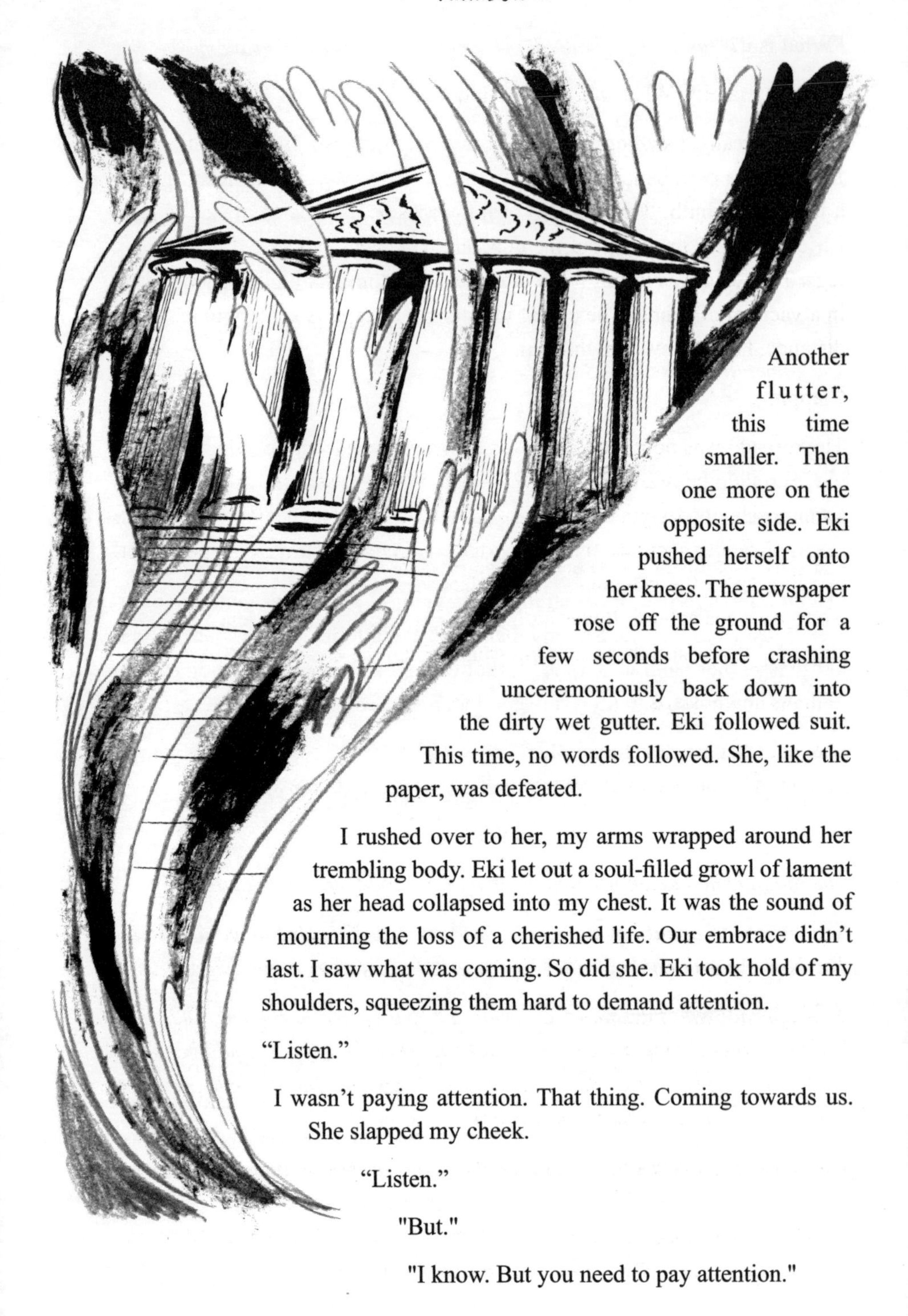

Another flutter, this time smaller. Then one more on the opposite side. Eki pushed herself onto her knees. The newspaper rose off the ground for a few seconds before crashing unceremoniously back down into the dirty wet gutter. Eki followed suit. This time, no words followed. She, like the paper, was defeated.

I rushed over to her, my arms wrapped around her trembling body. Eki let out a soul-filled growl of lament as her head collapsed into my chest. It was the sound of mourning the loss of a cherished life. Our embrace didn't last. I saw what was coming. So did she. Eki took hold of my shoulders, squeezing them hard to demand attention.

"Listen."

I wasn't paying attention. That thing. Coming towards us. She slapped my cheek.

"Listen."

"But."

"I know. But you need to pay attention."

"What is it?"

"Find my family. Whatever you do, find them."

I wasn't really listening. A small tornado of rubbish and vegetation had formed by a park bench. The vortex moved along the street, flickering like a faulty light bulb. It did a sharp turn towards us, jerking from side to side. I tried to get to my feet, but the concrete pavement had sealed itself to my legs. The wind was in full force now, but everything had fallen silent. I was in a vacuum of sound. The eye of the storm. Except. A solitary tone. In the distance. Faint. Slow. Rhythmical.

Clapping.

The tornado was now only ten yards away. My eyes were playing tricks on me. Through the twisting tunnel of leaves, I could just make out a building. Grandiose in its design, the entrance paid homage to Greek architecture with seven Corinthian pillars that supported an imposing triangular pediment. Leading up to the ostentatious entrance was a concrete staircase. Twenty. No thirty steps at least. It was hard to tell between the flying debris. And the clapping. It was still there, coming from behind the closed door.

"This is how it starts."

I never got a chance to turn around and ask what Eki's broken whisper meant. The tornado lurched over my frozen body and everything went dark.

*****

The old lady had taken her time walking back to St. James's Square.

She wanted to avoid having a conversation with Eki. One move at a time. The board wasn't ready for that reveal yet. This strategy required patience.

As she turned into the square, everything had returned to normal. The wind had died down. Eki had gone. She pondered where, hoping it would be to the most obvious place after the dancing paper episode. These whole series of next moves hinged on that journey of desperation.

The old lady's heart grew heavy as she stood on the pavement by the wet newspaper. Bending down to touch the gutter, she could feel the pain of Eki's destroyed hope. Creation remembers. It always does. Hopes crushed? Maybe. Maybe not. She looked at the paper still chained to its wet master.

It quivered before stretching itself towards the sky. The sight of it soaring through the street brought a smile to her face.

"There is always another side to a tale."

She watched the paper turn towards the park bench, before settling back on the ground. The old lady never quite understood why people rarely believed in the magic of stories. But then again, it made her job easier. It gave her the opportunity to make surprising moves, such as this. No one would see it coming.

And Abrahams was walking right into it.

STAVE 2
BEFORE THE DECISION

CHAPTER 14
NOWHERE

"Do you understand, sir, do you understand what it means when you have absolutely nowhere to turn?"
(Fyodor Dostoyevsky, Crime and Punishment)

WHERE?

I was feeling groggy, lying on the floor. A throbbing headache had made itself at home and was now setting up for the night. I tried opening my eyes, but the faintest of movements sent a sharp pain across the front of my head.

Where?

The question repeated itself. My open palm could feel the rough texture of dry ground. There was a warmth coming from the dirt. I was somewhere hot. The dry, intense heat was making my clothes soak up the onset of sweat. But this place didn't feel like home.

Home?

I was struggling to piece together where I had just come from. London. But this wasn't London now. How did I know that? The dirt. There's dirt in London. Yes. Except, I was on the pavement before coming here. Alone? No. With someone. A woman. She gave me an object. What object? A watch. Have I still got it? I think so. My hand scrambled around trying to find the watch. The sudden movement was accompanied by another stab of pain. The memories continued. This time, I was watching a tornado coming towards me. Inside the vortex was a building. My body tensed up.

“You alright, sonny? Mighty big fall you had.”

The male voice pressed pause on the terrifying scene.

“Who's there?”

There was no answer. I opened my eyes, accepting the pain that immediately dug its claws into me. Nothing was in focus. All I could see was a blur of colourful shapes. Without thinking I frantically rubbed my eyes, trying to wipe the blanket of mist away.

“No. No. Don’t do that.”

It was too late. Every movement dragged invisible grit across my eyes, along with a scream.

“Rubbing just makes things worse. You visitors never learn. Your landing brought with it a cloud of dust. It’s in your eyes now. A right big layer of the ugly stuff.”

The mysterious voice was in front of me. It was a mixture of an East End market stall trader and a carnival announcer. His ‘cheeky-chappie geezer’ tone could sell anything off the back of a lorry, including a season ticket for a one-night-only show.

“The answer is to blow the stuff out. A good huff and puff. It just sucks if you’re on your own, if you get my drift.”

He had a little chuckle to himself before his blurred outline bent over me. His hands grabbed hold of my face. Every one of his stubby fingers had a ring on them. No doubt another back-of-the-lorry deal. He stretched my eyelids and gave a long blow. Then two more for good measure.

“There. As good as new. Next time, shut your eyes when you fall. Like I said, you visitors never learn, no matter how many times you visit.”

The question returned. Where? This time, it brought a friend.

How many times had I been here?

*****

His breath had the strange mixture of stale coffee, cigarette smoke and a fresh mint sweet.

I hadn't smelt that aroma in years.

My father was one of those old-school men, born during the last years of the Second World War. He believed it was his duty to provide for his family. His payoff for such chivalry was a quick half at the local pub and a few hours alone in the garden shed during the weekend.

By the time I had come along, he had bent the rules a little more to include the odd cigarette. Mum didn't mind the smell of alcohol, but nicotine was off limits. That was the devil's aroma. She barred it from the house, so Dad resorted to a sneaky smoke on the way home from work. He would try and cover up his dance with the devil by taking a few mints. It was the worst cover-up. Even I knew what he had done. But Mum played along. I think she appreciated that he remembered the mints.

She knew giving Dad a little slack was important. However silly it sounded, that cigarette was his way of dealing with one of those life-sucking ten-hour factory shifts he did every day. He was a stubborn git. Mum offered to work, but Dad refused. Providing food on the table and money to pay the bills was his domain. Take that away and he would feel less of a man.

I think that's what killed him in the end.

The memories stopped. Going on any further would only bring tears. Tears and dust don't mix well.

*****

The coffee-infused blow worked.

I opened my eyes. They were still sensitive, but that didn't matter. I was just relieved that I could see again. The first thing that greeted me was a beaming smile. It was a grin that sparkled with three gold teeth on the top row and two on the bottom.

"Pleased to meet you. My name is Trott. Trott by name and Trott by nature."

Trott by speech as well. He reached out his ring infested hand and helped me up. His beaming smile widened as he dusted off my clothes. Trott was just under five foot, but his height didn't match the strength of his voice. The power of his vocal chords made his overhanging belly wobble with each phrase. Unlike his hair. That mop stood its ground due to the thick layer of wax backcombed into a homage to Elvis.

His clothes lived up to his carnival voice: a chequered waistcoat and flannel trousers. The crisp, bleached white shirt had a frayed collar from overuse. His shoes, dark brown, were heavy enough to settle any disturbance if needed. The final touch was a brown trilby hat. He worked it as an expert, waving it around his head to emphasise whatever point he wanted to make. The whole image may have looked random, but he had purposely chosen each item. It was all part of the show. And Trott lived up to it with perfection.

"So, I guess you are wondering where you are?"

Trott move his trilby hat around in the air for the big announcement. I instinctively held my breath.

"Except."

The hat dropped to his side.

"The problem is, this place lost its name years ago. Title-less, if you get my drift. And that messes with any grand introductions. So instead, I gave it a nickname. 'Nowhere.' And believe you me, this place lives up to its name."

Trott was right. This place did live up to its name. But it had been Somewhere once. The flat foreboding central plain carried all the hallmarks of a long drought. There was the occasional green patch of hope, but as with all levels of faith, optimism was in the eyes of the beholder. And I had none.

The dry spell had hit this place hard. Every bit of the land was down on its knees, begging for rain. To my right, there were the remnants of activity long gone. Rusty machinery. Abandoned work sheds. An engineless pickup truck with three flat tires. Past residents had tried to make something out of this place, but those farmers had departed years ago.

I tried to imagine what it must have been like living in this film set of the apocalypse. Every day must have been a kick in the head. Failed harvests. Dust storms. Random power cuts. You couldn't even put your wet clothes out to dry. Whatever tried to keep people here, its promise of a reward wasn't good enough. This piece of land had breathed its last breath. Watching your neighbours leave two by two must have been tough. Only the hard nuts or plain stupid remained until the end.

So what did that make Trott?

CHAPTER 15
TROTT'S WONDERLAND

"Never question the truth of what you fail to understand, for the world is filled with wonders."
(L. Frank Baum, Rinkitink in Oz)

"IT WASN'T ALWAYS LIKE THIS."

Trott sensed my disappointment with the place as I scanned the horizon.

"I remember when this land was full of green trees and harvest fields. And where you're looking right now, that dust bowl used to be a crystal lake. Such a beautiful spot and great for fishing."

He took a pause, clearing a lump in his throat. His trilby hat gently tapped against his leg.

"At its height, there were over eleven-hundred residents in this place. It was one of those towns that people always wanted to visit and never leave. I first came here as a kid. Later, when I set up my business, I thought of no better place to call home. Those were the days. I would rake in the cash. Some years I would make enough profit to take the missus on holiday for three months.

Then the drought hit. The residents left and visitor numbers dropped. My business, like so many others, suffered. I hung on for a few years, but one day my missus told me she was leaving. I didn't blame her, I was a miserable bugger and also stubborn. Everything I had built up was running on empty, but I refused to accept defeat. I stayed in the town, thinking she would come back. She never did. Neither did the crowds."

The hat stopped trotting.

"I heard on the wind she had found another fella, someone who treated her well. That's good. As for me, I'm stuck here with nowhere to go. Geez. The past. It sure messes with the head."

Trott snapped out of his sombre reminiscing as he looked over my dust-covered clothes. He stretched wide his mouth. The rays of the sun hit his golden teeth, turning his wince into a bright spotlight. It was as if I was on stage, all eyes watching my performance. He turned his head and the spotlight switched off.

"Hmm. You need a new shirt; it's ripped. I have a spare one in my caravan. It's just a ten-minute walk."

He didn't take his arm off my shoulder as we moved. The display of affection made me uncomfortable. I couldn't help but think this was all part of his sales pitch. His business.

And I didn't have to wait for long to hear what he was selling.

They delivered the bad news.

Abrahams had gone. Lost. And as They predicted, He wasn't pleased.

The only saving grace was that They were delivering the report separated by a locked study door. A silent 'Amen' was offered in thanks as the sound of glass smashed against the wooden frame. THEY turned and left.

He had many names, but his favourite was The Magician. He liked how it had a magie élaborée to its sound. The theatrical was something he adored, even though he hated the theatre world; an ironic twist.

Following Abrahams was his way of scratching a doubting itch which hadn't gone away. The last visit had been memorable, but there had been loose ends. Some of those unresolved issues had given The Magician hope. Others, not so. The finale had gone off as planned. Even the little twist He threw in at the end was impressive. But when Abrahams returned home, The Magician couldn't shake off the feeling He had missed something.

And now that doubting itch was keeping him up at night.

He had been in these situations before. The finale in The Theatre was never as cut and dried as people hoped it would be. But if things went wrong, it usually meant the involvement of other people. So who was messing with Abrahams' story? He had a hunch about Pevensie. When The Magician got word from his helpers that the drunken fool was at the library, it only confirmed what He already suspected. Pevensie had chosen sides.

The old lady.

Otherwise known as The Storyteller.

So what was She up to? It would have been easier if his helpers hadn't lost Abrahams. He needed to confirm how the boy had returned. But The Magician had learnt the hard way not to rush into things. To play the old lady's game, one needed to be patient. Sooner or later She would slip up and reveal too much. Until then, He needed to wait. Anyway, there were other things to prepare for. Abrahams had returned to PARADOX and The Magician needed to brush up on his performance.

The boy always liked his magic show.

*****

"Here it is, my pride and joy."

Trott was in his element. His trilby hat waved around his head as his beaming grin complimented the bounce in his step.

"My Carnival. I call it 'TROTT's WONDERLAND OF FUN'. It's the greatest show in the world."

It didn't exactly look like a wonderland of fun. A rickety scaffold sign precariously announced the name. The only wonder it conveyed was that it was still up in one piece. Health and Safety would have had a field day with their clipboards.

Behind the fragile structure was a carnival that had seen better days. Just like 'Nowhere'. The booths which once welcomed punters with bright colours and teasing lights were now held up with brown tape and prayer. Most of the bulbs had long since burnt out. The ones still working, flickered randomly as if powered by a generator running on the fumes of memories gone by.

In between the sad looking monuments of forgotten joy were six questionable rides. There was a little rollercoaster for under 8's, a medium-sized dodgem circuit, a Ferris wheel, two heart-thumping twists, and a family carousel. Rust was the dominant colour around the steel frames. It acted as a silent reminder for any punter to check their life insurance policy before taking a seat. And there lay the catch twenty-two for visitors. All the lawyers had already left town.

Steel wire held up a speaker system that Trott must have stolen from the lorry called 'the seventies seaside bingo hall'. Distortion was the prevailing sound. Occasionally, a pre-recorded 'fun announcement' would break up the generic piped music.

ROLL UP. ROLL UP. TROTT's WONDERLAND OF FUN.

THE RIDES ARE GREAT. THE RIDES ARE FAST. SO SUCK UP THE JOY AND SCREAM.

Except, the announcement came from a warped tape reel. YOU and SUCK came across louder than anything else. It flawlessly captured the spirit of the park.

I felt sorry for Trott. The drought had hit his pension plan hard. No punters meant no cash. The empty pot of funds led to his rides looking like anything but fun. And so started the vicious circle of life. Who in their right mind would set foot in this place? The park was empty. But Trott still believed. His eyes were alive with pride and excitement. He loved this place and, like any adoring parent, blindness was a prerequisite to how much of a brat the kid was.

We stood under the scaffold sign for a few moments. The trilby hat was once again trotting against the leg. He was thinking. Reminiscing.

"I'm trying to remember when I last had a visitor. This Christmas? Or was it the one before? Old age. It plays havoc with my head."

Not remembering troubled the carnival owner. It was just a niggle, but enough to show.

"Ahh, anyway. It will come to me, always does. So, what do you say? Want to have a look around? The first ride is on me."

I looked up at the sign again. So I finally got my answer to where I was: TROTT's WONDERLAND. But it didn't make sense. I was still walking blindfolded, feeling an invisible hand guiding my way.

*****

Trott didn't like how his memory went off for long walks.

The last few years had become difficult. He had seen some of his friends go the same way. It started with the odd date and nameless face, then slowly morphed into whole timelines saying goodbye. Trott's condition hadn't got that bad yet, but it was coming. Dates and names were his things at the moment.

He wanted to ask the stranger's name but felt he already knew it. Maybe thinking back to his last visitor would help. It worked in the past. He called his system 'the index card trot'. One memory card led to another. Build up enough rhythm, and he could kick-start the cards that were refusing to come out and play.

His mind focused on a silhouetted figure. When did that nameless character visit him? Last year. Christmas? They were angry about something. Damn. Trott lost his train of thought. He started his 'index card trot' again. Christmas. Visitor. Angry. About? They wanted to find someone. No. It wasn't just one person they were after. Two people. The Twins. Trott shivered under the sun's heat. He remembered that the visitor wanted to hurt them.

Trott didn't feel proud of his system this time. He didn't want to remember anymore, but the cards kept turning. More memories were coming back to him. He knew the name of his angry visitor and recognised the face.

And now that visitor had returned.

CHAPTER 16
PLASTIC BELL

"When you're twenty-one, life is a roadmap. It's only when you get to be twenty-five or so that you begin to suspect that you've been looking at the map upside down, and not until you're forty are you entirely sure. By the time you're sixty, take it from me, you're... lost."
(Stephen King, Joyland)

'TROTT'S WONDERLAND OF FUN'.

Walking under that rickety sign was like travelling back to my childhood. I remembered how my Dad used to love taking me to the various funfairs when they turned up to town. I don't know who was more excited to queue up for the season pass. He would invent some cock-and-bull story about it giving him an excuse not to think about factory work. But I could see behind that beaming smile and wide eyes, this was his version of joining the circus. The funfair was an invitation to walk on a land beyond his borders. Every jock operator had travelled far and wide. They had pitched up in places that were probably not even on the map. Those touring shows were a doorway into another world, full of adventurous tales only whispered in secret. And for a few hours, my Dad wanted in.

So did I.

My first visit to a funfair was when I was six.

Dad had taken a day off, supposedly sick. He wanted to introduce me to 'MR. BARNEY'S PLAYPEN'. It visited our town every year, just as autumn hit. Crisp air. Fallen leaves. And the idea that Christmas was just around the corner. It made the whole week feel magical.

My young eyes had never seen such a place before. The atmosphere freaked out my senses. I was on the ultimate sugar rush. Everywhere I looked, there was a tale. Some stories carried the joys of prizes won; others brought the tears of tired kids and worn out parents. The best tales were the ones that involved the ride jocks themselves. These people dressed differently, spoke differently, watched people differently. They were the guardians of mystery.

The first brightly coloured canopy we visited was the coconut stall. My excitement must have been evident. The jock was an old guy with a baseball cap that had the carnival's logo printed on it. A big fluffy bear. You could tell he hated the hat but loved seeing the kids have fun. When we had finished, he came over and placed a small plastic bell in my hand. He whispered it was magical. All I needed to do was to ring it whenever I wanted the funfair to come back to town.

Needless to say, I rang the bell a few times. It took a long time for them to respond. I blamed the plastic clapper. It didn't have a loud ring.

I was eighteen when I made my last visit to the funfair.

My love life was facing one of those heartbreaking moments. I was dating a girl called Laura. It was our final night together before she headed off to university, halfway across the country. We could've gone anywhere that evening, but the lure of the visiting show was too much. It also gave us the excuse of not having to think about the inevitable. We both knew our relationship would not last the three-hundred-mile round-trip. The funfair avoided awkward promises we would no doubt break by the end of the month.

The place called itself 'SAILORS', even though there wasn't a single ounce of a nautical theme to it. My childlike wonder had transformed itself into the scepticism of a late teenager. The jocks weren't mysterious any more. Instead, they were just plain weird, with kidnapping eyes and questionable fashion taste. The rides got the same cynical stare. All the thrill of the fair has disappeared. The only thing I was interested in was winning a prize.

Regardless of the cheap rides, flaky paint and the terrible music, I was still happy to be there. For hours we went from stall to stall, ride to ride. We drank sugared drinks and abused our bodies with food that rejected every good nutrient. The final stop on our visit was a coconut stall. Seeing it made me feel nostalgic about childhood. I couldn't resist having a go. Lady luck was shining down on me that night. I won a prize.

A cheap plastic bell.

Nothing changed. Except for one thing. There was no magical story attached to it this time. The jock sensed my scepticism. Laura wanted me to put the crappy thing in the bin, but I couldn't throw it away. Memories. What goes around comes around. A humble, mass-produced plastic bell became the most sentimental of gifts.

It beautifully bookmarked my childhood years.

After 'SAILORS', came adulthood and Margaret Thatcher.

The Iron Lady barged into my childhood playground and turned the funfair into a segregation camp. Long steel fences of personal wealth divided the haves and have-nots. I got sold on the idea of the yuppie dream and the intoxicating desire of putting myself first. And the best part of it? I could wash my conscience clear each night by believing in the beauty of trickle-down economics.

By the time I bought my first imitation leather Filofax, I had already maxed out my credit limit – and not just the financial one. My conscience was in the red, but I wasn't interested in paying off the debt. No matter what I saw on the news or in the streets, I happily lived in ignorance. The coal-dusted faces fighting for their existence never impacted me. I saw them only as spoilt brats not wanting to embrace reform. As for long queues of people waiting for ill-fitting job leads, they were nothing but slackers and benefit cheats. Shockingly, I convinced myself that whatever a person sows is what they reap. I was the living embodiment of the Poor Law, Scrooge to perfection. My bah-humbug declaration was the unquestionable belief in the power of

SELF. Instagram had nothing on us Thatcher kids. We invented the ultimate 'selfie' before Zuckerberg got out of his nappies. I just never considered the lives I was ignoring as I kept looking at myself.

One of them being my Dad.

He lost his job. The factory went through a restructuring, sold as 'remodelling for the future'. His golden handshake was a discount voucher for computer training. My dad lasted two sessions before the trainer gave up on him. Apparently, he wasn't the right type of person for this brave new world.

The broken fifty-four year old eventually found a job, an out-of-hours shelf-stacking position with a supermarket chain. My dad's worth was the minimum wage. He felt useless and a burden on society. I think the only thing that got him through each day was the dignity that he could still bring food to the family table.

As for myself, I was too busy taking another 'selfie' to notice how my father's eyes had changed. I even missed that his breath had stopped smelling of fresh mints. Whenever I visited, the majority of my monologue was about how great I was doing. My mother dropped a few hints, but I never listened.

Until.

The phone call. She told me that the police had found his body. Heart attack. The midnight shifts were too much for him. I cried when I heard the news. Not sure if it was because of the shock or that he died the same way as he lived. Run-of-the-mill.

I helped Mum clean out his study. She didn't want to do it on her own. We found some letters. My Dad must have known his days were being called in. He could tell his body wasn't working right. These letters were his way of signing off to the people he loved.

The letter told me how important it was never to lose the dream of another world. One where hope and imagination crafted every valley and hill. He urged me to hold onto the wonder of being a child because it was the only way to see how fake this present life had become. My Dad went on with his revolutionary plea. The worth of a person had nothing to do with their monetary wealth. Neither was education just about English and Maths. Never equate success to a fancy car and a big house. And finally his commission: 'It is all an illusion. Pull the curtain back and you see what is real.' Dad loved *The Wizard the Oz.*

The postscript told me to look inside the bottom desk drawer. Inside was the plastic bell from our first funfair visit. The thing looked cheaper than I remembered it, but I still wanted to ring the bell. I cried for a long time in that study. Thatcherism and the yuppie dream had lost its glamour. I saw the selfish king walking down the street for what he truly was. Naked. The desire to be like Dickens took on a whole new dimension after that. I wanted my words to shout out as loud as they could, that the king had an ugly arse.

That's what birthed my first book.

It hadn't taken me long to forget those tears in my Dad's study.

After the success of the first book, I wasn't interested in shouting out at the king any more. If the illusion broke and his naked butt ran off down the street, so would my advance for the next book. I couldn't let that happen. So I sold out.

Again.

*****

"Memories. They sure mess with the head."

Trott's remarks caught me off guard. I put his psychic ability down to the dazed look on my face. He was right. The memories were messing with my head, and they hadn't finished with me yet. He directed me to the stall nearest the entrance. On the shelf, behind the trestle table was the selection of prizes. There at the back, as though it had been there for years, was the story of my life.

A cheap plastic bell.

CHAPTER 17
FANCY A PLAY?

"Who turns his back upon the fallen and disfigured of his kind; abandons them as vile; and does not trace and track with pitying eyes the unfenced precipice by which they fell from good—grasping in their fall some tufts and shreds of that lost soil, and clinging to them still when bruised and dying in the gulf below; does wrong to Heaven and man, to time and to eternity. And you have done that wrong!"
(Charles Dickens, The Chimes)

TROTT KNEW how to emphasise a moment in time.

He wasn't afraid of silence, giving me enough emotional rope to tie my mind into a knot of confusion. I couldn't take my eyes off the plastic bell, struggling to understand what I had walked into. This had to be a dream. Maybe. Or was I swirling around in a world of concussion as I lay on the concrete floor outside the library? A muffled cough from behind his jewel-covered hand brought me back from the unending questions.

I stood in front of the trestle table. The mixture of sun and spilt drinks made the green baize look ready for the skip. In the middle of the table was a neatly stacked pack of cards; certainly not fifty-two in the deck. At a guess, half that amount. I assumed it was part of his budget cutbacks, post-drought. Trott adjusted my position a little. He then ambled around the table to the other side. The whole movement was orchestrated to build up anticipation for the impending game.

"Fancy a play?"

His fingers tapped the stack of cards. My hesitation resulted in his continued sales pitch.

"I know. A card game at a funfair is asking for trouble. But that's why it's so exciting. You get to see if you can beat the odds."

Trott picked up the cards, shuffled, then explained the rules. They seemed simple enough. We each pick a card. The highest wins.

"I call the game, 'The Chimes'. Named it after my favourite book."

Colour drained from my face. Trott noticed the change, accompanied with a slight smile.

"Ever read it? In fact, I'm in it. Well, not me exactly. But I do share the same name as the lead character. Not only that, the funfair is themed around the tale."

The cards fell onto the table. Trott gathered them up with a look of embarrassment. He hated how his body wasn't functioning like the old days. The shuffling continued.

"I wish I could take credit for it, but it wasn't my idea. Some storyteller used to own this place. They were selling. The P&L looked good but the fair needed a fresh coat of paint. So they knocked down the asking price and I bought it. The storytelling seller had just finished reading a book and thought the name of the lead character would help with the revamp. When they told me the story, I couldn't believe my luck. Not only did I share the same name as the hero, but it was a bloody good tale. When they suggested theming the funfair around the book, I couldn't wait to get started. The rest, as they say, is history."

"And did it bring in business?"

Trott's hand slammed on the table, spreading out the shuffled cards in one graceful action.

"Of course it did. It brought you."

*****

"Pick a card. Any card. But DON'T turn it over yet."

Trott's eyes never left my hand as I made my choice. I pulled the facedown card towards me. After a nod of approval, he made his selection.

"This game is like the opening chapters of *The Chimes.* And as all good stories should start, in the beginning there is a courier by the name of Toby 'Trotty' Veck. In a Victorian world where status is everything, our hero is a working-class man through and through. One day he sits outside a bell tower waiting for odd jobs to pay his way. But the last thing on his mind is work. News has come through that there's been an increase in crime and disorder, and the working-class are to blame. This sends him into a spiral of despair, wondering if this is a sign from heaven that God's favourite children are the upper class."

Trott's dramatic pause added to his slow build-up of the game. He wanted to make sure I soaked in everything he said.

"His daughter, Meg, and her fiancé, Richard, turn up. They inform him of their marriage plans. What should have been a joyous time upon those bell tower steps became crushed underfoot by a high society gentleman, Alderman Cute. He informs them they have no right to marry. He evens goes one step further by suggesting that their birth is considered a curse upon society. The Almighty God has deemed such things. It is their worshipful duty to accept that the lower-class are to live in the shadow of the favoured ones. Tears follow. And so does a job. Alderman commissions Trotty to deliver a letter."

"What a jerk."

"Who? Alderman?"

"No. Your namesake. Fancy taking a job from a guy that said all those cruel things. He sold his soul for the sake of money."

"And you've never sold your heart for some cash?"

I didn't reply. Trott gave me a wink. I couldn't tell if it was a joke or a sign that he knew more about me than was letting on.

"Let's see your card then."

I turned my choice over. JACK OF SPADES. I smiled.

"Impressive, but not good enough. Without even looking at my card I can guarantee my win. Tell you what, let's raise the stakes. If I turn the card over and it's lower, you get the funfair. Deal?"

It wasn't the greatest of prizes, but I played along. Trott turned over his card. KING OF HEARTS.

"Dealer wins. Told you."

"That was luck."

"Not luck. Something else. Want to play again?"

We did the same routine another four times. At every turn of his card, the dealer won.

"The game's rigged."

"Well done. You're getting close, but still not there yet."

Trott gathered up the cards and continued with the tale.

"There is a backstory to why Dickens wrote *The Chimes.* He based the high society Alderman on a real-life character – a famous magistrate renowned for his harsh viewpoints towards the poor. There was one case in particular that revealed the true nature of that judge's heart.

A mother came to court, her crime, a failed suicide attempt. She wanted to end her life because she couldn't face the workhouse system that The Poor Law was pushing her towards. The magistrate's disgust for not only her actions, but also the social class she belonged to, was shocking. But that wasn't the talking point of the town. The mother had lost her child in the failed suicide attempt. His dismissal of her pain and the worth of the young life took disgust to a whole new depth. It was only a matter of time before it grabbed Dickens' attention, and that of his imagination."

"But that still doesn't explain the cards."

Trott sighed.

"It tells you everything about the cards. The reason the dealer wins is the same reason Alderman and the magistrate said those cruel words. If you believe that the cards are dealt out according to personal worth, it's amazing how your view of others impacts the game."

"What game?"

"The game of life. All of us have done it. Stacked the cards in our favour. The dealer always wins."

"Prove it."

My reply took me by surprise. I was suddenly feeling defensive; the story was too close to home. Trott gave a little clap of excitement. His jewels made a dull sounding clank revealing that the plastic bells weren't the only cheap things at the stall.

"Thought you would never ask. But for that, we need to move on and play the next part of the story."

He bounded out from behind the table. Things were getting interesting for him now.

"You never know, you could even win a plastic bell."

CHAPTER 18
THE SOUND OF THE BELL

"Most travel, and certainly the rewarding kind, involves depending on the kindness of strangers, putting yourself into the hands of people you don't know and trusting them with your life."
(Paul Theroux, Ghost Train to the Eastern Star)

WE HADN'T WALKED more than fifty yards before Trott stopped mid-stride.

"I know the next chapter is around here, somewhere."

He did a three-hundred-and-sixty-degree scan of the fair. At first, his face found the whole hunt rather amusing. It made me think this was another part of his routine, to build up the act. But as he completed the circle, another expression rested on his face. Concern. Followed by fear. Trott noticed my stare and replaced his anxious look with a fake smile.

"That's the only problem with old age. Occasionally I forget where I put things. Not to worry, it will come to me. We just need a little walk to jog the memory. They don't call me 'Trott' for nothing."

He found the joke amusing, but it didn't hide the concern lingering behind his smile. We carried on walking. I followed. He talked. Now and then he would take a breather, looking for clues as to where we should be heading next.

"So, where were we? Yes. Our friend Trotty delivers the letter to another of those high society folk, Lord Bowley. He then waits for a reply while listening in on the man's conversation. Trotty finds out that Alderman is asking for permission to imprison a homeless man by the name of Will Fern. Lord Bowley agrees and Trotty delivers the response. And here is where everything changes."

Trott stopped walking, holding his breath as I crashed into his back. Checking I was OK with an apology, he continued.

"Walking back home, Trotty bumps into a ragamuffin carrying a young girl. As they apologise to each other, Trotty realises that the homeless man is the person Alderman wants to imprison. What a coincidence, eh? Overcome with compassion after hearing their tale, he invites Will Fern and his orphaned niece, Lilian, back to his home for the night. Who would have thought something as mundane as bumping into a stranger could shape the next scene? That's the power of what is usually ignored. A random conversation. Someone bumping into you at a funfair. Or..."

Our eyes fixed on each other.

"…even a stranger who asks you for some spare change."

Trott hoped his teasing observation would get a reaction.

And it did. The onslaught of questions kicked his 'index card trott' into action. His memory wasn't functioning like the old days, but that didn't mean he wasn't able to join a few dots together. Little things were coming back to him. He had played out the 'mundane' scene before. What triggered the memory was his visitor crashing into the back of him. But it was the first time he had used the 'spare change' line. There was a new character in the story. A homeless woman. Or not so new if truth be told. He had seen her before.

There was a magic within the funfair, something he never let on to punters. He could see things. Stories. Trott had no idea how it worked, but there were no complaints. It meant he could keep one step ahead in all the games. The magic enabled him to look into the lives of everyone who visited. It was as if he was there, outside the library, watching the scene play out.

As the questions continued about how he knew about the homeless woman, he batted them away with the usual, distracting excuse. 'It's all part of the show. We are in a funfair after all.' Dismissing it as an act seemed to work. But he wanted to make sure. He sealed the deal by adding the line, 'I was going to say, spare change for a shopping trolley, just never got a chance before you jumped in.'

A few more memory cards revealed themselves. He recalled the visitor's name. Abrahams. A writer. But hadn't he gone by another title during the last visit?

It would come to him. As for the homeless lady, Eki, she too went by a different name. But he could remember that one already. Trott hated the thought that his disease had moved on from just erasing names and dates. That filled him with fear. He had seen enough of his friends go down the same way, wandering around in a forgetful fog. That couldn't happen to him. His job depended upon a good memory as he guided people around the fair, preparing them to hear.

"The Chimes."

He repeated the words, trying to recall the location of the next ride. His face lit up. The 'index card trott' still had a bit of life in the old beast yet.

*****

Trott grabbed hold of my hand.

We hurried down the canvas-lined alleyway as though we were late for a deadline. Past the Hook a Duck. Ball in a Bucket. Tin Can Alley. And Coconut Throw.

"I know it's down here. You will love it. All we need to do is take another right."

His words trailed off as we came to a sudden stop. We were standing outside a funfair ride I hadn't been on in a long time. The Ghost Train. Even with Trott's 'Ooohhhh' expression, it didn't live up to the build up. Fluorescent painted ghouls and bats on strings weren't going to scare anyone these days. The world of horror had changed. We were now the kids with mass murderers living in dreams and crazed villains torturing victims through games. Trott didn't care. He was proud of this monument to the age of *Hammer House* and *Universal Monsters*. It was evident upon his gleaming 'Ooohhhh' face.

"I know it's dusty, but it sure packs a great scare."

Right on cue, a shallow scream came out of the public address system. The ride doors to the left opened and a carriage shuddered its way forward. It was another redundant design living in the past. This time with flaked black paint and a stuck-on spiders web. Trott walked over to the guardrail and pulled it up.

“I call this beauty 'The Sound of the Bell’. Wanna’ ride? Wanna’ scare? Makes you wet your underwear.”

I let out a little chuckle at his cringe-worthy sales pitch. At that moment I forget the weirdness of everything that was happening to me. This was an old-school ride – a monument to my childhood when carriages came from beaten metal, not moulded plastic. There were no CGI effects or over-explained plot lines for our microwave attention span. Instead, we had to rely upon conjuring up the scare through imagination alone.

Before I knew it, I was taking my seat. My imagination received a kick start from the cold industrial steel. The ghost of death had forged the ride's metal frame. A graveside coffin had provided the wooden planks for the seat. Then came the handrail. The most fearful part of all. It was critical I didn’t hold on too tightly. I would never know when it would transform itself into a metallic hand that wouldn’t let me go. And what about how these rides would save the best scare till last? A tingle of excitement danced upon my skin as I recalled the lure of the final turn and the rush towards the concrete wall. And then the electric dance faded away. It was a tragic day when I figured out that the wall would always open.

The guardrail came down with a metallic clank – a ghoul was hammering a nail. Another scream came out of the speaker, tortured souls were waiting for me beyond the gate. The carriage shuddered forward. Two goblins of hell were pushing me into the abyss.

The doorway opened. My imagination welcomed a three-minute click-clack journey into another realm.

CHAPTER 19
SCREAM

"Yet even when his eyes were opened on the mist and rain, on the moving patch of light from the lamps, and the hedge of the roadside retreating by jerks, the night shadows outside the coach would fall into the train of night shadows within. Out of the midst of them, a ghostly face would rise..."
(Charles Dickens, A Tale of Two Cities)

DISORIENTATION is the ultimate scare.

I couldn't get my bearings. Without any lights or fluorescent hanging bats, there was nothing to visually cling onto. The carriage was hurtling down a never-ending track of dark terror, as my body got pushed from side to side. There was a sudden turn to the left. Or was it the right? Left. I was certain of it. Or was I? The metal wheels made an ear-piercing screech. We were picking up speed. Suddenly there was a stomach-churning dip in the track. I lurched forward, my wrists banging against the rail. A shot of pain, an extra beat of the heart. The click-clack sound of the track encouraging the carriage to pick up its pace.

A scream of relief escaped my lips. In the distance I could see the faint glimmer of light. A silver object. And then it was gone. The track made another turn, throwing me into the dark once again. Dip. Right. Left. Dip. My hands clung to the rail as though my life was about to blow away. Another dip, then an incline. There it was. Just for a moment. A silver light. Closer this time.

A bell?

The carriage made a sharp turn to the right. My ears picked up the sound of static, the struggling P.A system had kicked into gear.

"Did you hear us?"

The voice-over artist sounded as cheap as the speakers. This must have been their big break, making sure they delivered each word as though it was destined for the Oscars.

"Well, did you hear us?"

Turn. Dip. Pick up the pace.

"Answer us."

A different voice this time, but the same dramatic delivery. In amongst the cringe-worthy production, there was a uniqueness about it. Whoever had recorded this message made it sound like the voices wanted a conversation with the punters.

"Really. Is that what you think?"

My throat went dry.

"Who said I was a recorded message. Never jump to conclusions, or you will miss what is in front of you."

The voice was close. I tentatively reached out my hand, half-hoping that this was all in my head. Thankfully, the only thing I felt were the coffin plank seats.

"Oh, come on. You can do better than that. Where are the screams?"

"Yes. We want your screams."

A third voice joined in. I jerked back; something had touched my arm. My hands scrambled around in the thick darkness. The carriage made a sudden turn to the left, and my body slammed against the side. I screamed with pain, verging on terror. The voices giggled with glee.

"He's getting close."

"Yes. Soon will be *That* scream."

The carriage slowed down. My hands gripped the handrail again, urging the metal coffin to keep going. But to no avail. We juddered to a stop. Silence. The air was heavy with anticipation. I knew the voices were out there. Waiting. That's what made the stillness terrifying. Whatever future was before me, it was only a matter of time before the whispers revealed the punch line.

"Don't you remember us, Abrahams?"

My name! The whispers giggled as they continued the conversation between themselves.

"Trust us. It's the least of your worries we know your name."

"Yes, least of your worries."

"And he always forgets."

"I know. But maybe things will change this time."

"Doubt it."

"But what if he hears us?"

"What? You mean like Trotty in *The Chimes*?"

"Yes. He heard us. And he changed."

"Ahh, but Trotty had Dickens to guide his way."

"But so does our little Abrahams. He just needs a little nudge to work it out."

The whispers fell silent again.

Darkness.

Nothingness.

Stillness.

A calmness settled. I didn't move. Nothing moved. We all waited.

Then.

An ear-piercing scream filled the dark void.

"HEAR US CHIME. HEAR US CHIME."

A silver bell came hurtling towards me. I raised my arms to form a protective cocoon, only to feel invisible hands pull them back down. Another pair of warm palms grabbed hold of my face, fixing my gaze towards the approaching bell. The impact was only seconds away. Five metres. Four. I closed my eyes. Long, thin fingers scurried across my face, pulling back my eye-lids to stare upon the approaching fate. The whispers wanted me to soak in every drop of terror. Three metres. Two metres.

And then it stopped.

My relief was short-lived. CHIME. CHIME. The hypnotic resonance of each clang punched hard in my stomach. I doubled over in pain as the bell sounded out again. The chimes were inside me, smashing against my ribs as they attempted to break out of their human cage. I tried to yell out for the ringing to stop, but just opening my mouth amplified the torment inside. The whispers started up their twisted conversation again.

"To stop will cause even more pain."

"Because if we stop, you will see."

"And if you see, you will hurt."

"Don't you remember?"

"It's the reason you left The Theatre the way you did."

I was going to be sick. My throat could taste the battered insides of my gut.

"Throwing up won't work."

"Neither will mouthwash."

"You should know that by now. You've been living with that taste in your mouth for a long time."

*****

The bell hadn't finished with me yet.

Its hypnotic sway dragged my eyes, left and right. The slow movement was drawing me into its silvery world. I watched, transfixed, to the metallic surface as letters etched themselves onto the bell's skirt.

T. H. E. A. P.

Each character chimed inside me as they slowly took their form.

P. L. A. U. S. E.

"The Applause."

Speaking it out sent me deeper into the hypnotic swing. Behind the words, I could make out another series of marks. The ravages of time had faded most of its carved-out lines, but I didn't need to look hard to recognise the image.

That image.

The faces of those two children looked as real as if they were standing in front of me. Their expressions of tortured pain tore into my soul. The young boy's head buried itself into his chest, not wanting to look my way. As for the girl, her bulging eyes wouldn't leave my sight. Her look spoke a thousand words, but only one came out.

"Why?"

An overwhelming sense of guilt flooded over me. The question was a plea to understand why I had been so cruel to her. I was speechless. It had to be a misunderstanding. She was just a girl from a 19th century picture. How could I have hurt her? She turned her head. *That* image faded away. I sat looking at the bell. The only thing staring back was my silver reflection. Judging. Asking the same terrifying question.

The carriage shuddered forwards. There was one final turn. The ride didn't need any big finish with a fake wall. It had already produced its biggest scare. The bell's surface was a mirror. Its reflection had said it all.

That image was inside me.

CHAPTER 20
RUMOURS

"It is the obvious which is so difficult to see most of the time. People say 'It's as plain as the nose on your face.' But how much of the nose on your face can you see, unless someone holds a mirror up to you?"
(Isaac Asimov, I, Robot)

TROTT *couldn't take his eyes off the Ghost Ride.*

The funfair owner was nervously pacing up and down, wondering whether the ride would work. For someone who had heard the chimes as many times as Abrahams, ears eventually grow deaf to the call of the bell. But not this time. The screams were a good sign, easing his concern. Maybe the rumours were true.

Rumours.

PARADOX was full of them these days, especially after Pevensie had chosen sides. Depending upon who Trott talked to, the messenger was either best friends with The Storyteller or loyal to The Magician. Both opinions were clutching at straws. Nobody knew, apart from the three central characters involved. But that hadn't stopped Trott from speculating himself. And his hunch had grown stronger since laying his eyes on Abrahams again. His return to the fair was not by accident.

Another rumour concerned The Theatre. The building was going through some renovations, and not just with the decor. To the casual eye, it looked like a fresh coat of paint. But for those who could remember the old tales, it was clear the owner was attempting to bring about a promise made many years ago. It wasn't the first time the building had gone through alterations. Each attempt failed. But this time was different. That explained the increased tension in the town.

Trott was thankful that his funfair was out of town. He was far enough away to keep his head down but close enough to hear the whispers in the wind. That's how he liked it. Especially now. His ears had picked up the warm front coming from the eastern wind. The rains would soon be here and with it his final days. Nobody lives forever, and he knew what he had signed up to when taking over the fair. He wanted to hang around a few more years, just to see the end game. But not if the price would be his memory. What was the use of sticking around if he couldn't even remember what he was looking for?

The Ghost Ride doors opened, revealing a subdued Abrahams. Trott waited a few seconds before walking over. He felt the strangest feeling of destiny's entwined.

Trott wasn't the only one who was facing his final days here.

I wanted to be mad at the funfair owner for not telling me about the ride.

But other things were on my mind. Everywhere I looked I could see the faces of those two children staring back at me. Their question lingered in the wind. Why? I tried lifting the carriage bar so I could stand up, but my legs gave way. Trott reached over and caught my arms. I didn't thank him. I didn't deserve help. Behind that one word question was a tale of torture. Their torture. By my hand. It couldn't be true. I wouldn't do such a thing. Trott helped me over to a nearby bench. Each step was a reminder of the throbbing pain in my chest. The bell may have fallen silent, but its chimes were still playing inside me. As we sat down, my hand touched the wooden planks, bringing back memories of the coffin seats.

If their question was true, I deserved the grave.

Trott could see the anguish on Abrahams' face.

He had witnessed that look many times. But illusions can be a powerful thing. They make a person see what they want to see. There were no guarantees.

Trott played with the brim of his hat, buying time. He didn't want the visit to end. Continuing the storyline would bring them one step closer to waving goodbye, and with it his own. Had the age of the funfair finally come to an end? It felt like it. His rides were out-dated. Soon, someone else would take over, change things up for a new batch of visitors. They might even move locations, build a fancy entertainment complex. Who knew?

One person did.

If these were his final days, at least he could go out with a bang. He would make this last visit mean something. For the both of them.

"The next part of the tale is sad."

Trott was looking down at the dusty ground, watching the effects of the wind craft a new miniature landscape. Out with the old, in with the new.

"After settling his guests, Trotty hears the haunting chimes of the nearby church bell. It was summoning him to the tower. There he stands accused of believing the words of Alderman about the worthlessness of his social class. Then comes the judgement. Trotty has to watch the results of his belief upon the lives of those around him."

Trott pauses his tale to look back at the ride.

"You heard the bell, right?"

I nodded, unsure of what it meant. Trott focused back on the ground. The wind had shaped a tiny mountain ridge by our bench. He gazed upon that landscape as though he was wondering what was beyond the horizon.

"And it showed you its judgement?"

I didn't respond this time. How could I? This funfair had turned my world inside out. I didn't know who I was anymore. Trott nodded. His eyes made a quick side-glance towards a white tent at the far end of the fair. Checking for something. Worried about something. He continued.

"Our lead character watches in despair as the chimes reveal how his life entwines itself with others. Homeless Will goes in and out of prison. Lillian, the niece, turns to prostitution. Trotty's daughter, Meg, does indeed marry, but her union is not one of joy. Her husband becomes an alcoholic, with all the hidden baggage that curse brings with it. And even after the birth of their child, it doesn't turn the disease around. After her husband's death, Meg continues to feel the painful rejection that only those who have walked that addictive path understand. Distraught, she stands on the ledge of death and stares into the so-called unforgivable sin…

…Suicide."

Our silence amplified the significance of those final scenes. Meg wasn't just the daughter of Trotty. She was the mother who was harshly judged by the card dealing magistrate. Fiction and real life. It's all part of the same family.

A gust of wind blew Trott's hat onto the ground. This *mise-en-scène* moment, where every part of the scenery joins in with the show, added to my guilt. If only it were that simple to wipe away life's dirt as brushing the dust off a hat. Trott glanced over to the white tent again. His mouth squeezed in and out, thinking through what to say next. I couldn't tell if this was part of his showman act. If it was, then he had mastered the authentic look.

"Listen."

He whispered the words. I hunched down.

"In that church tower, Trotty saw something. A secret as plain as day. It's the thing that will change the game. Dealer wins, but not in the usual way."

"I. Don't."

"Understand. I know. Give it time. You will. Find The Twins."

*****

That felt good to say.

Trott didn't know if he had overstepped the mark, but that didn't matter. He had nothing to lose now that his days were almost over. His act of rebellion against the rules wasn't just selfish. Trott genuinely wanted to help the lad. He would miss Abrahams. Against all the odds of his forgetful memory, he could still recall some of the past visits. Most of those occasions carried fond echoes, especially the early days. There was lots of laughter, endless sugared drinks and cheeky refusals to get off the rides. Each goodbye brought with it a tear, never knowing if those departing hugs would be the last.

Trott considered Abrahams a friend, aware that such a close relationship would be asking for trouble. That's why the recent visits brought with it pain and disappointment. Trott tried to help, but he could see the writing on the wall. Every visit turned ugly, leaving tales of damage in its wake. Damage that not even Trott could repair with sticky tape and paint.

And then came today. The surprise visit. Abrahams wasn't supposed to be back; unless one believed the rumours. These tales were bigger than the funfair, Pevensie and The Theatre. Something was in the wind. A change was coming.

He could feel it.

CHAPTER 21
A DREAM WITHIN A DREAM

"We have, as human beings, a storytelling problem. We're a bit too quick to come up with explanations for things we don't really have an explanation for."
(Malcolm Gladwell, Blink)

"IN THERE, that's where it will begin to make sense for you."

Trott didn't look up as his head nodded towards the white tent. I looked over at the ominous structure. There were no flashing bulbs or tempting signs. Just a blank canvas that begged for the imagination to conjure up what could be lurking inside. Even though the land hadn't seen rain in a long time, green mould had stretched out its eerie claws down the side of the pale sheets. This tent looked forgotten. On purpose.

"But you don't have to go in there. You can stay here a little longer, if you want."

Trott's boot played around in the dirt, drawing a solitary line up and down.

"You never finished the story."

"Huh?"

"The story. What did Trotty do after seeing his daughter about to commit suicide?"

The brown boot stopped half-way along another pass of the line.

"He faces what we all have to face during life: a decision."

"You mean he saves her?"

Trott looked up, but there was no smile.

"Maybe. Maybe not. You see Trotty realises that Alderman is wrong about the poor. These people are not wicked by nature. Neither are the fruits of poverty brought on by the seeds of their actions. The problem lies with society's selfish heart and how many accepted that it was OK to throw the weak and vulnerable to one side.

Holding onto that truth, Trotty decides to change how he sees himself and those around. He leaps out of his vision, just in time to catch Meg from falling to her death. The vision concludes and he is back home, waking up from a deep sleep."

I felt like a hammer of disappointment had just slammed into me. The type of feeling one gets when a binge-watching marathon ends with the corniest of finales.

"It was all a dream?"

It was half question, half shout of frustration. My whole experience in this funfair had left me with more questions than answers. I had been emotionally ripped apart and left in pieces. The only saving grace was my belief that before the end, I would find some solace – a line in the conclusion that would point to a saving peace. But a dream! All this and I get 'a dream' to send me on my way? I felt short-changed. Angry. Trott put his hand on my knee.

"It's not like that. Dickens leaves a question hanging that he doesn't answer: a dream or something else? It's left for the reader to decide. That's the twist. How you answer his question determines how you deal out the cards."

I disagreed. The twist didn't deal out any answers, it only brought another series of confusing questions.

I couldn't take my eyes off the image that Trott had drawn with his boot: one line and seven small circles at the top. There was something familiar about the picture, but the mental prod didn't bring any memories back. Trott waited a few seconds, hoping I would say something. Nothing came. He sighed, then stood up. Whatever response he had hoped for disappeared like the profit line of his funfair. A gust of wind blew his picture away.

Sensing the time, he searched in his pocket for a little gift. Moments later, he pulled out a plastic bell.

"Stop me if you know the tale already, but this plastic bell is magical. You just have to ring it and..."

"…the funfair comes to town."

It wasn't the kindest thing to do. Finishing his sentence had knocked Trott off his stride. The magical bell story seemed important to him, his big finish. I didn't have to spoil it for him. But I didn't care. I was still trying to come to terms with what had happened in the Ghost Train. Worrying about Trott was bottom of my checklist. I took the bell. The cheap plastic feel hadn't changed. Neither had the clapper that made more of a 'dud' sound instead of a 'chime'. It was just like the old days.

I handed it back.

There were some things better left forgotten. The bell was one of them. After my father's funeral, I believed in its magical power once again. It produced a book that my dad would have been proud of; a carbon copy of his final words to me. But then the bell kicked me in the balls. No matter how many times I rang that stupid clapper, nothing came except tears and questions. My words hadn't changed a thing. People still got hurt. Injustice continued. And my paragraphs became sound bites. Worst of all, I stopped believing in the funfair and its moral compass to guide my imagination. One night, I lost the bell. Accidentally on purpose. I watched it float down the river, with a bottle of champagne to toast its demise.

Trott normally loved surprises.

But not this one. Abrahams wasn't supposed to hand back the bell. That had never happened before. And it wasn't a good sign. The bell was more than just a link to the past. It was Abrahams' compass to find what he was looking for.

We stopped outside the moss-covered tent.

My refusal of the bell had affected Trott more than I had expected. He looked worried, unsure of his steps. Even seeing all this, I still didn't offer to take the bell from him. Those days were long gone. Trott made the first move. He leant in to give me a hug. His embrace was strong. Emotional. Deep inside it felt like our last goodbye.

He pulled back the canvas door and waited for me to walk inside. We shared one final look – that silent stare to imprint memories. Trott's eyes had lost all their sparkle. All I could see was doubt. Doubt of what was coming. Doubt of his cherished funfair. Doubt in who I was. Maybe I was just like all the other past residents of 'Nowhere' – the ones who had given up hoping that the rain would come. Faith, the evidence of things unseen.

What wasn't I seeing?

The inside of the white tent carried on the crumbling theme of the fair.

It was nothing more than a bargain version of a Hall of Mirrors. Or to be exact, a Hall of only One Mirror. All of the other frames were broken, no doubt from disappointed punters who used a hammer as a comment card.

The surviving mirror looked odd – probably the reason it hadn't endured the same fate as the others. Its thick wooden frame had one continuous carving around the edge. A single path, weaving to the right, to the left, and then on repeat. It had no start. It had no end.

I followed its hypnotic trail. Round and round the frame. To the left. Then to the right. There wasn't any reflection staring back at me. Left. Right. Left. Right. But there was an image caught within the frame. Left. Right. Left. Right. A tall tower with seven paths leading off its majestic column. I knew this place. It was good to be back. Left. Right. Left. Right. Then in one hypnotic moment of perfect clarity, I walked through the mirror. One step at a time.

Left. Right.

Left. Right.

*****

Trott counted to ten before opening the canvas door.

It seemed a silly thing to do but he wanted to check. Just in case.

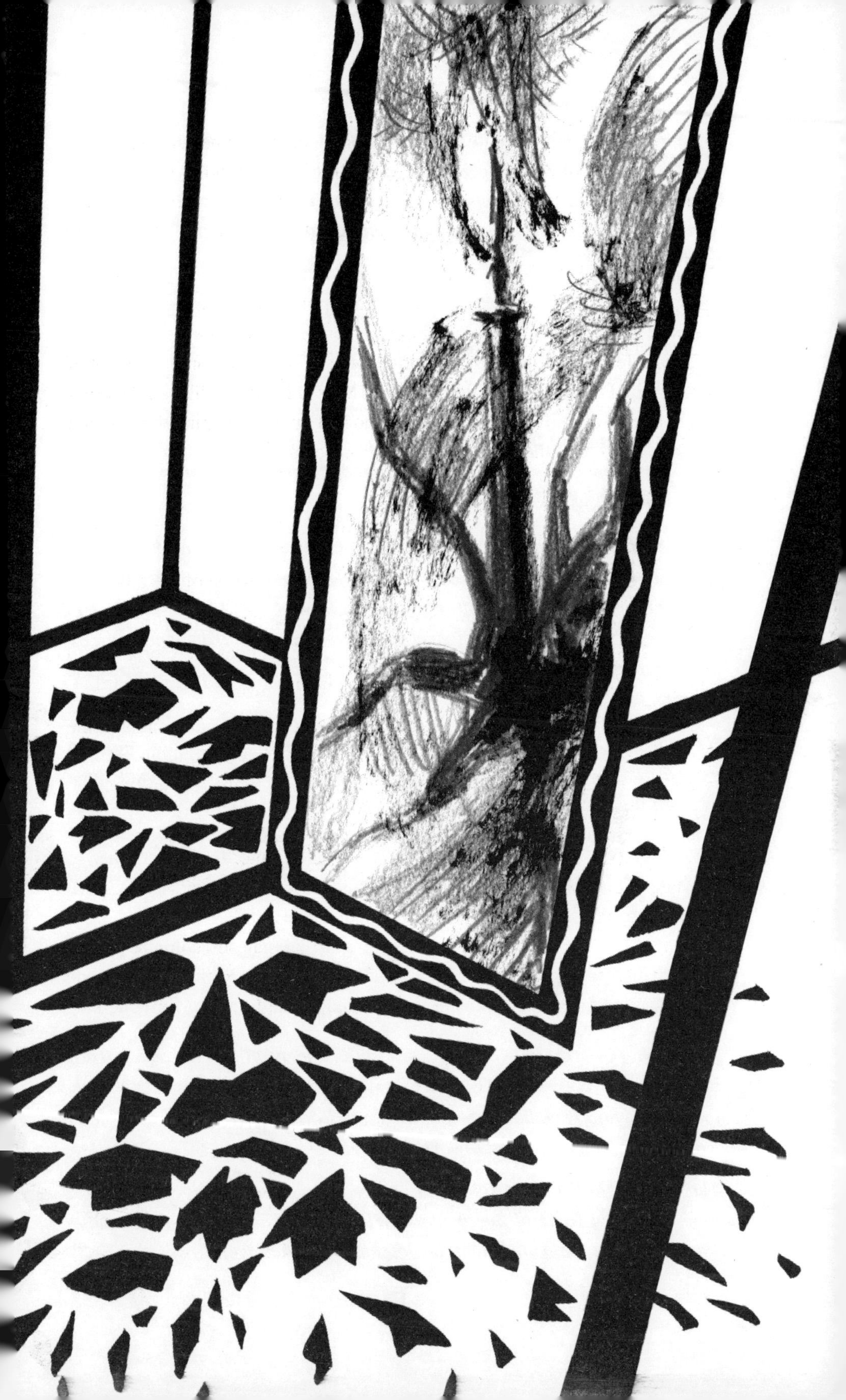

As expected, Abrahams had gone. The last remaining mirror had a long crack down the centre of it. At least it hadn't smashed like the rest of them. The previous visits by Abrahams had left many broken shards of glass. He wondered why this mirror hadn't gone the same way.

Change in the air?

Trott took his time walking back to the scaffold entrance. He wanted to visit every corner of the fair before his next visitor arrived. This person would not be falling from the sky in a cloud of dust. Their arrival would be by foot. His eyes kept scanning the horizon, occasionally breaking away to look back at the fair. He had already forgotten the name of his last visitor, and the 'index card Trott' wasn't helping. Something about a mirror and a Ghost Ride. Damn. It will come back.

A silhouetted figure appeared on the horizon. It was good to see them again. It had been a long time since they had met. He waited by the entrance until their usual embrace. By now his memory of the last few hours had gone entirely. His visitor asked a few questions, but Trott couldn't give any satisfactory answer. They ambled into the funfair, heading towards the caravan that Trott called home.

He pulled back for a moment, looking at the carnival baby he had nurtured for most of his adult life. A tear ran down his cheek. He didn't understand why. An invisible hand was already hard at work wiping away any mental connection to the place. But it had left one or two echoes. On purpose.

Blessing or a curse?

Trott couldn't tell.

Two hours later, The Storyteller locked the gate of the funfair.

A sign hung over the entrance. 'Closed until further notice.' It was a sad day, but one that was coming. The news would spread across PARADOX that the funfair had finally come to an end. Rumours would follow and The Magician would respond just like HE always did.

The old lady didn't want to leave until Trott had closed his eyes for the last time. No doubt some of the upcoming rumours would include the line that 'he had to face the punishment for breaking the rules.'

That didn't bother her. Let people think what they wanted to believe. Her visit to the fair was personal. They had business to conclude.

And now She had a game to win.

I walked through a mirror.

It wasn't the most original of ideas. Alice had perfected it beautifully in Through The Looking Glass. There she was, sitting sleepily in the armchair, playing imaginative chess with her black and white cats. And then it happened. The 'curiouser and curiouser' curse of the inquisitive. She stared into the mirror and wondered what world lay just beyond sight. The teasing thought placed her feet firmly upon a chessboard of adventure.

Her story was more than just a tale for a child's imagination. It was a beautiful metaphor concerning fate. Lewis Carroll, her creator, wanted to explore the ultimate question we all face. Do we have free will? He bottled out on delivering the punch line, aware that upsetting the governing power of the church would cause him problems. They, of course, had the keys to everlasting life. But he couldn't resist leaving the image of the chessboard in the mind of every reader.

Who did move the pieces on the board?

Were we all part of some elaborate game of the Divine?

And more to the point, could the rules be broken?

CHAPTER 22
WHEN SEVEN IS NOT SEVEN

"The stranger who finds himself in the Dials for the first time... at the entrance of Seven obscure passages, uncertain which to take, will see enough around him to keep his curiosity awake for no inconsiderable time..."

(Charles Dickens, Sketches by Boz)

PEVENSIE *sipped his double espresso.*

The café window seat on Monmouth Road was the perfect spot to watch the world pass him by. He loved the history of The Seven Dials District in London's West End.

Long before Las Vegas was a twinkle in the mafia's eye, 17th century London was the world's most famous gambling table. Real estate was its high-stakes game as the city expanded with the promise of wealth and fame. The favourite table to play was a square one. If a punter designed a series of buildings around an equal-sided field, they could guarantee a jackpot win. The bonus came if they stayed at the table for a few more hands. That's when the Victorian Hipster, the Aristocrat, moved in. Investments always tripled with their fancy tastes. But like most sure wins, once people figured out the formula, the jackpot lost all its shine. The game cried out for a joker card.

Enter Thomas Neale.

This rebel reimagined the game itself. He changed the precious square table into a daring series of triangles. Neale called his gamble the Seven Dials District; seven streets converging into one beautiful centrepiece. The star of his show was a monument, made up of six clock dials.

This intriguing design meant that he could demand extra rent, as aesthetics superseded space. The daring plan almost worked until all hell broke loose. Raging fires of greed turned exclusive castles into tenement housing. Buildings were sub-divided, then divided again; there was never such a thing as a room being too small. Black market trading became the currency of the district. And the seven streets became a metaphor for the seven deadly sins.

When hope lost sight of any redemption, a Phoenix rose up from the ashes of violence and selfish greed. This beautiful bird of the human heart flapped its wings of creativity as artists and dreamers reshaped the area. The Seven Dials District became a living badge of contradiction. Injustice rubbed shoulders with creative compassion. Selfishness walked the streets with sacrificial love. That's why Pevensie loved this place.

Contradiction – the magical paradox of life.

*****

I don't understand.

The image in the mirror was of the The Seven Dials District. One Pillar. Seven Roads. But as I stepped out of the frame, the sickening feeling of not knowing where I was swirled around inside. This wasn't London.

My eyes looked towards the central pillar. A massive wooden post had replaced the concrete monument. There were still six clock dials, but their faces were now abstract paintings. The roads had also changed. Gone were the bustling streets. Instead, simple dirt tracks stretched out from the wooden post. At the end of each path, stood a metal gate. And beyond that? Fields. Every one different.

To my right was a vast marketplace. Forty, maybe fifty stalls. At first glance, it was an artisan's haven, full of homemade products with that appealing personal touch. Looking a little harder, I saw the subtle con. Every stall had already sold their soul to the franchise beast. That didn't seem to bother the punters. This place carried an energy as if Black Friday was in full swing. Road rage had nothing on these rush-hour market lanes. It was everyone for themselves, as whispered curses became their agitated car horns.

The market traders were oblivious to this. And who could blame them? The cash was flowing freely. They all wore the same uniform. Another nod to the franchise curse. Their long green cloaks and velvet top hats must have come from a supermarket episode of *The Twilight Zone*. The only thing missing was the name badges giving the apathetic statement, 'Have A Nice Day'. A chill ran down my back. I was wrong. There was something else missing. Every trader had positioned the brim of their top hat to cast a shadow over their face. They liked to watch everyone, but hated anyone watching back. And what about myself, were they watching me right now? The creepy feeling of hidden eyes looking me up and down caused my throat to tighten up.

I turned away.

Pevensie ordered another espresso.

This time, a single. He needed a clear head, not one jumping off the walls. His eyes scanned the busy streets around the monument. The district fed on tourists and hurried shoppers like a consumeristic beast. People didn't stand a chance against its drooling mouth of lust.

"I wonder how many of you see them?"

It was only a whisper, but loud enough to make the waitress quickly head back after dropping off the drink. Pevensie leaned into the window. He wondered where Abrahams would go first. The marketplace. It was the most obvious choice. Pevensie then looked to his left. In this world, he was staring at a shoe shop. But in PARADOX? Pevensie drank his espresso in one gulp. He wasn't here to rehearse his version of Alice going through a mirror between two worlds. Distracting himself with reflections would only make his day longer. There was a job to do. Find the Twins. They were here.

Somewhere.

I looked around to see if there was a building I recognised.

The Cambridge Theatre? What about my cherished coffee shop on Monmouth Road? Nothing. They were all gone. Replaced. But in a strange way.

I could feel the place moving. Brick by brick the walls changed their form. The first Act of this architectural magic show was an ancient Mediterranean town. Its rustic designs with clay tile roofs burst into life, as the aromas of fresh produce pushed my senses overboard. Right in front my eyes I was living out a childhood holiday. I was ten years old, my family's first overseas trip. Even the hotel that we stayed in made an appearance, complete with the all-you-can-eat-buffet.

The buildings changed again for Act Two, but they still carried the same Mediterranean feel. This time, it was the little village I stayed in after my first book went to print. I adored that place. It was where I tasted food from the gods and wine from their lovers. I became addicted to citrus fruits and carried bruises from heated café debates. And now I was back in its land. The taste of the wine swirled around my mouth. Even the bruises on my arm felt fresh. This memory was real and in the present. But how?

The third Act followed. Then another. Each changing scene was like watching the greatest hits of places that I loved or wished I could visit. Act Five was in New Jersey, 1964. I was outside the shrine to jazz recordings on Sylvan Avenue. Inside, John Coltrane was recording history with *A Love Supreme*. My ears picked up the track *'Psalm'* playing through the streets. It was beautiful. My favourite track of all time.

Act Six took me into Gad's Hill Place, Kent. I had always wanted to travel back in time to the final days of Dickens. It wasn't out of some voyeuristic desire to relive the scandal of his death – was it in Kent or with his Peckham mistress? My only interest was to hear his sign off to the world. What would the great man say during those final hours of life?

I closed my eyes, trying to get a grip on what was happening. Some invisible architect was rummaging through every mental note. Hopes and dreams, experiences and regrets. Nothing was off limits to this inquisitive robber. But what were they hunting for? My body quivered with a terrifying thought. I tried to close my mind, but the unknown architect had already found the prize.

Act Seven moved in. 19th century London.

CHAPTER 23
WAR, WHAT IS IT GOOD FOR?

"Four score and seven years ago our fathers brought forth on this continent a new nation, conceived in liberty and dedicated to the proposition that all men are created equal. Now we are engaged in a great civil war, testing whether that nation or any nation so conceived and so dedicated can long endure. We are met on a great battlefield of that war."
(Abraham Lincoln, The Gettysburg Address)

EVER SINCE A CHILD, I wanted to travel back to the days of Dickens.

It came from the idea that the grass was greener on the other side. This mantra for the non-contented loved the imagery from the yearly influx of Christmas Cards and my safety-tower of books. The idea of walking through those picturesque scenes of human warmth often made me consider how ugly modern life had become.

Back in Victorian England, charcoal fires would fill the crisp, fresh air with a welcoming glow. Children played with toys that weren't made by nameless faces from the other side of the world. Friendly banter filled the cobbled lanes, and a chimney sweep's song turned a frown into a smile.

Buildings were the mouthpieces for wonder and delight. Exquisite window frames presented a stage for the Englishman's castle. People dressed to impress. Not because of a vain attempt to get one up on their neighbour, but because fashion proudly declared that the nation had never been so prosperous. These were the days when the glorious empire had an overflowing vault of riches that its citizens could walk into. London streets shone with paving stones of gold, and everyone glittered with diamond rings of joy. That's what the Christmas Cards told me.

But not this strange town.

The grass wasn't greener on the other side. My invisible architect had used the blueprint from my dreams but had spilt coffee on some of its instructions. Gone were the charcoal fires of warm greetings. In its place was a reddish fog complete with a sulphurous smell. It was the kind of odour that gripped the back of the throat, then collected the residue for safekeeping. A couple walked by me. 'An evening stroll before dinner and port, darling?' A picture-perfect postcard scene, but only if you narrowed the lens. For the rest, the fog was a killer. Particularly for those living outside in its vaporous grip every night. It was the children and elderly that got the raw end of the deal. They had the best seats in town for the fog's final trick. Instead of a multi-coloured handkerchief pulled out of their mouth, they had the joys of a rib-rattling cough that spat out blood. It was the thick, smelly kind that came from the pit of the stomach. If lucky, a person would cough up enough to fall into a deep sleep and never open their eyes. Few had that luxury. The show would drag on for months towards a slow and painful bloody demise.

The streets of London weren't golden. I would call them more a shade of crappy brown. People had to navigate between piles of disused coal, horse manure and the remains of yesterday's meal. While eyes avoided stepping onto anything unpleasant, the pickpockets would gladly do their work. Hitched items fed into a black market economy. In a twisted Victorian Robin Hood sort of way, it worked. Rob from the rich to feed the poor. Many survived cold nights thanks to the friendly highway robbers. Food. Clothing. Even a few backhanders to doctors and landlords. It was a silver lining to a corrupt and evil system.

The black market was open for business to all walks of life. From the wealthiest to the poorest, they were just one handshake away from a deal. Restaurant owners loved the odd cheap cut of meat to help with cash flow. As for landlords, advance warning about a property coming on the market was always beneficial for the pocket. A lovely dress for the wife or mistress? What about some cheap alcohol? And don't forget those rooms hidden from sight, the ones that took the visitor on a trip outside their mind. Everyone benefited and everyone got screwed. The underground system gave the people what they wanted, but it also took their soul.

And the worst part of it was that everyone knew the evil secret. Human trafficking was the backbone of the black market economy. The tools for slavery varied, from debt collection, food distribution, medicine and a roof for the night. The list seemed endless. Some parents had to sell their oldest kids as foot soldiers just to avoid their youngest from going hungry. Others just never returned home one night. Kidnapping was rife. And few cared enough to change a system that provided so many helpful things. The poor were the rejects of God's favour, fodder for everyone else to have a comfortable life.

From broken windows in a derelict home to the broken heart of human hope, life was bloody tough for those outside the small ring of wealth. These were the many that were deemed not worthy to have a membership card to the British Empire Club.

It was the Victorian social caste system in all its selfish glory.

The town added its final touch.

A ragged clothed charity collector walked up to me holding a battered donation box. On the side was a scrawled out message: 'GIVE FOR THE UNSEEN POOR'. I instinctively rummaged in my pocket for change. I dropped a few coins into the box. He never reacted as he walked off towards a nearby shop. The cheek of it. I would have at least expected a thank you. The shop lived up to its name, 'A Little Store of Wondrous Things'. Its front window glistened with sparkling beauty, but the charity collector didn't seem interested in what was on display. All that glistened wasn't gold. His eyes were staring past all the objects and focusing on what was inside. I blinked, not believing what was in front of me. There was a sweatshop behind the pretty items on sale. It was in plain view, yet hidden from sight. Another blink and it was gone.

The charity collector banged his hand against the glass sending a static ripple across the window. He could recognise someone inside. Before the reverberation ended, the shopkeeper rushed out, pushing him away like a stray dog. The collector fell to the floor, his box smashing to pieces. His pitiful collection of loose change scattered across the dirty floor. The shopkeeper continued to shout at the crying man, grabbing the money as compensation for the dirty window. I did nothing but watch. Just like everyone else in the town. A few seconds later, the charity collector scurried off. His existence returned to the shadows of a nearby alleyway.

There was an uneasy tension in the air.

The town was on edge. I imagined the scene when guns had fallen silent during World War One. In that stillness, the heavens would be dense with anticipation. Everyone knew what was coming; they just didn't know when. Soon, the inevitable whistle would sound and people would run into an indescribable slaughter for a few yards of ground. In that stillness was peace. A strange peace. A dangerous peace. For a split second a soldier could think the war had finished. That's when heads would appear over the trench walls, having a look to see if the hopeful dream was real. No one survived that look. There was always a bullet. And if the bullet didn't get you, then the madness of waiting would.

I felt the same nervous tension covering this town. I was standing on a battlefield where the guns had fallen silent. There was an awkward truce. But who were the sides? The rich against the poor? Or was it the bullies against the victims? No. A battle was being played out, but the strategic minds had yet to show their faces. What worried me the most was that I was standing in the middle of it, and didn't even know which way to run.

CHAPTER 24
THE MARKET

"There is only one thing in the world worse than being talked about, and that is not being talked about."
(Oscar Wilde, The Picture of Dorian Gray)

I CHOSE MY SIDE without even knowing it.

The market square drew me into its chaos. I was intrigued by the shoppers rushing around for never-ending deals. They showed no mercy as arms and legs flung out in anger as they tried to claw back lost seconds to a potential bargain. I stepped closer into the chaos, wanting to see more. A stab of pain dug into my left leg. Someone had intentionally kicked me. The flustered face of a middle-aged shopper was staring right back at me. Their eyes wide open, a volcano of anger ready to erupt.

"WHY ARE STANDING STILL? YOU TRYING TO STOP ME ON PURPOSE?"

The man was irate. His veins were creating a topography of fuming passion over his forehead and neck.

"WELL?"

Words failed me. So had the natural response to fight back. The after-effect of their kick was still unleashing its injection of pain. I bent down and rubbed my shin.

"ANSWER ME YOU..."

His shopping partner in crime interrupted his volcanic flow of words.

"Clive. Clive. Don't be silly. I've just heard the Froadest Stall is about to open. Get over there right now and grab us the stuff."

I looked back up. Clive's face was turning a deeper shade of crimson red, complete with a sprinkle of sweat. He was struggling to decide between wanting to unleash another round of frustration or head over to the stall. Deep inside Clive knew every wasted second changed the odds of getting his treasured bargain. What to do? He had to choose. And quickly.

"Come on, Clive. Leave the jerk. He's probably working with those Hannon Brothers, trying to distract us from the best deals."

That sealed it for Clive. He nodded while scrunching up his mouth in utter disgust. I wasn't worth it. He barged his way through the crowds, kicking and punching like a human juggernaut. Fellow shoppers responded in kind, some more capable of holding their ground than others. Clive fell to the floor, his legs sweeping around to take as many people down as possible. No bargain for him after all.

I was watching a living experiment in human greed. All the market stalls were close together. The narrow shopping lanes stretched out like a perfectly designed maze. Whoever had put this market square together wanted to observe the human heart under the extreme pressure of limited stock. What would win out, compassion or greed? The laboratory experiment was in full effect. The catchy one-liners from the stall owners added to the chaos.

"Cheap now."

"Six for the price of four."

"Not a monkey, not a rhino, but a bargain commodore."

The last call hooked me. It was a bargain. Not £500, not £250, but only £15. A burning passion welled up inside me. I had to get one of those 'commodore' deals. Panic set in. Did everyone hear the offer? What if they did, would I miss out? That would be disastrous. It never occurred to me as I pushed my way through the market lanes that I had no idea what was on sale.

"Come and get a bargain commodore."

I was getting close. The kick of adrenaline was just what I needed. A gentle push here. A less than gentle kick there. I was on a mission and pity any poor fool that stood in my way. No mercy. It wasn't my fault if they got hurt. They knew what they were signing up to being here. It was every one for themselves. I turned left, past two stalls, then a sharp right. Follow the voice.

Follow the 'bargain commodore.'

"You?"

It was a strange way to greet a customer. I didn't care. The important thing was that I had arrived and there were no other shoppers at the stall. That meant the offer was mine. I eagerly scanned the table. My heart instantly dropped. It couldn't be. The table was empty. Had I missed the offer?

My mind raced through the last few minutes. Hadn't I rushed off as soon as I'd heard the offer? Yes. Straight away. What about the other shoppers? They were going to different stalls. But what about the group I had to barge through? Crap, I had lost valuable seconds there. And some of them refused to move at first. Why? I bet they had links to the Hannon Brothers. Or what if they were working with Clive? Yes. He took my 'bargain commodore'. My hands gripped the edge of the table. I wanted to find Clive. I wanted my offer.

"Is it really you?"

The market trader's question snapped me out of a head-on crash into a mental wall. I looked up at him. The trader shuffled a few inches. He didn't like being watched. I put the laboured move down to the green uniform. It looked heavy, covering every part of his body from the neck down. There were slits at each side for the arms, but they remained shut. It added to the mystery of what lay hidden under that green shield. Even though the shadow of his top hat covered his eyes, I knew he was examining every single part of my body. His eyes were tearing through each layer to find the hook for his next sales pitch. His mouth formed into a stretched-out smile that looked as fake as the grin from a used-car sales lot. There was a little glint of white behind his smirk.

I felt the tug.

"Do they know?"

The green-clothed trader leant forward. My chest tightened. The tug had become more like a hand, rummaging inside. It was pulling out drawers and opening the doors of my memories. He was searching for the answer and had no interest in tidying up afterwards. I tried to step back. The grip only tightened. I winched in pain. This was another part of the market lab experiment. Teach the specimen the concepts of consequence and reward.

He still was coming up blank. Desperate times called for desperate measures. Out of the shadow of the top hat, his eyes pierced through the darkness. They were brilliant white with bright green pupils. Those small circles had captured untold secrets from countless customers, and his camera shutter blink was now taking snapshots of my hidden vault.

"Don't fight it."

A shopper pushed by, eager to see what offers were on the table. It took one look from those green eyes to emphasise that this was a private sale. The unwelcome guest left as the world closed tighter around me.

"Tell me, who brought you back?"

Another shutter blink. He still couldn't find the answers. His rummaging hand inside me shook with frustration.

"Tell me!"

A droplet of spit ran down the side of his mouth as he stretched out the last two words. He was craving knowledge and could taste the anticipation of its nectar in his mouth. A short, diseased tongue pierced through his lips, gathering up the evidence of his lust. Without warning, he jerked backwards. I screamed out in pain as the invisible grip ripped itself free from my soul. The trader's face fell back into the shadow of the top heat.

"Santiago."

I staggered around to see what had made him back away in fear. My unexpected rescuer had a look in his eyes.

And he wasn't pleased to see me.

CHAPTER 25
MEET SANTIAGO

"Have you ever lost someone you love and wanted one more conversation, one more chance to make up for the time when you thought they would be here forever? If so, then you know you can go your whole life collecting days, and none will outweigh the one you wish you had back."
(Mitch Albom, For One More Day)

4:00AM

It was never a good time to wake up.

In the world of insomniacs, this part of the morning had another name. 'The unhappy hour'. It was neither too early nor too late; the no-mans-land of sleep. Santiago knew 'the unhappy hour' well. It was both his long-term friend and nemesis. And this morning was no different. He looked over at his bedside watch. Santiago hated this hour. The groggy state of his mind was in no fit state to fend off what was coming next.

Regrets.

*****

4:30am

Santiago stepped out of his rented room. This sad excuse for accommodation should have been a short-term let. After three months, it changed to mid-

term. He signed the long-term contract four months after that. His death warrant. Before arriving in PARADOX, Santiago had a great apartment. It was one of those buildings that symbolised everything he had pursued in life. The shelves were crammed with memorabilia that backed up the tales he told to his friends. Everything had been perfect. Apart from the nightmares. His dreams told a different tale, and they eventually became true. And now his reward was being locked away in some ramshackle place. A dodgy boiler. Badly fitting windows. Noisy neighbours. It was no wonder he struggled to get a decent night's sleep.

He turned right and ambled down the deserted lane. He knew where he was heading. It was the spot he would always go to during his 'unhappy hour' walks. The market square. He liked how the place provided a distraction from all the thoughts running roughshod through his head.

Santiago sat down in the usual place. The market traders were busy setting up their stalls. They exchanged glances, but never words. The lust for those items had faded a long time ago. It was a compromise that suited everyone – a way of keeping the peace. His hand rubbed along the side of the wooden bench. It had seen better days, but that's what made it special. It reminded him of the old times. Visiting the seat was a daily self-induced torture. But it was essential to endure the pain. This ugly piece of furniture was the only thing left that made Santiago's life stand for something.

4:45am

Santiago wasn't his real name. The nickname came from his love for walking. It verged upon a religious experience. Hence the name in honour of the pilgrimage of St. James.

PARADOX was also a nickname, but no one could remember its original term. He thought it was a fitting title. The place was notorious for its unique ability to morph into whatever the heart desired. Good. Bad. Beautiful. Ugly. Take your pick. It relished exposing the crazy contradictions that resided deep within the human soul.

Every traveller was wary of this place, but none could avoid it. PARADOX was the starting point for every journey in this land. Maybe that's why the town had its magical morphing ability. It provided the first real test for any adventure. Would the journey end before it even started? Santiago had often said to himself that the day a traveller dies is when they stop walking. PARADOX could do that to a person. Why see the world when what you are seeking is already in front of you? The longer someone stayed in the town, the harder it was to distinguish the real from the fake. That's why Santiago never deviated from a silent rule with every visit. He would only rent an apartment on a short-term lease. But this current visit hadn't gone as planned.

For the first two days, PARADOX had done its usual show. There was nothing like a dip into self-indulgence. But then came a surprising twist. The town dared to question the precious walk itself. This terrifying exposé into why Santiago kept pursuing his pilgrimage cut deep into his heart. It mocked his cry for redemption. He wasn't blind to his flaws. But didn't everyone have a dark side? That was the paradox of life. People could be selfish and yet full of love, all at the same time. His regular walks upon the pilgrim track was his way of earning enough brownie points to kill off his demons once and for all. His heart was good; it just needed a helping hand. A helping walk, so to speak.

But PARADOX saw it differently.

Santiago had watched in terror as the town pulled back the curtain on his cry to become a better man. It wasn't the mockery that hurt him the most, but its insistence on telling him how the storyline would end. Failure. No matter which Path Santiago took, it would always end with disappointment. Nothing would change. He was, and forever would be, selfish.

At first, Santiago refused to believe in the town's prophecy. Adding a few extra months to his rent agreement was his way of buying time. He needed to find another way to prove that there was an element of goodness left within his messed up life. But just as PARADOX had revealed, every journey led to people getting hurt. There was only one last thing he could do. On the day he signed the long-term rent, Santiago inflicted the cruellest of all punishments upon a pilgrim. A traveller dies when they stop walking.

So he broke his own feet.

10:00am

'The unhappy hour' moved into its sixth unhappy repeat.

Sitting on the uneven bench was a way of reminding him he must never walk again. This mundane looking object acted like a holy shrine on a pilgrim route. His first walk had started with a wooden seat and now his last needed to end with one. The only difference was that he was now sitting alone. No old lady to talk to. His lament would have gone on all morning if it hadn't been for the new face in the marketplace. New face?

Old face.

It was the last person Santiago had expected to see in PARADOX. There was no other option but to intervene. But his actions would have consequences. The uneasy truce in this place would come to an end, and he had no idea what would follow.

"What are you doing here?"

The middle-aged man looked confused as he hobbled over towards me.

My unexpected saviour was in his late forties. His skin carried all the hallmarks of emotional wear-and-tear. The bloodshot eyes told tales of late nights and endless worry. Whoever this man was, he was someone who had willingly beaten himself up with self-judgment, then came back for seconds. It made me wonder how many times had he stared at a bottle of pills or the ripples of a dark blue river. The closer he got the more I realised that his eyes already carried the answer. He had faced that demon many times. It was only a matter of time before the poor sod would carry out his final wish.

"Why? Why are you here?"

He grabbed hold of my arm, pulling me away from the market stall. The mysterious man kept looking back towards the booths. The traders were getting agitated. Three of them had come together now, murmuring, pushing customers away. I pulled my arm free.

"What's going on?"

It was a lame question, but the only one I could muster up. As I asked it, I wished I had never opened my mouth. The reply turned my world upside down.

"Everything. You shouldn't be here Peccadillo."

Peccadillo! How did he know *That* name?

CHAPTER 26
MEET PECCADILLO

"There is no greater agony than bearing an untold story inside you."
(Maya Angelou, I Know Why the Caged Bird Sings)

TO EVERYONE ELSE, my name is Abrahams.

But to my mother, I was Peccadillo.

It was a secret term of affection between the two of us. She never used it in public, and rarely when we were alone. But when she did, I would listen. It was a signal that she was sharing something valuable. Not her words, but the spirit behind it. She was digging deep into her soul, drawing out the purest of love towards me. After my father died, the name took on a new meaning.

She refused to alter her husband's study. Friends insisted on the need to redecorate, telling her it would be therapy for the soul. But she hated wiping his memory away with a shade of cornfield white. Instead, she took over his antique writing desk as her quiet sanctuary. There she would write letters. Long. Short. Official. Friendly. Sometimes she would sit there all day.

After my first book pay-out, I bought her a desktop computer. She had always insisted on using paper and pen. When I next visited, the computer was back in the box. Modern machines were apparently from the devil, tempting her to speed through life and forget the importance of shaping each character and form. Tapping on plastic keys didn't carry the same ache and indentation that a perfectly weighted pen would leave upon her hand. It was important that she couldn't erase ink with a delete button. The blank sheet of paper held an importance that no white screen could ever match. It was the canvas of eternity and it demanded something magical.

Vulnerability.

She was old-school and I respected that. It still didn't stop me from thinking she was a little crazy. Her way required patience. My way brought instant results. Apple Mac instant.

Sunday lunchtimes were sacred. No matter what else was happening or clogging up the diary, this weekly gathering took priority. It was our way of honouring a dear member of our family. A table for three. We never removed 'his' chair. It was over a roast chicken dinner that my mother dropped the news. She started off by talking about her admiration for letter writing and how a piece of paper could become an agent for change. Her favourite example was *Romeo and Juliet*. She wondered whether the ending would have been as powerful if the letter had arrived in time. We agreed it would have sucked. She then handed over an A4 piece of paper with the blue logo of the hospital at the top. My eyes only registered one word.

Terminal.

Sunday lunchtimes changed after the letter. We still met, but I would stay longer. Usually into the evenings. Our conversations altered. They got real. My mother could tell I wasn't coping. Even when she had every legitimate right to think about herself, she still put her son first. What I hated most was the waiting, wondering when the next hospital letter would come through the door. It was as if the sword of Damocles was hanging over my mother's head and I couldn't do a single thing about it. I needed someone to blame. The government was first on my list. Cutbacks in public healthcare. Longer waiting times. Air pollution. No matter what I rallied against, it still didn't soothe the pain. So I turned my anger towards God. By the time my mother started her treatment, I was in His face.

In His Divine wisdom, this God who my mother had prayed to daily, had invited death's messenger to take his time. During those last months of her life, I witnessed her breathing become tiresome and her movements, painful. Weight loss meant that her clothes hung onto nothing but saggy skin and bones. The hair never came back, neither did the dignity to go to the toilet on her own.

But she never stopped praying. And she never stopped looking out for me.

In her worst state, when we both knew it was only a matter of weeks, she handed me a scallop shell. When she was nineteen, she had walked the Camino de Santiago pilgrim route. One of the things she had brought back was the symbol of a pilgrim. Another was a story.

There was once a dreamer called Peccadillo. Every day he would walk towards the hills and stare at the beauty that was the created world. When looking into the distance wasn't enough, he would walk. At first, he took short journeys, coming back home for dinner every night. But soon those walks grew into two days. Then three. Eventually, months would pass before he would return. And when he did, not only his family but the town would come out to hear his tales. These stories were full of adventure, inviting the listener to believe in the power of mystery. People were inspired. People believed. People dared to walk into the unknown.

Then during one of his explorations, Peccadillo stumbled and fell. Not badly. But from that day on, a subtle pain never left his foot. The irritation was enough to make him aware of what he could, and couldn't do. He stopped running through the fields. If there were shortcuts, he would take them instead of seeking the more extensive trials. The journey became more about getting to the end, than the walk itself. And when he told his stories, they were practical instead of mysterious.

Without knowing it, the subtle pain became a master over his heart. He lost the love of walking and eventually he gave it up to sit on a hill again. One day, he came across a scallop shell. As he stared at its groves reaching towards a single focal point at the bottom, a little voice spoke to him. All roads lead back to the start, no matter how many detours one takes. He put the shell in his pocket and looked out across the horizon. I wonder what's out there, he said. And with that, he went for a walk.

I knew what my mother was getting at, especially when she told me that Peccadillo meant 'broken feet'. Subtly was never her forte. She had watched her treasured boy stare into the horizon, dreaming that one day I would become a writer. Not just any old author, but someone who crafted words that valued the quietest voice and the humblest heart. My long walks made her proud.

But then I stumbled over the rock called SELF, and soon its subtle pain became my master. I wrote words that would never upset the readership. Keeping up sales was important and also my rent payments. On paper, I spoke about social justice, but at the ballot box, I went for the best tax cuts. Compassion poured itself from a measuring jug. People deserved help, but only enough so I didn't feel left out.

I had one question as my mother handed me the shell.

"What use is a journey that takes you back to the beginning?"

Her laugh was wonderful. I hadn't heard that sound for a long time. Her words back to me were just as precious.

"It is the most important part of the journey. The beginning is when our dream is the most real."

From that day until her funeral five weeks later, Peccadillo became something different for me. It represented my mother's hope that I would walk into the unknown once more.

I buried her on a Tuesday morning. The rain had stopped before the service had finished. My walk to the graveside was on a saturated field of mud and tears. Tuesday lunchtime, I was in a trance-like state holding onto a plastic plate of untouched food. People kept coming up, sharing their condolences. I knew it was well-meaning, but it felt as flimsy as those tuna sandwiches on my plate. By Tuesday afternoon I was back at her house, replaying the same scene as when my father had died. I sat in the study and wept. The scallop shell came with me that day. Holding it in my hand was just like clinging onto the plastic bell. Hope. Lost hope. Some journeys could never come back to the start. I had ventured too far off course. One month later I signed the papers for the sale of the house. I kept a few things, including the desk.

And the scallop shell.

The first time I sat at the desk, I understood why my mother had taken up writing letters after my father had died. His note to her meant everything. She wanted to keep hearing his voice. The shell was my way of keeping her alive. I wanted to hear my mother call me Peccadillo one final time.

CHAPTER 27
TIME IS UP

"Try to imagine a life without timekeeping. You probably can't... Man alone measures time. Man alone chimes the hour. And, because of this, man alone suffers a paralysing fear that no other creature endures. A fear of time running out."
(Mitch Albom, Time Keeper)

"TELL ME. How do you know that name?"

It was my third time of asking. The first and second was a request. The third was a demand. Santiago continued to look as though he had seen a ghost. He reached out and touched my face, checking I was real. The confirmation tipped him into the arms of panic.

"You shouldn't be here."

"Tell me. How do..."

"You need to leave."

"But I need to know."

Santiago spun around, checking the marketplace. Two more traders had joined in with the huddled conversation. Angry shoppers didn't appreciate the impact this was having upon their treasured stalls. Trouble was brewing.

"You need to go."

Even though I could sense the mood change in the air, I had no intention of leaving. I needed Santiago to tell me how he knew *That* name.

A handful of brave shoppers had now taken matters into their own hands. This small band of protestors walked up to the traders, demanding they get back to work. Raised voices sent the crowd hurtling towards the stalls, but the traders never moved. Metres away from fists finding their target, an eerie silence suddenly fell over the place. I couldn't believe what I was seeing. Every shopper had stopped running, their feet stuck to the floor. They were in a trance, gently swaying from side to side. I turned back to Santiago, wanting to understand.

Fear gripped my heart as I watched him gently sway.

Buy time.

Pretend.

Santiago knew what the traders were capable of. He had seen them do this magic before. They loathed everything the shoppers represented; pitiful creatures who had sold their soul for the cheapest trick the world had ever seen. Lust. If any of them had put up a fight, then maybe the traders would have had more respect for them. But that wasn't the case. They had given up their eternal dignity without even a whimpering cry. And that deserved punishment. The trance was their way of judging the scum. Nothing elaborate, just a simple thought that would drop into their pathetic minds. "We can always take the deals away." And the results would always be the same. Complete obedience.

He continued to sway. It was helpful knowing their tactics, especially now. He needed to get a grip on what was happening. Peccadillo's arrival had caught him off-guard. But so too the traders. That didn't make sense. Why was everyone in the same position?

The question knocked his concentration. Santiago's rhythmical sway went out of sync. The traders noticed and made their move.

*****

"Nice try."

The inquisitive trader who had reached inside me, was now moving slowly towards us. His colleagues followed behind. I couldn't believe what Santiago had done. He faked his sway. Was he selling me out to save his life?

"Don't come any closer."

Santiago's command carried the conviction of impending death. I just didn't know who had the shadow of the grim reaper. The trader continued to inch his way forward. Santiago grabbed my arm then pushed me further away.

"*They* mustn't get you."

I refused to move.

"Please. I beg you. Go. Now."

The trader's laugh echoed through the stalls.

"You pathetic man. Begging doesn't suit you."

Santiago's grip tightened around my arm. I could feel his panic soak into my skin.

"Our dear Santiago. Why make this hard for yourself? Your little friend is ours. Just step aside."

*****

Santiago could taste their desire for fresh meat.

Nothing would stand in their way.

"Come on Santiago. You had your chance. And we had a deal."

They were right. There was a deal, but only for him. Not Peccadillo.

His eyes looked over towards the wooden pillar. Was it possible? The game had finished. That was the deal. It didn't make sense. He continued to stare at its rough bark. Within the shadows, watching spectators. People he hadn't spoken to in a while. He would give anything to visit that place again, but it was out-of-bounds for someone like him. For a moment he allowed himself to believe that things had changed, and then silenced the hope.

They were coming closer.

I needed to run. We needed to run. But Santiago refused to budge. He kept glancing towards the pillar, mumbling words as though trying to solve a cryptic clue. I tried again, but he continued to stand his ground. Behind me I could feel the traders moving closer towards us, their camera shutter blink tearing into my back.

“For God’s sake, move.”

Santiago took one final look then put his hands together. I watched in terrifying disbelief at the unfolding scene. Panic tore through the group of traders as their rhythmical walk came to a sudden stop. Their leader’s green cloak shivered as a wrinkled hand slowly emerged out of the slit. It writhed around the gap like a new-born baby gasping for air; breathing in, breathing out. A thin line of blood worked itself through the veins. Colour was coming back with a faint shade of pink. His long, bony finger stretched out in a command.

“Don’t you dare.”

“But I can. Can’t I?”

“No. That gift has long passed.”

“I don’t think so.”

“The price of disobedience is high.”

“But worth it.”

“No. Just stupid. You’re giving it all up for an empty dream.”

“I don’t believe you.”

“You should. We all know the ending.”

Santiago hesitated. Those words carried an impact. He glanced back at the pillar before fixing his eyes on mine. His smile was one of the warmest I had ever seen.

“Maybe.”

The trader’s outstretched finger quickly drew back. The shade of pink in his skin turned a brilliant white as his clenched fist drained out all its blood.

“DON’T.”

But Santiago wasn’t listening. The screams of every trader filled the marketplace as he pulled back his hands and clapped.

TIME IS UP

*****

Santiago couldn't believe the crazy idea was working.

He thought that magic had ended long ago. But he was wrong. It felt good to be surprised, just like the old days.

Old days.

What a beautiful thought – a time when he had believed in the impossible and stared into the unknown. He had taken those days for granted, always believing they would come around like Groundhog Day. And now for a fleeting moment, it had returned. But for how long?

The air was getting heavy. In a few seconds, everything would stop. He wondered if he would see it, or whether it would just be reserved for his surprise guest. Deep down he knew the answer, but liked to pretend that he stood a chance. His hands continued to clap, slower now. It was hard to push through the invisible sludge. He could hear a faint noise coming from the pillar. Another sign that it was about to arrive.

It – the best description to give to something that could not be defined.

Santiago tried one last clap, but couldn't make it. His right leg buckled, then his left. The fall wasn't bad. The heavy air acted like a cushion. With wide eyes he gazed upon something he thought he would never see again. Another surprise. And then everything went black as he closed his eyes.

The Applause had arrived.

CHAPTER 28
NOW RUN

"My dear, here we must run as fast as we can, just to stay in place. And if you wish to go anywhere you must run twice as fast as that."
(Lewis Carroll, Alice in Wonderland)

SOMEONE had pressed a giant pause button in PARADOX.

I struggled to take in all the sights. Dust clouds and falling leaves glued themselves to the blue sky canvas. Butterflies and birds hung frozen on an invisible string. And in amongst this spellbinding static display, the traders looked like statues caught in mid-stride. My eyes lingered on their green cloaks, following the lines of the motionless fabric hills and valleys. Even in their harmless state, *They* carried the stench of death.

"Santiago. What's happening?"

His non-response didn't register with me. I was distracted by the way my voice bounced around a lifeless PARADOX. I followed its direction to the wooden pillar. A red glow was rippling through its bark. The deep vibrant colour looked alive as it tried to find cracks to break through. Suddenly a crimson beam burst through its cage. Then another A third ray, narrowly missing my arm. There was a sound within the light. A deep rumble.

The Applause.

It was calling me to come closer. Pushing against the heaviness of the air, I put one finger into the beam. Then another. Soon my whole hand. The red light danced over my palm. I could feel its heat warming my skin. The deep rumble reached into my gut as my body stepped deeper into its call. Beyond where beyond stopped, I could see a building. Greek architecture. Corinthian pillars.

As if I was watching inside a dream, I floated gracefully up the steps, hovering in front of the large doorway. I looked around for a handle, but there wasn't one. A gentle push against the door was followed by a harder one. It wouldn't open, but I wasn't surprised. For some reason I already knew that no one walks in unannounced.

The Theatre was by invitation only.

Behind the doors I could hear the sound of applause gradually coming to a end. One by one the clapping hands fell to the side. It was a pitiful way to conclude a show. A slow demise that outstayed its welcome. I couldn't explain it, but I had the strangest feeling that silence was the mark of the show's success. Without warning, my body lurched backwards. It was time to go. The light faded and I was standing in the marketplace again. I looked at the pillar. There were no red beams or deep rumble. But there was one thing I had brought back with me. An invitation.

And whoever was in The Theatre, they were waiting for my RSVP.

I called out to Santiago again.

This time his silence got my attention. His hunched up body looked like a discarded rag doll. I clawed against the thick air, dragging myself over to him. I took hold of his limp hand and pressed it against my chest. A weak pulse. He was alive. Thank God.

I remembered back to the bedside of my dying mother. The hours of that final evening with her were the worst of my life. We both knew there wouldn't be a morning conversation. She didn't have the energy to speak, so I had to do the talking for both of us. Except, I didn't know what to say, so I just held her hand. The silence in that room was deafening with the sound of connection. A raw connection. And it was the same now. For some unknown reason, I carried a force of compassion for Santiago. There was an unspoken union between us, something that ran deep. But why? I had never met Santiago

before today, and yet my emotions were all over the place. Tears ran down both cheeks as I willed him to open his eyes. In that hushed moment inside our protective cocoon, I never noticed that the outside world was slowly coming off pause. Dust clouds worked themselves free from the canvas glue as falling leaves gently landed onto the ground.

And in the distance, long, bony fingers moved.

Seeing Santiago open his eyes sent the warm touch of relief over my worried body.

His lips quivered as mumbled words dribbled out. I leant forward to hear the unintelligible sound, then told him to rest. His arms swayed about like a puppet on a loose string, protesting against my advice. He turned his loose head to the side. The wide-eyed expression was enough to understand his fear.

Beyond the shadow of the top hat, the trader's camera shutter blink worked overtime. He still couldn't move his arms and legs, but that didn't stop him from reaching into my soul. Like a fish gasping for life on dry land, I tried to wriggle out of his grip. Santiago flung his rag doll body in front of me, breaking the invisible cord. The trader screamed out in frustration as he worked hard to free his arms and legs. I had seconds, maybe a minute left.

"Run."

"No."

Santiago looked heartbroken at my refusal.

"I'm not going to leave you."

Again, his arms swayed in protest, begging with his eyes for me to run away. A cold chill touched my back, then burrowed its way into my spine. Streams of ice trickled up and down my bones as the terrifying realisation sunk in.

"There. There. There. No need to struggle."

The trader bent down, our faces only inches away. His shadowy features were in full view now. I couldn't take my eyes off how his skin had a battered look to it, but it wasn't from outside elements. The internal bruising told only one tale: he was withering from the inside out. I pulled away in disgust. He leant forward. Our mouths were almost touching now. I could taste the foul smell of decay from his rotting insides. His tongue slid out and licked my lips. The stench from his sticky saliva made me retch, bringing the sickly leftovers of my stomach back into my mouth. This brought further delight to the trader, his lick accompanied with a perverted giggle. His companions joined in the laughter. *They* were tasting my soul.

"Hmmm. Fresh, with the seasoning of regret. Just how we like it."

He leant back, loosening his invisible grip. Sensing my chance, I scrambled to my feet and ran. Anywhere. Somewhere. The pillar.

I had only staggered a few meters before I realised what I had done. Santiago! I screamed out his name. The weight of guilt for leaving him grew heavier as the traders circled around his defenceless body. My shuffling feet caught themselves in the brambles of indecision. I wanted to run back, but knew it was a fool's folly. Outnumbered. Weakened. And completely at a loss with knowing who I was up against. But.

He's my friend.

The thought sneaked up on me unnoticed. I didn't push back. It was true. Somehow. And yet I still turned my back on him and ran. Guilt wasn't a new thing for me. I had felt its weight many times. The shame of who I was had just added another link to Marley's chain.

*****

The pillar was only yards away now.

I turned around to see Santiago dragged feet first back towards the marketplace. As he disappeared between the stalls, only one trader remained at the scene. It was the same inquisitive being who had grabbed hold of me earlier. From under the shadow of his hat, he gave me a grin before raising his hand to wave goodbye. He was enjoying seeing my body wrapped up in shame.

“Run. Run. Run.”

It was his mocking wave that made me realise it wasn't my strength that had broken free from his grip. He had chosen to let me go. Why? The trader picked up on my revelation.

“And it finally sinks in.”

Mustering all my strength I sprinted towards the haven of safety. In the distance, I could hear his departing words, begging they weren't prophetic.

"You will come back to us. You always do."

STAVE 3
DURING THE DECISION

CHAPTER 29
HOW THE PILLAR CAME TO BE

"The iron that has entered into our souls has gone too deep for you to find it. Leave the refugee alone! Laugh at him, distrust him, open your eyes in wonder at the secret self which smoulders in him, sometimes under the every-day respectability and tranquillity of a man like me – sometimes under the grinding poverty, the fierce squalor, of men less lucky, less pliable, less patient than I am – but judge us not. In the time of your first Charles you might have done us justice – the long luxury of your freedom has made you incapable of doing us justice now."
(Wilkie Collins, The Woman in White)

EKI KEPT IN THE SHADOWS.

It was second nature to her, an abnormal benefit of living on the streets. For the last fifteen minutes she had followed Pevensie through the Seven Dials District. Something hadn't felt right about the message outside the library. It felt unfinished and she needed to know why.

Monmouth Street. Shaftesbury Avenue. Then left onto John Street. Eki knew this route well, but like most of her painful story, she hadn't walked those paths in a long time. Her return hadn't been pleasant. There were many haunting memories lingering within the pavement cracks. Some of those shadows told tales about her past. Others, her present. The ones she cared about most were the shadows revealing the future. Where was Pevensie heading to?

Her answer came quicker than expected.

Pevensie stopped outside a townhouse on Doughty Street. He scanned the terraced building up and down, trying to find signs of life. Even from a distance, she could spot the look of disappointment on his face. Deflated but not defeated he carried on walking down the street. Eki had seen enough. Pevensie's mysterious hunt wasn't a mystery anymore. Doughty Street was where Dickens had lived for a few years, birthing Oliver Twist.

And.

Eki's face lit up. She was conscious that already her mind was joining two-and-two together to make ten, but she didn't care. Even if most of her equation was wrong, it didn't alter the hoped-for answer. She waited until Pevensie turned a corner before walking up to the house. Could it be? What an amazing question to think about after all this time. A tingle of anticipation ran across her dirt-stained skin. This was the street where The Twins first introduced themselves to Dickens. And if they were back... Eki drew in a deep breath, calming her excited nerves.

There was no need to follow Pevensie anymore. If her hunch was right about their hiding place, the old man was heading in the wrong direction. It felt strange to think her story could be coming round full circle. Back to the Seven Dials monument.

Or should she say, The Pillar?

*****

Many years ago, before time became constrained within minutes and hours, the town folk of Codicia came across a strange man. They called him The Magician. His nickname came from the peculiar choice of clothes he would wear. A frilly white shirt. Black penguin suit. Velvet top hat. And shiny dark shoes. The whole outfit had the feel of the theatrical. So did his arrival into town.

The Magician had set up a big top tent in the middle of the field, then left it there, closed, for three weeks. Rumours filled the town, complete with unconfirmed sightings of the peculiar man. And then, on a cold Sunday morning, posters appeared. The conversations over breakfast were about nothing else.

FOR ONE NIGHT ONLY, A SHOW NOT TO MISS.

HOW THE PILLAR CAME TO BE

It was a sell-out. Standing room only. Not only did the whole town of Codicia turn up, but also the folk from nearby Rico and Ilodi. With the mixture of a travelling salesman infused with a TV Evangelist, The Magician's blend of magic and prophecy captivated the crowd.

Act One was the warm up. He picked out six audience members and recounted what their last twenty-four hours had looked like. Asking as though He already knew their answers, the Magician offered them the opportunity to see their future. People always accepted the chance of turning to the last page of the book.

Act Two was where the real magic kicked off. It only took one word from The Magician to silence the audience. "Rain!" The heavens obeyed without question, opening their clouds with a downpour bouncing off the canvas roof. Another command. "Light!" In the evening darkness, the tent lit up with a mystifying beam from outside. A standing ovation followed, expecting the show to end. But the two acts had been designed for one reason only.

To set people up for Act Three.

In hushed disbelief, The Magician told the audience they too could be people of magic. Together they could create something that no one had ever seen before. A town like no other, continually shaping itself to whatever was in their hearts.

Welcome to PARADOX.

People came from far and wide to visit the new town.

The tales of wonder and delight were infectious. Bright lights and fancy shows captivated the eyes. That's why nobody noticed another strange figure walking the streets one night. They planted a seed just outside the marketplace and then left. The following morning a wooden post appeared. It caught everyone by surprise. The town's folk took an instant dislike to it. Not only was the wooden post dull, it had also become a meeting point for anyone who had fallen upon hard times. The rejects. The refugees.

The others.

People tried to clear the undesirables away, but every day they returned. Then came the barriers, trying to stop the increase in numbers. That didn't work either. Rumours followed. An evil magic was at play. So they called a town hall meeting to deal with the problem once and for all. Some were worried about the impact it would have upon business. Tourism was important. The sight of the down-and-outs would mess with the image of their town. Others spoke about how 'those type of people' made them feel unsafe – it was important to think of the children. During the worried outbursts, someone described the post as though it was immovable, just like a pillar.

The name stuck.

When the town meeting looked like it would end in disappointment, He appeared, like magic. The Magician reminded them how PARADOX came into being. They were all magicians and could simply magic the situation away. Ignorance was one of the strongest spells a person could cast, and if performed correctly, their beautiful landscape would return. All they needed to do was ignore what they didn't want to see.

And it worked.

The Pillar was always on show but never seen.

Gradgrind never wanted to sit down at The Pillar, but her 'Hard Times' ticket had only one destination.

In a former life, Gradgrind had been a successful businesswoman, turned teacher, turned PARADOX governor. She had seen her job as one that taught the importance of facts. "Facts alone are wanted in life. They weigh and measure the value of human worth." Her approach to hard data had won many admirers, including The Magician.

The day Gradgrind received an invitation to visit him in his study was like winning the lottery. There was no small talk in this honoured meeting. The Magician went straight to the point. HE was working in secret on a new trick and needed someone to pull a few levers behind the scenes. Figures. Data. Profit and Loss. It was critical to know whether his latest trick would bring the house down. Figuratively? The Magician never confirmed.

Weeks blurred into months as the data flowed and the paycheques arrived. Yet Gradgrind grew concerned with what she was uncovering. Yes, this would be the greatest trick, but at what cost?

Human cost.

Gradgrind attempted to change the bottom line, but the results would always come out the same. Fait accompli. She didn't know what to do. Saying something to her boss would incur his wrath, and she had seen his anger before. If that happened, then unemployment would soon follow. She couldn't let that happen; her family was reliant upon the income. Telling others would break her contract of secrecy, but keeping quiet would be just as bad. Her only option was the 'old' trick again. Ignorance. The magic worked for a while, until her family fell on the wrong side of the data. Gradgrind waited until the kids were in bed to tell her husband. That night, they planned their escape.

The visit in the morning came as a surprise. The Magician already knew what she was up to, reasoning with her to change her mind. She had read the data wrong – no need to be worried about her family. When his words fell on deaf ears, He opened up a secret file. A reminder of things best forgotten. She asked for time. They agreed to talk the next day.

That was ten years ago.

Or was it fifteen? Maybe twenty. It was hard to tell. Every day blurred into the next. 'Hard Times' at The Pillar felt like a lifetime for Gradgrind. But it was a price worth paying. The important thing was that she had been able to get her family out of PARADOX. Unfortunately, the same couldn't be said for her. The Magician knew too much about her life. There was no way she could've left without her world, and her family, falling apart.

Within weeks of staying, she gave up her job. It wasn't the easiest decision to make, she had become accustomed to the fine things PARADOX could bring. But it became clear that the only way to be reunited with her family was to expose The Magician's new trick. From The Pillar, her prophetic call echoed through the streets, calling on people to leave this dangerous town. As months turned into years, she started to doubt. There had been no new trick or devastating event. And the house hadn't fallen down. She couldn't understand how she had got it so wrong. Her search for answers created a new role. She set herself up as a guide. Helping other travellers around PARADOX gave her a chance to collect data again. She was good at analysing figures. With data came information. And with information, the possibility to see what she was missing.

Was The Magician a villain or hero?

It was still too early to say, but another stream of data was now running towards her. Maybe this familiar face would be the final clue.

CHAPTER 30
THINGS HAVE CHANGED

"'You have been so careful of me, that I never had a child's heart. You have trained me so well, that I never dreamed a child's dream. You have dealt so wisely with me, father, from my cradle to this hour, that I never had a child's belief or a child's fear.' Mr Gradgrind was quite moved by his success, and by this testimony to it."
(Charles Dickens, Hard Times)

WHO WAS THIS WOMAN?

Standing next to the wooden post was an enigmatic figure. Rigid. Slim. Dressed in black. Her stern schoolmistress face carried the lines of someone who preferred life to be neat and orderly. She scanned me up and down with her narrow, deep-sunken eyes. It made me feel like I was a human spreadsheet of data, her poker face expression never letting on what my figures revealed.

Back in the day, her managerial dress code would have sent the strongest heart into a nervous meltdown. Not today. The tailored black suit was nothing more than ragged cloth. Overused pockets shaped the jacket to look one size too big. Her white blouse was more of a dirty grey. It had a splattering of food stains around the edge that provided a practical history lesson concerning her dietary preferences. Broken hems around the long skirt brought attention to the handmade Italian-leather shoes. These once statements-of-status had seen their fair share of DIY fingers. Tape and prayer were the only things holding the repairs in place. The whole visual package told the story of an out-of-luck woman hanging onto a rich faded dream. Whoever she was, her life had hit hard times.

She liked to refer to herself as The Guide in these situations.

It was her way of keeping the priorities in order. Any interest in the person came second, this was all about data. Data for learning. Data to get her family back.

Seeing Peccadillo again had been a surprise addition to her established lines of data. He wasn't supposed to be back, and now her old friend had paid dearly for his return. She choked up a little as she watched Santiago disappear behind the stall. They hadn't spoken in a while, courtesy of them both having stubborn personalities. Somewhere in all their historic mess, they believed time would resolve things.

Maybe not after all.

The Guide felt a tug on her jacket. She looked down and gave a warm smile. It was rare that anyone saw what she was looking at, including Santiago. That was the reason for their falling out. And what about the returning Peccadillo? If only it were that simple. She was angry at him. It wasn't his fault, but who else could she blame.

Santiago was the only piece of data that made sense to her.

Her introduction was sharp and to the point.

She was holding back, double-checking and triple-checking each word before delivery. I had the sense she blamed me for what had happened to Santiago. For a split second I even thought she had choked up. The Guide kept looking down at her side as though acknowledging an invisible friend. Her lips quivered, giving the impression she was having an imaginary conversation. Whatever she heard, it changed her attitude towards me. She still carried a stern expression, but there was a warmth in her cheeks. The Guide told me to wait as she scurried around The Pillar. Seconds later, she came back with a clipboard and pen. Adjusting her clothes and straightening her shoulders, she feverishly flicked through the pages. Her pen tapped on the lines of text, signifying essential data to remember. Satisfied things were in order, she looked up in deep thought.

I stood dumbfounded by the whole thing. Although there was a moment of genuine sadness, she was acting as though nothing else had happened. Couldn't she see the state of confusion I was in? PARADOX had frozen then come back to life. What about the red beams from The Pillar or the terrifying words from the market traders? How cold could she be? The Guide picked up on my confused agitation.

"Spit it out, boy. I hate..."

"Didn't you...."

"Manners!"

The pencil slammed against the clipboard.

"Where are your manners? One does not interrupt. One listens then replies. It's the order of life. Black, white. Front, back. Up, down. Listen, reply. Life is all about order. Understand?"

In any other circumstance, I would have given her a piece of my mind, including the ironic nature of her interruption. Not today. I didn't understand what was happening to me, but I sensed she was my ticket out of here.

"And now the boy doesn't speak when spoken to. Shocking."

"I'm. Sorry."

The Guide leant forward, her sunken eyes stretching out of their sockets.

"Speak up. Stuttering. Mumbling. All signs of a bad upbringing."

"I. Just."

The pen slammed down again in frustration.

"You're attempting to say, you don't know where you are or what is happening. Well, I can answer one of those questions, but I'm more interested in the one I can't yet answer."

She spun around. Another invisible tug on her jacket. Her stern expression immediately changed to a deep show of affection. She bent down and angled her head to listen. A one-way conversation started up in a two-way invisible world.

"I know. Agree. But I don't trust him. Long time. That's dreaming, nothing else. See the eyes. Nothing's changed. I agree, but not when it involves..."

She stopped the conversation mid-flow and looked up at me. I didn't know who was staring back through those sunken eyes, the stern looking schoolmistress or the woman who had that imaginary game inside her head. She turned away.

"Told you. We shouldn't. It took a long time to pick up the pieces. I know. Well."

Her tone changed again, so too her flow of words. She placed a lot of respect upon what was being said to her.

"If you say so. You know my feelings though. Thank you. Me too. The future is. Unclear. If you're happy with that, you know I will always be here for you. OK. I will. And what about Santiago? Thank you. That means a lot."

The Guide stood up and straightened her clothes again.

"Come this way. We have data to collect."

*****

The Magician hated the new name.

What was Gradgrind thinking of? The Guide, a self-appointed helper of people. But she wasn't self-appointed, was she? It was an illusion, just like everything else in PARADOX. The Guide took orders, regardless of what she thought. And if she discovered what He knew about that relationship, her righteous world would come falling down with no show of mercy.

The Magician was still kicking himself for not seeing that relationship before it happened. The ability to foresee every step was something He took pride in. His ego had taken a hit, but He adjusted and played along with her new role. The Guide had her uses.

And He needed that use today.

As predicted, she couldn't resist the collection of data. Peccadillo was an accountant's dream formula. But for everything to work, The Guide and her comrades-in-arms needed to think they were acting on their own accord. Welcome to The Magician's sleight-of-hand. Santiago. The man played his part to perfection. Nobody would suspect a thing. And now everything was falling into place for Peccadillo's return visit to The Theatre.

CHAPTER 31
THE PATHS

"You cannot judge the beauty of a particular path by looking at the gate."
(Paulo Coelho, The Pilgrimage)

"SEVEN PATHS. One destination."

The Guide whispered the words like a haunting soundtrack. Her hand rubbed along The Pillar, feeling every bump and indentation of the bark. It was a touch of memories and she was falling deeper into its endless labyrinth. So was I. The way the Paths fanned out from The Pillar reminded me of a scallop shell and the cancer-filled Sunday lunchtime chats with my mother.

"I doubt you remember this place. I can tell from your eyes."

Her fingers rested over a series of markings. Letters. Etched into the wood. Faded with age.

"I don't blame you. Even I struggle to recall the first time I walked from here. Adventures have a way of sneaking up on you then thrusting a blunt-edged dagger into your back. I thought these Paths were an answer, but I was wrong. They are a curse."

She looked down at her side. Her invisible friends were tagging along. We lingered by the etched letters. My fingers rubbed along the worn-out lines of the first word. Maybe that's why she was The Guide. I would have easily missed them if it wasn't for her pointing them out. The bark felt warm, residue from the red light.

'Path of the Mystery.'

Without thinking, I carried on dragging my hand along the rough surface. I became nervous of the energy lurking behind its wooden cage.

'Path of the Twist.'

'Path of the Mundane.'

'Path of the Demand.'

'Path of the Godot.'

'Path of the Tristan.'

And.

The Guide touched my hand. She spoke out the final name.

"Path of the Decision. You walk that one at the end."

*****

Walking around The Pillar had softened The Guide.

Uncertainty does that to the heart. I kept replaying her words about how The Paths had stabbed her in the back. Whatever this place represented, her belief in it had changed. She was now caught up in the unforgiving space of doubt.

"To leave you must walk the Paths."

"What is this, some test?"

There was an unintended lightness in my reply that provoked a heated outburst.

"How dare you! You have always treated this place with such... such... Damn You. Your return has hurt too many people already."

People? Not just Santiago. Another tug on her jacket calmed her down. She had a look on her face that children get when told to apologise. The Guide compromised by pretending the outburst never happened. She told me to follow her as we slowly walked down the first Path.

The Path of the Mystery.

The Guide was in front. I followed a few metres behind. At the end of the lane was an iron gate. The design tipped its head to Temple Bar, the famed Christopher Wren's arched gateway that Dickens used in *A Tale of Two Cities.* In the book, severed heads hung down to deter any criminal. There were no such signs of punishment on this one, just a door of mystery that hid whatever was lurking behind.

As I kid, I loved the lure of the unknown. For a few years, gates bizarrely represented that for me. They were doorways into an adventure. It didn't matter whether they had an exquisite design or were just a pile of bricks and broken twigs. They all said the same thing to my passionate heart: imagination and adventure walk hand in hand. That excitement wore off as an adult. I got bored with gates. They became a nuisance more than a precursor to an adventure into the unknown. Some days, when I was feeling melancholic, I would imagine what lay behind those gates. Fantasy was enough. I didn't want to get my shoes dirty.

"There it is. Mystery awaits."

She was back in her reflective mood as she opened the gate.

"Why can't I just skip to the seventh Path?"

I still didn't want to get my shoes dirty.

"No shortcuts. Every Path has a reason for existence. Put them together and you open up the seventh."

Her laboured words trudged through the thick mud of weariness. She had said those lines many times. It flicked on a memory for me too. Distant. Out of focus.

"I've been here before?"

I didn't know whether I was making a statement or asking a question. The Guide replied with a surprising smile.

"What's so funny?"

"History. You say the same thing about this gate every time we meet."

*****

The Guide had rules.

She had broken one of them already. Open the gate and say goodbye. Her job here was to guide any traveller towards the gate and then collect the data that followed. Getting caught up in their life story complicated her goal of getting her family back safe.

But she struggled today to keep the rule. Standing by the gate had brought back memories of when she had walked Peccadillo down this Path for the first time. That had been a good day for both of them. There was so much hope for the future. But she got too involved, wrapping herself up in a battle that wasn't hers.

The Guide pulled out her key and looked at its metal form. How many times had she opened this gate for him? Many times. Times of hope. Times of despair. And this one? Peccadillo wasn't supposed to have come back. His last visit had sealed his choice. That's how PARADOX works: one continual loop until the eyes see the place for what it is. It had taken a while for The Guide to get over the loss. She vowed never to blur friendship with data ever again.

Behind that entrance lay a storyline of pain and betrayal, written by Peccadillo's hand.

*****

"I will be here when you return."

The stern expression had returned. She never looked me in the eyes. Her stare fixed upon her DIY shoes. This was not a warm send-off or tearful goodbye. The Guide wanted me out of here for her own peace of mind.

I pushed the gate open; its greeting back was a high pitched screech.

*****

Now what?

The Guide closed the gate and turned the lock. It was important she kept focused. Every visit from a traveller brought little changes to the data. Hidden within those small adjustments were the answers that revealed The Magician's end game. Villain. Hero. She needed to know.

For years she had trusted his opponent and look where that had taken her. Nothing had changed. Her family were still in hiding and she was stuck in this god-forsaken place. The Storyteller had promised her freedom from the secret that held her in PARADOX. But maybe she was seeing this all wrong. What if the old lady was the one holding the key and not The Magician?

Stop!

"Talk like this corrupts the data."

She needed to focus. PARADOX was alive with rumours. Messy rumours. And in times like this, it was important to keep the head clear.

It was important to live by data alone.

CHAPTER 32
TSHILABA

"Inside us there is something that has no name, that something is what we are."
(José Saramago, Blindness)

OPEN FIELDS of Mediterranean grasslands surrounded me.

God had experimented with His colour palette on this place. Every colour of the rainbow was present. Red, yellow and blue bushes clashed with the purple and orange blades of grass. Golden flecks of mystical paint rested on the vegetation like an acid-inspired morning dew. As for the trees, they got in on the colourful action, replacing their brown coverings with multi-coloured coats. The uncluttered blue sky was the only thing that looked normal. There was not a cloud in sight as the sun made sure that all of Creation knew who was reigning supreme. I didn't feel unpleasantly hot. The dry heat had a gentle breeze. It was tempting to stop and soak in the sweet aroma of summer.

But the lure of mystery got the better of me.

Squinting, I could just make out that there was a fork in the road. It wasn't the only thing waiting for me. Between the two trails was a woman. She was standing with her back towards me, next to what looked like a traditional Romani caravan. With each step, the traditional horse-drawn Vardo revealed layer upon layer of its captivating beauty. The exquisite and practical design welcomed the bright colours of painted flowers in bloom. I could almost hear the whispers of haunting stories, housed within those curved walls. Many a traveller would have stumbled upon the gypsy lure and given their soul to find a fortune.

The woman turned around. Her dramatic reveal brought my walk to a sudden stop. She was stunning. An Eastern goddess. Her dark skin was the perfect canvas for emerald green eyes. Those shining crystals of heavenliness that reflected the sun's rays blinded my heart. Dark, red lips became monuments of passion on the top of a neckline of graceful elegance. The cooling breeze gently blew her flower-patterned dress. A quick adjustment of a crocheted shawl revealed a golden bracelet with two charms. One was a cross, the other a broken heart.

She wore her beauty with persuasive ease. A mermaid of love that happily sang her song on sharp, jagged cliffs. It didn't occur to me until she spoke, that my static feet had walked up to her. That's how sailors lost their lives to the mermaid song. Enchantment is a dangerous thing.

"Welcome. My name is Tshilaba. I'm sure if you think hard enough, you will remember that."

What a heavenly voice. I was the spotty kid at a school dance again, standing opposite the prom queen. Everything in me wanted to talk to her, but instead, the only thing I could muster was a nervous sigh. In front of her was a wooden crate with a small cardboard box on top; a sign propped against the edge.

TSHILABA'S MAGICAL MYSTERY CARDBOARD BOX.

WHAT'S INSIDE?

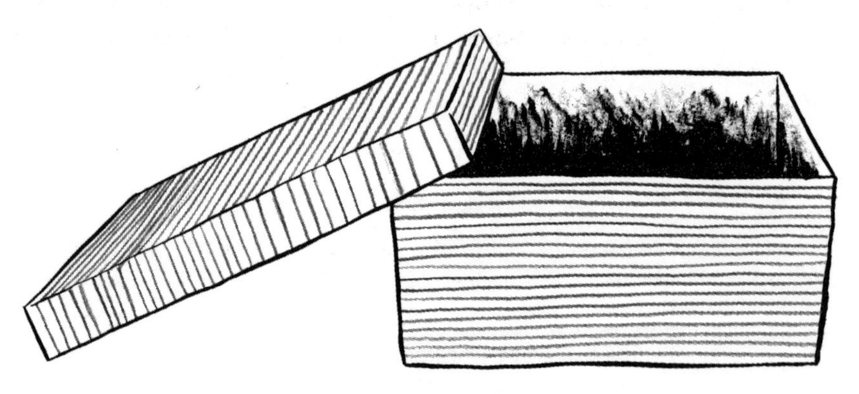

My inquisitive look was her cue to continue with her sounds of the divine.

"Open the box to see what is inside. Or… Maybe the clue is in the name."

Her words only added another layer to my curious look. Tshilaba fidgeted with her charm bracelet. Her fingers were rubbing the edge of the broken heart.

"I thought I would never see you again, not after last time. But you don't remember, do you?"

Her soft voice carried another silent question behind it. *How could you NOT remember?* She masked her emotions well, but not well enough. What had happened between us? Tshilaba waited for my reply. I longed to give her the response she was craving for. Her beauty was fragile and I felt somehow responsible for the marks of pain she was covering up. My silence only made it worse. The look in her eyes was enough to bring guilt and I still didn't know why. Her answer back sent me further into the dark cell of the unknowing.

"My sweet Peccadillo. How could you not remember? You nearly killed me opening this box."

*****

The scar on her leg was long and clean. It started just above her knee and ended at the ankle.

"I have another scar as well."

Tshilaba continued to touch the broken heart charm.

"You said some awful things. Things that cut deeper than any physical scar."

She was mistaken. I would never have done something like that! Never? My mind flashed back to Terri. Words maybe, but never physical. I went into self-defence mode, looking for a way out. That's when I focused on The MAGICAL MYSTERY CARDBOARD BOX. *Déjà vu.*

"You're remembering."

Tshilaba was right. God, she was right.

"We were arguing."

My eyes never left the crate as I spoke out the swirling memory.

"It was because of this box. I wanted something from it. You told me, begged me not to do it. I remember the fight. And..."

Unspeakable. Inexcusable. I didn't want to say the final words. My mind played out the scene of me pushing her to the floor. I watched in horror as she screamed out in pain. Shame twisted my gut as the echo of myself walked over to the box, not caring to even turn around and come to her aid. I closed my eyes. The scene paused. A close up of my face. Pure selfish lust. Such an evil look. My hands began to shake. So many emotions were ripping my heart apart. This wasn't right. It couldn't be right. An illusion. It had to be.

Please God let it be!

But my face. The truth was in those evil eyes wanting to see what was inside the box. But it didn't make sense. It was just a bloody box. Nothing more. How could I do such a thing to her? Tshilaba took hold of my hand. The soothing balm of her touch gently laid over my shame.

"Come and sit down. Please."

She led me to a couple of overturned apple boxes. We sat in silence. I looked back up the road I had just walked. The vibrant colours had lost all their wonder now. Nothing but darkness – the dark night of my soul.

*****

"We used to sit here for hours."

Tshilaba joined in looking up the road.

"There were days we would just watch the sun go down over that hill and tell each other stories. Happy stories. Painful stories. When you were feeling brave, your heart would open up. In those moments you were as a child, dreaming about changing the world. It was beautiful. Special."

Her words carried the cry of lament for what we once had. She gathered herself, then continued.

"I guess nobody notices the change until it's too late. You used to bring me a present every time we met. Remember? It was a story, the latest tale in your head. But then you started bringing me physical gifts that you picked up from the market in town. One of them being this bracelet. It was as if what was in your heart wasn't good enough anymore.

We still talked about your books and hopes, but rarely about changing the world. Occasionally there were moments of vulnerability. You spoke a lot about what happened with Terri. It was the same about the death of your mother."

My stare silenced her words. How did she know all of this? Tshilaba pressed harder down on my hand, her soft skin like a warm blanket of reassurance.

"But I can see in your eyes the reflection of a child. You're still in there.

Hanging on.

Hanging on to mystery."

CHAPTER 33
MYSTERY BOX

"The magical mystery box... It represents hope. It represents potential... I find myself drawn to infinite possibility... Mystery is the catalyst for imagination... Maybe there are times when mystery is more important than knowledge."
(J.J. Abrams, TED 2007)

TRUTH IS A PAINFUL THING to hear when it touches upon shame.

As I sat on the upside down apple crate, Tshilaba recounted the tale about how she got her scar. My desperation to open the Mystery Box had taken her by surprise. She thought I wasn't like that anymore.

My first few visits to her caravan were pleasant. We would sit on the crates and talk about the mystery of life. There was always the offering of opening the lid, but I never did. Our stories were enough to live with the tension of the unknown. But by my fifth visit, things had changed. I was older, more of a cynic. The world had beaten me up too many times and I now had different priorities. I wasn't interested in fantastical tales or wasting my hours away staring into a blood red sunset. Life was about getting ahead and then staying ahead, regardless of who I clambered over. I craved to know what was inside the Box, convinced it was some magical formula for success. After lifting the lid, I walked away, not even saying goodbye. Visits six and seven followed the same routine. All I wanted was the contents in the Box. Nothing more. Tshilaba was just a means of achieving my goal. How quickly the eyes can eradicate the humanity of a life.

But Tshilaba continued to have faith that things could change. As the visits continued, she would drop out little storylines that would make me stop and wonder. Just for a few seconds, but that's all she was looking for. Stories have a way of acting like yeast in the soul. I would still open the Box, except it felt more like a routine than a desire. There was hope.

Until Santiago.

His surprising decision to side with The Magician had hit me hard. During my last visit, I wanted nothing more to do with PARADOX. It was everyone for themselves. And I wanted it all. Tshilaba pleaded with me not to open the lid. Doing so in my current state of mind would have an irreversible consequence. But I craved what was inside the Box like a hungry beast. Hating that I had wasted my time listening to stories of mystery, I pushed her to one side as I rushed over to my goal. Her cry of pain was a needless distraction. I never noticed her leg crashing against the caravan wheel. After opening the lid, that's when HE came for me. The Magician asked if I had anything to say to my crying friend; words seeking forgiveness or concern for her pain? I told her she meant nothing to me, then walked away.

Tshilaba thought I would never return after that.

*****

"But you did."

Her soft voice carried undertones of the unknown. My return wasn't in her plan and the temptation to seek answers had a familiar pull. She looked over at the Box. Her hand, over mine, trembled.

"Never underestimate the power of mystery. I have seen many empires fall trying to open its lid."

I believed her. Even though it looked like a cardboard box, I could already feel its invisible tug. So could Tshilaba. She wanted to know why I was here. Maybe the answer was inside. I wanted answers as well, not just about PARADOX but why I believed her story about me was true.

"It's strong, isn't it? We all want to know what's inside."

She looked away, back towards the horizon.

“The only way to resist opening the lid is by remembering what the Box is all about. We used to tell stories to each other about it. Remember?”

I couldn’t, but I longed to. Strangely.

“That’s OK. Let me remind you.”

*****

“Once upon a time there was The Storyteller.

She had an incredible skill for magic that would amaze the eyes of the universe. All of Creation longed to gaze upon illusions that declared the majesty of her imagination. But there was dissent in the camp.

The Magician.

He was the opening act for her, and felt short-changed on recognition. His sleight-of-hand performances were a favourite with the crowds. The Magician believed the only reason the audience erupted in applause every night was because his act had warmed them up perfectly. But *She* never acknowledged his contribution.

Rumours turned into arguments and soon it disrupted the show. The Magician laid down a challenge. For a ‘one-time-only’ performance, the two of them would reveal their greatest trick. Winner takes all. Loser exits stage left. The Magician went first. His performance was what the audience had come to expect, a dazzling display of lights and special effects. The conclusion brought the entire room to a standing ovation. Then came The Storyteller, who did the unexpected. There were no pyrotechnics, no heart-thumping music. *She* merely brought out a box and stood beside it. The audience watched as The Storyteller wrote something on a piece of paper, then placed it inside. There was a pause. Followed by a bow. The trick was over. And the audience fell silent. The Magician pushed his way back onto the stage. It was clear who had won the challenge, it was now time to claim the prize. But most of the crowd greeted him with jeers and boos. The ultimate trick wasn’t gauged by a standing ovation, but by the unknown. What was inside the Box? The very question led people into a world of imagination, taking them beyond their restricting picture frame. The greatest trick of all.

Mystery.

The Magician refused to leave the stage. *He* believed there was only one rightful winner. Shouting towards the crowd for support, half of them stood up. His departure was menacing, letting everyone know this challenge wasn't over. *He* would prove to the universe that *She* was nothing but a con-artist. Words followed and then came the threats. The Magician would take no prisoners. This house, and its stage, will eventually fall down!"

It was a captivating story.

I didn't believe it was real, but then again, I was in a world that transformed itself to my desires. Could it be true? I started to doubt my doubts. A memory lingered about the note inside, the one written by The Storyteller. I had seen it. It was the reason I had kept opening the lid, believing it would help me with my book. After all, the mysterious note came from the ultimate storyteller. It would be a sure-fire bestseller. But my fogged-up memory told me it hadn't turned out the way I expected. The note was... different.

My mind's eye tried to make out the mysterious words.

"It's no use trying. You will never see the note unless you open the lid."

Tshilaba was watching my every move.

"Maybe you could do something different this time and leave the lid shut."

My eyes fixed on the Box, willing the lid to open up.

"What use would that be?"

"Mystery is stronger than knowledge."

CHAPTER 34
A STRANGE PATH

"I come from under the hill, and under the hills and over the hills my paths led. And through the air, I am he that walks unseen."
(J.R.R. Tolkien, The Hobbit)

I MADE three unexpected moves.

The first was that the Box lid remained shut. I wished it was down to some new found love for mystery. It wasn't. Even though everything in me wanted to peer inside, shame for what I had done to Tshilaba got the upper hand. We sat for a while. I didn't want to leave. There was so much that hadn't been said. Unspoken things. Redemptive things. It was Tshilaba that suggested it was time to go, telling me that it would only cause us more pain if I didn't end this journey.

The second unexpected move was taking the broken heart off her bracelet. I wanted to do something that would show my remorse. But the gesture was a poor substitute for the real thing. How could I make amends for such an act? Tshilaba kissed me on the cheek. It was gentle. Forgiving. And yet. There was distance, as though the damage would never heal.

The third unexpected move was choosing the left fork in the road. Tshilaba told me that both routes took me back to The Pillar. Turning right was the easy way. Nothing to see and amazingly quick. She refused to tell me what was down the left fork. I chose that route, not because of mystery but punishment. I had stared into the abyss of my actions and hated what I had seen. My life didn't deserve a painless walk back home. The least I could do was serve penance for what I had done. Another empty gesture?

I was about to find out.

*****

Regret kicked in almost immediately.

Turning left was the wrong choice. This open trail I had been walking on had now transformed itself into a narrow, bramble-covered track. My desire for a painful penance served itself with thorns piercing through my jeans and digging into the skin. The bushes that arched their branches into the sky blocked out the broad vista of golden fields. Everything felt enclosed. Unsafe. Out of the dark came the feeling of watching eyes. I tried to catch out the voyeuristic stare with a quick turn to the left and right. My foot slipped on the uneven ground, sending me off balance. As I steadied myself, blaming the moss covered stones, a strange thought made me look down. The rock had moved. Not a wobble, but a jump.

"Mind where you are bloody well going."

I pretended I couldn't see the talking stone. Acknowledging it would only make the crazy truth real.

"Yes. You. You big fat loaf. Always do that, eh? Trample on heads?"

Two big chalk eyes stared directly at me. These uneven circles had all the markings of a child's drawing. There wasn't a nose, but the mouth had the same pre-school view of perspective. Overcompensated in a logical way. Bizarrely, I stepped back and apologised.

"Damn right you should. Nearly wiped my… OH HECK. YOU DID. YOU BLOODY WELL WIPED MY NOSE CLEAN OFF!"

The illogical farce and its Cockney accent made me laugh.

"Yes. Yes. Yes. Laugh it up. It's alright for you, big nose. You never get to lose your features. As for me, I have to go through a facelift every few years. The weather plays havoc with my lines, and don't get me started about people not looking where they are going. The worst thing is, I now have the whole evening ahead of me without smelling the good cooking that my missus has for me."

His impassioned speech added to the comical nature of the moment. I couldn't stop laughing. That made him more agitated. It was a vicious circle.

"Think it's funny, eh? I'll tell you what's funny. Ever heard of the guy who thinks he can walk but has broken feet?"

The cutting remark did the trick of shutting me up.

"What's happened? Did someone wipe away your mouth? That's right. A girl did. Not just any girl, but one with a box. That Box. And did you open the lid like last time?"

The stone signed off his delivery with a deep sigh.

"Sorry. I shouldn't have lost control like that. One of my shortcomings. I'm just sensitive about broken promises."

"Promises?"

"Yeah, you owe me something. Now take a seat. It hurts looking up at you from down here."

*****

"Haven't you grown up!"

The stone was acting as though I was a long-lost relative that had returned to the fold. Because of that, I was expecting open arms of verbal affirmation. Instead, the follow-up was a download of disappointment.

"What a shame. Maybe my wife was right after all when she said your inner Pan had finally grown up."

Rumour had it that J.M. Barrie, the author of *Peter Pan*, had played with the idea of writing a sequel where Pan becomes an adult. Spielberg took the concept and made it into a film about the sad demise of imagination. I wondered if this dig from the stone was just another reminder of how willing I was to dismiss the magic of the plastic bell.

"I'm guessing you still haven't bought your pencil?"

"What?"

I wasn't paying attention to what the stone was saying. In amongst the thoughts of childhood carnivals, I had begun to worry about where I was sitting. Loose dirt. Damp moss. A new pair of jeans. There was no sign of my inner-child as I cried out for a chair. Back in my younger days, I would have gotten into the mud without thinking. Who cared if my clothes got dirty? That's what they were for anyway – adventure. But not today. Only adult sensibility.

"Yep. Just as I thought. Grown up and with no pencil. Shame. Years ago you promised me a beautiful hairline. My missus got well excited about it. Said it would take years off me. I haven't forgotten that promise."

The stone gave a little sniffle as he held back the tears. Crying was dangerous, it would ruin his eyes. He gathered himself and shuffled to the right. One jump. Then another. He was now facing down the Path.

"Head down there for about a mile. Next to a big tree stump, you will see two kids playing. They sometimes have a tea-party, but I haven't heard that sound in a while. Have a chat with them. And while you are there, see if they have a pencil."

Childhood.

Those strange ten minutes of talking to the stone were like a flashback to being young again. Imaginary friends, adventures in the woods, drawings in the ground and talking trees. Nothing was impossible and everything astounding.

In those early years of life, a simple walk would take me hours. I was infatuated with Creation. This living organism of adventure was a majestic symphony being played out within the cracks of getting from *a-to-b*. The world was more significant than the four walls of my school classroom, louder than a chart single and more creative than a computer game. I had magic beans.

Then I gave them away, one by one.

It happened slowly with each passing year. The wonder of a moving clock hand replaced my excitement about sitting under a tree. I had jobs to do and a career ladder to climb. My gentle walk became a powerful stride that saved a few vital seconds. High speed. Tunnel-visioned. Everything shaped by an ever-demanding calendar.

Maybe the author Mitch Albom was right when he wrote his disturbing tale about Father Time. In those pages, the mystical being was a man whom the universe punished for creating a mechanism of slavery. Time can be a curse. It was for me. And yet, on this Path, however illogical and stupid it sounded, I yearned to be young again. Peccadillo. A man with broken feet. Learning to walk again with baby steps.

Tshilaba would be proud.

CHAPTER 35
MEET THE KIDS

"'Children, you are the future,' he said, and today I realise he did not mean it the way it sounded. The reason children are the future is not that they will one day be grownups. No, the reason is that mankind is moving more and more in the direction of infancy, and childhood is the image of the future."
(Milan Kundera, The Book of Laughter and Forgetting)

THE TWO KIDS, A GIRL AND A BOY, looked about seven.

They were twins.

The Twins?

Couldn't be. They looked harmless. The girl had dungarees on with a chequered shirt. Her blonde hair tied back into a pony tail. Confidence naturally shone out of her as she issued instructions to the boy sitting beside her. He had on shorts and a t-shirt. The crew cut hairstyle made his face look round and pudgy; his look, finished off with black-rimmed glasses. The boy rarely looked up. His freckled face staring in concentration at the task at hand. The two of them were drawing.

There was a messy pile of stones next to them. Some had half-completed faces scribbled on their smooth surface. Others just needed the finishing touch of an eyebrow and ear. The kids didn't seem to be in any rush to complete their works of art. Whatever stones they were working on gave them the opportunity to delve into a backstory of imagination.

The girl called her stone Kelliko. It was a robot, turned human, turned stone. Kelliko was on a secret mission to find the lost treasure of Glop. This magical wealth could convert the land into ice-cream. A perfect world. The boy called his stone, Cedric, an artist who liked painting flowers. Cedric's backstory was that he had woken up and realised that he was too tall to see all the beautiful things that were growing close to the ground. To rectify that, he visited the woodland elves who agreed to magic him down to a more appropriate size. What Cedric hadn't realised was that elves could be mischievous. They thought it would be funny to turn him into a small stone.

I could tell that the two kids knew I was standing next to them, but they tried hard to pretend I wasn't there. The boy was the first to blink in this strange game. He looked up, just for a split second. His imaginative eyes suddenly turned to fear.

Little did I know he had every reason to be scared of me.

The ancient oak tree was magical.

It was their favourite place. Every day, between lunchtime and dinner, the two kids would run through the fields to make sure that their magical spot had not disappeared. It never did. The oak tree just grew older and greener as the days passed by.

One day a visitor arrived. This mysterious man sat in their favourite spot. The two kids weren't nervous. It was exciting to have a new friend. Both of them would have preferred someone younger. Not an adult. It took the 'big' people a little longer to see what was so special about the tree. And true to form, their 'big' friend just wanted to sit under the overhanging branches and rest. He had walked a long way. But the kids didn't mind being patient. The magic would come. And it did. When their friend eventually saw it, he was like a child again. The man's imagination had no bounds. But then came That visit.

The one when the man brought an axe.

*****

"Can I sit down?"

"Anything in your hands?"

The girl replied without looking up. Her voice wobbled a little as she silently played out a backstory. The uncertainty of her tone reminded me of Tshilaba. I felt a wave of unease.

"Don't worry. He hasn't brought it."

The boy answered for me. Unlike the girl, his voice wasn't masking anything.

He didn't like me.

The two kids watched from a distance.

They thought it was just an act at first, part of their friend's imaginative play. When the blade dug into the bark, the fantasy turned into a living nightmare. It was the boy who ran back to the tree first, followed by his sister. He tried to stop the man, screaming to find out why he was doing such a thing. None of it was making sense. Hadn't their friend seen the magic of the tree? Yes. The man even knew its name. It was The Heart Tree. The tree that everyone leans up against.

The three of them had played by this tree many times. They had ventured into imaginative worlds, had numerous illogical tea-parties that made Alice's Wonderland feel sensible. At times they even shared happy and painful backstories over a cup of invisible tea. During one of those illogical tea-parties, the man had told them about his childhood. He too had a special tree, somewhere where he had played magical games. Then one day he thought it was time to grow up. After that, the man couldn't remember the way back to his special place. The two kids told him that no one loses their Heart Tree; the magic just plays hide-and-seek. When people get old, the tree gets smaller. That's why so many adults think it's lost. They just have to look a little harder for it.

But now the man was cutting down the tree. He was screaming that he didn't believe in this stupid thing anymore. The man suddenly looked older than the kids remembered. They ran in front of him, trying to stop the axe. He laughed in their face, then turned his attention to the table that was laid out for their Mad Hatter party. Cups of invisible Earl Grey tea and lemon cake flew across the ground. In amongst the splintered wood was the ruins of imagination. His attention now turned back to the tree.

The kids feared for their lives. They could see in the man's eyes that he hated everything their young lives represented. The only safe space for them was the nearby field. They watched with tears as the magical tree fell to the ground. Their hearts broke at the sight of a fallen dream. The Heart Tree does indeed become lost.

"You abandoned us. Made us into something we hate."

The girl was staring right back at me. Gone was her childhood innocence and playful imagination. Her face was full of pain and heartfelt revenge.

"Do it!"

The shout came from the boy who was sitting upright with a big smile. He was relishing this moment as his sister pulled out an axe from behind her back.

"Do it!"

"WAIT."

I screamed back at her. Then to the boy.

"You're mistaken. You've got the wrong person."

"DO IT. DO IT. DO IT."

The young boy wouldn't stop screaming as he rocked from side to side. Spit ran down his chin like a rabid dog. He hated me and wanted to see me cut into pieces. I scrambled backwards. My legs struggled to coordinate any movement as I crashed down onto the ground.

"You made us into something horrible."

The young girl's face scrunched up in anger. Her arms now raised above her head. The axe, pointing towards the sky.

"DO IT. DO IT."

I stretched out my hands, trying to buy time and mercy.

"Please. I did nothing to you. You have the wrong man."

A smile appeared on the girl's face.

"I hate you."

Her whisper cut deeper than any blade. With those three words, my hands suddenly dropped. So did her axe onto my head. I didn't even have time to scream.

The brother and sister waited in the fields.

Even though the man had left, they gave it another hour before the two of them walked back towards the fallen tree. The axe was leaning up against the stump. It was his leaving present.

Amongst the broken table and overturned tea-party was a bowl of water. It was the young girl who saw her reflection first. The boy followed, wanting to know why his sister was crying. Seeing his reflection sent him into an emotional meltdown. They cried a long time by the tree stump. Their beautiful world had changed. So had their skin. Age had set in, and not just with wrinkles and bags under the eyes. It was the worst kind.

The kind that twisted life's canvas and destroyed the heart.

I opened my eyes.

No one was around. For a few seconds I wondered if it was all a dream, but I knew otherwise. Next to the tree stump was a pencil. I picked it up and walked back to the talking stone. It was getting late. He was already fast asleep. I bent down and drew his nose, followed by a big quiff. Part of me wanted to wake him up so I could feel a little affirmation. I needed someone to tell me I was a good guy.

"Hmm."

The stone stirred. His eyes half-opened with a tired expression.

"Did you find the two kids? Bet they were pleased to see you. Hope the tea-party was fun. The Twins don't get many visitors these days."

CHAPTER 36
DOT-TO-DOT

"You can't connect the dots looking forward; you can only connect them looking backwards. So you have to trust that the dots will somehow connect in your future."
(Steve Jobs, Stanford 2005 Commencement Address)

PEVENSIE *didn't want to knock on her door today.*

He often visited her, usually with jokes and hugs. But this conversation would be different. It would bring with it some bad memories. She too could travel between the worlds and, like himself, she worked for both sides. Her name depended on her mood. Mystery... Tshilaba... amongst others. They all meant the same thing – seeker of knowledge – and to find knowledge, one must first embrace mystery.

Pevensie waited a few seconds before knocking. Music was coming from behind the door. 'Pure Imagination.' She did like to dream of another world. He stepped inside. There were no hugs this time as they walked into the parlour. Pevensie always thought her house resembled a scene from a Dickens' novel. Very Victorian with the touch of an old curiosity shop. Tshilaba pulled up the stylus from the record player. The music stopped. She already knew the reason for the visit.

I found the way back by myself, wanting to find Tshilaba.

She wasn't there. I didn't blame her. The two overturned apple crates were the only remnants of our time together. I sat down looking at the fork in the road, my eyes examining the path that would take me quickly back to The Pillar. The sun was still high in the sky. Long shadows covered the dusty track. It felt an analogy for how my heart was feeling. In my head I replayed every scene that had just happened. For someone who loved his own company, I hated being alone with my shadows.

*****

"I'm not interested."

Tshilaba's reply didn't surprise Pevensie. But her tone did. It was distant. Uncaring. She knew the importance of finding The Twins. Peccadillo's life hinged on it. So why was she so dismissive? Pevensie got his answer.

"He had his chance. In fact, he had more than his fair share of chances. And he blew them all. Surely you know that as well as I do?"

He did. He had. And yet. She continued.

"I saw his eyes. He still wants to open that lid."

*****

"Want to know a secret?"

I turned around. No one was there.

"Down here."

On the floor was another stone. A woman's face. Out of breath.

"Took me ages to jump over to you. Left my hubby sleeping. Bless him, he's getting on a bit and needs the rest."

It was strangely good to see a friendly face, even if it did have mismatched eyes, a square nose and a squiggle for a smile. This Path had ruined me. Or maybe I was ruined already and just didn't know it until now. Either way, any bit of comfort was welcome. I picked up the stone and gently placed her on the second crate. Her squiggle smile widened.

"Ahh, thank you love. Very kind. And thank you for my hubby's quiff. That was nice you remembered."

I wanted to blurt out every reason why I didn't deserve her thanks. Her hubby's new hairline was only there by chance; a pencil was left and I wanted to get back to Tshilaba. But I could tell in her oddly shaped eyes that she already knew the reasons, but didn't believe they were by chance alone.

"Your tree isn't lost. That's the secret. Like The Twins said, it's just harder to find this time around."

Just the mention of their name made me shiver.

"They wanted to kill me."

I delivered the line slowly. Each word took an effort to come out as I played the scene in slow motion. The stone jumped closer towards me.

"I know. And not just you. When their pain is too much to bear, they lash out. Left to their own devices, I think PARADOX would have gone years ago."

There was a slight nervousness in her voice.

"I must admit, it surprised me that you saw them so young and full of life. They don't look like that now. That's why I came to find you. I thought maybe this time you were different. You know, my hubby's hairline and the way The Twins looked. I even reckon you have a different walk."

"Is that why you are being so kind to me?"

"It's not you I'm being kind to. The Twins deserve their pain to end."

Pevensie stepped onto the pavement.

Behind the closed front door, there was music again. It was a different record this time. Something more appropriate for the conversation that had just happened. 'Fake Plastic Trees' by Radiohead. The chorus repeated its haunting melody. It was the soundtrack to Tshilaba's life. The fake world WAS wearing her out.

He understood her reluctance to help. She had seen her fair share of disappointment, her fair share of fake plastic trees. Pevensie had often watched from a distance as she tried to convince people they were buying nothing but cheap imitation knock-offs. She never preached her message, just dropped out hints. Sometimes it worked. People saw The Twins. But how quickly did the lure of the fake world come back?

He admired her commitment to the cause. A lost cause more like it. Far too many people sold her out, but she still carried on sitting by the caravan, telling her tales. Then Santiago happened. The betrayal was more than just a scandal. It cut deep. As deep as a scar. And now she believed Peccadillo would go the same way.

Pevensie looked down the street. No one was around. That was a good sign. Just like The Storyteller had told him, Eki would follow then leave. He wondered if she would head back to the Seven Dials. If so, someone would be waiting.

"I've got something for you. Do you mind putting me down."

I placed the stone back on the ground. She shuffled over towards an acorn designed charm resting in the undergrowth.

"Out of something small, a big oak tree can emerge. Remember to plant it in good soil when you get back home. I mean it. You never know what will grow up from the ground. Look at young Digory Kirke when he returned from Narnia. He planted a small seed and a tree grew. And from that wood…"

"...came the wardrobe."

The stone giggled then jumped down the Path a few yards. She yelled out a goodbye and another thanks for remembering her hubby's hairline. I bent down and picked up the acorn charm. It had the cheap feel of the jewellery you get at a seaside gift shop or travelling funfair. But sometimes those things are the most precious to the heart.

I walked back to The Pillar in silence. In no time at all, The Guide greeted me then led my steps to the gate of the second Path. She never asked what had happened; her analytical eyes had already gathered the data from my sunken face. The metal railings opened and I stepped through.

Tshilaba stared at her mantelpiece.

Her hand touched the empty shelf space to the left. She had taken the picture down a long time ago. It was safely hidden away in the drawer. Out of sight. Out of mind. That image. Maybe it was time to bring it back. The dull thump of the finished record continued to play out its hypnotic rhythm. Even when things had come to an end, a new sound would always come through.

"But only if you have ears to hear it."

CHAPTER 37
THE PICTURES

"But there's a story behind everything. How a picture got on a wall. How a scar got on your face. Sometimes the stories are simple, and sometimes they are hard and heart breaking."
(Mitch Albom, For One More Day)

THE SECOND PATH wasn't like the first.

Open fields with wild colours were replaced with a narrow lane walled with dark green trees. The ominous tunnel gradually transformed itself into a corridor inside a run-down house. I didn't question the visual evolution. Somehow it felt natural. Expected. A return to a place that I once knew well.

This stately home was now a sad excuse for a building. It clung to a past grandeur that no one could see apart from its delusional owner. The peeling wallpaper of lost wealth revealed crumbling walls and a rotting wooden frame. There had been the odd repair, but the task at hand was evidently too much.

Along the corridor were many doors, but only one that opened. I stepped into a large room, but the dark wood panelling and half-closed shutters made everything feel claustrophobic. In the corner was another door. Next to that, a small fireplace. The crackling wood played out an atmospheric soundtrack that harmonised with the gentle tick of a grandfather clock. It was the only thing that brought comfort to this living prison cell. The photo frames that hung up on the walls added to the owner's mystery. I wasn't staring at the usual portraits of family and friends. Instead, each frame had a torn off calendar date written in bold red type on a brilliant white surface.

The rattling sound of a cough spun me around. Next to the door I'd just walked through, covered in shadows, was a middle-aged man hunched over a wooden desk. The marks on his face and arms told the tale of severe beatings. And they hadn't been quick. I could only imagine what cuts lay under his ripped clothes. The beatings hadn't ended with a fist or stick. Every move had the consequence of pain, even his decision to remain still. Rest was temporary.

Summoning up a prophetic courage for upcoming pain, his shaking hand tried to write a few words. The crumpled paper revealed the history of his attempts, with the spasms of pain following each stroke of the pen – a sadistic merry-go-round. His sheer commitment to the cause made me feel sad. I was witnessing the final days of a man crafting the words he felt important to share.

Except no one was around to hear his dying voice on the page.

A painful expression shot across his face as he looked up. That simple move took effort and he was now reaping the consequence. Unlike the rest of his battered body, his eyes carried a raging fire of passion. Full of life. Full of a southern revival tent preacher that could scare the hell out of a congregation with just one look. His altar-call-stare was captivating, but his days of convincing people to run up to the front crying for repentance had long gone. The 'preacher man' was struggling to keep his head held high. Every passing second added to the agony gripping his fragile life. A series of coughs, followed by a cry of pain, heralded a perverted form of solace for the man. I ran towards him as his body slumped over the desk.

His altar-call did bring a response after all.

It took a while before he could speak.

His staggered, short breaths meant his lungs never quite got all that they needed. As his head rested on my shoulder, I looked at the paper. Most of the sentences were illegible scribbles, but I could make out a few words. On the top of the page was a little drawing of a heart. Below that, a question: 'Way Back Home?'

The paper was less thoughtful prose and more a messy worksheet. The further down I went, the shakier the hand. Desperation soaked into each line of text, every doodle. Time was short for this preacher and he was fearful that it would end before he found his answer. At the bottom was a hand-drawn map. The haunting weight of fate pressed down onto my shoulder, pushing me closer towards the scribbled lines. I didn't want to believe what was on the page. A tree with two children playing next to it. Seven paths leading away from them, all taking different routes. And then. Each trail, heading to the same destination. A building – the one haunting my every step.

"The Theatre."

The preacher's slow southern drawl had lost none of its convicting power. For a moment, his face came alive with memories from behind the pulpit. Then came the punishment for his actions. A coughing fit brought with it a splatter of blood. He looked embarrassed as his trembling hand unsuccessfully tried to wipe the dark red stain from the map. Exhausted, his head collapsed back onto my shoulder. I wanted to hug him, but knew every touch would send another bolt of suffering through his body. The dying man picked up my concern. His fingers tenderly rested on mine, showing a silent but voice-filled cry of gratitude.

*****

Roho didn't consider himself a preacher, more a teacher.

He hated the confines of the pulpit and the enclosure of a tent crusade. That's why, in the days of his youth, he had taken his sermons into the open, exchanging pews for tree stumps. He enjoyed encouraging anyone who would listen to see beyond their small world. The greatest lesson life could ever teach was the tapestry of life itself. This love of open spaces was the reason why he despised this room. His punisher knew how to inflict the worst kind of torture upon a dying heart.

The world had become smaller ever since he'd been locked inside this rectangular box. But that hadn't stopped Roho from bringing reminders of the open plains into his prison cell. The wood panelling represented his pulpit of trees; the open fire, the late night conversations under the stars. When the heart-breaking realisation came that his punishment would not be short-lived, he lined the fireplace with pictorial tiles. Small details, but it meant a great deal. It was a subtle homage to Scrooge's journey towards freedom. For the businessman's heart to be ready for Marley's visit, he first had to stare into the fire and follow the story on its tiles. Thankfully, his punisher thought all the alterations were signs of a man going senile, so nothing was taken away.

Another touch of assumed madness was the calendar dates around the room. Roho feared the loss of connection to the life beyond his prison cell. The system he came up with was simple but effective: important dates to remember became framed masterpieces on the wall.

"You need to pick a date."

I felt guilty hearing Roho push through a barrier of intense pain just to get his words out. If it wasn't for me, he would be resting. Yet my presence drew out of him the need to guide my next steps. A small part of me wanted to tell him to keep quiet. Shamefully, the larger part became intrigued with his cryptic request. Selfishness has many expressions.

Looking around the room sent a chill through my veins. Every date carried a link back to my life. One of the picture frames marked the day when I started secondary school. Another, my first job. Memorable kiss. Cruellest breakup. To my right, the date of my parent's wedding anniversary. The next two noted their deaths. On the other side of the room were my moments with Terri: our first meeting at the library, book club dates, Natasha's hug and my cowardly walk away. Picture frames continued… dates not in my lifetime, but events that inspired my walk. An encyclopaedia of history. Cromwell's Revolution. The Civil Rights Movements. World Wars. Political change. It was a disturbing sight to behold.

"Pick."

Roho grew weary of my indecision. I was struggling to come to terms with the stories of my life on display. My eyes rested on a date. A safe choice, so I thought. The 'preacher man' looked up.

"February 1837. Funny thing about running away from something: the past will always catch up with you."

CHAPTER 38
KNOCK. KNOCK. WHO IS THERE?

"You are part of my existence, part of myself. You have been in every line I have ever read, since I first came here."
(Charles Dickens, Great Expectations)

BANG.

A heavy fist smashed against the door opposite me. I jolted back against the wall.

"You grabbed his attention."

The tired preacher took the commotion in his stride. To him, the logical follow-up to choosing the date was the knock on the door. There was one more heavy thud, followed by silence. I looked at the door, expecting another knock. The wait was excruciating. Nothing came. I glanced back, hoping for answers. Roho had closed his eyes, his body twitching with a painful rest.

The silence was terrifying as I edged closer to the door. I couldn't shake off the feeling I was in a B-move slasher film. These low-budget flicks would have the soon-to-be victim walk up to a door, knowing their killer was lurking in the shadows. It was the craving to confirm their hunch which made them disengage logic and turn the handle. Three seconds later the axe would fall. A predictable formula. And I was repeating it right now. Someone was behind that door. I needed to find out who.

"Quick, we don't have much time."

The axe fell, but not how I was expecting it. I recognised the voice and his stale breath. It was the one from my vision. The clothes gave away his name. A frilly white shirt. Black penguin suit. Velvet top hat. It was the wardrobe of theatre. I was face to face with The Magician.

BANG.

Another knock, this time from the door opposite. The Magician's jewel-covered fingers gripped my arm. I could feel the cold sweat on his palm pressing down. It was the dew of panic.

"We need to go."

His dark brown pupils widened as another heavy knock resonated through the door. Whoever it was, they were desperate to come in. *He* tugged at my arm, but I wasn't moving.

"Please. You've got it all wrong about me. We have to go. Once we are safe, let me explain. After that, if you still want to run away, I won't stop you, I promise."

His words were sincere, but that didn't remove my distrust. The story from Tshilaba had made him out to be a dangerous character who wanted revenge. It didn't make sense. Neither did the worrying question as to why *He* was interested in me? BANG. The door lock couldn't handle too much more. Opting for the lesser of two dangers, I followed him out of the room. His 'thank you' strangely soothed my unease.

We ran into the shadows just as the other door opened.

*****

Fear-filled running.

We turned right. Down a narrow corridor. Around the corner. Into another hallway. To the left of me were dormitory style rooms. The doors had long gone. So had the occupants. Rusted bed frames bolted to the floor were the only things left. I only needed a glancing look to know that whoever had designed the rooms, space had been foremost in their mind. Each bed position was less about personal comfort and more about numbers. No wonder the doors were kicked down. People couldn't wait to get out the rooms quick enough.

Down the stairs. Turn right. Running.

We were now in a rabbit warren of small rooms. Offices? Classrooms? Difficult to tell. The broken furniture that lay scattered across the floor looked Victorian. There was an eerie feel to the place. Whoever had kicked down the doors of the dormitories had also paid a final visit to these rooms. It had been their leaving mark. Utter destruction. Pure hatred. The rooms still carried the emotional echoes of the rampaging crowds.

Our strange tour ended at two large wooden doors. The Magician took a deep breath as *He* gripped the iron handles. Sweat was running down his brow as *He* bowed his head in silent prayer. Awkwardly I waited. Seconds later, a forceful push and the doors flung open.

"No one will look for us here. This place is forgotten."

We walked into a large empty hall. A quick scan of the room suggested that it could seat around three-hundred people. Maybe a few more, at a push. Along the sides of the walls were a series of thin, crumbling pillars. These precariously propped up a half-destroyed mezzanine floor. Every wall had windows, but the place still felt dark and enclosed. The only bright colours in the room came from a beautiful stained glass window at the far end. It had an image of a well-dressed Victorian man giving food to a beggar and his family. Once there had been an inscription too; it looked like a verse from The Bible. Broken panes had erased much of the inspirational message.

The hall had seen better days. It's damage done by Mother Nature and human hands. Moss covered stones gave away the cause of the smashed windows. The surviving glass panes were now home to cobwebs and dirt. Damp, uneven floorboards partnered perfectly with the grey shade that covered the once whitewashed walls. And then there were the pigeons. The birds had found a cosy home in the corner. Thankfully, they had kept their droppings to that part of the room. Collectively, these signs of decay added to the magical feel that all derelict buildings carry. The untold history was tangible as I walked around the room, taking in every mark and scuff. If only the walls could talk. But they could. Through The Magician.

"It was something to behold back in its day."

He was standing in the centre of the hall, slowly panning around. Panic had left his voice. The warm tone of reminiscing was a mixed blessing for him. Fond memories blended with sadness for its loss.

"You should have seen this place when it was up and running. Full of activity. Never a dull day. Nearly four hundred people would sit behind wooden benches, eating until they were full. And over there…"

The Magician pointed to the pigeon occupied corner.

"...that's where people registered for health care and medicine. It was a beautiful sight, hundreds upon hundreds accessing a service they couldn't otherwise afford."

Pride coloured his cheeks.

"I saw many lives saved. Old. Young. Fathers. Mothers. Children."

There was a pause as *He* turned around.

"Even twins."

I stumbled backwards. His outstretched hand felt like a supportive friend – a friend who knew about The Twins.

A friend who could save me from their axe.

*****

"What is this place?"

"This place, as you say, is the reason why we are both being played."

"Played?"

The Magician nodded, emphasising his point. I didn't understand what *He* was talking about but recognised the belief in his voice. This wasn't a game.

"Some people used to call this place a 'building for welfare support'. Others labelled it a 'workhouse'. Either description received the same level of hatred. Such a shame. Always misunderstood."

I was battling to match my understanding of these buildings with The Magician's fond description. Victorian Workhouses were notoriously cruel towards their occupants. Shareholders and owners would keep people off the books so they could avoid employment law and safety requirements. Just like the dormitories upstairs, utilisation of space took priority over human life. The individual was a commodity for the middle-class and wealthy. This system separated families to motivate production. And all of it founded on an ideology that stated poverty was the sign of an evil heart. The workhouse was the perfect mechanism to beat the living sin out of every poor soul.

None of this storyline was in The Magician's voice. He saw a different side to these buildings. To him, it was a place where people found help. When medicine and health care were only a luxury for the wealthy, workhouses provided their own form of free healthcare. Education was no longer a divine right just for high society. Now, even the poor could access a learning programme that would help them develop a trade. With apprenticeships came the opportunity to provide. And with the toil of work, the human heart would eventually find redemption. I listened as The Magician reeled off the statistics. The numbers of transformed lives sounded impressive. But numbers could lie. And *He* knew it.

"It's true. The numbers don't tell the whole tale. This place had its flaws. The whole system did. Its Achilles Heel was the owners. A good, compassionate owner could shape these places into a blessing from heaven. But the news only focused on the bad apples. This programme of reform could have worked if it wasn't for..."

His face twisted with utter hate.

"...a boy. He ruined it all. He made The Twins into something they should never have been."

CHAPTER 39
THE BOY

"Bleak, dark, and piercing cold, it was a night for the well-housed and fed to draw round the bright fire, and thank God they were at home; and for the homeless starving wretch to lay him down and die. Many hunger-worn outcasts close their eyes in our bare streets at such times, who, let their crimes have been what they may, can hardly open them in a more bitter world."

(Charles Dickens, Oliver Twist)

"DO YOU PLAY CHESS?"

The Magician's question caught me off guard. I had played the game as a kid, but those days had long gone. Patience wasn't my thing.

"Never mind. It's more of a stage prop anyway."

I followed him to the stained glassed window. Walking through the technicolour rays of dusty light, I felt like a volunteer stepping onto the stage. An electric shock of anticipation went through my body as the hushed audience readied themselves for the trick. In front of me was a small table. Placed in the middle, a chessboard. There was one piece on show. A pawn; its simple design standing out on a board made up of sixty-four squares. The Magician ushered me to the other side of the table.

"Ready?"

I nodded, not sure what I had agreed to.

"Good. Now keep your eyes on the pawn as I tell you a little story."

*****

"The year is 1837.

England is near the end of a hundred-year rollercoaster ride of social transformation. The Industrial Revolution. Chaos and beauty. Hope and fear. This timeline has it all. During these years, the population of the county will increase from nine million to forty-one million. It is the best and worst of times, so to speak.

Cities and towns are taking the greatest hit from the demand for more homes and jobs. Family businesses have the tough task of adapting from backyard operations to factories of mass production. This radical change in manufacturing is opening up new forms of employment. Flexible careers. Multiple trades. The only limit to work is the confines of imagination. Some people are worried, and rightly so. Change is not always pretty. Not everyone is finding the treasure at the end of the Empire rainbow.

But a surprising transformation is taking place, regardless of the cost. This radical shift in work practice is bringing with it the rise of the middle class. England's aristocracy is facing a revolution. Nobility refuses to accept this new class of people as worthy equals. 'Gentleman never work.' The wealthy refuse to open their private clubs to new members. And yet, as they settle back and sip their port, the nobility fail to recognise that the middle class have learnt their lesson well. The tools of the aristocracy are not exclusive anymore.

"Money talks, especially to political power."

*****

"Following the story?"

I couldn't speak. The Magician was flawless in his performance. *He* was a true master of the stage, acting out every sentence with passion and belief. I could feel the turmoil of the Industrial Revolution, sense the emotions of every character. The story was real. And I wanted to know more.

"Still keeping your eyes on the pawn?"

My nod stretched out the smile on his already beaming face. *He* was enjoying this moment as much as I was.

"Good. We've only just begun."

*****

"Work: it's a funny old concept.

You must understand that until this cultural shift, the idea of 'working for a living' is nothing more than a social stigma. The commonly held belief is that God only shines His blessing upon those deemed worthy to rest from the toil of the land. In other words, the aristocracy.

Then comes the middle-class with their bulging purses and lofty ideals. They change the way people see 'work'. It's now a moral virtue. The ability to purchase property, goods and security are all signs of a godly lifestyle. Work hard and The Almighty will reward you. Slack off, accept His curse. This shift impacts the poor. The inability to provide for oneself is a sign of weak morals and questionable lifestyles. Charitable acts need to adapt. It's not good enough to just give a cup of water to someone who is thirsty. Acts of charity have to include the encouragement to get back to work.

Moral Work.

And so the Poor Law is born.

This law has a good heart, even though some of its methods are questionable. Its design is simple. Place all forms of welfare support in the structure of the workhouse system. These buildings have harsh regimes. On purpose. The brutal conditions are there to encourage all of its inhabitants to seek work for themselves. A firm but loving hand is used to eradicate any temptation to live off benefits permanently. Spare the rod and spoil the soul. Through the provision of healthcare, education programmes and the development of skills, the poor find redemption.

That is until *That* boy comes along."

*****

The MAGICIAN paused the story.

"Keep watching."

The pawn was changing. An invisible hand chipped away at the wooden piece. Small shavings of wood fell onto the board. The chess piece twisted to the left, then to the right, providing perfect angles for the unseen tool to do its work. It was an impressive trick. I couldn't see any string or gadgets from The Magician's sleeve. This mind-bending show lasted thirty seconds. I picked up the perfectly weighted piece, now shaped like a boy, to check if it was real. Genuine.

"Everything changes with the boy.

He is born into the workhouse system due to his mother dying in childbirth. The father is unknown and wants to remain in the shadows. At the age of nine, he moves onto the factory floor. Very soon he's identified as a bad apple; evil to the core. The boy causes trouble wherever he goes. He rarely shows gratitude for any charity that comes his way. The tipping point for discipline is his request for a second helping of food.

Harsh love is the only way forward and it is outworked through a cruel apprenticeship. Through its Draconian measures it is hoped that it will bring forth redemption. It doesn't work. The boy runs away to the city. Evil attracts evil, like moths drawn to a flame. He finds himself in the underbelly of the criminal world. A robbery goes wrong and he gets arrested. Undeservingly, a magistrate shows kindness and places him in the care of a charitable man. Life is good, but not for long. The boy's evil world catches up with him and tries to draw him back into the grime of where he belongs. But something unexpected happens.

The kid discovers the truth about his birth. His mysterious father is none other than the charitable man who has taken him in. According to society's belief, the inheritance that then comes his way should reveal the evil nature of the boy's heart. His weak morals should lead to excess spending and selfish living. But the boy shows mercy. Humility. And love.

Everything the poor should not be."

The Magician snatched the chess piece from my hand.

His eyes were a laser beam of hate burning into the wood.

“This stupid little pawn changed the nature of the game. His story made people see the poor differently. Worse still, many questioned the legitimacy of the workhouse idea. Tough love became an outdated concept. And it was only a matter of time before buildings like these fell into ruin.

I watched angry mobs run through this place, smash its furniture and destroy everything it had worked hard to achieve. Owners became objects of contempt. The public was judge and jury. They weren’t interested in hearing any defence case. All they wanted to do was free the poor from the so-called oppressor’s grip. And as they did, everyone fell right into the trap.”

The chess piece smashed onto the board.

“Never underestimate the sleight-of-hand. The boy’s story was nothing but misdirection. Take away the structure of the workhouse, and what do you have left? All of a sudden there was no free healthcare or welfare support for the poor. Education returned to being just for the wealthy and blessed. Some people stepped up, but not many. And what they provided was never as comprehensive as the torn-down system.

What should have happened was an adaption of the workhouse system, not its eradication. People were so intent on knocking down its walls that they never noticed the poor souls lying damaged in the rubble. Including two little children. The Twins. These poor souls had no one, left to fend for themselves.

And that, my dear friend, was the plan all along.”

The Magician looked traumatised. His bony index finger flicked the chess piece onto the floor.

“The misdirection had a purpose. It made new villains in the story. People like me. Once that happened, it was easy to keep up the illusion because no one could tell what was real or fake. Right or wrong. Friend or Foe. We are all getting played. My regret is that I never saw it until it was too late. I watched the board but never noticed the move that changed everything. Never trust pawns.

Especially the ones called Oliver.”

CHAPTER 40
THE WHOLE BOARD

"They sometimes forgot what happened if you let a pawn get all the way up the board."
(Terry Pratchett, The Last Hero)

THE MAGICIAN WAS WRONG.

On all fronts. The workhouse wasn't some just system for the poor, and neither did it hurt The Twins. There was only person those children blamed.

"I know what you're thinking. The crazy fool is wrong."

His reply made me nervous. What else could *He* read from my mind? The Magician pulled out a small box of chess pieces from under his sleeve, then placed each item on the board.

"Let me ask you a question. What if you're not seeing the whole board? This twisted game we are in is all about illusion, including making you think it's your fault."

He stood back and observed the pieces in perfect symmetry.

"Listen. I like you. Like you a lot. And I think it's horrible how you're getting played. That's why I'm going to help you out. Just this once mind you. Have to be careful not to break the rules. Then it's your choice which side you take."

He picked up two chess pieces.

"Choose a side."

I picked his right hand.

"Black it is. You go second."

"I haven't played in a long time."

"Doesn't matter. Chess is like riding a bike. The game never leaves you."

*****

The Magician made the first move.

Pawn E2 to E4. I responded. Pawn C7 to C5. Instinct. *He* looked impressed.

"Well. Well. Well. The trusted Sicilian Defence."

I wished I had planned the strategy, but the move was the first thing that had come to mind. There was no way I was going to own up to the fluke. The Magician was doing a little bit of street banter as though *He* was playing in New York's Washington Square Park. Suddenly I was feeling competitive.

"Did you know The Sicilian Defence is a rather intriguing strategy?"

He was playing with me, trying to distract my mind. I ignored him.

"The Sicilian Defence carries the sophisticated strategy of placing Black in a position of vulnerability. Not a great way to start the game. Or is it? Did you also know the strategy signals to the opponent that Black is focused upon attack? So one never quite knows what the player is up to. Is it a vulnerable mistake or an attacking move?"

Pawn D7 to D6. My response, Knight G1 to G3. The Magician continued his street banter jive.

"The strategy made its debut appearance back in the 17th century. At first, people considered it a flawed idea. Vulnerability never gets rave reviews. But then as time passed, players understood its long game. If played right, and patiently may I add, the subtleties of the strategy reveal another side. Bet you don't know what it is?"

We silently played another five moves as I battled with the desire to ask him to continue. Chess is lethal. It takes no prisoners. I moved my Queen.

A show of strength. The Magician responded by moving one of his pawns. I just about contained a smile that was craving to break out across my face. *He* had made a mistake. My Black Knight moved up the board. I was now only one move away from taking his Queen. If *He* tried to defend it, then I had options to capture either his Castle or Bishop. I eagerly watched the board as *He* presented his Castle for sacrifice. Taking his piece was pure joy.

We were both staring at the right side of the board. All the activity of the game had centred around a few squares, and I was now ready to do the final push towards victory. I could see his exposed King. If this was his way of giving advice, it wasn't going well for The Magician.

Then I saw the smile.

He reached his hand towards the boy-shaped pawn on the left side of the board. It only took one move and my show of strength crumbled with a whimper. His street banter added to the insult.

"The beauty of The Sicilian Defence is that it teaches us that in weakness you can also be strong. When you captured my Castle and then saw my exposed King, you took that as confirmation of your strength. But weakness can also be a misdirection.

You see, my dear Peccadillo, the other side wins when you don't see the whole board."

*****

It took another two moves for The Magician to check-mate me.

"Want to know who I learnt that lesson from?"

"Oliver?"

"Ha, If only. Pawns are dangerous, but only because of the hand that moves them."

The Magician drew in a long breath. His wheezing had returned. It didn't take me long to figure out who *He* was referring to. I could see it on his face. The story from Tshilaba only went so far in capturing the tension between the two sides. Hatred and anger burrowed under his skin, twisting his features to tell a deeper tale. This was more than a disagreement about a trick.

The Storyteller and Magician were at war.

"*She* outplayed me. I never expected a move up the left side of the board. All the activity was on the right. Here I was, thinking the workhouse system would come under threat from violent protests and political debates. And all along, I never saw a writer crafting a story about a boy. *Oliver Twist.* The hero of the story is the most insignificant lead character society could ever imagine. A child. And not just any child. Someone who is poor. Rejected. Disposable.

A pawn.

And the bloody title of his book still rubs salt into my wounds. *Oliver Twist: The Parish Boy's Progress.* No one could have made it any more obvious. I forgot the first rule of The Sicilian Defence. Always think about the long game. The strategy only works if a person trusts the 'progress' of the journey. It's not just about the two moves ahead, but the tenth and twentieth."

The Magician picked up his winning pawn and rolled it around his long fingers. It changed back to its usual form. Oliver was history.

"I never saw the twist in the story until it was too late. It's the long game that gets you in the end."

*****

We took one of the side doors off the great hall.

The Magician told me it was a secret way out, away from prying eyes. Was it my suggestion that I wanted time to think before heading back to The Pillar, or his? *He* had a subtle way of guiding my steps.

Framed letters from past occupants lined the narrow hallway. Every note was thanking the workhouse for giving them the opportunity to find employment. Some notes carried tales of restored hope. Others shared their excitement concerning the future. I was about to move on when something caught my eye.

"Same handwriting."

I spoke out the words, not expecting a reply. It made sense coming from the same hand. Not many people knew how to write. The workhouse must have employed someone to capture their stories. But I still felt uncomfortable. I had missed something. Leaning in, I carefully examined the note. My eyes darted to another frame. Then a third. The handwriting.

"It's mine."

"You're right. I wish I could tell you why, but you will need to discover that for yourself. Rules my boy."

Frustrated and confused, I turned around.

Like any good magician, *He* had disappeared.

Make the audience crave for more.

It was The Magician's motto in life, and also a helpful reminder to know when to leave. He loved the stage, and because of that, often overstayed his welcome. What use is a show if the audience leaves feeling content? Where's the repeat business? A good show is like a drug. One injection is never enough. The dosage increases, but the craving never dies away. Except in the grave.

It was good to be back in his study. This place helped him think. Before placing the chess box back on the shelf, He took one final peek inside. His fingers rummaged through the pieces to find another pawn. Locating it, He could already feel its form begin to change. By the time The Magician pulled it out, the pawn had transformed into the figure of a man.

Peccadillo.

He waited patiently. Slowly. Centimetre by centimetre, the figure changed colour. The Magician was proud of this move. Amazing how one piece can alter the game if it changes sides.

CHAPTER 41
TIME FOR CHURCH

"Death must be so beautiful. To lie in the soft brown earth, with the grasses waving above one's head, and listen to silence. To have no yesterday, and no tomorrow. To forget time, to forgive life, to be at peace."
(Oscar Wilde, The Canterville Ghost)

THE GUIDE *wasn't prone to worrying.*

But today was different. The evening was about to set in and Peccadillo hadn't returned from the second Path. Delays were all part of the journey. But this didn't feel like a typical day. She peered down the Path. Still no sign. Her mind went back and forth trying to figure out what to do next. She could feel herself getting drawn into a battle she didn't want to be part of.

"Get a grip."

The emotional pep-talk sounded weak. She didn't believe a single word coming out of those tense lips. Every rule carefully put in place to protect her from temptations such as this one were now up for debate. Logic told her to stay at The Pillar and not get involved. Her heart disagreed. But breaking her rules would mean taking sides. And that couldn't happen. Her plan counted on it.

She made her way to the third Path, just to check everything was in order for when Peccadillo did finally return. Her slow, torturous walk speeded up as soon as she saw what was waiting for her.

The next gate was already open.

*****

I needed time.

And this was the best way.

I wanted to avoid The Guide. Talking to her would only cloud my mind. This world made no sense and I was struggling to know who to trust. Before the workhouse, The Magician fitted perfectly into the arch-villain role. *He* was anything but that now. I felt sorry for him. His sense of loss and being misunderstood resonated with my own screwed up journey through life. We shared the same type of story. Hadn't I tried to help someone in need, Terri, and what did I get in return?

That image.

I looked down the third Path. The Path of the Mundane. The bland, dusty track went on for miles. That suited me fine. The walk would be good for my soul, giving me space to work out what to do next. I hated the feeling I was a pawn in someone else's game. But who could I turn to? The person I trusted at this moment specialised in creating illusions and that felt like a recipe for disaster.

My walk slowed up after thirty minutes. The landscape hadn't changed; all I could still see were open fields and a dusty track. I estimated another hour of light as dusk heralded the onset of evening. Without a torch, I wouldn't know where to walk. But what other option did I have? Going back now would mean I would have to face questions from The Guide. I wasn't ready for that.

Picking up my pace, I carried on down the track, eager to get to whatever destination lay ahead. I hadn't gone fifty yards before I heard a snap from behind. Someone had stepped on a twig nearby. I turned around. Nothing. The air felt heavy with silence. Oddly, every insect and bird ceased their call, waiting for the next SNAP. This time the sound came from the left. I spun around on the spot, my eyes scrutinising every divot and hill. There were no spaces to hide. Had I imagined it? SNAP. SNAP. In front. No. Behind.

And then.

My heart was beating faster than ever as I watched the air in front of me ripple as though caught in a heat-wave. The shimmering reflection of the track carried an eerie feel of something mystical lurking behind. I stepped back but didn't run away. Its magical ripple of intrigue had a hook in me. Inch by inch, a figure gracefully emerged through the distortion. This translucent figure, dressed in white robes, was holding an iron door knocker. The object gently swayed from side to side as the ghost-like figure floated across the track.

Strangely, I didn't feel scared. If there was ever such a thing as a friendly ghost, I was staring at it. This other-worldly figure was an elderly lady. One of those dear sweetheart types I would often pass by as they sat alone at a bus stop. I could imagine her being someone who would make a Victoria Sponge Cake for the community fair, and then knit a baby-grow for her neighbour's new-born child. As she passed by, I stepped to one side, giving her room. She nodded her head in gratitude. I nodded back. Quietly, almost a whisper, she hummed a tune. I instantly recognised it. My mother had asked me to sing it to her on that final day in hospital. *Shall We Gather By The River,* was one of those old-time gospel tunes that brought comfort to any listener. *'Soon we'll reach the silver river, soon our pilgrimage will cease. Soon our happy hearts will quiver, with the melody of peace.'*

SNAP. Out of the ripples came another ghostly figure, a man in his twenties. He too was holding a door knocker. Humming. The old Gospel hymn. One after another, a procession of translucent figures drifted slowly down the Path. I counted thirty-four. When the final one passed by, I felt an inner tug to follow. Seconds later I was joining in with their song.

The Guide locked the third gate.

In the distance, she could hear the faint sound of that old faithful hymn. The air currents had carried its melody across the land. Her shaking hand rechecked the lock; she couldn't remember if she'd turned the key. It wasn't like her to get distracted, but hearing the tune meant only one thing.

Peccadillo.

Why had he avoided her? Nothing like this had ever happened before on his visits. A drop of curiosity fell on her dry, data-driven mind. There was a moment's temptation to open the gate and run after him. Why was this journey different? Without thinking, another voice kicked in. 'Stay out of it. Your job here is to collect data.' She agreed, speaking out her purpose in PARADOX.

"Data brings knowledge. Knowledge brings safety. Safety brings my family back."

Another check of the lock. She adjusted her clothes and made her way back to The Pillar. Peccadillo would return in his own time; then she would gather the relevant information. No matter the urge to help him, she needed to keep her purpose clear.

"And my family's return brings an end to this curse."

It was a picture postcard scene.

The ghostly possession walked up to an old white chapel surrounded by a picket fence. Trees were in full, pink blossom as birds sang out their evening chorus. The bell tower on top of the chapel was a simple construction. Four pillars with an angled roof. The bell silently swayed in the gentle breeze; its clapper, missing.

Attached to the postcard chapel was a series of steps that led up to the front porch. In its heyday, I imagined how those simple planks of wood welcomed the rich and poor, young and old, into its gospel home. There would be a friendly preacher shaking hands, dressed in white. His wife would have been playing the organ. Their kids, looking down in shame after being told off for getting their Sunday best clothes dirty. As I walked up the steps, I felt humbled at the thought of the countless stories that had soaked themselves into the grains of wood. People, seeking hope. People, needing love. People, craving redemption. Was I also one of those seekers?

The doors opened with a gentle push. Inside, the chapel was one rectangular room. Three-quarters of the hall comprised of wooden pews, with the final part housing a little stage and oversized mahogany pulpit. The ghostly figures had already taken their seats by the time I arrived. I looked around to see where I could sit. Fifth row. There was only one person there and he wasn't a ghost.

But he was back from the dead.

CHAPTER 42
SURPRISE

"The church consists of a brotherhood of imperfect, simple souls wanting only to be a voice of compassion in a world spinning out of control."
(Dan Brown, Angels & Demons)

SANTIAGO.

Impossible. I reached out and touched his hand. My trembling fingers felt flesh and bone.

"You found the chapel. Thank God."

It was good to hear his rough voice again, but there was no pleasure in seeing the hallmarks of a severe beating on his face. The bruises were raw and the cavernous cuts painful. He was keeping his right arm away from me. It was still tender.

"What happened? I thought you were dead."

One of the ghostly congregation leant forward. The pale looking businessman told us to keep our voices down; the church service was about to start. Santiago whispered our apology. The figure settled back into the pew, satisfied. A look of discomfort flashed across Santiago's face as he turned around to face the front. His right arm dropped into view.

"My God. Who did that to you?"

"Shhh."

The businessman reminded us where we were. I gave him a stern look before focusing back on Santiago. Blood and puss had encrusted itself around the ripped fabric of his sleeve. Every movement yanked another strand away from the wound. His arm looked as if a drunk surgeon with a blunt, rusty knife had hacked away in a spirit-induced rage. It was a small mercy that the majority of cuts were only a few millimetres deep. Santiago responded to my look of horror.

"Don't worry. I've had worse."

"But who did this?"

"Long story and you wouldn't believe me even if I told you."

Santiago timed his reply to finish just as the preacher took to the stage. His little smile made me think the timing was more than a coincidence.

*****

"Welcome dear brothers and sisters. It is so good to sec so many of my beautiful friends hcre."

The preacher wasn't what I was expecting. There was no designer suit paid for by the kind donations of the congregation, or a diamond-encrusted gold watch dangling from the wrist. And the preacher wasn't an adult.

The teenage girl dressed as if she had just walked off stage playing Dorothy in *The Wizard of Oz*. Her teeth braces reflected the chapel lights, which in turn became a spotlight shining on her freckled face. She stood on tiptoes as her head peered over the oversized pulpit. There was a ripple of giggles from the expectant congregation as she pushed the adult-designed world to one side.

"Elizabeth. Johnny. Mary-Anne. And is that you, Walter? How wonderful. Precious saints, all in one place."

There wasn't an ounce of fakery in the girl's voice. Another first from a preacher.

"Would anyone like to share a witness?"

My face lit up with a smile. I hadn't heard a line like that in a long time. When I was still wearing shorts for school, my mother would take me to an old Pentecostal church. She thought the music would be good for my soul, so too the discipline of greeting the Lord Almighty every Sunday morning at 9.00am. I hated the early start, but my mother was right about the music. Tambourines, organs and a Hallelujah sweating preacher was a sight to behold. Ladies, young and old, thin and not-so-thin, would dance down the aisles. I would take bets on whether their hairpins would fly out and hit someone. Occasionally they did. The Spirit did indeed move in mysterious ways. Although the music was great, the best part of the service was the 'witness time'. This was where the floor opened up for anyone to share a few words. One could never guarantee what would come up. Heavenly appeals for a lost cat. A cry of healing for haemorrhoids. Deliverance and a thunderbolt for noisy neighbours. My favourite as a kid were the ones delving into the world of conspiracy theories: Elvis was alive and needed the salvation touch. The older I got, the more I appreciated another side of the 'witness time' tales. These were the ones that recounted the mundane and honest aspects of life. A lost coin found. Food on the table. A peaceful sleep. In a modern world where fame, the dramatic and lies are role models to follow, it was refreshing to hear a frail voice value the simplest of things. Blessed are the meek. Blessed are the poor. Blessed are the boring folk and the ones overlooked.

'Witness time' started.

The congregation turned to face a translucent elderly lady called Doris. She was one of the meek, poor and overlooked boring ones. There was nothing special about her appearance. A hand knitted cardigan and chequered skirt blended in with her plain shirt and thick tights. She held a door knocker in the shape of an archway covered with flowers. Her nervous grip tightened as she recounted her day.

It was sweet to hear what time Doris had woken up. The contents of breakfast. What the morning paper had reported. And, which sections had grabbed her attention. Her voice had risen with excitement when explaining how the article on flower arrangements had been most enlightening – even the youngsters are joining in. Apparently

I learnt about her journey into town, the people she had met and the random, sometimes intentional, conversations that had taken place. Her voice broke as she concluded her story with describing the book she had been reading at bedtime. It had come from the library. Renewed three times. Doris was a slow reader.

"I thank God for a peaceful day, but..."

Doris sniffled. She was holding back tears.

"But, I do so wish I had been more useful to those around me."

That should have been the cue for the congregation to sign off the witness with an 'Amen' chorus. Except, this time, there was only silence; the weight of Doris' words tangible in the room.

I was about to find out why.

A young, translucent mother stood up. Claire. She too was holding a door knocker. This one, shaped like a heart. Her soft voice broke the silence as she gave witness about her Tuesday morning. She had been sitting on a bench, waiting for a bus. The eight-fifty to Larson High Street was late. It was the last thing she needed. The morning had already been exhausting. Claire's child had woken up early and that meant her own 'special time' became lost in sleepy tears. The bus delay only added to that stress. Sarah, her child, struggled with waiting.

An elderly lady sat down next to her. They talked, even laughed. It was rare that people would sit down next to Claire, let alone speak to her. She put it down to having a disabled child that was noisy. Their conversation moved on to how flower arranging was good for the soul. According to Doris, it had to be true; it was in the morning paper. When the bus arrived, Claire had expected the conversation to end. She was wrong. Flower arranging turned into the cost of living, which then moved into the importance of creating things of beauty. Before Doris stepped off the bus, she bent over and whispered how wonderful it had been meeting such a creative person and caring mother.

The timing of that conversation was amazing. Claire struggled with depression. The demands from twenty-four-hour care had taken a toll on her exhausted life. One question laid heavy on her heart. Was she failing as a mother? Even though Sarah was six years old, her child often seemed in pain and distress. Claire rarely was able to provide enough comfort. Then came the conversation with the sweet elderly lady. Affirmation. And the reminder about flower arrangements. Claire remembered her childhood fascination with that same hobby and how it had helped her communicate to others.

She tried it with her child. The beautiful things they created later that day weren't held just in a vase. Claire broke down in tears as she spoke about the transformation between mother and daughter. She never met Doris again. But the ripple effect of that conversation changed the course of the young mother's life.

And Sarah often smiled after that Tuesday morning bus ride.

Doris gingerly walked over to Claire.

They embraced. Two became three as they bent down and hugged Sarah. For over an hour I sat in the chapel as witness upon witness spoke of how Doris' life had impacted others. Random conversations. Homemade gifts. Cakes. The list was endless of her mundane beauty that radically changed lives. But there was a catch. Doris had changed the world and she hadn't even known it. Until now.

After death.

CHAPTER 43
THE MAGICAL MUNDANE

"When a man understands the art of seeing, he can trace the spirit of an age and the features of a king even in the knocker on a door."
(Victor Hugo, The Hunchback of Notre-Dame)

THE BROKEN CHAPEL BELL rang the leaving call.

One by one in ordered procession, the ghostly congregation made their way out. Their door knockers swayed in time with the chimes. Santiago remained seated. I followed his lead. As the teenage preacher shut the door behind her, he turned around and placed a door knocker on the pew. It was in the shape of a chess piece. A pawn.

"Few people get to see a scene like that during their first life."

"First life?"

"The life before the short sleep."

"You mean death."

"Maybe. It seems such a weak word to describe the colour behind our limited palette."

I didn't follow up on his cryptic response, I was more concerned with how he was looking at the door knocker. His face revealed a series of words yet to be spoken. He softly tapped the iron pawn, gathering up the courage to continue.

"I thought I had lost this. A friend found it by The Theatre steps. When he brought it to me, I knew what I had to do."

CLANK. The door knocker moved across the pew. Santiago's eyes were red from holding back tears of regret.

"Forgive me, but I had no choice."

"What do you mean?"

Panic filled my words as the door knocker continued to move across our wooden seat. Santiago shook his head, repeating his apologetic words. I asked again.

"What do you mean? Tell..."

CLICK.

My mouth sealed up with fear. The light by the chapel door switched off. CLICK. Another light at the far end of the aisle went dark. I felt my throat tighten with the terrifying realisation of what was happening. Betrayal. CLICK. CLICK. Darkness engulfed the room as the last bulb went out.

Alone, with my apologetic Judas.

*****

Charles Dickens needed to take a break.

It wasn't easy for him to write any more. He was feeling old and the dizziness was hitting him more frequently now. People had told him that fifty-seven was a good age. There was still life in the old bones yet. But he knew better. The last twelve months had pushed his body to the limit. His 'Farewell Reading' tour had been tough, both physically and mentally. That wasn't an excuse to quit. The message he had to tell was too important to keep silent.

Dickens looked around the study. There were so many objects scattered around the room; precious memories he had collected over the years. One piece caught his eye. It was on the mantelpiece over the fire. A picture. Had it been that long? Many things had happened since he had placed it there. Everything Dickens had done, the writings, the work, even the tour; every road led back to That image. The picture had gathered a thick layer of dust now. On purpose. Cleaning it would have given away to any visitor the significance of the piece. If all 'this' was going to work – his tour and legacy – then it had to be for eyes willing to observe and not just see.

Dickens pushed himself up from the chair. He could almost hear his bones creaking under the strain. His shaking hand rubbed along the nearby bookshelf. Third row down. Half way across. There it was. 'Sketches by Boz: Illustrative of Every-day Life and Every-day People.' He loved this book, even though the critics deemed it as one of his lesser pieces of work. 'Sketches' was a collection of observations written under a pseudonym back in 1836. These pages were far from polished with weak paragraph structures and wandering narrative arcs, but that didn't matter. This was the book that set him up to eventually see The Twins.

His shaking fingers reached behind the book and touched a metal object. A smile appeared on his worn, aged face. The iron door knocker landed on the desk with a metallic thud. Of all the things Dickens had written about, this plot device was the one he was most proud of. He wasn't the sole author of it, but at least he could take credit for dropping it into every one of his books.

Dickens had stumbled upon the door knocker by accident. It had started with a casual walk, noticing someone playing chess by themselves in the park. After introductions, he joined in with the game. The person opposite him talked about appreciating the mundane. The idea lingered long after Dickens lost the game. On the way home, he noticed the front doors that lined the street and wondered what lives lived behind those mundane wooden gates. What he discovered broke his heart. The only thing he could do was to write down everything he saw. 'Sketches' came soon after. He had purposely crafted the opening paragraphs to talk about the different types of door knockers that were in a neighbourhood. It was his way of challenging the reader to consider the unheard stories behind what they pass by every single day. There were so many tales of pain hidden within the mundane. His walks continued after the book came out, always looking at the door knockers. That was why he stopped by the alleyway. Another wooden door, this time propped up against the wall. His discovery in the shadows changed the course of his writing forever. The Twins.

Memories.

Dickens sighed. His face scrunched up in discomfort. Breathing wasn't so easy anymore. He slumped back in his chair as his body welcomed the rest.

The chess player had set him up, knowing he would eventually notice a wooden door in a forgotten alleyway. However painful that journey turned out to be, he was thankful for being a pawn in someone else's game. It gave him the perfect opportunity to figure out the two sides. He dropped hints in every one of his books, trusting that eventually, a reader would join all the dots together. The plan was simple. Use the mundane, just like door knockers, to keep under the radar – a pawn moving up the board unnoticed.

And the end game? Dickens looked back at the mantelpiece.

That image.

*****

CLICK. CLICK.

The lights came on. One by one. I was no longer in the chapel. Neither was this PARADOX. I was back in London. Present-day London. I breathed a sigh of relief. The nightmare was finally over.

It was early evening. I was standing on a suburban street overlooking a gated park. To my left, a row of terraced, four-storey houses. The type of owner and income level matched the state of the buildings. Some walls were pristine, with perfect paint jobs. Others had crumbling brickwork and rotting window frames. Rich and poor, together, but never sharing anything else in common except the park.

And door knockers.

Every house, regardless of its look, had an antique iron knocker. If it had just been one or two, I would have put it down to a weird coincidence. But every house? Number Seven had a door knocker shaped like a cat. I wondered if the owner was an animal lover. Number Twelve had an old castle. My mind wandered through images of the occupant being afraid, building up an emotional wall to fend off visitors. Or were they just a lover of history? I continued to walk down the street, surprised by how such a simple object could cause such imagination.

There was a park bench a few yards down. Santiago was waiting for me. Maybe this wasn't my return home after all. He was sitting opposite Number Sixteen. I looked over at the front door. The place looked familiar. Had I passed this house before? I couldn't remember. The sound of the clanking door knocker in Santiago's hands was telling me to walk over to the house. I shook my head. It was a silly thought. Door knockers don't talk.

Do they?

CHAPTER 44
GAME CHANGER

"If you challenge conventional wisdom, you will find ways to do things much better than they are currently done."
(Michael Lewis, Moneyball)

NUMBER SIXTEEN was one of those 'not so wealthy' houses.

There was no front garden, only a few concrete slabs that were big enough for the uncollected council bins. Broken bags of rubbish had emptied onto the ground, leaving a trail of food wrappers and toiletries. Sodden cardboard sheets covered up two broken window panes, with another three rotting frames ready to go the same way. Someone had kicked in the front door a few times. Jilted lovers. Lost keys. I could only imagine. Whoever had repaired the door hadn't finished their woodwork course. MDF wasn't the best material to use for outdoor weather; neither was a blunt saw.

The only thing of beauty was the door knocker designed to look like two delicate flowers. I couldn't take my eyes off its metallic petals, even when the unbelievable happened. The flowers blossomed, sending a sweet scent into the air. It was like the early days of spring breaking into December. No sooner had I breathed in its refreshing fragrance, a blast of cold air circled me. Shivering, and with a sense of shock, I watched the wind's icy touch work its winter magic. Iron petals fell to the floor. Grief welled up inside as I watched their haunting death. I somehow felt responsible. Gently, I reached down and picked up each flower. Everything in me wanted to turn back time. Frantically, I pushed the broken metal pieces back onto the knocker, praying they would come back to life. Every failed attempt heightened my sense of loss.

Behind me, I could hear Santiago crying.

*****

Santiago considered it a holy ritual.

Every Saturday, after the matinee and before The Theatre's evening show, he would sit on the park bench outside Number Sixteen. His liturgy started and ended with reflection upon everything that had happened behind that closed door. The petals would always fall to the ground. And every visit, he would cry.

It was a tough call to bring Peccadillo to this holy spot. The last thing Santiago wanted to do was to betray its memory. And yet his lost and found door knocker was evidence enough of a change in the game. No one knew he had re-discovered this place. That meant that the secret way to the next Path was still open: Path of the Demand. All Peccadillo needed to do was walk inside. Santiago wiped away his tears. He could already hear the soft call coming from behind the door. His heart skipped a beat, yearning to go through himself. Drawing upon a strength that could only come from regret, he gripped the bench and remained still.

This time, the call was for Peccadillo.

*****

I could hear a female voice.

It was soft. Whispering. And familiar. The cold wind had died away, but I could still feel its chilling touch. I recognised the voice. Six words. Repeated. Her broken-heart tone, full of confusion. The door opened and I stood frozen to the spot. In front of me was a woman I thought I would never see again. She wore the same clothes and expression on her face as the day she had said those same six words to me. Terri was back. And so was her question.

"Why did you do it, Abrahams?"

*****

The day I walked out of Terri's life was the day I heard those six words.

But like any line that shapes a person's destiny, there is context.

Sixteen months before that fateful day, Terri opened up to me about her Dickensian tale. Just like Dickens, her childhood dreams were robbed by the chains of debt. Three days after her thirteenth birthday, her parents announced that they had to move. The doormat had too many overdue rent payments, credit card bills and betting slips carrying failed hopes. She thought the move would just be down the road. Same school, same friends. She was wrong. For the next three years, the family moved from one temporary accommodation to another. Lousy credit references had a way of making a stable home just out of reach. The landlords only cared about one thing – rent payments. Maintenance was a side issue. The family couldn't do much about it. Complaints led to the prospect of being kicked out. So everyone had to grin and bear it. Eventually, the pressure got too much. Arguments between her parents soon followed.

That's how she remembered her teenage years. That, and her father jumping off Hungerford Bridge when she was sixteen. His note didn't say much. It was mainly full of apologies for being a failure. The final straw for him was pinning all his hopes on a horse called '*Sleary's Hope*'. It should have changed everything. The horse was a sign. It referenced his favourite Dickens' story, *Hard Times.* Some sign. It came in fifth and with it, an IOU slip to some dangerous people. Her father never gave a reason in the note for choosing that specific bridge, but Terri knew. It was the place where Dickens felt the greatest childhood pain.

That's when Terri broke off her story to check on Natasha. It gave me time to scribble down notes. I thought she was none-the-wiser.

Flash forward a year. My writing career had picked up. I landed a new deal for my fourth book and the advance on my outline brought with it a nice cheque. That afternoon I put down a deposit on an apartment. It was a special moment because of its connection to Terri and how we had first met at the library. She was there to arrange a protest for what was happening to her neighbourhood. I was there to hear a sales pitch about a new apartment complex nearby. It was destiny. And now my upcoming book had put down a deposit on that very same apartment. The move-in date was just before Christmas, along with an invite for Terri and Natasha to move in with me.

My new place had four bedrooms, so plenty of space. It was also next to the estate where Terri lived in her cramped, rented and ill-suited flat. That meant school and her sentimental library were close by. I had rehearsed my sales pitch to her all day.

"No pressure; just stay until you can find somewhere that isn't damp."

I didn't factor in Terri putting all the pieces together.

We argued after her refusal. She couldn't believe I was so blind. Didn't I realise what she had been protesting about in the library?

Before the first brick of my trendy apartment complex had its layer of cement, the development had hit the local papers. The council had partnered with a property company to help with regeneration. Their first task was to demolish an ugly 1960's social housing tower block and replace it with state-of-the-art living quarters. The private developers were doing the city a favour. How does the saying go? If you want to attract the best, get rid of the mess. It attracted me.

The first story from the paper was how the council dealt with the ex-social tenants. Their offer was one alternative property within the Borough. If rejected, the tenants were pretty much told to bugger off to another part of the country. It didn't take long for the reports to hit the headlines telling of unsuitable alternatives, children having to leave school, families being split apart. Then came the protests on the estate. The unrest would've faded away within weeks if it hadn't been for a controversial policy. For building companies to win housing contracts, they needed to commit a percentage of apartments for low-income families and social tenants. This was to demonstrate that all parties were being socially responsible. To ensure the building company kept the exclusivity of their key target audience happy, they would adopt a two-door entrance policy. The front door led into a spacious and opulent foyer, set aside for the full-paying tenants to use. Down the side alley was the second door. It was still exclusive, but this time only for the less wealthy. The papers labelled it 'The Poor Door'. Funny how history repeats itself. Charles Dickens would have been turning in his grave.

Personally, I didn't get the whole protest. Didn't most things in life have a two-door policy? Hotel check-ins. Loyalty schemes. Why pick on an apartment block? Terri didn't see it that way. She saw injustice. Blatant, unsympathetic brutality. The poor were getting treated as second-rate citizens. Landlords and developers were happily placing profit on a higher pedestal than the well-being of those in need. It brought back painful childhood memories of seeing her parents treated just the same way. She hated that apartment block and everything the redevelopment stood for. It was part of the system that destroyed her family. Her father.

It was the Hungerford bridge all over again.

Our argument ended with her chucking the glossy brochure into the kitchen sink. Her eyes were full of pain and disappointment. But most of all, I saw broken trust. She knew what was in the outline of my new book. My secret scribbled notes weren't so hidden after all. Just like her father, I was always after the next big thing while forgetting to see what was right in front of my eyes.

"Why did you do it, Abrahams?"

I couldn't answer back then.

And I still couldn't answer as I stood outside Number Sixteen.

CHAPTER 45
THE FOURTH PATH

"I see a beautiful city and a brilliant people rising from this abyss. I see the lives for which I lay down my life, peaceful, useful, prosperous and happy. I see that I hold a sanctuary in their hearts, and in the hearts of their descendants, generations hence."
(Charles Dickens, A Tale of Two Cities)

INSIDE NUMBER SIXTEEN was the outdoors.

A blast of heat caught the back of my throat as I stepped into a blazing hot desert. My glands instantly dug for saliva, but their excavation came up short. The endless yellow dunes had death written into the sand. A stretched out silhouette came up from behind. I turned around, already knowing who I would see.

Terri.

We faced each other in silence. For a writer, I suddenly found I had no words to convey the gut-wrenching mixture of guilt and joy of seeing her again. She looked just the same as I remembered, and yet behind that external display of beauty I knew I had broken her heart. My fingerprints were all over those shattered pieces.

Terri dropped her journal at my feet. I had seen its well-used, battered cover many times before during our kitchen table chats. Her silent stare was piercing. She wanted me to pick it up and read. How could I? It was her private journal. But it hadn't stopped me in the past. Reluctantly, I bent down and flicked through the pages. There were so many entries I recognised. One page stuck out. Terri bent down, her finger outstretched like The Ghost of Christmas Future in front of Scrooge's grave. We both knew what that entry meant.

A betrayal of trust.

Terri had a strange way of keeping a journal.

She would mix fiction with non-fiction by blending a Dickens tale with her storyline. Occasionally she would show me a page. I appreciated her trust in me. But for Terri, her open heart was a way of healing herself from the painful baggage she carried around. Over a glass of wine one night, she opened up her journal and let me into a part of her life I had never seen before. On the top of the page was the title 'Love's Demand'. A catchy line, and as usual she had drawn upon fiction to delve into her thoughts. This time *A Tale of Two Cities.* Terri loved that story by Dickens. Until that night, the only two things I knew about the tale was its connection to the French Revolution and that it had one of the best opening lines ever penned.

'It was the best of times, it was the worst of times, it was the age of wisdom, it was the age of foolishness, it was the epoch of belief, it was the epoch of incredulity, it was the season of light, it was the season of darkness, it was the spring of hope, it was the winter of despair, we had everything before us, we had nothing before us, we were all going direct to Heaven, we were all going direct the other way.'

Her synopsis of the story captivated me.

A Tale of Two Cities follows the lives of Dr Manette, his daughter Lucie, and two male suitors for her hand: Charles Darnay and Sydney Carton.

Dr Manette, recently released from the hated Bastille prison, becomes friends with Darnay. The young man successfully asks permission to marry Manette's daughter. To make things complicated, Carton also reveals his love for Lucie, but recognises that her affection is for someone else. He makes an oath of sacrificial love to her, promising that he would *'give his life to keep a life you loved besides you'*. Before the wedding day, Darnay confesses his backstory to Dr Manette. He tells him how he shed his aristocratic identity out of protest for how his family treated a stranger. They both agree that it will be kept secret between them. France had lost its love for the nobility. These were dangerous times. The marriage went ahead. After losing one child, the couple gave birth to a daughter named 'little Lucie'.

Welcome the plot twist – the storming of the Bastille.

The revolutionary mob discovers a document about Manette's imprisonment. It reveals how the old man was always innocent, sent to prison because Darney's father and uncle wanted to protect their family name. A cry of justice rises up, arrests soon follow. There would only be one judgment for Darney during a time when a nation's lust calls for the guillotine. Manette's attempts to save his son-in-law fall on deaf ears. To make matters worse, Carton overhears a conversation that the courts won't just be calling for Darnay's head. Lucie and the daughter were in danger too.

Carton arranges for the family to leave and then visits Darnay in his prison cell. Drugging the prisoner to sleep, Carton changes identity with him, due to their similar looks. He calls for the guard and watches Lucie's husband taken out to a waiting carriage. The final scene is that of Carton's execution. Dickens captured the beauty of sacrificial love perfectly.

'It is a far, far better thing that I do than I have ever done. It is a far, far better rest that I go to than I have ever known.'

Carton kept his promise to Lucie. He gave his life for her.

It was a good story, made real by what Terri told me next during that kitchen table chat.

She recounted her tales of sacrificial love, especially towards her daughter. Her best and worst of times brought me to tears. Life was hard for them and yet Terri continued to see the world through the eyes of love, putting others before herself. That night, back home, I scribbled down a story on my yellow pad. The outline built up from there with the aid of a few more secret reads of her journal. I had the content of my next book. Her story, but with the names changed.

The reason I gave myself to do such a thing was that people needed to wake up to what was happening in society. It was a good excuse, but only partly true. I was desperate. This next book had to be a hit. This story gave me a fighting chance. And my agent loved the title.

'Love's Demand.'

Santiago continued to sit outside the closed door of Number Sixteen.

He knew Terri well. Like Peccadillo, he came across her at the library. It was the first time he truly saw the raw reality of the benefits system. Unlike the tales he had heard on TV about scroungers, Terri's benefit support didn't go on Cable TV and fashion trends. She stretched out every penny in a makeshift allotment of second-hand goods. Their two-bed flat had all the budget hallmarks of a property set aside for the DSS support system. Apart from the grim and questionable heating, the biggest thing they struggled with was the smell of damp. They had moved enough times within the system to know that if you complained too much, then the landlord would kick you out. That was the way it worked. There was no such thing as social housing anymore, just private landlords who didn't care about the moral right that everyone should have a home.

For the first few weeks, Terri spent time making the flat liveable while Natasha was at school. By the second month, it felt like a home. It still didn't meet the criteria for letting other school parents see the property though. Terri could handle the looks, but Natasha was too young to face the judgmental comparisons of wealth.

Even with the constant uphill trudge of life, there was an inner conviction that someday things would get better. She would not give up hope as her father had. But it was tough to keep believing. Then came the moment which every parent dreads – the inability to mend a child's broken heart. Natasha needed new school shoes. Her current ones were falling apart. Terri had no money. It ruined her seeing her daughter give that 'It's OK Mummy' smile, knowing full well that her precious child would later cry out the disappointment within the privacy of her bedroom. No child should be spoilt, but neither should a young life be collateral damage within a biased financial system. The tissue used to wipe away those tears was a legalised loan shark. It was so easy to do. Interest payments built up. Another loan followed.

Santiago remembered the time when it became apparent that Terri's sacrificial love was prioritising food. When Natasha asked why her mother wasn't eating with her, the reply came that she would cook something later. It wasn't a lie. She did eat, but it was a stretch to call it dinner. Bedtimes were the hardest. The prayers always made Terri cry. It was the only time when Natasha felt brave enough to tell God how she was feeling. Santiago had tried to help with the odd envelope of money and trips to the supermarket. Terri thanked him, but also made it clear it was only temporary. When he tried to pay off the loan sharks, she didn't speak to him for two days. Shame does that to the heart.

Tears came hard and fast down Santiago's face. These memories carried pain. They always did on the bench outside Number Sixteen.

He knew the punchline of the story.

CHAPTER 46
THE ABANDONED PLACE

"That's when I miss you most. When you're here. When you aren't here, when you're just a ghost of the past or a dream from another life, it's easier then."
(Neil Gaiman, American Gods)

TERRI *called the desert 'the abandoned place'.*

It was a play on words. There was always life here; one just had to observe it.

Deserts had always been a thing for Terri. It started at school when her geography teacher told her about these magical landscapes made out of sand. Ever since, nature's mysterious dunes had captivated her mind. She loved that deserts defied logic. They embraced the extremities of hot and cold, crushing rocks into tiny pieces. Their vast canvas drained expansive seas into barren lands. And when a traveller dared to set foot upon its work, the desert challenged the very notion of what it meant to be strong. For the only way someone could ever get to the other side was to trust in something higher than their understanding.

The oasis.

These beautiful watering holes broke all the rules. Against the odds, they survived when everything seemed to be against them. In the vastness of endless sandy dunes, a refuge forms out of nothing, welcoming the traveller just at the right time. Some even say these saviours move across the desert, positioned like chess pieces to help move a traveller's journey forward. That's why no map could ever successfully plot the location of an oasis. The only way to discover such a prize is by walking. Trust the desert rhythm. But sadly, humanity rarely sees such beauty. Who wants to find a magical refuge in a land that demands that one must first let go of control?

For as long as Terri could remember, her life had felt like a desert. She had experienced the extremities of the blazing heat of humanity's greed and the cold shoulder of disgust. Her heart knew what it was like to have a hammer of rage slam down and leave a trail of tiny pieces on life's floor. And she had lost count of the vast ocean of dreams that had slowly drained away. But her 'witness' had also been one of setting foot upon this sandy landscape and staring at a beautiful oasis. These places of refuge had come in many forms – this latest one, taking her breath away.

I rummaged through the deep crevices of my heart trying to find the words, any words, to tell Terri how I felt. Every sentence I cobbled together felt empty. There was nothing I could say that would blot out the glaring truth of my betrayal. I had pimped her precious story to the highest bidder. Even my stated reason for doing so, the desire to be her knight in shining armour, couldn't hide the reality that I wanted that bestseller badge again. That's the difference between charity and compassion. Both do the right thing, but only one changes the selfish heart.

In my silence, all I could do was stare. Her skin glowed, just like how a mother's face lights up when she secretly carries a new life inside. The eyes must have gazed into heaven's crystal lake because its reflection had etched its majesty back into her life. I had never seen her so alive. Was it a mirage, a trick of the desert? It had to be, but I begged inside it wasn't. There was so much to say if I could find the words.

Terri took hold of my hand. Her cool touch instantly refreshed my heated skin. As she leant in, some of her hair rubbed against my cheek. I could smell the fresh scent of her shampoo. This was no optical illusion. My heart leapt for joy, before beating fast with apprehension. This was the moment of reckoning I had dreaded since walking out of her front door.

"I wish I could…"

Turn back time? Never write that story and walk out of her door? I wanted to say all those repentant things, but the desperation to explain my reasoning won out. Yes, I had taken her story. But weren't some of my motives good? What friend would I have been if I had left the two of them living in a flat that was falling apart with damp? Terri had been drowning in a raging sea of debt. She needed help, and her answer, whether she could see it or not, was the book. The royalty cheques and the new apartment weren't just for me. I wanted to give them a safe home; something that would set them up for a new adventure in life. And maybe with me alongside them.

I did it for love.

No. I did it for SELF.

I never finished off my sentence.

Terri let the silence speak volumes before pointing towards a rippling shadow on the horizon.

"That's my home. Would you like to walk with me for a while?"

I nodded, somewhat confused. It seemed an odd place to live. We only took a few steps before the dry heat gripped tighter around my throat. I needed water and fast. Terri noticed my discomfort.

"Don't worry. There's water ahead. The desert will keep you alive today."

Right on cue, my tired eyes focused on a welcoming oasis shimmering in the distance. It didn't look like the mythical watering holes from my childhood picture books and adventure films. The sprawled out city went on for at least two miles. Frustratingly, we never picked up the pace. Terri made sure that our amble kept in rhythm with the movement of the sand under our feet. She occasionally dropped out comments about the destination we were heading to. It left me with the impression she was preparing me for what was inside.

"The oasis is rarely just a watering hole. Within its borders are wells, homes and commerce too numerous to count. Some are permanent, some are temporary, but everything is equal."

She laughed when I told her about my assumption of a few palm trees and a pond. Myths like that, she informed me, were humanity's attempt at trying to define something that is undefinable.

"There are rules," she continued. "Simple rules that both traveller and resident must obey. All are welcome and everyone is respected. Regardless of colour, race and theological differences, equality reigns supreme. That goes as well for warring factions. All weapons are to be left at the city gate."

In amongst the discomfort of thirst, it was good to hear Terri's voice again. God I missed her.

"The oasis governs itself. It uses campfires, bustling bazaars and communal tables as the counsel of wisdom. These sacred spaces are a place where people share stories and work out their differences. Break the rules and the traveller must leave."

Her hand pulled me to a stop.

"Don't fool yourself. This is holy ground you are about to enter."

*****

The oasis city was alive with colour.

My senses couldn't take in the mixture of an old Mediterranean town and a bartering Middle Eastern market square. The symphony of musical tones and smells told the tale that no street or bazaar was the same as its comrades-in-arms. Each tent-covered table was a mysterious Aladdin's Cave. But Terri was walking too fast for me to explore.

We darted through side alleyways and bustling streets. I could tell she was making sure we avoided certain places. Because they were off limits. Why? She yanked my arm as we quickly turned left. We squeezed through some tables then down a narrow brick-walled alley. The reveal was spectacular.

The communal patio was a kaleidoscope of colour. Hanging baskets and potted plants brought a sense of peace to the place. Scattered around by the walls were three tables and sixteen chairs. Clay water jugs rested on top, filled with the one thing I was craving most of all. I rushed over and took a drink. Then another. By the third beaker, I slumped onto the chair and took in the surroundings. This place was urging me to slow down, its irresistible peace calling me to 'be still and know'. Terri sat down opposite me.

"There is something you need to know."

Her expression told me I would not like what she was about to say.

"You need to know what happened at Number Sixteen."

CHAPTER 47
NUMBER SIXTEEN

"All endings are also beginnings. We just don't know it at the time."
(Mitch Albom, The Five People You Meet in Heaven)

"IT STARTED WITH A KISS after you left."

That's how Terri began her story. My mind had already written the next line. A lover. Hidden affair. But I was wrong. The kiss was on Natasha's forehead. For five weeks her daughter had been suffering from one of those coughs that disturbed sleep then lingered throughout a tired day. At first, she told herself that it was 'just one of those things kids get'. It would soon go away.

Except. It didn't. And it was getting worse.

The doctor gave Natasha some medicine. When that didn't work, the next appointment focused on whether she was eating well and keeping warm. Terri didn't need the test results to know the cause. The newspapers nicknamed the cough 'The Refugee Growl'. It was a terrible title, but spot on with the description. It became headline reading for a few weeks because of the refugee crisis across Europe. As makeshift camps sprung up and aid workers moved in, people noticed a growling sound lurking behind their breath. Damp conditions. Lack of sleep. Sporadic food intake. These all brought with it a cough that people couldn't shake off. Young and old. Everyone had it.

The myth was that it consigned itself to the camps.

But the same sound echoed around the cramped lanes of privatised social housing and the revamped benefit system. Damp conditions. Lack of sleep. Sporadic food intake. On the streets, the cough had a new nickname.

'The Poor Growl.'

*****

Terri got the cough a few weeks later.

She contacted the landlord, aware of the horror stories from others who had done the same thing. The first few calls bought nothing but broken promises and the occasional excuse. Eventually, Terri complained to the authorities. The response was a two-month notice period and a lousy tenancy report. Without the funds or decent references to put down another deposit, Terri couldn't find a place near her daughter's school. The local council stepped in, finding a temporary room – 'room' being the perfect description. It was a bed-sit in a converted four-storey townhouse.

Number Sixteen.

Just like before, Terri worked hard at making it a home. Each corner had a theme. There was a dream area, reading den, cooking fun and the play-till-you-drop corner. But no matter the creativity, it never removed the reality that the bed-sit was situated in a property that was anything but welcoming. The adult world that Terri's little girl saw every day paid little attention to a child's innocent imagination. Each bed-sit carried a story of pain and rejection. Passing the neighbours in the hallway brought eye contact into the abyss of lost hope. Noises through flimsy wall panels were just scary sounds in Natasha's ears. For Terri, they painted the image of violence. This was a world a child should never hear.

Night time's were the worst. Bedtimes had a heavy blanket of fear as the outside world pressed against the walls. Creaky floorboards by her door moved in time to sinister whispers. The imagination played cruel tricks in the dark, especially when the shadows stopped outside the front door. Terri tried hard not to show her anxiety, always telling herself that the place was only temporary. They were on a list – 'The list for housing' – and because they were a family, they were near the top. A few more days. Maybe a couple of weeks. Then it would be over.

But it wasn't.

Housing was in short supply and private landlords were choosy. That was about the time when Terri tried calling me. She decided not to leave any messages. The machine wasn't the place for recorded cries of help. Then came the letters. Terri opened her heart on those pages, sharing her fears about that bed-sit and the constant coughs. She never knew I had thrown her notes straight into the bin without reading them. To her, my non-existent reply was nothing but rejection.

The harshest form of dismissal to such vulnerable words.

*****

Weeks turned into months.

The disturbed nights and fearful days made the themed corners of the room lose their magical appeal. Terri's answer was the local park opposite the bed-sit. It was an oasis. A refuge from the horror. Just behind the park bench was a group of trees. The way they had formed over the years made an enchanting woodland circle. To most adult eyes it was just dead space full of fallen leaves. But for the two of them, it was a magical kingdom waiting for their imagination. Woodland fairies. Teddy bear tea-parties. Adventurous princesses and buried treasure. Their kingdom became sacred.

The wood was the place where they could dream about another world. A new house, somewhere that was warm and safe. They would have lots of friends, too many to count. In this 'other' world Terri had a great job, one that used her creative skills and paid enough to live. For Natasha, this world also included me. We were all friends. I would take them out every weekend. One such trip was to the stage performance of *A Christmas Carol.* That's where the idea of the postcard came from. The imaginary theatre was selling them after the play.

Natasha struggled to separate reality from fiction. Although Terri tried hard to persuade her daughter not to send the postcard to me, it fell on deaf ears. The letter that accompanied *That* image was from Terri, begging me to reply and not destroy a little girl's wonderland. This woodland dream world was important to her.

To them.

*****

The night before I received the postcard, their electricity went off.

They could hear the anger through the partitioned walls. Then came the heavy breathing in the corridors. Terri knew where those angry sounds of lust would lead. They gathered up whatever warm clothes and blankets they could find and headed to their woodland circle. Torches provided light and the sheets over the branches created a den. Within minutes, a sleepover with the fairies was the evening treat. They were safe.

The plan was to stay out there a couple of hours until Natasha was in a deep sleep. By then, the electricity would be back on. Terri could hear the deep breathing of her daughter. She hadn't slept that heavy in a while. The rattle in her chest was still there, but thankfully it wasn't bothering the restful child. In the distance, the noise from Number Sixteen faded away. Sleep was closing in. So was the cold. Another blanket helped. The drop in temperature didn't seem too bad.

Fade in. Fade out.

The world blurred into a swirl of colours.

In her dream-like state, Terri heard a voice. A whisper. It was soft and caring. Trustworthy. And then everything fell quiet. When they opened their eyes, neither of them were in the woodland circle anymore. Terri and Natasha were home.

The home they'd always hoped for.

*****

"That's where we live now."

Terri pointed towards a building on her left. If ever there was a dream house that fitted her heart, I was staring at it. It put my sterile apartment to shame. This brick and clay building embodied love and appreciation. Not too big, not too small – everything centred around releasing the heart to sing towards the heavens.

"Natasha loves it here. She has wonderful friends and we have so many things we can create together. "

"Mummy?"

"Coming."

I recognised the voice from behind the curtained door. It was the sweetest sound I had heard all day. She was happy and full of life. Terri answered my question before I even asked it.

"Sorry, but I can't take you in. It would raise too many questions."

I nodded, although I didn't want to accept what had dawned on me. I let out a sorrow-filled cry of grief, overwhelmed with the sense of loss. Terri leant forward, my head nestled into the ridge between her shoulder and neck. Her embrace was full of forgiveness. I didn't deserve such love. If only I had picked up the phone or read her letters.

If only... I hadn't been so selfish.

Natasha called out again. Our embrace ended.

"It's time for you to leave."

I clambered around for the right words, but nothing could come close to the depth of grief ravaging my soul. Terri pressed her hand against my heart.

"It's not the time for words. The real change happens in here."

I put my hand over hers.

"Remember those kitchen table chats we used to have in my flat."

I nodded.

"My favourite time was when we read *A Christmas Carol.* I loved how we tore into the scene when Marley tried to help Scrooge find the real meaning of life. *'The chain I forged in life... I made it link by link, and yard by yard; I girded it on of my own free will, and of my own free will I wore it.'* Oh, my dear Abrahams. You can still forge a different way to live. The choice is always there."

"Please let me stay."

Terri wiped away my tears with her soft, cooling hand.

"I'm sorry. The oasis is not for you at this time."

One kiss on the cheek and then she told me to close my eyes. When I opened them, I was back at The Pillar. Terri and Natasha were gone. But not forgotten. Their deaths now engraved into the chains around my heart.

'Guilty'.

CHAPTER 48
THE MAGICIAN

"Without music, life would be a mistake."
(Friedrich Nietzsche, Twilight of the Idols)

THE MAGICIAN *slowly walked around his study, taking in every carefully arranged item.*

He considered this place a continuation of his show, giving considerable thought to its design. To the left was a small collection of books, perfectly arranged so it would be the first thing any visitor would see. Each edition, purposely chosen: a few classics and a scattering of modern fiction. Not too many to overwhelm, but enough to give the impression He was well-read. And rightly so. Stories were important to him.

On the dark oak-panelled walls were seven shelves, and on each shelf, a selection of handcrafted chess pieces. Just like the books, not everything was on display. The Magician had learned the hard way about the power of mystery. This study was his version of that dreaded trick all those years ago.

Under the large bay window on the opposite side of the room were an elegantly carved cherry wood desk and a traditional coaster office chair. It had taken him a long time to find the perfect pair, but that was all part of the joy of getting this study 'just right'. The uncluttered desk was all about focus – an antique banker's lamp, notepad and fountain pen. Scribbled thoughts filled the paper, thick lines connecting one observation to another. Evidence of a trick-in-development.

Before walking over to the chair, He bent down to his most prized possession: a Victor Talking Machine gramophone. His fingers carefully placed the needle on the 1975 vinyl recording of Fauré's Requiem. Five bars into the music He sat down and bathed in its sound. By the time The Magician opened his eyes again, the performance by Sir David Willcocks conducting the King's College Choir in Cambridge had just moved into the fourth movement. Its choral masterpiece of 'Pie Jesu in B-flat Major' floated around the room. Exquisite. He loved this recording because of its grand illusion. Listeners, too many to count, assumed the concert took place in King's College Chapel. And why shouldn't they? The title did include 'some' of those words.

"Misdirection."

The sound of The Magician's whisper blended in with the Requiem. There was a sense of satisfaction as He considered how people see what they want to see. Just because the choir from King's College was on the recording, didn't mean the concert took place in that grand historical hall. Nobody paid attention to details any more. The performance was in fact held in the smaller and less glamorous Trinity College Chapel. It was a perfect illusion; get the audience to create the scene themselves.

The Magician had a soft spot for Fauré, especially his Requiem.

He liked how the composer screwed the system and got away with it. Back in the 19th century, a Requiem, or mass for the dead, was part of the controlling hand of religion. The composer and church would set the music up to scare the listener into thinking about what happened to them after death. In their quivering state, the church would then emerge as their all-knowing saviour. The ticket to heaven usually came with a price tag, but beggars couldn't be choosers. So the listener paid up. It was a fool-proof system. The profits rolled in.

Then along came Fauré and his infamous sleight-of-hand.

His Requiem was more like death's lullaby. He replaced fire and brimstone imagery with the gentle thoughts of a Divine Being rocking His children into eternal bliss. The church lost a lot of money because of that piece of music. They could still sell their travel cards to heaven, but happiness was never as profitable as fear. Slowly but surely, the walls of religion's power crumbled away.

"The first rule of any illusion: use the very thing one opposes to change the nature of the game."

The seventh movement started. 'In Paradisum.' The Magician gently sang along to the Latin liturgy:

'May the angels lead you into paradise; may the martyrs come to welcome you and take you to the holy city.'

It was a good line. He wondered how many people had suddenly woken up from their deep sleep to find that eternity had nothing to do with the travel cards they had bought from the church. The chains one crafted in this life were the only currency in the sweet-by-and-by. His eyes glanced over towards the book collection. One title stuck out. He never really liked that Christmas story, but Dickens was spot on when he penned the line, 'I wear the chain I forged in life.' The Magician never worked out how the writer had discovered such a gem. Marley's prophetic speech had ruffled a few feathers in PARADOX when it first came out. Not so any more. Over the years the whole story became more like a song and dance number than a haunting Christmas prophecy. People see what they want to see. That's how He liked it.

A knock on the door brought his mind back to the present. Fifteen-minute warning. Was it that time for the show already? The Magician let out a long sigh of tired inevitability. There was a time when He used to relish these performances. Not so any more. The audiences had become predictable; there was rarely a raucous crowd. And even when The Magician showed them what was 'up his sleeve', they pretended it wasn't there. Illusion trumped reality. Easier for him, but where was the challenge? That's why He needed to change the show. A new trick.

Another knock on the door. Ten-minute warning.

The trick had been developing nicely. A few more performances and hopefully it would be ready for the grand unveil. For years The Magician had slipped his new idea into the act. This living experiment adapted with every performance as He scrutinised every intake of air and grip on the seat. What worked? Did the audience see? Would it...

"Bring the house down?"

The drawn-out words brought a smile to his face. He appreciated the ironic nature of the whole thing. With eyes wide open, the audience would still not recognise the roof falling on top of them. A perfect illusion.

A deadly illusion.

Another knock on the door, final call.

He ignored the summons. His mind was elsewhere. Peccadillo. The traveller often visited PARADOX, but his last journey through these lands was supposed to have been his final. He didn't mind that the wanderer had returned. It gave The Magician a chance to tidy up loose ends. Sealing Peccadillo's fate wasn't his finest closing move, but it did get the job done. Just like so many others who had gone the same way, the chains of seeing but not observing was a wonderful way to seal the gateway back into PARADOX.

What caused him concern was not the return, but the decisions that Peccadillo was making. Usually, one could pretty much guess the route and response along The Paths. Just like chess, He was always five moves ahead. But not this visit. Something was different, as though an unknown hand was helping the traveller. The Magician had the uncomfortable feeling of misdirection.

But where was it coming from?

Certainly not Peccadillo. Chatting with him at the workhouse confirmed that the guy was still as ignorant as ever. He never even recognised his own furniture as they ran through the offices. That left The Storyteller. Her fingerprints were all over Peccadillo's return. But wasn't that the whole idea of misdirection? Get the opponent to look at the most obvious thing, and then come up on the other side of the board.

With a pawn.

There was no doubt in his mind that The Storyteller was involved, but who was That pawn? He didn't like the idea that a mysterious someone was playing him from the shadows. The Magician tried to keep his thoughts on track as the stagehand entered.

"Sir, it is time."

Maybe the unknown hand didn't belong to a stranger after all. It would make sense using someone He wouldn't suspect.

"Sir? Time to go on stage."

The Magician turned around, his trail of thought evaporating into the final chords of the recording. Right on cue, the Requiem of illusion finished. He stood up and greeted his friend. His sidekick. The Magician had many partners to help him with his act. That was the unique thing about the show. Each audience had its own special stagehand.

"Santiago. It's good to see you. May I say, you are playing your part to perfection."

CHAPTER 49
TIME FOR GODOT

"Let's go. We can't. Why not? We're waiting for Godot."
(Samuel Beckett, Waiting for Godot)

I WAS BACK at The Pillar.

Santiago was gone. I didn't care. What was the point? My whole body felt numb, weighed down by the guilt of what I had just seen. Terri. Natasha. I could have helped them. If only. My legs buckled. Tears dripped onto the dusty ground as my hunched body heaved with judgement's gut-wrenching cry. For years I had served out selfishness to the world around me, not sticking around to see the after-effects of my revolting recipe. Now, in this nightmarish place, the fruits of my life were on full display. I couldn't avoid it; my actions were a signature on death's warrant card.

"NO!"

There had to be a mistake. It wasn't me who caused Terri to spiral into a world of debt. Neither did I turn the electricity off or encourage them to go into a dangerous field on a cold night. Death couldn't blame me for a crumbling social housing system or the increase of greedy landlords. Yet the judgemental tears continued to come. Those droplets of regret told a different story, forming from the inner-most part of my soul. In a world which seemed so big and distant, the human universe was a network of cause and effect. An ignored phone call here. A cry of desperation there. The desire for investment as I climbed the housing ladder.

My fist pounded on the floor, a passionate statement of innocence. Yes, I was guilty of stubborn selfishness, but never of death. Their deaths.

"YOU!"

I lurched on all fours towards The Guide who had just walked up from a nearby Path.

"How could you? You knew what had happened to Terri. Why didn't you tell me?"

The guilt inside needed to lash out at someone other than my broken heart. She soaked up every angry word without responding. It was the confused look on her face that silenced my cry. She joined me on the floor.

"How did…? You weren't supposed. To go. There."

The Guide struggled to finish her sentence. She looked even more unsettled when I told her how I got to Number Sixteen. Apparently I wasn't supposed to see Terri, only hear about her story. And as for Santiago, she couldn't understand why he was breaking the strict rules on interference. We sat in silence after that. Her, trying to work out a new string of data. Me, wishing I could wake up back in my bed of ignorance.

The evening sun bowed its head towards the moon. Its chemical red blanket of light changed the whole feel of PARADOX. The town lost all of its mysterious charm and nervous tension. Nothing it could throw at me now could hurt as much as what I was feeling inside. The market traders were packing up their stalls. A few shoppers lingered around, trying to find a last-minute bargain. Their frustrated expressions at not having enough time in their day made me feel sad for them. Was this the most important thing in life? How little did they know? As the final shoppers departed with bags full of disappointment, The Guide stood up and walked over to her invisible friends. She pretended to wipe their brows. In the deathly silence of the market, I stood up. This nightmare needed to end. I signalled to The Guide that I was ready for the next Path. The Path of the Godot. Three more to go, and the sooner I walked them, the sooner I would get home.

Our walk to the gate was quicker than expected. The lock opened, but I didn't move. In that moment of stillness, we shared a look. Both of us felt it. Time was ending. I tried to dismiss it. This Path was only the fifth. The Guide's eyes said differently. Things had changed. Her data had revealed something she wasn't letting on. We briefly shook hands. I stepped through the gate, wondering what was waiting for me. Or was it the other way round?

Was something waiting for The Guide?

*****

So I had finally arrived.

I recognised where I was standing: outside The Theatre. The building looked even more impressive than my vision. The eight Corinthian pillars supporting the triangular pediment, made me feel as though I was gazing upon a world of high art. Everything about the structure was self-selective, including the grandiose steps leading up to the palace-type doors. This was a place that made anyone question their suitability even to come close. Were my clothes fancy enough? Had I enough income? Did I know enough about the arts? It was always about not having enough. Just staring at The Theatre erected mental guards inside me. I wanted that VIP access, just like how I had wanted that key code to the front door of my apartment block.

Or did I?

Terri.

My foot hovered over the first step. Seconds later, I pulled it back.

*****

The Magician looked down from the stage.

ROW 6. SEAT 22. It was empty. That was strange. Peccadillo should have been there by now. What was taking so long? The unanswered questions had spoilt the show. It wasn't his best performance. He couldn't wait to get off the stage. Back in his study, The Magician called out for Santiago. There was no answer. He too was missing. That was no coincidence. There was only one thing to do now: take the game in a different direction. His next move made him sad. He liked The Guide. They had a history together.

But sometimes the player must sacrifice a piece to win the game.

*****

Sitting on the steps were two smartly dressed men.

Both were wearing black bowler hats, pinstripe shirts and bright red cravats. Their suits had the exclusive tailor look written all over them. As for the shoes, polished to perfection. They gave me a questioning look as I walked over. Neither of them hid their disappointment when I was close enough for a better inspection.

"Bother."

"It's not him."

"Told you."

"No, you didn't."

They talked to each other like a rich man's version of Tweedledee and Tweedledum. I asked if they were waiting for The Theatre to open. The man on the right laughed first, followed by the second. Back and forth, the tag-team approach was consistent.

"Did you hear that?"

"Yes. What a preposterous thought."

"To walk up the steps."

"Why would we do that?"

"Especially when we are expecting a visit."

"Yes. A most important visit."

"A visit from the man himself."

"The conductor."

Their faces suddenly dropped. Gone were the smiles and pompous mockery. In their place was a picture postcard of a child who had missed seeing Father Christmas and was now beginning to disbelieve the magic.

"Except."

"He hasn't turned up yet."

"Been a while."

"A long while."

"He did say he was coming."

"We just needed to wait."

"But it wasn't him who said it, was it?"

"You're right. It was the other fellow."

"I still believe him though."

"Yes. So do I. The conductor is coming. I think."

"He has to come."

Their back-and-forth conversation rehearsed the steps that had led them to this peculiar waiting game. It all started when they had bumped into a young man called Boi. In the middle of apologising, they discovered that he was the bag carrier for their favourite conductor. This was an exciting discovery. Especially when they heard the conductor was making a comeback. It had been a sad day for the two gentleman when this famed musician had retired. Nobody knew the exact reasons why he had hung up his baton. The rumour was that it had been down to frustration with the audience. Most of them were more interested in the status of his shows than the appreciation of what he had composed and the stories it would tell. Boi told them that there would be a special event, just for the conductor's 'real' fans. If the two men waited, they would get front row seats.

"It will obviously be in The Theatre."

"Such a grand building."

"Nothing less will do."

"We're waiting here for the tickets."

"Yes, but that was three months ago."

"Really? I thought it was four."

"Has it been that long already?"

*****

I joined them on the steps.

The rectangular piazza The Theatre joined onto was a thriving collection of human life. On one side, a café haphazardly scattered its tables and chairs around the walkway. Just like The Theatre, there was a feeling of self-selection for its clientele. Their menu stubbornly offered Cappuccinos in the morning and Espressos for the rest of the day. If you didn't like it, tough; there was always some diluted franchise down the street. Opposite the café was a series of boutique shops. Whatever these places offered, the crowds loved it. So did the proprietors. Maybe that's why my eyes moved towards a small shop in the corner. It was the only building that nobody seemed interested in.

"That's Micawber's shop."

"His shop is never busy."

"Folk here think he's a bit strange."

"And he always has odd things in his shop."

"Don't know why he still sticks around."

"I heard he is…"

Their faces went ghostly white.

Micawber was standing in the doorway, looking straight at us. He raised his index finger in the air, signalling me to come over. The two men never said a word as I stood up.

They had better things to do. Waiting for tickets.

CHAPTER 50

AND THE STORY GOES ON

"Stories you read when you're the right age never quite leave you. You may forget who wrote them or what the story was called. Sometimes you'll forget precisely what happened, but if a story touches you it will stay with you, haunting the places in your mind that you rarely ever visit."
(Neil Gaiman, M Is for Magic)

MICAWBER *had a love-hate relationship with PARADOX.*

Lousy luck had brought him here. Or was it fate? His last business went under after someone posted a negative review online. It only took two hours before a thousand people saw the report. By teatime, the view count went up to five thousand, plus comments. After that, people stopped turning up to his pride and joy. Apparently, his rides were old fashioned. The funfair racked up a hefty amount of debt. Micawber tried to find the money to pay off the loans but kept coming up short. The collectors sensed blood with their foreclosure-notice teeth. One day before the deadline, an elderly lady turned up and offered to buy out the business. She had always wanted a funfair and apparently this one was perfect. The lady gave him an excellent deal. He told her that She was paying over the odds, but the lady insisted. For his honesty, She offered a bonus payment. All he had to do was a keep a promise. 'On my next visit, you can't refuse to hear my job offer.' It was an odd promise to make, but Micawber needed the sale to go through. He also factored in that the lady was old. Death's door was close by.

A pocketful of cash brought him to PARADOX. This shop was up for sale. The owner wanted to remain anonymous but was willing to accept offers for a quick sale. Micawber sent in his bid, a very low bid. Two days later, he received the keys to the place. He first tried selling kitchen equipment. Everyone cooks, right? Not in this town. Next was a clothes boutique, but fashion was never Micawber's forte. A supermarket followed next, then a chemist. Each one, a failure. The town folk didn't seem interested in either him or his shop. When every idea came up short, a visitor turned up.

The elderly lady had returned to remind Micawber of his promise.

The job was both interesting and odd.

He was only to stock items in his shop that travellers had lost or discarded. It wasn't a hard thing to do. There were plenty of objects on The Paths. The problem lay with the next part of the promise. He was never to sell any of the goods. This lost and found treasure trove was free. The inevitable question followed: how to make money? All expenses covered. That suited him fine. And so began the strange business. Occasionally, a traveller would return and claim their item, but on most occasions the visitors would stare at a once treasured object then walk out with a pained expression. There was never a dull day. Micawber went on lots of wild adventures to claim those mysterious items. He could have written a book or two. He just hadn't found the time. Yet.

The old lady visited once a month, checking how things were going. He didn't mind her subtle interference or long chats. She had a way of communicating that made everything feel like a story. Over time Micawber pieced together the reason for doing his strange job.

PARADOX was never the same for him after that.

It was taking longer than expected for Eki to reach The Seven Dials.

The warning tug inside her refused to go away. Usually, she would have listened to its cry, but not today. Desperate times, desperate measures. She needed to get back to PARADOX. Her compromise was to stay in the shadows, taking a few detours to buy time. She needed to prepare herself for whatever was waiting at the other end. The tug got stronger as she turned into Earlham Street. One more minute and the monument would be in sight. Her feet dragged along the evening pavement.

'Listen to your inner voice. It's always served you well.'

She winced at the thought. Her inner voice hadn't always served her well. It screwed everything up in The Theatre. She was determined not to make the same mistake again, especially after finding that her chess piece was still in the game. All she needed to do was to claim her ticket back to PARADOX and that non-stop pass was waiting for her at the monument. The Twins, hiding in the one place everyone expected them to avoid.

Except.

Her ticket wasn't there. The Twins had already left, but someone else was sitting in their place. Waiting. The tug suddenly disappeared. There was no more need for it any more. Eki paused before walking over to her.

She.

The Storyteller.

*****

11:00pm

Pevensie raced back towards to The London Library. The phone call had changed everything. He had expected Tshilaba to eventually help him. But so soon? She had found them. The good news was they were alive and well. He couldn't contain his nervous excitement as he arrived outside the building. Tshilaba was sitting on the steps outside.

"Are they in there?"

"I'm good. A little cold, but OK. Thanks for asking."

The flustered face of Pevensie turned a deeper shade of embarrassed red. Sweat poured down his forehead and neck as his short intakes of breath buttered out an apology. Tshilaba absorbed the moment.

"You need to exercise."

"Got enough running here."

Pevensie rushed up the steps and gripped the handle.

"Wait! They're fragile. You can't just go barging in. It's not right to demand this of them. They have a choice. You understand that, right?"

Pevensie nodded, but couldn't promise. He wanted this to work. Every previous move today hinged upon this meeting. If everything fell into place, his job was complete. The only thing left was to return to PARADOX and face the consequence of what he had done over the last twenty-four hours. Tshilaba sensed his worry. She stood up, kissing him on his flustered cheek.

"It will be fine."

A half-smile broke out on his face. Their brother and sister-like friendship went back a long way. Both of them worked together over the years, covering each other's back when things got tricky. They had spoken to each other at great lengths concerning Pevensie's decision. Taking sides meant he could no longer perform his role as messenger between opposing camps. That decision impacted more than just his job. The ripple effects would be felt on every relationship, including their precious friendship. Tshilaba wasn't worried – on the surface. They had been in worst scrapes than this one.

"Remember the time when we helped that Paramedic enter The Theatre through the side entrance?"

"Sally."

"Yes, that's her name. Well, we got through that unscathed, even if it did mean keeping ourselves hidden for a while."

Pevensie nodded, but not fully convinced.

"Serendipity. It could have turned ugly if it wasn't for her being on call that night. Finding those two bodies in the woodland circle would have broken the hardest of hearts. We got Sally into The Theatre that night already changed."

"Exactly. And we can do it again."

"Except this time there's no hiding my loyalty."

"And She will protect you. Us."

"It's not The Magician I'm worried about."

Tshilaba knew what her friend was referring to. She carried the same fear. Pevensie quickly changed the subject.

"How did you know The Twins would be in the library?"

Tshilaba touched her nose.

"Mystery."

Pevensie looked put-out. She knew it would get a reaction, so waited a few seconds to put him out of his teased misery.

"You should have figured it out yourself. The destination always starts at the beginning. That's where mystery first plants the seed."

"And?"

He could tell it wasn't the full story.

"And a visitor helped as well. She was an elderly lady this time. I liked the new image."

"But why would The Twins come back here?"

"Isn't it obvious? Their story hasn't finished yet."

Tshilaba pulled out a long, iron key and opened the door. Mystery has a way of doing that to something locked. Pevensie held her back.

"Listen. About that Paramedic. Her story. How she found those two bodies."

"I know. I thought I saw them in the shadows too."

Micawber lived up to the code of having 'no favourites'.

He considered every traveller a friend, and because he took an interest in every story, the shopkeeper was willing to do anything to help. That included travelling to the furthest edges of PARADOX to find those lost and discarded items. He believed in second chances. And third. Fourth.

There were no set amount of visits for each person, but he could often tell when the journey was on the final leg. Peccadillo was one such case. His last visit carried all those hallmarks. How could a person undo what had happened with Santiago? Then came the visit from The Storyteller, telling him to see if there was anything outside The Theatre. It was obvious that there was something waiting for him. Micawber obeyed, finding the iron door knocker on the bottom step. He hadn't seen that pawn-shaped item in a long time. What he didn't factor in was the surprise addition.

He knew what to do with the knocker, hand it to Santiago. But the second item? The only thing he could think of was to place it in his shop and wait. Surprise, surprise, Peccadillo was now walking towards him, playing out The Storyteller's move. But it wasn't that simple. It never was. He knew not to take the old lady at face value. The person who posted that first negative review online about his funfair was the one and only Storyteller. She orchestrated every move to get him to this place. And now She was doing the same thing again. Moving pieces.

But to what end?

CHAPTER 51
MICAWBER'S SHOP

"'Gentlemen,' returned Mr Micawber, 'do with me as you will! I am a straw upon the surface of the deep and am tossed in all directions by the elephants – I beg your pardon; I should have said the elements."
(Charles Dickens, David Copperfield)

ODD.

It was the first thing that came to mind as I stood inside Micawber's shop. The second word. Sinister. This enchanted emporium could have been designed inside the mind of Stephen King. It looked innocent from the outside but was purposely vague about what lay within its shadows. I couldn't shake the sensation that there were more '*Needful Things*' hidden than on display.

The shop had everything and nothing. Mint-scented soap? Of course sir, by the piece of string made out of gently combed horse hair. What about a jewel-encrusted copper kettle? You're in luck. I picked one up yesterday from a travelling salesman on route to the Far East. It's just behind the willow peg basket made by woodland fairies, a chicken coup and a signed baseball card by Justin Verlander. Go Detroit Tigers. There was a strange sound in the air, making the hairs on my skin stand up with an electric charge. The soft whispers came from the crooked shelves around the store. Not just one voice, a chorus. Haunting. Lamenting. Travellers' tales, recounting hopes and regrets.

Micawber's gaze tracked my every move. His eyes had the discomforting touch of lust rubbing across my skin, opposite to his cheery, almost cartoonish appearance. Round face. Round belly. Almost round arms and legs. His stumpy, wriggling fingers adjusted small oval glasses as his plump, red cheeks acted as a safety net for a nose too chubby to hold the thick lenses in place. Innocent on the outside. Purposely vague about what lay within his shadow.

"You like what you see?"

He eagerly waited my reply. Micawber's little feet shuffled in excitement as his fingers once again adjusted his glasses. With each passing second of silence he struggled to contain any sense of verbal control, eventually snapping as the invisible clock hand reached half-a-minute.

"I mean to say. Well. That. I hope you like what you see. This IS the shop of the one and only Micawber. Not exactly the one and only. That would be a silly statement, wouldn't it? There are obviously others who share the same name. For example, Jerry Micawber who runs the sweet shop in the next town. Then there's Catherine Doreen-Micawber, the one who insists on using her double-barrelled name on every letterhead. She's the town planner. Oh, the number of times I have forgotten to call her by the correct..."

Micawber pressed pause on his lips. This verbal rabbit hole he had fallen down had made him forget why he first started the conversation. His eyeballs moved up and to the right as he tried to find helpful hints in the recesses of his mind. Two blinks later and he was back on track.

"Yes. The greeting. I was welcoming you to this humble place of mine. Well, maybe not humble. That word can sometimes imply inferior or low quality. These items are certainly neither of those descriptions. You would not believe some of the…"

Micawber caught himself.

"Ha! Forgive me. I get excited whenever a visitor turns up. Non-stop talking you know."

He took a deep intake of air. Then another. I shuddered as the whispering sounds of travellers' tales lingered behind his panting, almost round, breath.

Act? Not an act?

Micawber struggled to tell any more. When he first opened the store, his performance of a bumbling shopkeeper encouraged people to drop their guard. How else would he get unfettered access into the hearts of all the travellers? But over time, fact and fiction blurred together. He put it down to three things.

Reason one: the items in his store. Finding lost or discarded objects on The Paths may have been exciting, but there was a catch. Each had a story attached to them. Micawber could hear every whisper of joy and pain. He had no one else to blame except himself for allowing those voices inside his head. Detaching himself from work would have been the easy solution, but he considered that disrespectful. These were the lives of people he had placed on the shelves. Their stories were remarkable. Why would he silence their voice?

Reason two: excitement. He loved putting a face to the story. When a traveller turned up to his store, Micawber already knew their backstory inside out. The conversations that followed would bring him up to date with recent developments. It was a human version of binge-watching a whole TV season in one sitting. Often the travellers never recognised him, even if they had visited his store three, five, ten times before. That was hard, but he was OK with it. This shop was never about himself. Some visits were short. Others prolonged. The saddest part was watching everyone leave for The Theatre. They were family. Or were they prized collections?

Reason three: addiction. This one worried him the most. He was hooked on stories. Micawber tried to control the craving but rarely succeeded. The excitement of seeing people come through the door was rarely that innocent. He lusted after their news; every detail sucked up through a small paper tube. If that didn't get into the body fast enough, then he would find ways of injecting it directly into the bloodstream. That explained the voices of past travellers that lingered in every pant of breath. Sometimes he would wake up at night not sure if he was dreaming his dreams or that of others. The Storyteller warned him not to get too close.

"When you see behind the veil, you can't help but go deeper inside."

Micawber learnt the hard way. Once he was that deep there was no way he would turn his back on their journey. Rain or shine. Joy or tears. He was with them all the way. Looking back, his 'hits' started from the right motive. Micawber wanted to help the travellers, especially as they climbed

The Theatre steps. But just like a seasoned junkie, his assistance also ended up with being too high even to say goodbye.

So what was the reason for his loose mind today? One, two or three?

Micawber couldn't decide. His dry lips twitched with the prospect of another 'hit'. Peccadillo's story had been a fascinating one, especially after what had happened with Santiago. He lived off that injection into the bloodstream for weeks. But the crash hit him hard. Then came the knock on the door from the old lady telling him to collect those two items. What a beautiful move, under the radar and away from prying eyes. That sweet needle was sharp and thin, just how he liked it. Inside those objects was a story so pure and fresh that his body lusted for its Sicilian Defence touch. Victory in defeat. But it had been out reach, locked away, until Peccadillo's return. And now that the traveller was here, Micawber would do anything for his fresh tale.

STOP.

He was better than this. Junkie or no junkie, his heart still had a bit of dignity left in it. He loved that Peccadillo was back. The last time the traveller walked up those Theatre steps, Micawber had been face-down on the shop floor. Next to him, an empty needle; the story of Santiago's betrayal injected into his blood. It always pained him that he never got to say goodbye. Today was that moment. There had been a new move on the board. He couldn't quite understand what was going on, but it felt good. 'The ultimate hit.'

Maybe The Twins would finally get their hands on Santiago after all.

CHAPTER 52
ORDER IN CHAOS

"Chaos was the law of nature; Order was the dream of man."
(Henry Adams, The Education of Henry Adams)

IT WAS BY ACCIDENT that my foot kicked the wooden fruit box.

I apologised, then bent down to straighten up the container. Inside was a collection of vinyl recordings. Every one of them, the dreaded 'second album'. I pulled out a few. Nirvana's *Nevermind.* Radiohead's *The Bends.* Van Morrison's *Astral Weeks.* I smiled at the subtle compilation, admiring the person who had put it together. Each recording had stuck up two fingers to the age-old myth that an artist couldn't better their first outing. Second chances. Never underestimate them. Putting the records back I wished it could be true for everything. My eyes moved along to the next crate, hoping to find another profound moment. All I got in return for such longing was disappointment. This box was full of different sized screws and the odd nail. The story of my life.

I couldn't get my head around this shop. And yet the place had an ordered chaos to it. There were no matching display cabinets or shelving units. Figurines lay hidden behind kitchen utensils, while books found a space next to electrical leads. If I wanted to locate any postage stamps, then I needed to look towards the toy car collection next to the little glass statue of the Eiffel Tower. The store operated a strange loyalty card scheme. Serendipity. I had to trust in its magical power. The shop asked for patience and an open mind. I had neither as I carried on walking through its chaotic lanes. Frustration was building up inside. It wasn't the disorder that was bugging me, but the sensation that I was close to something. Had I been here before? It felt like it. I turned around to ask Micawber but never got around to opening my mouth.

My eyes spotted a desk in the far corner. This flat-pack, mass-produced piece of crap wasn't anything special to look at. On top were three piles of scrap paper and trashy magazines, the only thing worth keeping on something so worthless. Yet I couldn't take my eyes off it. No matter where I explored, I kept glancing back to its unimaginative design. A question teased my mind. What was inside those drawers? The left one. No. Right. Bottom right. I could feel its presence. Calling me.

I couldn't hold out any longer, rushing over to open the drawer. Curiosity led me to the desk, but fandom kept me there. I couldn't believe what was in front of my eyes. Inside the drawer was a treasure trove of memorabilia. A shrine to Charles Dickens, crammed full of his notebooks and rough drafts. My heart was already skipping a few beats as I cleared the work surface and laid out the papers. On the desk was an ink tapestry of how the mind of Dickens worked. It was all there: his motivations for writing a story, the rationale for plot lines, and the ideas that formed his beloved characters. What writer wouldn't want to throw themselves into this sea of creativity?

I could think of one as I stared down at four words.

Micawber watched with interest.

Peccadillo had found the second item, but there was a subtle difference between finding and observing. He wasn't worried. It was only a matter of time; he could already taste the intensity of emotions seeping out of Peccadillo's pores. His tongue licked the edge of his cracked lips. The changing atmosphere in the store tasted sweet. A new chapter in a person's story always had spoonfuls of sugary anticipation. His body quivered with delight. And worry. He was finding it hard to keep his lust under control. The dark shadows in his mind were creating images of claiming what was rightfully his. He owned this story, not Peccadillo. The traveller had given up that right long ago when he threw his tale away for what was in that repulsive building across the square. Who had stayed up in the midnight hours, listening to the whisper's lament over lost hope? Micawber. Who had found the traveller's story and treated it with respect? Who knew the true worth of that injection into life's bloodstream? Micawber. Micawber. And how dare Peccadillo take that beauty away from him! This was his moment. HIS. A self-inflicted pinch on the skin brought sense back to his raging mind. He needed to keep control. It would be a travesty if everything collapsed now, just because he couldn't keep his desires in check. He edged closer to the desk. Micawber wanted to see where Peccadillo's curiosity had taken him. His friend and holder of the ultimate 'hit' was pressing his fingers hard down on the page. Blood drained from his shaking fingers. Had he seen it? God, he hoped so.

Micawber needed this new chapter as much as his friend.

Four words.

'Ignorance and Selfish Want.'

The lines of ink pierced into my heart, its judgemental stare refusing to look away. I knew those words well. It was a narrative masterstroke from Dickens when those four words took their starring role in *A Christmas Carol.* The Ghost of Christmas Present had just taken Scrooge on a shocking tour, laying open the hidden stories of pain that people, strangers and friends were living with. Scrooge's unrepentant heart needed a helping hand. Emerging from under the cloak of the spiritual guide came two malnourished children: *Ignorance* and *Selfish Want*. In just one scene, Dickens declared to every reader why injustice flowed throughout the streets of society. For humanity's inner-Scrooge to find redemption, the heart must decide to live a different way. Love's demand: it eradicates our ignorance and selfish desires.

It was my favourite scene in the book. I'd always wanted to write something so hard-hitting and concise. Maybe that's why Leech's illustration of the two children, *That* image, stuck in my head. And now that horrific picture was back. This time as four words. But it said the same thing.

Nobody wants to think of themselves as a modern day Scrooge.

"You see it, don't you? Dickens' scallop shell. All roads lead back to one destination."

Micawber was right. Every scribbled plot and story arc on these pages had a line of ink leading back to those four haunting words. My finger rubbed along Dickens' rough ideas for *Hard Times, Bleak House, A Tale of Two Cities* and *Great Expectations.* Did all these stories have...? It couldn't be. I was struggling to take in what was in front of me. The elegant prose and haphazard statements revealed a man on the verge of madness. Whatever he was planning on these pages carried a weight too heavy to bear. The rough outlines continued... *Oliver Twist. Little Dorrit. Edwin Drood. A Christmas Carol.*

And.

Every story had the same characters. *IGNORANCE* and *SELFISH WANT.* Circled. Underlined. Dickens deeply cared for these two people, evident by the softness of his pen. They might have looked different in each story, even had their names changed. But they were there. In the books.

The Twins.

CHAPTER 53
POUNDING THE STREETS

"There lay, in an old egg-box, which the mother had begged from a shop, a feeble, wasted, wan, sick child. With his little wasted face... and his little bright attentive eyes, I can see him now, as I have seen him for several years, looking steadily at us. There he lay in his little frail box, which was not at all a bad emblem of the little body from which he was slowly parting – there he lay quite quiet, quite patient, saying never a word... He lay there, seeming to wonder what it was all about. God knows, I thought, as I stood looking at him, he had his reasons for wondering – and why, in the name of a gracious God, such things should be."

(Charles Dickens, speech on 9th February 1858, before his reading of A Christmas Carol)

DEEP THOUGHT.

That's how Dickens described his moments of meditation. His world had changed because of four words. And now, in his twilight years, he was once again wondering whether he could put an end to the chains of regret around his heart.

Dickens took a deep breath, followed by his face wincing in pain. The burning sensation inside his ribcage was getting worse. Not long now. The doctor's visit had not delivered good news. But there was a strange comfort in that. He had nothing to lose now by going back to The Theatre. One last visit. And this time, he wouldn't fail. CHIME. CHIME. The sound of the clock on the mantelpiece flung his mind into the past.

"I was pounding the streets when I heard the sound."

His whisper was soft as he flicked through an index card of memories.

There was no such thing as a mindless stroll.

The young Dickens devoured the streets, hating the idea that a journey was just getting from a-to-b. Life happens within the cracks. He put his religious fervour to soak in every sight and sound down to his broken childhood. How many times had people passed by him when he had worked in a shop window as a child? Forget the idea that children were seen but never heard.

The sound of The Applause came in the form of an elderly lady. She was holding a sick child that was hours, maybe minutes from meeting the cruel God that had allowed such injustice to happen. The young body was malnourished. He had one of those coughs common within the backstreets of London. The pitiful sight was enough to break his heart. Minutes later, Dickens returned with some food. The lady was too old to be the child's mother, yet cared for the wasted being as though it was her very own. She had a way of telling a story that made him feel relaxed and at peace. He had only closed his eyes for a moment. Opening them, he wasn't in London any more.

That had been the first visit to The Theatre, but it wouldn't be his last.

On his return from PARADOX, Dickens looked for the elderly lady and child. Gone. There were so many questions that needed answers. Also regrets. His devouring walks through London occasionally glimpsed the old lady. One day She was sitting on a bench. Another time, feeding the ducks in the park. Dickens would run over to her, but by the time he arrived, She had disappeared.

The return from The Theatre had been tough on Dickens. Every day he pounded the streets, trying to understand what he had seen. And every walk just added to his frustration. But all that changed when he bumped into her again playing chess. She guided him to two scruffy children. They were in plain view and yet easily missed by hundreds of people walking by. It was like Dickens was back in the shop window of that blackening factory all over again. Why were people so blind? The two children introduced themselves as The Twins. Their faces were young, innocent, full of life and hope for the future. But their stories were the opposite. They told tales of living on the streets as if their hearts were carrying the hurts and injustice of the unseen many. Dickens couldn't just leave them there, but The Twins refused that kind of help. They had a different proposition.

A weekly walk.

The strange partnership started every Monday at 11.00am. Dickens would bring food. They would eat, then venture onto the streets. The Twins opened up London like a map, taking him to places he never knew existed. Such pain. In open view. Everything Dickens saw and experienced, filtered back into his writings. His words received high praise, his insights into society were put on a high pedestal. But it was never down to him alone. The secret ingredient was always the two children.

Dickens loved them as his own family. That's why he struggled as the walks continued. The Twins were dying. With each weekly outing, the life of those precious children slowly drained away. No matter how much Dickens pleaded for them to stop, they refused. There was a determination from them to show him the very things that were destroying their fragile lives.

All that Dickens could do was watch. And then write.

A Christmas Carol.

But he couldn't finish it. His second journey into PARADOX had made him forget the deeper storyline. He questioned what he was doing. Soon, he stopped turning up to the weekly walks. The manuscript would have gone into the bin if it hadn't been for the elderly lady leaving the bundle of tatty papers at the grave. His journal, outlining everything he had learnt on The Paths.

When Dickens found The Twins again, their bodies were eaten with disease. He tried to help them, bringing doctors and politicians over to their alleyway home. There was no miracle cure. Most of the people informed him he was going mad.

"No one is there ... It is just your imagination ... Take a holiday and rest your mind."

Rarely did people see the two children. But an illustrator did. John Leech. He brought over blankets and food with every visit. The Twins were appreciative, but they were more interested in another form of help from Leech. A picture. That image.

It was all part of their plan to help end The Theatre show.

There was no popping of the cork when A Christmas Carol went on sale. The Twins had disappeared. Without warning. Leech and Dickens pounded the streets for days trying to find them. By the end of the week it was clear that the children had gone. For good. Everywhere Dickens walked, the streets echoed their lives. That image. He couldn't avoid it. The only comforting thought was knowing that's how The Twins would have wanted it. Their story. In plain sight.

The third trip back to PARADOX coincided with hearing news about the book sales for A Christmas Carol. They were impressive figures. Dickens entered The Theatre thinking the plan would finally work. But he underestimated the power of what was on stage. The only thing that followed was failure. Again.

And again.

And again.

Over the years, telling the stories of The Twins in every one of his books was his way of helping others not to fall for the same damn trick. There were good days; he saw political change. Businesses adopted fairer work practices; and things like food distribution and healthcare provision filtered into the forgotten backstreets of the city. His passion for child safety brought dramatic shifts in public awareness. Some even declared this was a golden age of social transformation. But every day another tale would filter through the cracks, letting him know that the trick was still as strong as ever.

He needed another move.

CHIME.

The memories faded. Dickens slowly opened his eyes. It was time. He tried to stand up before collapsing back into his chair. A shot of pain went through his left side. His body was fighting a losing battle. All sides knew it and that's what he was counting on. Against doctor's orders, he had continued with his reading tour. Every element of his writings led up to this moment. His swan song.

His final move against The Magician.

Dickens tried standing again. This time, success. Gingerly, he walked over to the fireplace and picked up the picture from the mantelpiece. He wiped off the thick layer of dust. That image. It was in plain sight now. Even though it was no bigger than a postcard, this picture could fill the world with stories. Leech had captured The Twins well. People needed to see what their hearts, his heart, had done to those two little children.

THUD. THUD. THUD. Footsteps, climbing the stairs.

The smile on his face eased the pain. Dickens knew The Magician was already writing the author's obituary. At the grand old age of fifty-seven, the expected thing to do was to sip brandy and happily watch the world screw itself through a window of retirement. But that wasn't Dickens. And The Magician would never expect the move coming up. Against great expectations, Dickens had found The Twins again. He might be weak, but the game wasn't over. The Sicilian Defence. Victory in weakness.

All the ravages of old age dropped off Dickens as the study door opened. It was good to see their childhood faces. They embraced, shared laughter, even tears. The three of them were about to do their weekly walk again, pounding the streets. It was time to remind the readers that every story has a Change Agent.

That image.

The Twins stood at the back of the building.

Dickens, old and frail, was about to give his Christmas Carol reading to the hushed audience. They were ready for the famous Marley opening line. But it didn't come. Dickens started with a different story, something he had used many times on his tour. His tale was about an elderly lady holding a dying child. The introduction gave a context to why he wrote the Christmas adventure. Nobody expected it. But every ear was attentive. Dickens ended his tale with four words. After that. Silence.

And then.

A sound. In the distance. Dickens looked towards the back of the building. The Twins were smiling. The Applause.

There was hope after all.

CHAPTER 54
COURT IN SESSION

"Deserves it! I daresay he does. Many that live deserve death. And some that die deserve life. Can you give it to them? Then do not be too eager to deal out death in judgement. For even the very wise cannot see all ends."

(J.R.R. Tolkien, The Fellowship of the Ring)

ENOUGH.

I didn't want to think about those four words any more. If this shop wanted to remind me of the regret ravaging my body, then it had come too late to this party of self-inflicted hell. I couldn't take any more, but as I lifted my hands off the page an invisible force pushed them back down. Shock, then fear gripped my skin. Underneath my fingers I could feel the four words wriggling around. They were trying to break free. My fingers moved up and down as these black-inked characters clawed themselves onto the surface before rolling across the page like fish out of water. I stared down in horror as beetle-like creatures writhed in agony, giving birth to four, six, then eight legs. They scurried across the page, relishing their moment of freedom. Suddenly, they turned around, their legs, pounding the papyrus surface in a static march. They were waiting in excited anticipation, ready for orders. For what? A call. Coming from my chest. A deep rumble? No. The sound of clapping in an echoing chamber.

Ignorance
and
Selfish Want

They lurched forwards. Their legs, running up my fingers then across my arm. Sharp claws dug into me. Footprints of congealed ink and blood trailed across my skin. I tried again to raise my hand, but the page's grip only tightened. Frantically, I waved my head from side to side as their continual pounding burrowed their jagged feet into my neck. The creatures moved up my face. They circled my eyes as though my pupils were a warming fire in the night-time air. Slowly and orderly, each one inched their way forward. Two of the creatures stretched out their legs, pinning my eyelids back. The remaining beetles opened their mouths and dripped warm ink into my eyes. I screamed in terror as everything went black. There was a tug from the page. My hand sank into its grip. Then my arm. Chest. Body.

Dragged.

Into the darkness.

*****

I knew this place.

The photo frames with torn-off calendar dates inside gave it away. Why was I back in Roho's cell?

"Judgement of your heart."

The preacher man was gingerly putting up a new frame with today's date.

"Funny what we remember and how quickly we forget."

KNOCK. KNOCK. I frantically spun around.

"You better let them in."

"Who?"

"Your guests."

Roho paused, considering his words. He turned around to rectify his mistake.

"Prosecutors."

*****

The sight of Peccadillo's slumped body over the desk would have shocked many.

Not Micawber. He had seen this scene many times. In a few minutes the traveller would wake up, but for Peccadillo it would feel like hours. Torturous hours. The shopkeeper gently lifted his friend's head and placed a pillow underneath. A small comfort for a painful journey. God knows he would need it.

"Urrghh."

The murmur indicated that the court session had begun. Would this time be any different? He hoped it would. Micawber let out a long, tired sigh. So much hinged upon this moment. Yet all he could think about was self-hatred for how his lust for a continuing storyline overshadowed his concern for a friend's soul. But that's what he was – a junkie who would sell anything for a fix. Except... This story carried something beyond the broken needles and temporary highs. There was a tale behind the tale, one that spoke of grace. Micawber could never understand why The Storyteller pinned so much faith on this illogical idea of countless chances. Too many people had used the excuse of pressing reset to repeat the same mistakes, over and over again. But Micawber had to keep hoping that grace would work its magic. He too needed another chance.

Grace.

*****

The Twins stood in front of me.

Gone were their young, innocent faces. Their malnourished bodies looked terrifying. *That* image's nightmarish disease had touched every part of their skin. Burst blisters had spread a layer of hardened puss over their arms and legs. A stomach-churning odour lingered from the open wounds. One of the boy's feet had a cut spanning his heel. There was a piece of glass sticking out from the injury. The infection was already spreading across the foot. Two of his toes had no nails. A stream of blood trickled onto the floor. Heavy laden eyes told the tale of sleepless nights. His broken teeth and discoloured enamel hid behind cracked lips covered with flesh-eating scabs. The girl's face was almost identical to her brother's. Except. Her eyes told of a horror beyond just sleepless nights. I didn't want to know, but that was all part of her pain. It wasn't that she had no voice to cry out for help; I, the world, just wasn't listening to her. My stomach heaved at their pitiful sight, not knowing if I should feel disgust or compassion. These children existed, but this wasn't a life worth living.

The girl smiled with anticipation. Her cracked lips broke a layer of skin sending a trickle of dark blood down her chin. She didn't mind the stab of pain. The girl had waited a long time to stand face to face in this room. A rush of panic seized my body as she raised her scar-covered arm above her head. The axe? Relief. Short-lived. Her hand was empty, but it did bring down a terrifying blow. She rubbed her rough palm along my cheek. I stepped back, sickened by her diseased touch.

"Have you figured it out yet?"

Her breath was stale, as though she had tasted the evilest and most disgusting things of a human soul, then swirled it around in her mouth. She leant in closer. I could hear the air running up and down the trackways of her nose, dragging with it the loose mucus of sickness and death. And behind that repulsive sound, another. Clapping.

"Look around."

"He will never get it."

The boy chipped in, watching me scan the room for hints. Roho? He had taken his seat behind the desk. The poor man looked weary. Another round of beating had recently taken place. What about the pictures? There must be something about the latest addition with today's date. My eyes darted between the two doors. One led to the workhouse. And the other one?

"Want a hint?"

"That's cheating."

The young girl gave a stern look back at the boy. He stopped his protest.

"A little clue… You know the owner of this room."

I still didn't understand. The young boy hobbled up, examining the confused look on my face. Satisfied, he turned and faced his sister.

"Told you he would never figure it out. He doesn't even recognise his own..."

The boy caught his loose tongue. I looked at him, the girl. Then the old man. It couldn't be. The girl continued.

"Welcome to our case against you. The human heart is a fantastic thing. It can store the most precious or violent of thoughts. What we allow in here brings us comfort or an endless torture which beats our flesh to a pulp. You want to know what beast would do such a thing to Roho?"

I didn't want to answer back. Keeping silent kept reality at bay. The girl refused my feeble attempt.

"Let me introduce you to him. YOU! And if YOU did this to your own heart, how worse is your cruelty to those around?"

I stumbled back, falling to the floor. My hands and feet scrambled to the far corner of the room.

"No. No. You're wrong."

"Look at this pathetic creature, still not owning up to what he has done to himself and others."

There was a look behind the bloodshot eyes of the boy. Pure hatred. He loathed my refusal to own up to what I had done. And because of that, he craved the gavel of judgement to bang upon the desk. His sister walked over and wiped his pulsating brow.

"It's OK. I know he deserves nothing less than this disease that has ravished our bodies. But *She* won't allow us to judge him. That's her job. Our job is to be the voice of all those he has hurt. Including ourselves."

She turned her gaze towards the second door.

"Here ends our case."

CHAPTER 55
THE CABIN

"You're off to Great Places. Today is your day.
Your mountain is waiting."
(Dr Seuss, Oh, The Places You'll Go)

"AND DO YOU THINK you're guilty?"

Roho's question bounced off the courtroom walls like a repeated record. With each passing echo, its piercing cry pressed harder against my heart. Every framed date confirming what The Twins had just said. My history told the tale of selfish desire. Even my most charitable actions and acclaimed achievements had the bitter aftertaste of putting myself at the core. I wanted the right hand to know what the left hand was doing. And yet. A rush of blood sent my heart into defensive overdrive. This didn't make me an evil man. Everyone is selfish. No one is a saint. Just because I wanted a sniff of recognition or financial security, didn't negate my good deeds. This whole court case was a sham. The only thing beating up my heart was self-pity. But I already doubted this impassioned defence. The prime witness had her own tale to tell about my selfish betrayal. Terri. Hearing the footsteps from behind the second door added to approaching dread of the verdict. My judge and jury were about to arrive. The Storyteller? It had to be. And The Twins were the ones who would then throw away the prison cell key.

Another surge of defensive strength filled my resolve. Screw this court and its bloody judgement. PARADOX had made me out to be someone I wasn't. The only way to survive this charade was to run away. With stumbling feet and staggered breath, I rushed through the other door to the one place that knew how it felt to be on the wrong side of a biased belief.

The Workhouse.

*****

My head jerked backwards.

The painfully slow focusing of my eyes brought with it the disorientating reality that I was back in Micawber's shop. The shopkeeper's narrow pupils had a lust for knowledge which was driving him crazy. His gaze tore through my skin, trying to find clues about what had happened in the courtroom drama. Standing up was harder than I expected. Flashbacks of The Twins' prosecution still had its terrifying hold on me. Knocking the treasured memorabilia to the floor, I rushed towards the front door.

"Wait!"

Micawber's panicked voice attached itself to a grip desperately holding onto hope. Our physical struggle morphed into a fight of words.

"I need to know."

"Get off me."

"Who was there?"

"Let go."

"Tell me."

Our eyes met once again. This time, he got his answer. The redness in his face drained away as he pieced all the unspoken clues together. Seizing the moment while his mind was distracted, I pulled my arm back and flung open the door. I didn't look back, even though his cries to stop carried a genuine tone of concern for me.

His cries intensified as the wind picked up. Without warning, the heavens opened with a downpour of rain. The Piazza instantly became a battleground of flooded drains and overturned bins. Discarded rubbish violently swirled around the square looking for a new home. The elements of nature relished this open canvas as the inhabitants of the town quickly sought cover. In the midst of the howling wind, I could just make out Micawber's plea for me to come back inside. This time I turned around as a moment's doubt halted my run.

Memories.

The familiar swirling leaves and twigs brought home the awful truth of what was happening. My fists clenched onto a hope that I was wrong. Seeing nothing but the wind's destructive force lifted a heavy weight off my shoulders. I could handle the battering of the storm, just as long as there was no... Hope ripped itself from me as it swirled off into the grey clouds. The thing I dreaded, remembered, appeared in front of me.

Micawber watched with a face of devastated hope as the tornado swept over Peccadillo.

As quickly as the storm arrived, it disappeared into nothingness. The only evidence of its existence was his soaked clothes and the tablecloth of destruction scattered across the square. He ran towards the spot where Peccadillo had once stood, praying that somehow the traveller had darted out of the way. But who was he kidding? The only reason the storm had stopped was that it had found its prey. He knew the calling card of The Storyteller well.

His fingers twitched; a familiar sign that his body had already registered the bad news concerning the lost 'hit'. But his inner pain was more than just a junkie's regret. He crumpled to the floor, struggling to come to terms with what had just happened.

Grace.

Finally broken.

There was an end to the countless chances. Micawber dreaded what that meant for his own story. Every day he had held onto a redemptive hope as he stuck another needle into his body. He comforted himself by believing that tomorrow would be the day he would finally kick his habit. But now, as his trembling body curled up on the square, there was no more tomorrow. Just today. And his needle.

He looked across the Piazza towards the two men sitting on the steps. They hadn't left. Come rain or shine, they still clung onto the dream of a returning conductor. Micawber wondered how many chances they had left to work it out. The two men had patiently sat waiting for a ticket, and yet the conductor's new work was already being played out in front of their eyes: The Symphony of Life. But they never noticed a single bar. The Storyteller had given up playing in The Theatre a long time ago. People saw what they wanted to see. For many, She had taken the form of a grand, elegant conductor. Male, of course. The ticket holders deemed one's image important. It was usually the cheap seats that got the real HER, but even then, the lure of the building narrowed their gaze. Taking the symphony to the streets was a way of smashing the frame through which the world so narrowly defined itself. The only catch was that one must first recognise the frame.

Micawber considered walking over to the men, telling them the punchline. Then he had second thoughts, instead heading back to his shop. There's always tomorrow. He gently closed the door and flicked the dangling sign to CLOSED. In one graceful move he pulled down the window blind and turned off the lights. The darkness covered his tears, but it never muffled his cry.

His inner demons had finally come out to play.

Where was I?

On a bench. Opening my eyes would have provided more answers, but for the first time in this crazy world, I felt at peace. Above me I could hear the sound of wind chimes. The soothing tone floated on the waves of a cool breeze. I breathed in the fresh, clean air as the evening rays of the sun warmed my face. Tranquillity. I adjusted my position and felt the bench swing to a new rhythm. The surprise made me open my eyes and sit up. A thick patterned quilt covered the white wooden planks, making it ideal for cool summer evenings staring into a sunset. This homemade piece of furniture was a thing of beauty, something to hand down from generation to generation. It carried a history; stories of evening hours staring into the horizon. I rubbed my palm along the edge. And what stories would it keep from me?

CHIME. CHIME.

The wooden porch was the perfect size for a gathering of friends – an outdoor living room that had 'welcome' written all over it. It was a place of rest.

Somewhere to think. A home of safety. Opposite me was a rocking chair, older than the swing bench. The battered wooden frame had seen its fair share of use, but it was still going strong. Beside it, there was a small table with a half-finished glass of lemonade. Homemade? Had to be. This whole place screamed of authenticity.

The cabin was in the middle of a fruit orchard. I breathed in the citrus fragrance that lingered in the breeze. My mind went back to days of youth when seeing such a field meant only one thing. Adventure. I missed those days. Why did I ever give them up? Sitting on the porch had stripped back life to its most beautiful and profound beauty. Simplicity.

CHIME. CHIME.

I leant back, letting the natural swing of the bench gently rock me into a blissful state. Thinking. Dreaming. Remembering. Trott? The Chimes. Didn't they call people to see something? CHIME. What did they want me to see now? CHIME.

"That's a simple question to answer."

I sat upright, my back straight like a plank of wood. The voice came from behind the cabin door. It opened. Footsteps. Then a face.

"The chimes want you to see me."

CHAPTER 56
SHE

"I don't know if you've ever noticed this, but first impressions are often entirely wrong."
(Lemony Snicket, The Bad Beginning)

"FRESH LEMONADE?"

The elderly lady hobbled towards me, precariously balancing a wooden tray. I offered to help. The look *She* gave back to me revealed her displeasure at the subtle suggestion of not being up to the task. I apologised. Seconds later, a sly smile broke out on her heavily wrinkled black face. *She* had a sense of humour.

There was a unique look to her. The small, wire-framed glasses that balanced on the end of her nose had a frayed piece of string looped around her neck. Practical, but not visually appealing. A ribbon would have worked better. But it was clear *She* didn't care what people thought about her image. Her jumble sale clothes had taken one garment from every stall and decade. The eighties, power-shoulder-pad shirt hung above a flower-patterned skirt from the seventies. Her trusted ball of frayed string came in useful again, this time as a makeshift belt. Crumpled around her ankles were green woollen tights. I could only see a few inches, as the dress followed the rule of 'below the knee only'. They had seen better days. Fluff balls outnumbered the small rips, which themselves outnumbered the repairs.

However odd those clothes looked, it was the shawl that stood out. Unlike everything else, this hand-woven Middle Eastern garment was spotless. My mind played back the time in the oasis, passing the magical bazaars and whispered tales of the desert. There was a mystery woven into its fabric. A ripple of light danced between each strand. Alive. Hypnotic. And talking. It was as if I was listening behind a wall to a room full of people. I couldn't make out what they were saying but could sense the diverse range of emotions. Some voices were happy. Others, sad. There were cries of fear alongside statements of hope. If this was the person I thought it was, it made sense that *She* carried those stories with her. The old lady adjusted the shawl around her shoulders. My eyes blinked and the spell fell silent.

"Lemonade? It's fresh, you know. Homemade."

I picked up the glass from the wobbling tray, not taking my eyes off her. The old lady walked back to the rocking chair, then paused. Her eyes focused on the table with the half-drunk lemonade.

"The last time you were here, you asked me who I was before I even took a sip. Why the wait?"

"I don't know."

The answer came out without a second thought. It seemed silly to acknowledge that I already knew the answer.

"I am indeed who you think I am. But your heart already told you that, didn't it? So you waited because of something else."

I took a sip of lemonade. A sugar rush set off a volcano of energy inside me. An unseen but felt force hurtled through my veins, like a chorus of voices funnelled down narrow lanes. My lips twitched, eager to sound out each passing tale. Nothing came out. The old lady expected nothing less. *She* nodded, then settled herself into the chair, struggling to get the cushion just right.

"Stories are hard to speak out. I think it's because they reveal a truth, and often we wish to stay within our comfortable world of fiction. What do you think?"

My lips had a dentist-like numbness to them now. *She* took a moment to stare back at me, pressing pause on her quest for comfort.

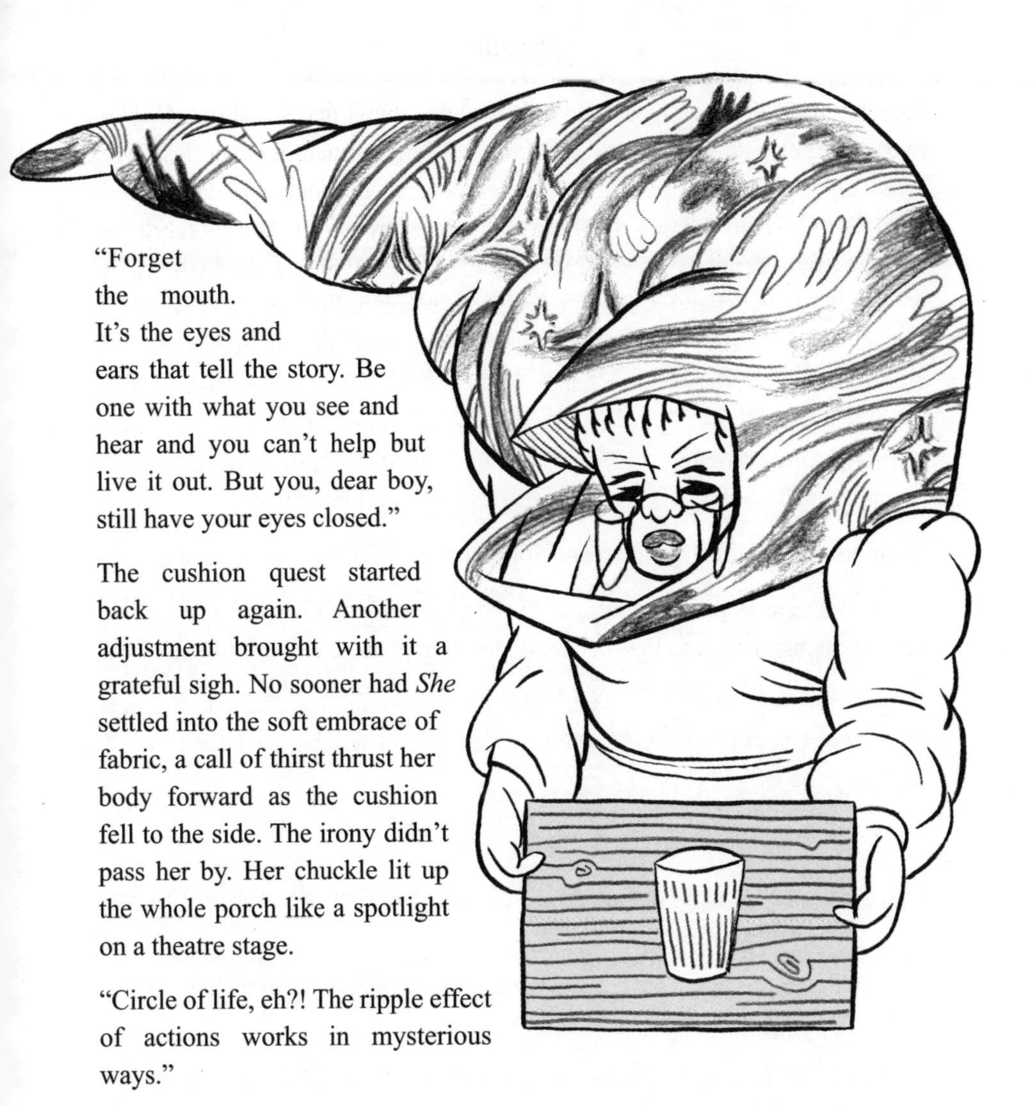

"Forget the mouth. It's the eyes and ears that tell the story. Be one with what you see and hear and you can't help but live it out. But you, dear boy, still have your eyes closed."

The cushion quest started back up again. Another adjustment brought with it a grateful sigh. No sooner had *She* settled into the soft embrace of fabric, a call of thirst thrust her body forward as the cushion fell to the side. The irony didn't pass her by. Her chuckle lit up the whole porch like a spotlight on a theatre stage.

"Circle of life, eh?! The ripple effect of actions works in mysterious ways."

She took a long gulp of lemonade; this time, finishing off the glass. The pursuit of clearing the dregs from the bottom revealed her secret of false teeth. Just like her clothes, *She* wasn't bothered about image. *She* happily allowed the teeth to fall to one side as she angled the glass for that final conquest. The finishing touch, a vacuum suck verging on blowing a raspberry. Satisfied, *She* placed her empty drink back on the tray.

"Dora. That's what you can call me. I know that many like to refer to me as The Storyteller, but come on. It's just like calling yourself The Magician or The Guide. Official twaddle. I prefer something simple. Friendly. Hence, D-O-R-A – Dora."

*****

Dora.

She loved that name. The whole Storytelling title complicated things. It sounded distant, sometimes verging on the dramatic. People loved the dramatic; that was the problem. With drama came the desire for spoilers. Dora could never work out why so many craved knowledge over mystery. For people to learn, they needed to be willing to unlearn. See the world through childhood eyes. Through mystery.

Through non-spoilers.

In the world of non-spoilers, a story could create its own ending – and then redefine assumptions of what that could even look like. Who said a story had to end with the final word? The last page could be a book in itself. With many versions. Contradictions. And questions. Dora often tried to mess things up with her tale, taking the form of someone that each traveller least expected. Male. Female. Young. Old. Poor. Rich. Able-bodied. Disabled. The list grew continually, and that was the point.

There were never just two sides to a tale.

*****

Santiago walked along the backstage of The Theatre.

His job was a simple one tonight. The Magician wanted him to check all the props before the show. Nothing could go wrong in front of Peccadillo. Signs of nerves from the big guy. Rumours had already come back concerning what He had done to The Guide. The excuse given was desperation, but that tale wasn't able to wipe the blood clean from his cloak. Santiago hadn't seen The Magician act like that since...

He doubled-checked the lighting board then glanced around the room. No one was there. He checked again. Better safe than sorry. Santiago bent down and pulled a small, battered book from under the board. It was only by chance he remembered its location – the good old door knocker.

Dora had given him the book a long time ago, during the days when his own tale carried hope. She insisted that he read it. Apparently it would explain the reason they often met at her cabin. He wiped the dust off the cover. The Woman in White by the Dickens' protégé, Wilkie Collins. It was a good book. A mystery story. A kind of 'whodunit' and unique for its time. The tale had kept him guessing through each page turn. Collins had taken what he had learnt from his mentor to a whole new level, employing a technique that shocked many critics of the Victorian day. His revolutionary approach was to tell one story through the eyes of many different people. The author wanted to dispel the idea that there were only two sides to every story. Success. Failure. Win. Lose. Dead. Alive.

The intricate tapestry of life.

And his daring experiment worked.

But would it work today? Santiago flicked through the pages, looking for reassurance. One story, many sides. One story, many sides. He kept repeating the mantra over in his head, hoping that comfort would kick in. What he was about to do would mean his final night in PARADOX.

Final?

In a way.

But then again, there are more than two sides to every story.

CHAPTER 57
MANY SIDES OF THE STORY

"The story here presented will be told by more than one pen, as the story of an offence against the laws is told in Court by more than one witness."
(Wilkie Collins, The Woman in White)

FIRST CAME THE STORIES in the lemonade.

Then came the memories. From Dora, recalling my visits to the cabin.

"There was a time when you would come running up to this porch. We would take long walks through the orchard, plucking lemons from the trees. You told me early on that you preferred oranges, but I knew you would eventually see the light – the third visit to be exact.

Our walks were always light-hearted. We talked about hopes and childhood dreams not yet fulfilled. Sometimes you gave me an update on the magical games you played with The Twins under the Heart Tree. We reserved more in-depth themes for the porch. This was our sacred place to share pain and regret; to stare into the fear which lurks within the hidden cracks of life. As the visits continued, our conversations changed. Shorter. Distant. Suspicious of one another. You barely said anything to me on the day when the Heart Tree fell to the ground. There was only one thing on your mind. The Theatre. You were so troubled on that visit. Want to know why this bench looks so fresh compared to my chair? After you smashed your glass of lemonade against it, I had to give it a fresh coat of paint. Anger has a way of eating into the wood."

"How many times?"

"Visits? My boy, that's not the question you should be asking. Does it really matter whether you've sat on this porch ten, twenty or even thirty times? The answer won't change a thing. But if you asked 'Why can't I remember these visits?' Well, that would certainly open up a mystery."

Dora left her teasing words out in the open, waiting for the bite. I never even questioned the visible hook inside the bait as I continued to sip my drink.

"So why can't I remember?"

The hook lodged itself in my flesh as I chomped down on the bait. There was a tug on the line, then the slow reel in. Fight it? What was the point? I wanted her to catch me into a net of answers.

"To begin, I must first tell you a story.

Imagine a place where every colour of the universe meets. It is a land beyond all lands, open to all. Everyone is equal as they walk barefoot upon its colourful soil. No one visits once. And yet there is also no beginning or end as we know it – just the present, outside of time. Entry to this place is mysterious. Some call the doorway an 'event'. I've heard others name it 'trauma'. Maybe another way to describe it would be the moment when you see your world outside of the constricting frame, like walking through a wardrobe or climbing into a mirror.

This is when the heart welcomes PARADOX.

Imagination takes the starring role in a world that cannot define itself through the confines of language. Each traveller gazes upon this land in their own unique way. A cabin for one is a hotel lobby for another. One day I'm an old lady called Dora, another it's welcome to Larry from accounts. The same goes for the Paths that each traveller walks. But every trail leads to the same destination.

The Theatre.

Because PARADOX exists for one purpose: to reveal the *real* before your eyes."

Dora picked up her empty glass, pondering whether to go into the cabin to pour another drink.

"You never answered my question. Why can't I remember?"

"Ha! Ironically, you've already heard the answer, but it's also the reason memories fade."

I looked blankly at the old lady. Even though I was sitting in this peaceful place, I was losing patience. Dora nestled the glass back in her lap, realising that a trip to the kitchen would tempt fate.

"To understand The Theatre, one must first understand the disagreement.

The Magician saw the stage for only one purpose – to receive praise from the audience. *He* was the best in his field, and wanted people to know it. Second billing to an old storyteller like me was an insult. So *He* challenged me to a duel of imagination and, as you know, my Mystery Box came out on top. What *He* failed to recognise was that the stage was never about the two of us receiving praise. We weren't the ones in the spotlight – the audience were. They were ones who carried a mystery within them, so profound that it could silence the universe with wonder. Each one of the audience, even now, writes what's inside the box. But the Magician refused to accept it. And so, what should have ended on that stage became a battleground of wills across the celestial canvas. A cosmic chessboard. On one side, The Magician. On the other, myself.

The Theatre became his new illusion. There, on the stage, *He* constructed a story that would corrupt the beauty of what resided in each beautiful life. The audience fell for his sleight-of-hand. They welcomed a life of ignorance and selfish want. But like I often say, there are more than two sides to a story. This cosmic chessboard has a twist.

We are not the ones moving each piece."

Dora paused, allowing the invisible currents of her story to lap against my skin.

It took a few seconds for the cold sensation of the hook to register what I had just heard. But this time, there was a desire to fight back against her approaching net. I didn't like the answer Dora had given. How dare this be just a game! It was like the Dickensian age all over again: the upper-class treating those 'below them' like pawns. While those two celestial beings happily sipped wine by a log fire, they never once considered the innocent lives that were crying out in pain. The deaths of Terri and Natasha deserved more than just two pieces taken off their twisted, perverse board.

I threw my drink against the bench; lemonade and shards of glass scattered across both wood and quilt. Why had I been so stupid to fall for her 'kind old granny' con? Dora was just as twisted as everyone else in this bloody world. It had to end. No goodbyes. No insults. *She* didn't deserve the energy. I rushed towards the orchard. Instinct told me this was the way out. One destination. The Theatre. And it wouldn't be The Magician bringing the house down.

They all deserved to go under.

Just like the last time.

Only worse.

The stain on the quilt was a new addition.

Dora couldn't work out if that was a good sign. Sometimes it's hard to know the difference between righteous anger and selfish rage. She had taken great care with her words; choosing what to say and what to leave out. Sometimes her role needed to be subtle. She dropped a few clues in the conversation, hopefully enough to spark thought. But would Peccadillo finally recognise it?

She gingerly pushed herself off the chair and walked into the cabin. A book just finished lay on the kitchen table. Dora loved reading A Christmas Carol, especially this edition; personally delivered and signed by the man himself. Number 1 of a 6,000 print run. A special edition. The old lady never had favourites, but She was immensely proud of her storyline with the author. It had filled her heart with joy when he finally figured out the real agent of change. Dickens even went so far as to drop his own hint into each story he penned. Well, two hints to be exact.

Dora looked out of the window towards the orchard. Peccadillo had gone. In a few minutes, this cabin would disappear and She would take on a different form. No more Dora. Until? She pondered the question, pouring out another lemonade. One long sip, but She didn't want to finish it off. Just in case.

Patience. She walked back onto the porch and placed the half-full glass on the table.

Stories.

One never quite knows when the end is finally the end.

CHAPTER 58
THE SHOW

"Hearts will never be practical until they can be made unbreakable."
(L. Frank Baum, The Wonderful Wizard of Oz)

ALONE.

Sort of.

The once bustling square outside The Theatre was now an empty frame. All signs of life had gone. No birds in the sky or shoppers gazing into windows. Every building, including Micawber's store, closed up for the night. There was a flicker of candlelight coming from his back room, but I had no desire to knock on the door. Whatever dark corners the shopkeeper had crawled into, that was his nightmare alone.

The two men were still sitting on The Theatre steps, waiting patiently for their tickets. We shared glances as I walked up the steps, but no words. Our silence confirmed what we all knew about this place. They could tell from my eyes it was time to leave. I understood their visible reluctance. Fake or not, who didn't want to cling onto hope? At least my tough love was saving two souls tonight from *That* twisted game. I pushed against the large door, knowing it would open; VIP ticket. A blast of cold air hit my skin, followed by the intense smell of damp. Whatever was waiting for me, its welcome sent a chill of disgust through my body.

The Theatre was in a terrible state. Derelict. There were row upon row of crimson velvet seats, but every one had lost their royal shine. Some had rips in them; others had repairs barely holding the seams together. The blanket of dust from years of neglect had comfortably made its home on the worn-out fabric. This four-walled time capsule told the sad tale of shunned love.

I carefully walked down the left aisle, trying hard not to trip over the ripped carpet. Pools of water from broken pipes created an Amazonian topography across the floor. Most of the seats in the middle of The Theatre had stains from the leaking roof. The smell of decay lingered in the room like a dense fog on a cold, damp night. It penetrated every part of the building. Dark stains of mildew stretched across the peeling wall, as lights which once gave the illusion of grandeur now dangled pathetically on electrical cords.

Coming to terms with what I was looking at was hard. Broken memories and distant flashbacks told me that I had seen this theatre during its heyday. I had walked into this building and gasped at its magnificent designs and golden paint. Its show of wonder and awe never started with the pulling back of the curtains; Act One was when you walked through the door. So what had happened? The chandelier was the only thing still holding onto the luxurious past. Its lights were on, but nobody was home.

Or were they?

There was an odd feel to the place. I swore The Theatre was wearing its derelict state with pride as though it was all part of the show. My feet stopped by ROW 6. Autopilot kicked in as I shuffled along the aisle to find SEAT 22. This was my usual spot. Dust particles launched into the air as I sat down on the comfy cushion. It was a perfect fit, just how I remembered it. My hand reached under the armrest. There it was, the rip in the fabric. There was a memory lodged somewhere in the dark about what caused the tear. It felt important, but at the same time too hard to find. I could think about it later. The comfy seat was encouraging me to settle into its welcoming embrace and forget the hassles of the world around. This was home. My place of safety.

Although The Theatre was empty, my mind had already created the image of a full house. The gentle buzz of anticipation bounced off the freshly painted golden walls, as people took their seats on smooth velvet fabric. Last minute arrivals scurried down the thick, carpeted aisles, trying to find their place. Ushers made one final check. Nothing could spoil the show. In front of me, the orchestra fine-tuned their instruments. The audience did the same, clearing their throats and checking that phones were on silent – a symphony of last minute adjustments.

And then.

The hush of excitement.

Lights dimmed.

The two-minute warning.

*****

Santiago watched from the side.

Dimming the lights was one of the many jobs he had as The Magician's assistant. Looking out into the empty rows of crimson seats, he knew Peccadillo would see a full house and repaired building. The Theatre did that to people; one of its illusions. Santiago had fallen for the same trick many times. Not any more. People only got to see this place in its true form when the game was finally over. His moves on the board had run out – so the rules had said.

He smiled.

CLICK. The lights at the back turned off. One-minute warning. The show was about to start.

Santiago braced himself.

*****

My hands excitedly gripped the armrests.

The tear widened.

I had seen this show many times before, but couldn't remember a single scene. All I could recall was that I was in for a real treat. A niggle in my mind caused the excitement to dial down a little. Wasn't there something I should be doing?

*****

Santiago noticed Peccadillo's hands tightly gripping the chair.

He then waited for the look on the face. It often happened that people forgot.

No matter what they intended to do to this place before walking through the doors, the illusion would prove too distracting. Peccadillo's own desire to bring down the house was already fading away. And even if it lingered, it would be a fool's folly. The Theatre always won.

I pushed the niggling question to one side.

Nothing would stop me from enjoying the show. I had waited a long time for this moment. A hush fell over the audience as the orchestra finished tuning up. The last few light bulbs over the seats switched off. A single beam focused on the empty stage. Goosebumps scattered themselves across my arms. There was electricity in the air. I took a quick intake of breath. Then one more. The show would be a good one. I could feel it.

Damn.

The niggle pushed its way back into the spotlight. I strained, trying to remember. Something about the end. Something I never do. Something I should do. This time.

The niggle left.

The Magician had thought long and hard about the opening act.

He had used the same routine many times for Peccadillo, but this particular performance had to be different. The traveller's return to PARADOX had complicated things. He had made some strange moves, lingering too long on the Paths. And then there was his meeting with The Storyteller. That shouldn't have happened, not after everything with Santiago. So He needed to mess up the board a little. Get the upper hand again.

The answer? A new opening act. It would be a surprise. Even for old ladies who like to play the long game.

It wasn't easy to craft such an opening. Reach the build-up of excitement too early and the anticipation for the final act would deflate like a punctured tyre. Overplay the tension and Peccadillo would get agitated and see too much.

Too much. That was the beauty of the new act. The Magician would reveal to Peccadillo straight away what was up his sleeve. It was a risky play, but also a stroke of genius.

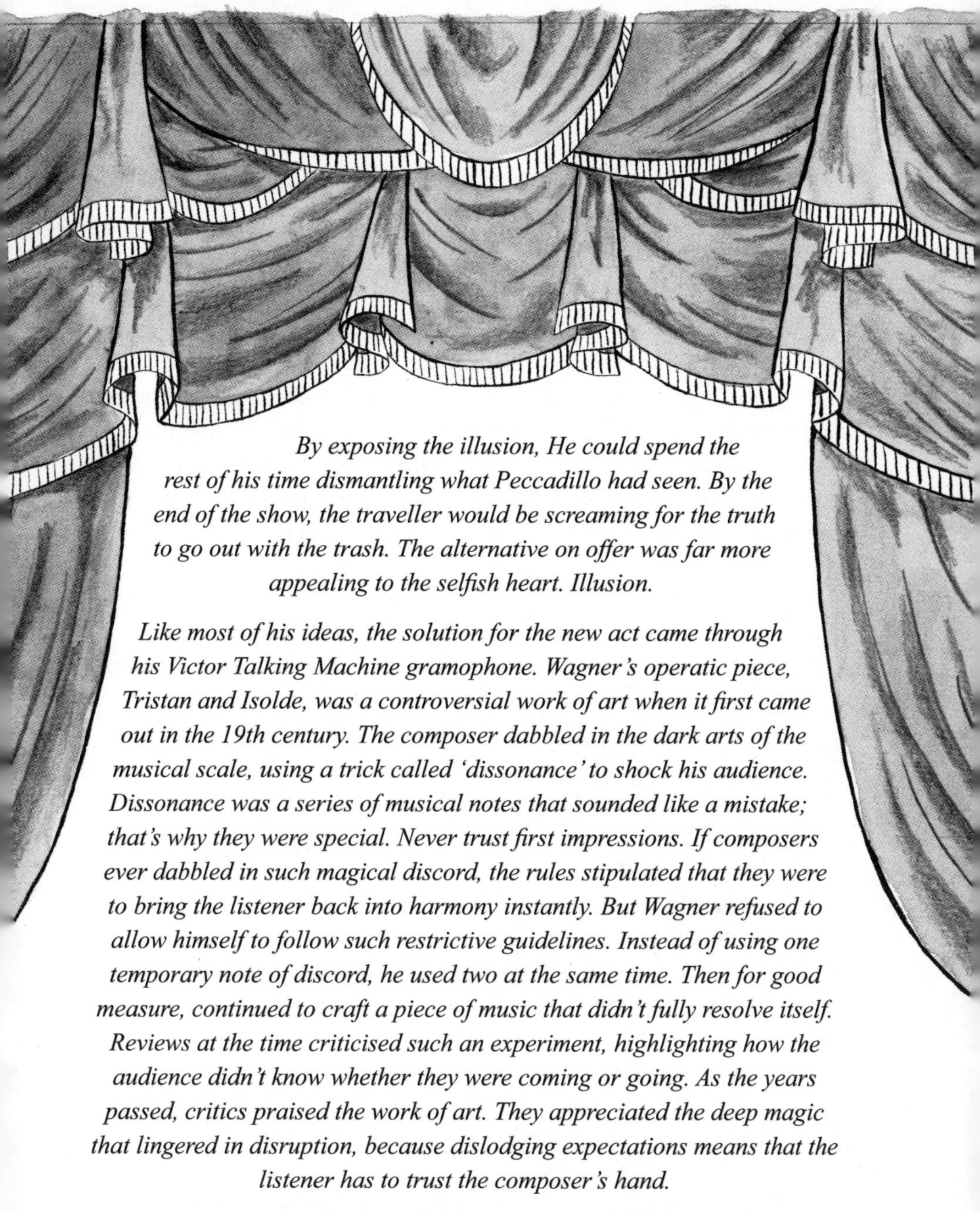

By exposing the illusion, He could spend the rest of his time dismantling what Peccadillo had seen. By the end of the show, the traveller would be screaming for the truth to go out with the trash. The alternative on offer was far more appealing to the selfish heart. Illusion.

Like most of his ideas, the solution for the new act came through his Victor Talking Machine gramophone. Wagner's operatic piece, Tristan and Isolde, was a controversial work of art when it first came out in the 19th century. The composer dabbled in the dark arts of the musical scale, using a trick called 'dissonance' to shock his audience. Dissonance was a series of musical notes that sounded like a mistake; that's why they were special. Never trust first impressions. If composers ever dabbled in such magical discord, the rules stipulated that they were to bring the listener back into harmony instantly. But Wagner refused to allow himself to follow such restrictive guidelines. Instead of using one temporary note of discord, he used two at the same time. Then for good measure, continued to craft a piece of music that didn't fully resolve itself. Reviews at the time criticised such an experiment, highlighting how the audience didn't know whether they were coming or going. As the years passed, critics praised the work of art. They appreciated the deep magic that lingered in disruption, because dislodging expectations means that the listener has to trust the composer's hand.

And The Magician would be using the same trick today.

Discord. But with a twist. Nobody wants their world to fall apart.

Ever.

CHAPTER 59
TRISTAN

"Was that a high C, or Vitamin D?"
(Groucho Marx, A Night at the Opera.)

ACT ONE.

The opening bars of music were awful. As soon as I thought I was following the melody, another note barged itself to the front, leaving me stranded in a tonal wilderness. The discord created a sense of being lost and unsure. Fear of the unknown settled over my tense body. I looked around The Theatre for moral support. All imaginary eyes were on the front of the stage.

To my horror, a silver mist twisted and swirled itself, forming dreamlike scenes from my past. One echo focused on my fear of not being a good writer. Another played out my endless worry of not having enough money. Scene after scene hit the boards as the mist revealed insecurities and hidden secrets of my heart. I sunk down into the chair, embarrassed to see such shallowness on display.

The performance grew darker, focusing on how I had manipulated people for personal gain. Lying. Cheating. And then repeating each betrayal for good measure. I saw my charitable donations exposed for the self-grandiose acts they were. I bragged to my friends about how much I cared for those in need, and yet when it came to the rest of my bank balance, I preferred to cross over to the other side of the street. The shops propping up the very system that caused such injustice were much shinier over there. I screamed out, not able to take any more. Nobody was listening. The all-access pass into my life was too good to miss.

The music softened. I breathed a sigh of relief as the mist drifted off the stage. The lights switched off. Darkness. I didn't mind. Anything to hide from the audience.

From myself.

*****

Act Two.

The silence was deafening. I could feel every eye on me. The audience had seen me at my worst. Or had they? One bolt holding my seat broke free from the floor. Then another. As the last bracket snapped, the chair lifted into the air. I gripped the armrest with dear life as I floated across the dark, voyeuristic sea.

CLICK.

The lights came up. I was outside Number Sixteen. Terri's temporary accommodation. Everything was translucent. I could see through walls and time. Every part of her life at that sad excuse for a house played out in front of me. Terri worked multiple jobs as she tried in vain to cover unpaid bills and the purchase of school uniforms. Sometimes the heating worked. Other times, she had to boil a kettle for Natasha's bath. Sleepless nights drained their daytime energy. Natasha struggled at school. The kids picked on the low grades at first, then moved to the tatty shoes and frequently repaired skirts. Natasha's lifeline was throwing herself into books, creating a world made out of ink. I wondered if she would become a writer, and then realised that I would never find out.

The tears came as I watched the two of them huddled around a single light bulb. Terri was writing a letter. Natasha, a postcard. There were bills by the door. I could see through the envelopes and read the FINAL DEMANDS. By the sink was a note from the council. 'Due to unprecedented demand, your place on the housing list is downgraded.' The detailed explanation assured them they were not forgotten. But the bullshit was clear. This place would be their home for a long time.

There was a knock on the door. Debt collector. Terri wouldn't answer. She never did when her daughter was around. When the payday loans stopped paying out, it was time to call on the backstreet lenders. They didn't care how the never-ending debt got paid. Terri hated what she had to do to keep the electricity on. Every payment resulted in her throwing up in the toilet afterwards. She knew that failure to answer the door would mean higher interest rates and darker demands. But she couldn't let him in, not tonight. Scum like that didn't care where their lusting eyes ventured. Terri covered her daughter's ears as the man shouted out a prophecy for his next visit. When he left, they continued to write.

My tears of regret turned to a gut-wrenching disgust for myself. I had left them alone in an evil world.

Act Three.

My seat violently moved from side to side. I was travelling again, rushing through the streets of London. In and out of buildings. Across green parks and bright blue lakes. I recognised the surroundings. My trendy, two-entrance apartment was straight ahead. Just like Number Sixteen, everything became translucent. I could see my double hunched over the writing desk, examining a spreadsheet. It was a complicated document, a breakdown of how my life carried an impact on everyone else in the world. An adjustment of affection here, an action of selfishness there, the ripple effect worked its magic. I could see my hand rub out numbers and adjust the lines. There was a simple goal I wanted to achieve.

The spreadsheet had to lean in my favour. It was another form of Trott's card table.

A letter floated down from the ceiling and landed on the desk. My double panicked. Its presence had messed up the spreadsheet; the bottom line had gone into the red. A cry came out of the envelope. It was Terri's voice, begging for help. He turned his gaze, throwing the message into the bin. A smile returned as the bottom line of the spreadsheet went to black. My seat moved a little closer. There was no way I could trace the countless cause-and-effect reverberations on the page, but its message was already clear.

My fingerprints were all over Number Sixteen.

Act Four.

The seat landed heavily on the floor. I was back in The Theatre. The lights turned on revealing the derelict state of the building and its water-soaked empty chairs. CHIME. The sound of a cheap bell echoed around the walls. My eyes followed its call to the stage curtain. Slowly, in a carefully rehearsed reveal, The Magician walked out holding a small plastic bell. *He* stepped off the stage and walked towards me.

"See? Observe?"

It was a question more than a statement. A big smile stretched across his face, flattening his eyes as though they were squeezing under a door. He brushed the dust off the chair next to me and sat down.

"Feeling guilty? I know the feeling. It's a killer seeing all that. Just when you think you've got a handle on this place, it throws a curve ball. Unfortunately for you, no excuses this time. It's true. Choices do have an impact on others, including strangers. That damn spreadsheet."

The Magician gently tapped my knee. His cold, bony fingers sending a shiver up my leg.

"But don't worry. It's not all bad. There is a way out. Just like you, I've grown bored with this place. I would love nothing more than to end it all. Good job I've prepared something on stage for such an occasion. Want to join me?"

He stood up, stretching out his arm. Even though I didn't trust him, it was an easy choice. I hated this place. As I took his hand, the niggle came back. Mistakes have a way of repeating themselves.

CHAPTER 60
THE TWO SEATS

"It matters not how strait the gate, how charged with punishments the scroll. I am the master of my fate: I am the captain of my soul."
(William Ernest Henley, Echoes of Life and Death.)

ONE TRESTLE TABLE.

Three chairs. Two on my side and one on his. The Magician motioned to me to sit down opposite him. I nervously obeyed, looking at the empty third chair.

"I know what you're thinking. It's always just been the two of us. Why the guest? Three is a crowd."

A picture of excitement covered The Magician's face. This was a big moment for him.

"I always looked forward to our little get-togethers on this stage. But this one didn't feel right. I thought it was me at first. You know, had I let myself go or not given you enough space? Oh, the hours of turmoil and self-torture. And then I figured it out. Fauré's Requiem."

His hand slammed down onto the table making me jump back.

"Two chapels. One illusion. Surely you know the story? Ah, it doesn't matter anyway. The important part of this story is the question that followed such a discovery."

"What question?"

He leant forward, his fingers drumming on the surface. The animated expression on his face dripped down onto every limb, causing a tingle of excitement to kick start fevered movement in his arms and legs.

"Could it be we were playing out this meeting in a different place?"

Silence.

Confusing silence.

The Magician happily allowed the deafening weight of the pause to work its magic. Behind me, I could hear the slow drip of water from a leaking pipe. I knew the building was empty, but it didn't stop me imagining the sound of feet moving through the aisles. The audience was getting restless. They were on the edge of their seats waiting for his next line. Feeling the wait had reached the perfect climax, *He* continued.

"When I saw this delightful sleight-of-hand, there was no other option but to admire the audacity of the whole thing. I had forgotten the first rule of this game. Always look at the whole board. If I had done that, then I would have saved myself a whole lot of trouble and soul searching.

You see, I knew you would get help in PARADOX, that's what the old lady and myself are here for. Assistance. Clues. But the rules are clear: we never make the moves. That's down to the player. Obviously there is a catch. Even though we don't push any pieces around, it doesn't stop us from knowing the mind of the player. Predictability is the name of the game. The heart is like a open book. But occasionally there's a surprise, an odd move."

The Magician stretched over the table, his lips almost touching my ear. I pulled back, feeling the cold decay of his stale breath tickle my skin.

"In your case, insider knowledge – from someone who shouldn't be helping you."

Santiago looked on from the side of the stage.

He was nervous about the approaching reveal. It wasn't because The Magician had worked out who was helping Peccadillo. That was all part of the plan; it was the only way to distract eyes from the rest of the board. The nerves came from uncertainty. Regardless of the careful planning, he had no idea what dark shadows lay at the end of this Path. And that worried him. He edged his way to the curtain's edge, waiting for the call. In those few agonising seconds, he played back his own journey on The Paths.

Santiago was a young man, full of dreams and certainty, when he had set foot in PARADOX. The first person he met was an aged traveller called James. He spoke many strange things, including tales about a mysterious box and a magical tree. The stories came with a plea – don't make the same mistakes as his old heart. Santiago ignored the advice. After taking the Box, he felt compelled to cut down the tree. Destiny. It was a surprise to find the old man again, crying on The Theatre steps. They never spoke. He was too ashamed to look into those red, broken eyes. It wasn't until Santiago took his seat on the stage that he finally figured out the identity of James. He wanted to rush back. Change things. But it was too late. The game had finished.

Santiago halted the memories.

The Magician was now banging his hands on the table like a human drum roll. A spotlight focused its blinding beam towards the side curtain.

"Ladies and Gentlemen, boys and girls. Let me introduce you to the star of the show. The one. The only. Santiago."

That was his cue. Quickly, he ran through all the moves in his head. Step onto the stage. Look shocked. Nervous. Add a sprinkle of concern for Peccadillo. But don't over-do-it, that would give the game away. And then? He pushed the uncertain thought to one side.

Santiago brushed himself down, giving a silent 'break a leg'.

What was he doing here?

"Peccadillo, meet Santiago. Santiago meet Peccadillo."

The Magician flippantly ran through the introductions, his hands waving from side to side. A tilted grin gave away the immeasurable pleasure of this moment.

"Oh, how silly of me, you've already met. But wait... WHEN did you meet? Hmm, interesting question."

"Why are you dragging this out?"

Santiago's question was more like a broken whisper as he tried to mask the nervous wobble in his voice. He sat down, paying careful attention not to look my way.

"How ironic it's you of all people asking that question. Trust me, I'm not the one dragging this out. This story should have ended with you on this stage."

The Magician's tilted grin suddenly levelled out as the memories of that scene dampened his excitement. I looked over towards Santiago. His face was just as heavy. What did I care? My eyes drifted back to the table and then to the side. All I wanted to do was to get home. And. Yes. For a split second, PARADOX faded away, and I could smell the welcoming aroma of fresh coffee on the stove. My safe little world.

"Am I losing you?"

My kitchen faded away into The Magician's question.

"You better pay attention, this is the good part. You don't want to miss this."

The Magician gave a piercing glance to Santiago.

"Do you want to tell him or me?"

It was clear on his face that *He* had no intention of giving way. But like any true showman, the name of the game was to add tension to the grand reveal.

"Now, what is it that the old lady often bores us with? That's right, more than two sides to every story. I hate that woman. And yet, I can't help but admire her stubbornness. Here I was, thinking that this particular story had finished, and a new chapter was already in play. The cheek of the whole thing!"

His words landed with a soul-freezing stare back at me.

"I have no idea how *She* got you to go The London Library, but I have to admit, it was a good move. And then there was your 'chance' meeting with Eki. A stranger."

Air quotes.

"A stranger integral to your journey. Who would have thought two failed travellers would meet like that – what are the odds?"

*****

The Magician pondered how much to say.

It was easy to go down many verbal rabbit holes and lose sight of the goal today. But what was the point in wasting time? Peccadillo's journey was about to end for good. And yet there was a slight sadness not being able to bask in the magic of PARADOX. He likened it to Alice stepping through the Looking Glass: two worlds existing at the same time. The first Alice was in the living room; the second, beyond the mirror. Both were real. Both co-existing.

And it was the same here.

Everyone Peccadillo had met along his journey had a mirror-copy back home. If someone looked hard enough, the clues were there. But even The Magician had missed the 'chance' meeting with Eki. Then again, why should He have been looking for it? Their stories had ended in PARADOX and back home they were nothing but strangers.

Strangers?

There was no such thing. That's what the opening act was all about. The spreadsheet of life; humanity connected in so many different ways.

He continued to ponder telling Peccadillo about the connection. Eki. The Guide. Surely the hints were obvious? Maybe. But no disclosure today. It would complicate matters, especially trying to explain what He had done to the mirror copy. Focus. This performance was all about the other connection.

The other mirror-copy.

The Magician drew in his breath for the big announcement. This was going to be good. The slow delivery was on purpose; a mixture of savouring the moment and making sure every word counted.

"Two chairs. One person."

Pause.

"One person. Two chairs."

Rest.

"Have you worked it out yet?"

Wait.

"Peccadillo."

And now the line.

"Or should I call you Santiago?"

CHAPTER 61
ECHOES

"You've seen the sun flatten and take strange shapes just before it sinks in the ocean. Do you have to tell yourself every time that it's an illusion caused by atmospheric dust and light distorted by the sea, or do you simply enjoy the beauty of it?"
(John Steinbeck, Sweet Thursday)

THE FIRST SIGN of madness isn't talking to yourself, it's continuing the conversation.

I was in the throes of insanity, bombarding Santiago with jumbled questions and nonsensical statements. Every one of his replies sounded like a cheap B-movie plotline as confusion led me into its padded cell. He told me that every visit from a traveller leaves an echo in PARADOX. My mirrored-copy was Santiago. His was an elderly man called James. This strange land had a thing about age. Echoes could never be young, something about eating the fruit of their decisions. Each reflection acted as a guide for their next self. Help or manipulation? One would never know. That secret would always remain hidden within the echo's heart.

Santiago believed the story he was telling me, I could tell from his eyes. Behind his sunken gaze there was a distant swirling universe of regret. His conversation with James was as real as my words to him today. But there was also a silence resting behind his voice. A secret. Unspoken.

*****

James waited by The Theatre steps as Santiago walked inside.

His breathing grew heavy. Laboured. The final tick-tock of time was drawing near. It wasn't supposed to end like this, on the steps. He had pictured this closing scene as a tranquil wood next to a crystal stream; a place that would gently rock his heart to sleep. But now all he had was a cold concrete floor reminding him that his past had finally caught up with him. He curled up on the second ledge, cursing himself that he had no energy left to burst through The Theatre doors and save... his heart. Through blurred vision he could make out the two 'Godot' men sitting on the far end of the steps. They hadn't moved since his last visit.

Nothing changes. Or maybe.

"Here. Take this."

The red-faced Micawber bent down with a glass of water and a thick wool blanket. He had seen the old man struggling on the steps. James refused the encouragement of moving somewhere warmer, like the shop. He knew the shopkeeper was thinking for the best, but there was also that glint in his round eyes which lusted after the sweet nectar of 'deathbed words'. Under any other circumstance, he would have given his junkie friend a final gift. But not today. Today needed to mean something more. If he couldn't get up the steps and into The Theatre, he would wait it out, catch Santiago leaving. One last chance to change things.

"He's not going to listen. He probably won't even stop on the way home."

Micawber spoke the words as gently as possible, aware it wouldn't be what a dying man wanted to hear. He had followed this storyline, often with tears. Before James, there had been Rich, then Manning and Allen. Each visit had become darker with tales of disappointment. Santiago was a lost cause – the fruit of all those visits. Because of that, Micawber wanted to protect his old friend from false hope, even if the tingle of a regretful tale danced teasingly on his lips.

"Please, let me take you somewhere other than here. Leave PARADOX in peace, not in tears."

"No. I have. To..."

James never got a chance to finish off his sentence. The Theatre door swung open. Moments later Santiago staggered towards the top step before collapsing to his knees.

I pushed Santiago for answers.

He refused all enquiries about James. It was off limits. The Magician silently watched from the other side of the table, enjoying every feverish minute. *He* wanted to join in, stir up the tension but knew his contribution would ruin the fun. This was between the two of us.

Between me and myself.

Fragile hope is a fickle thing.

Seeing Santiago on his knees unleashed a torrent of faith before it twisted itself into a heart-wrenching lament. The traveller hadn't collapsed in repentance, his body was just recovering from hitting the jackpot.

"You. You lied to me!"

Santiago's outstretched finger pierced through the air like a poisonous dart. Its accusation clinically hitting its target as he staggered down the steps. James winced.

"No. No. Everything I told you is true. It's all an illusion. You have to..."

"Believe you? You're even more of a pitiful creature than I first thought. No wonder my life has been so screwed up. But things are going to change. He showed me a way out. A way to make things right again."

"Let me guess. Wealth? Bestseller? New apartment? New lover?"

Micawber regretted his mocking words as soon as Santiago turned to face him. The picture of hatred sealed his lips.

"You hypocrite. I know your game. You only want the taste of a new story. There's not an ounce of compassion in you. And anyway, I saw in there your dirty little secret and why you will never get out of here."

Micawber's face turned a deathly shade of white. The smile on Santiago's face had all the hallmarks of a knock-out blow. He loved having the power to end a career. The words were just about to leave his lips when James grabbed his leg.

"Don't. You're better than this. I know your heart."

The exchange of looks pressed pause on the high-tempered scene. Buried within the broken eyes of James was the reflection of an equally broken man. In that vulnerable moment, both of them thought of another future – one where The Theatre stage had lost all its power. James dreamed of closing his eyes in peace. Santiago pictured returning home with a softer heart and someone to find. But moments don't last. Time moves on. The spell of exchanged glances eventually breaks.

Santiago pulled back. There was a moment of hesitation before he ran away.

He hated the show of weakness on The Theatre steps. With everything The Magician had revealed, that little exchange nearly messed everything up. That couldn't happen again. The solution to end any temptation came naturally to him – the Heart Tree needed to be chopped down. Just like Scrooge, he would then be able to walk through the streets focused on only one thing: personal gain.

In his plan, he never intended to see James again, but plans are subject to change. Micawber was resting the old man's head on a soft pillow of loose dirt by the exit that led home. All signs of life had drained away from his mirrored-copy. Once the soul leaves a body, the features of the human cage are barely recognisable, but he could still see the impression of a broken heart. There was no logical reason why Santiago had taken a souvenir from the chopped down tree. The small twig somehow found its way into his pocket, and now it rested on the chest of a dead man. Micawber returned an approving nod. It seemed appropriate to lay the last remnants of a good heart on a worthy soul next to the exit he forever longed for.

The walk through the exit joined the two worlds together in the usual way. Abrahams was back in London, Santiago in the marketplace. On the surface, nothing had changed. But behind the scenes it was as if PARADOX knew the show had finally come to an end. The pain in his feet was getting worse. He couldn't figure out what had caused the injury, but knew it started after chopping down the tree. Maybe it was a muscle strain. Temporary. His heart told him otherwise, so too the memories of his mother's tales.

Days turned into weeks. Santiago often wondered what his counterpart would be doing. If he thought hard enough, there would be an occasional release of endorphins; a signal that Abrahams was having a great time in his small world. The Magician had kept his promise. More like a curse.

Santiago kept himself to himself. He couldn't bear seeing what he had done to his colleagues and friends. They kept their distance too. It worked well for all parties. And somewhere in that swirling mass of time he ventured down one of the disused Paths and threw away the door knocker. He had no use for it now. An intense stab of pain pierced his heart, as though someone deeply loved had passed away. It surprised him. He thought his heart had become nothing but stone after his decision on The Theatre stage. Tears formed, then flowed. Through misty vision, a figure appeared in front of him. He hadn't seen The Storyteller in a long time. They went on a long walk. She had lots to talk to him about. Visiting Number Sixteen wasn't easy, but it explained the pain.

Except.

His question was still unanswered. Why was he feeling such emotion in his condemned heart? The Storyteller sat down on the bench opposite the crumbling house and offered to tell him the outline of a new story She was thinking of. But there was one condition. He couldn't tell a soul.

And he was still keeping that promise today during the barrage of questions.

CHAPTER 62
THE TRICK

"I know there's no way I can convince you this is not one of their tricks, but I don't care, I am me."
(Alan Moore, V for Vendetta)

"YOU WANT OUT? This is how."

The Magician pulled a pack of cards from under his sleeve. *He* had grown weary of Santiago not playing ball, and the distraction was taking his carefully planned show off-course. The cards danced between his long fingers. In. Out. Through and over. A flick of his wrist and the fifty-two cards spread across the table, face down.

"I'm proud of this trick. The cards read the desires of your heart. They paint fifty-two images, asking you to choose just one. And the prize? When you return home, your choice becomes reality."

The Magician adjusted his pride and joy so each card lined up in perfect symmetry.

"And the catch?"

Santiago's reply caught us both off-guard. He answered his own question.

"You live with your decision."

*****

Fifty-two pulls of the heart.

How could I decide? The purple and red patterned back of the cards all looked the same, but their individual tugs told a different story. Each one had a unique image, a treasure trove of possibilities before me.

My fingers moved across the cards, hoping to pick up clues. Just like a kid at Christmas being told to choose only one present from Santa's sack, I tried to feel and squeeze my way to the best. I hesitated over the tenth card. An image came into my mind. I was standing on the balcony of a large four bedroom apartment overlooking The Thames. In the distance, the lights of Big Ben and The London Eye reflected off the city mirror. It was a prime location that had the title of success carved into every wall. This could be mine? It was the mystery of greed that stopped me from turning the card over there and then. I wanted to feel and squeeze more presents.

My fingers stopped over the thirteenth card. A New York Times bestseller. Didn't every author want that? I could see my name in black and white. Next to it, a towering Number One. I had made it, beating Grisham, King and Patterson without breaking a sweat. Next stop, Oprah's book club. I could taste success on my lips and its sweet nectar felt good. The image continued, playing out the next few years of my life. No more chasing agents, they were calling me. Long gone were book tours in dusty halls, eating cucumber sandwiches. I now had a private dressing room, put up in the swankiest of hotels. Ticket only events. People paid to hear me read a few chapters, but they got a free, digitally signed copy of my book. Bargain.

Indecision. Which card was the best?

Annoyingly, the niggle had returned. Its irritating presence made me press down harder onto the card. A ripple ran across the image, taking me deeper into the future. Yes, I was at the top of my writing game, but all I could see was the look of loneliness in my eyes. Most of my friends had gone; used up and pushed aside so I could sit on that supposedly successful throne. The ones who had survived the purge weren't so close anymore. I pulled my hand away. The image left.

Dora was right, there ARE more than two sides to every story.

Slowly, my fingers went back to the tenth card. As before, I pushed down harder onto the image. The ripples took me deeper into the tale of my dream apartment. I lasted seventy-one seconds. Regardless of the fancy words I used for my purchase, nothing could hide the driving force of greed that signed the contract. This wasn't about having a home, but some self-centred lust which cried 'everyone for themselves'. Behind my purchase of an overpriced shell of bricks and mortar was a hidden cost to society's soul. When greed for profit and investment replaces the human right to have a home, it's amazing what the heart can justify in its quest.

The Magician shuffled awkwardly in his chair.

He usually didn't mind people seeing beyond the cards. What disturbed him was the timing. One could almost guarantee how the game would play out. The first few visits from any traveller would often lead to them going deeper into their heart's desires. With shocked eyes, they would stare into the cause and effect of every action – the wonderful spreadsheet of life. It was a beautiful thing seeing the soul battle with the lust of the heart. As the visits continued, the travellers time at the table would become shorter. They desired less of reality. Even though they knew the world they were choosing was just an illusion, they happily embraced ignorance to keep up the selfish charade. That's what made his trick so amazing. The decision said everything. Santiago's visit to the table had been a thing of beauty. He welcomed ignorance with open arms, not even wanting to go deeper into the cards. Peccadillo should have done the same.

Something had changed.

*****

Santiago watched intently to every twitch of emotion flashing across Peccadillo's face.

Details were important. The next few minutes would determine the future, for both of them. He too could see the images. One card revealed a charitable foundation that Peccadillo wanted to set up. Another told the story of a wife, two kids and a dog called Jasper. A donation to help fund a cancer support wing lay under card forty-two. But even with all those wonderful things, Santiago winced at the broader tale revealed within the ripples. 'Earn enough money, make a name for yourself, then you can help others.' Greed comes in many different forms.

His eyes focused in on card number six.

That card.

Every time.

Would the cycle ever end?

My hand moved up and down the table, dipping in and out of random images.

No matter where I went, my fingers kept coming back to one card. Number six. It was different to the rest. Instead of the future, it revealed my past. I was back in school; a bullied kid burying his head into the world of Dickens. The image zoomed into the book resting on top of my crossed legs. It was a collection of letters written by my hero. They were addressed to his friend and protégé, Wilkie Collins; sharing wisdom that could only come from pounding the streets in the most vulnerable of ways. Dickens had seen many things during his trips; aspects of life that had shaken him to the core. But there was one thing that was ringing out in his heart like a chiming bell. *'Everything that happens shows beyond mistake that you can't shut out the world...You are in it, to be of it.'* The image zoomed in closer to his final words. *'You get yourself into a false position the moment you try to sever yourself from it.'* The message from Dickens was clear: the spreadsheet of life. There can be no disconnection apart from selfish ignorance.

Suddenly, the image ended as The Magician gathered up the cards into a neat pile.

"What are you doing?"

"My favourite part. The end of the trick. Time to choose a card."

"But you've put them away."

"On the contrary. How does the saying go? The dealer always wins. I don't want you thinking I somehow manipulated the game. Your shuffle."

He pushed the cardboard tower of destiny towards me. After spreading the cards back on the table, there was only one future I desired. Once again, my hand hovered over each card. Halfway down, the warm sensation of destiny warmed my skin. I found it.

It was time to end this game once and for all.

CHAPTER 63
THE SETUP

"War is peace. Freedom is slavery. Ignorance is strength."
(George Orwell, 1984)

MY FINGER rested on the card.

'You can't shut out the world...You are in it....'

The words from Dickens drew me deeper into their scribbled lines of ink. Until. They appeared. Terri. Natasha. The two of them were walking out of Number Sixteen, heading towards the woodland circle. Their faces looked tired. My eyes wandered down to the clutch of dolls Natasha was holding onto with dear life. Their final sleep-over. In the distance, I could see the figure of another two children. I knew who they were. Natasha recognised the onlookers as well. They exchanged smiles and a nod of reassurance. She loosed her grip a little on the dolls, not so afraid anymore.

The image distorted with another ripple. This time I was at the bedside of my dying mother. Her rattling breath matched the rhythm of the sterile monitoring machine. Through whispered lips, I was telling her everything she needed to hear in those final hours. She wanted to die with hope, so I gave her that. My promise of living by the Scallop Shell sounded convincing in the room. Hearing those words now revealed the shallowness of my heart. The scene moved on, taking me back into my father's study. In the corner was his desk, a plastic bell resting on top. I should have done great things with that piece of junk, yet I sold its magic for a handful of consumeristic beans.

As long as I kept my hand on the card, the ripples continued. I was in school, too scared to help the new kid with his welcoming party of bullies. My spreadsheet was working overtime that morning, enjoying the break from fists and harsh words. Next, I was an adult, late for a meeting, passing yet another homeless person. The man in front of me grew frustrated with the blocked walkway, so he kicked over the cardboard cup of change. Silver and gold coins ran down the path and into the gutter. I would have helped gather them up, but my watch told me there wasn't enough time. Human life was secondary to my diary.

My finger lifted off the card. Was this my way out? It had to be. *'You can't shut out the world...You are in it....You get yourself into a false position the moment you try to sever yourself from it.'* With a straightforward decision, I could erase those painful words from my life. All my failures to act upon injustice, the self-loathing at the greed guiding my steps. Gone. And the inner turmoil, would that leave as well? Yes. How could I hear the voices of those hurting, if I was ignorant to their cries? It could all disappear with a flick of a card.

Including the guilt of Terri and Natasha's death.

'You can't shut out the world.' Yes I could

'You are in it.' But not be part of it.

'You get yourself into a false position the moment you try to sever yourself from it.' I could happily live with the illusion.

Ignorance and Selfish Want would be my way out.

"Is that your choice?"

The Magician leaned forward. *He* couldn't wait for the turn of the card. Neither could I. Santiago touched my hand, his eyes revealing a swirling sea of words urging me to stop. For a moment I dived in, letting the waves crash against any moral remnants of my heart. Its refreshing waters told me I could still change my mind. All I had to do was embrace the thing I feared the most.

Love's demand.

In love's water, the heart swims to the rhythm of putting others before self. Its current never ceases as it passes strangers and friends alike. There is only one destination this river leads to. The Twins. There, the heart embraces their pain, facing the infinite demand of compassion. And that's why I could never choose another card. Love has no end. Its challenge to life's spreadsheet would continually cause me pain.

Tears of sorrow ran down my cheek as I realised what I needed to do. The last of my life's goodness weaved itself towards my chin, then dropped onto the table. However hard it was to admit it, my heart couldn't meet this demand of love.

Santiago masked the emotions tearing him up inside.

After everything Peccadillo had seen, he was making the same mistakes again. Just like James. Just like himself. History was repeating itself. Hadn't The Storyteller told him this would happen? Yes. And She had also told him about a possible twist in the tale. But it required a decision. From him. His move alone. Because the cost would be great. And now that decision was upon him. So too, a hesitation.

What if The Storyteller was wrong about her latest tale?

Pevensie walked out of The London Library.

He looked up and down the street, checking no one was around. A hand wave signalled the coast was clear. Tshilaba came out first, followed by the young girl and boy. The Twins looked anxious. They could feel danger in the air. Pevensie sensed it too as he quickly scanned the streets again. The darkness was playing havoc with his eyes, making harmless shadows into outlines of The Magician's henchmen. There was no way the market traders would know The Twins were here.

Pevensie stepped back. He was missing something. His mind played out the route back to the meeting point. Abraham's apartment. Ten minutes, that's all it would take. The traveller would have returned from PARADOX by then, ready to embrace a life that would heal the wounds on those poor children.

Unless.

If the traders already knew The Twins were here, what did that mean for the destination? Were they waiting there as well? How did they find out? It couldn't be down to luck. And no one had followed him apart from Eki, and that was all part of the plan.

Unless.

Unless.

Pevensie didn't like where that word took him.

*****

Santiago lurched forward, pushing Peccadillo's hand away.

"NO!"

The Magician's scream was too late. Santiago turned over the card.

What now?

Judgement.

He had bent the rules a few times during this trip, especially taking Peccadillo to Number Sixteen. But this action at the table went to another level. He had not only touched the card, forbidden by the rules, but had turned it over as well. The consequences would be severe.

The rules of PARADOX stated that only one mirrored-copy could remain. James had departed once Santiago took residence. And he too would leave this land as Peccadillo waved goodbye to Abrahams' return home. The judgement would relate to the nature of Santiago's departure. There would be no peaceful death or gentle lullaby to eternal sleep. He had to become a lesson to the rest of creation. No shortcuts in this eternal game.

"There's a land across the border, shaped by our deepest mistakes."

He could hear the words of The Storyteller come back to him.

"Every echo has to take a Path through that world as they depart PARADOX. It's not pleasant, but there is an end with a pasture to greet the weary, heartbroken traveller. Not everyone makes it. Some give up. And some…"

Santiago paused the memories. This was his judgement for breaking the rules.

"…And some have to remain in that land, forever faced with the fruit of their lives."

When The Storyteller first told him her plan – turn over the card instead of Peccadillo – he baulked at the idea. Laying his life down for a destiny not set in stone meant he could be doing this all in vain. Abrahams could still live his life back home in the illusion of The Theatre. But isn't that what love's demand was all about? Compassion never seeks certainty.

Except, the sick feeling in his gut told him that things hadn't turned out well.

Pevensie clenched his fists.

Unless.

Betrayal.

"Not a betrayal darling. Just a setup."

He didn't want to turn around. Anyone but her. After everything they had gone through. Why? The traders moved out from the shadows and made their way towards the library. This was no setup.

It was an execution.

CHAPTER 64
IT ALL COMES TUMBLING DOWN

"I wanted to destroy everything beautiful I'd never have."
(Chuck Palahniuk, Fight Club)

I WASN'T THE ONLY ONE to hear the rumble under the stage.

All three of us looked down at the same time as floorboards broke free from their nailed masters. Crippled by fear, our bodies never reacted in time to the wave of wooden planks flinging the table to one side. Cards and chairs followed suit, throwing us headfirst into the destructive storm. The Magician disappeared under broken timber and fallen plaster. I scrambled to my feet just in time as wooden roof beams crashed down onto the stage.

"Santiago!"

I spun around, frantically searching for him. It was hard to see anything amongst the cloud of dust and flying debris. The deep rumble continued to shake The Theatre to its core. For a moment I thought its symphony of destruction sounded like people clapping. Another crash of concrete. This time from the far wall. Burst pipes sprayed their contents over exposed electrical wires. Seconds later, a fire broke out, its red and yellow hands eagerly touching the nearby canvas seats. Fear changed to panic, it was only a matter of time before it reached the stage. I needed to find Santiago and quick. Splintered wood and sharp edges of stone ripped open my hands as I pushed the fallen objects to one side. Seeing the mangled body under a wooden beam numbed any pain. I cried out his name. A fragile response of life came back. Next to his broken body I could see a large hole in the stage. Fire from the basement had already set the jagged edges alight.

"I will get you out."

Behind me, a loud metallic noise filled The Theatre. The chandelier dangling over the middle of the building broke free from its brackets and smashed down into the seats. The red canvas floor gave way, signing off with a heart-stopping fireball from the basement. As if in response to the impressive display, the flames next to us rose up in a standing ovation. The blast of heat pushed me back momentarily. I tried lifting the beam, but it wouldn't budge. Concrete boulders secured both sides.

"I'm not leaving you."

But in the heat of the approaching flames, I didn't know how I would keep my word.

*****

"RUN!"

Pevensie screamed out the order. The Twins didn't need any encouragement, they were already racing towards the square. Three traders ran after them. The fourth went around the side, trying to cut them off at the other end. Pevensie could see what was about to happen. He ran down the road, grabbing a large stone resting in the flower beds. Ten yards. Five yards.

Throw.

The shadowy figure staggered to his left. Right. Left. His legs buckled, sending his body crashing to the floor. Pevensie's face went white as he watched the head bounce on the pavement with a dull thud. A stream of blood trickled through the concrete cracks. He had never done something like that before – take someone off the board. Nobody removes a piece unless... He never got to finish the thought. Pain ran through his body, quickly followed by the sensation of liquid soaking into his clothes. He never heard the shot, didn't even feel the bullet tear into his skin. There was no time to look down at the damage. Everything went hazy as he felt the cold concrete floor touch his skin. Through blurred vision he glimpsed The Twins running into the dead end of a locked gate. Trapped. And he could do nothing about it. His eyes closed. The world slowed down.

Tshilaba stood over the limp body. Her hand, holding the hot gun. Two bullets left. That's all she needed. And then home.

She was expecting a visitor.

*****

Dora hunched over in pain, her stomach twisted with cramp.

Eki reached out to help her, but She pushed the woman away.

"What's happening?"

"My pieces."

She waved frantically towards her bag.

"Please, let me get you some help."

Dora refused, her shaking hands pointing towards the left corner of the bag. Eki searched inside, pulling out two broken pawns. A cry of grief burst out of Dora's wrinkled mouth. Her haunting tone echoed around The Seven Dials, making shoppers and tourists take a pause. The looks of concern didn't last – seeing a homeless woman has a way of making feet cross to the other side. But one person continued to stare. From the shadows. A solitary trader watching the unfolding events with great interest. He had lots to report back to The Magician. Everything had played out just like The Magician had planned.

*****

"The Applause, it's close."

Santiago's weak voice somehow pierced through the chaos of noise around us. I didn't care if there was a mysterious sound of people clapping. My only concern was to get him out of here.

"Close. Close."

His words tailed off. I was losing him. Screaming for him to stay with me, I pushed against the concrete slab, praying that it would move. Nothing. The heat from the basement fire was now turning the floorboards underneath us into fresh kindling. Crack. Snap. I lurched forward, grabbing hold of Santiago's hand just in time. The boards by the concrete slab went up in flames. Seconds later, another hole appeared, sending everything that had trapped my friend into the fiery pit. The weight of his limp body slowly edged its way over the edge.

"Hold on. Hold..."

The look in his eyes told me what he was about to do.

"Don't you dare."

His grip loosened a little. I scrambled around for his other hand, but he purposely left it dangling at his side.

"I had to turn the card over. It was the only way."

"Give me your other hand."

A little glint appeared in his eyes. His face lightened with a smile as the hand relaxed its grip.

"NO!"

There was no sound in my scream as I watched Santiago fall into the flames. Flickering arms wrapped themselves around his outstretched body and then he was gone. Dead. And for what? I couldn't understand why he would do such a thing, but there was no time for quiet reflection by the open grave. The fire at the back of The Theatre had now reached its brother-in-arms on the stage. One look around confirmed the sobering truth I already knew. There was no way out. I slumped down. Above me, most of the roof had disappeared. It was both strange and comforting seeing the peaceful night sky within the chaos. Fiery embers floated upwards, caught with the swirling clouds of grey smoke. They looked like lost souls finally hearing the call of freedom. And soon another one would float away. I wondered where the currents would take me. My head rested down on the warm boards. The smoke inside my lungs was acting out its closing ritual. Soon. Very soon. It would all end. My eyelids grew heavy. A blessing. It was better not seeing the final moment. Light sleep turned to deep sleep. And in the swirling fog of dreamlike figures, arms wrapped around my chest. Someone was dragging me through the burning Theatre and down concrete steps. I tried to open my eyes, but the world told me to sleep.

Sleep more.

Sleep well.

And then wake up.

*****

He had to do it.

For his friend.

Micawber had waited until the laughing Magician staggered out of the building before rushing through the flames. Taking Peccadillo back to The Pillar was the logical thing to do. There was only one Path left to walk – The Path of the Decision. Everyone would expect to see the traveller there. As for putting the card in Peccadillo's pocket, it felt important to do. A reminder. Just like the items back in his shop.

The shop.

It was time to close his business for a while. The building work on The Theatre would be noisy; that monstrosity wasn't going away anytime soon. Avoiding the upheaval wasn't the reason for the break, but it served as a good excuse to post on his door. His reason for leaving needed to be a secret; find out what The Magician had done to The Guide. She hadn't been seen since his visit.

Peccadillo stirred. It was time to leave. Micawber didn't want to be around when the traveller woke up. Inevitable questions would only lead to answers that were unhelpful. Sometimes mystery is the only way to walk the Paths. He stretched, then took one final look around the market square. All was quiet. Empty. PARADOX had done its job and was now resting. The game had finished. There was a winner.

Except.

It was too quiet.

The type of confident silence when someone thinks they know the outcome of the game.

STAVE 4
AFTER THE DECISION

CHAPTER 65
ONE YEAR LATER

"I may not have gone where I intended to go, but I think I have ended up where I needed to be."
(Douglas Adams, The Long Dark Tea-Time of the Soul)

16th October. One year later. 7:55pm

THE END.

I stared down at my hand-written sign-off. It was tradition to close the final draft with a pencil instead of an ink-jet printer. This was my fifth book and over the years I had adopted many weird traditions. Another was leaving the completed manuscript on the desk for seven days. I wouldn't touch it again until this holy time had said its final prayer of reflection and thanks. The double espresso I was now pouring out was another sacred routine. It had to be a particular roast, drunk while listening to John Coltrane's *A Love Supreme – Part Four* only. '*Psalm*' – it was his masterpiece. A recording that delved into the unknown realms of the spiritual world. His work of art revealed the beauty that human life could create if it tapped into the mystery of the hidden soul. That was my prayer after every book. Did I hear that voice?

Did I hear mystery?

Tradition also dictated that in a few hours I would pack my research notes away, colour coded and referenced. In the morning I would then take the boxes to a storage unit and lock the door to another chapter of my life. After that, a train trip to Berwick-upon-Tweed. The Northumberland coastal town was a hideaway for me. Two days of rest, walking along the shore with a bag of fish and chips. No writing, just reading and catching up on podcasts. I would stay in the same hotel. It was an odd place, caught in a time loop between the 1970s and '80s. But I loved it. It felt homely and reminded me of my parents.

These routines were important.

And they were important enough to break today.

It had taken me a year to get to this point.

Over the months, I filled in the majority of missing gaps that happened during, and post, The Theatre. At first, all I could remember was a burning building and the vague recollection of someone pulling me outside. Next, I was back in London, waking up on the path outside The London Library. I was alone. The date and time hadn't changed. It was as if I hadn't left the city. But I had. In my pocket was the chosen card: the destiny of *Ignorance* and *Selfish Want*.

The card wasn't the only thing I had brought back from PARADOX. London had changed, although on the surface it was all the same. That night, walking home, I couldn't explain the uncomfortable feeling inside. It took another month to find the right words. '*You can't shut out the world.... You are in it.... You get yourself into a false position the moment you try to sever yourself from it.'* Beyond understanding, I couldn't sever myself from what I passed by every day. Whether it was an article I read, something I saw on TV, a visit to the shops or an individual walking by – the spreadsheet of life wouldn't leave my sight. I felt connected to the world.

And I hated it.

Eki tracked me down during the second month. I never asked her how she found out where I was living. Somewhere in the back of my mind I was expecting her visit. We played quid-pro-quo. I shared some of my story, she revealed hers. It was an informal counselling session for both of us as we tried to piece together our fragmented memories. But behind her questions,

I could tell Eki had an ulterior motive, as though she was testing me. There was nothing random with her encouragement to share what was in my head.

My soul.

It was during her fourth visit that she asked the question, “And the sound?” To any onlooker, it would be a one-way ticket into the asylum. My response indicated that I was already there. The Applause was everywhere. Faint. In the background. But ever-present. In the shops. At a restaurant. On the phone. In my sleep. I couldn’t shake off the rumble of people clapping.

“People clapping?”

I had never thought about that point until her follow-up question asked for clarification. Eki was right. It wasn’t the sound of people clapping. Just one person.

Me.

I had woken up to the illusion.

That conversation changed the next ten months.

We met every week after that, slowly hatching a plan. Some of our meetings didn’t always feel truthful. There was an unspoken tension, especially from her. I had an unpleasant sense that Eki was taking orders from someone. But I didn’t ask. It felt like opening up a Mystery Box. Answers would come in a different way.

And now it was twelve months to the day that I had returned from PARADOX.

The first part of our plan was complete: my book. It wasn’t what I had expected to write. The story had a life of its own, sometimes demanding blood and sweat to follow its trail. I didn’t want to see, remember, everything it happily revealed, but I knew it was important to follow the ink’s Path. Because of watching eyes in the shadows, I wrote in secret. To keep up appearances that everything was OK, I also penned a second book. The one I should have written coming back from PARADOX. That book was predictable, a potential bestseller. I had seen its storyline play across the cards during that horrific night at The Theatre. It was one of the rewards of choosing a life of selfish ignorance; a page-turner that swung the spreadsheet in my favour. And now that the second book had served its purpose, it was time to destroy the manuscript. I didn't want the temptation of running into its welcoming arms. Success has a way of doing that. Pulling the box file from the desk drawer was harder than I was expecting. Even with everything I had pieced together over the last year, I still had *That* desire – the desire to choose the same card over and over again.

My phone rang. It was my sixty-minute warning. Eki was on her way. She asked if I had destroyed the book. My assurance that the task was in hand didn't sit well with her. She had assumed I had already done it.

Trust was fragile, both ways.

*****

I looked at the wall clock.

Thirty minutes left. There was still time to write the letter. I took a moment, sitting at my desk. Before I committed pen to paper, I wanted to savour these few seconds. This would be the last time I would be sitting here. Regardless of whatever happened tonight, I wouldn't be returning to this desk. What more fitting way to end a chapter of my life than to write a letter. My mother would be proud. All Paths do lead back to the scallop shell beginning.

There were still questions unanswered. The one foremost in my mind was also the one that had plagued me for the whole year. Why could I still remember my journey into PARADOX? The rules stated that memories fade. But things had become clearer as weeks turned into months. I had a hunch why this was happening. So too did Eki. We based our plan on that belief, and now it was time to see if it was right.

The intercom buzzed. Eki had arrived. I scribbled out the last line then laid the letter on top of the book. Traditions should never set themselves in stone. It is the very journey itself that shapes practice, and only when one walks that Path does the heart realise that the pilgrimage is ever-changing. And so, today, this manuscript would not sit on my desk, untouched, for seven days. In the next hour, I would give it to someone.

And then?

I walked to the intercom and pressed the door release.

The Theatre.

I hadn't destroyed it. My heart could still feel its presence inside me. I had to admit, its show was impressive. If it weren't for the lingering sound of The Applause I would have believed the building was in ruins. But that was all part of its show. The Sicilian Defence, taken to a new level. Fake your defeat.

There was only one way to end its twisted performance. As long as I believed its treasures of selfish ignorance were real, I would continually live in its make-believe world. I needed to call its show for what it was. An illusion. And what better way to acknowledge what's on the stage than to applaud it.

The Theatre was my heart; it's stage, the daily interactions of my life. Strange to think that what I considered real was just a clever sleight-of-hand. To applaud its illusion, I needed to live a different way. It wouldn't be easy. So much of my identity in life had bought into the con. But that was how The Theatre would fall. With a slow and steady hand-clap for the star of its show.

Me.

CHAPTER 66
THE APPLE SEED

"Grown-ups are always thinking of uninteresting explanations."
(C.S. Lewis, The Magician's Nephew)

"AM I LATE?"

Eki bypassed the usual form of greeting as she pushed by, heading straight for the kitchen. She still preferred being homeless but liked having constant access to a stocked-up fridge and warm shower. I understood why she wanted to remain on the streets. It was the same reason I wrote the second book – to keep up appearances. Homelessness went with her story of lost hope. The Magician's spies would suspect something if her life changed course. There was also another reason for her pavement home, although she never spoke of it. Just like my need to destroy the temptation of the destined book, we were not as strong as we wished we were.

"But she's late."

Her follow up observation had a hint of impatience to it. She was on a schedule, which surprised me. Eki hated living by the watch. Opening a tub of yoghurt she walked over to my desk. Her full spoon acted as a pointer device, taking aim over the secret book.

"Is that it?"

"Yes."

"And that one? I thought you were going to destroy it."

Eki pointed to the box file on the floor.

"I will, but not here."

She silently dug into the yoghurt again as she crashed down in the middle of the sofa. I could tell from the way she avoided eye-contact that she had doubts I would go through with it. If I were in her position, I would question my commitment as well. The track record wasn't great. But something had changed.

Santiago.

I rummaged in my pocket, checking they were still there – apple seeds. For the last few days, I had been carrying them around with me, a secret reminder to believe in the possibility of new beginnings. I didn't want to tell anyone, vocalising it would have sounded mad. This was between myself and the inner child that had long been forgotten. A plastic bell with a magical ring, version two. Instead of looking for a funfair, I had delved back into the books of Narnia. My childlike eyes soaked in the excitement of ships, wardrobes and mythical creatures. And weaving it all together, a whisper from a storyteller telling the reader that the tale is never over.

When Professor Kirke was neither a professor nor an adult, he entered Narnia. In the *'wood between the worlds',* he met the fierce but also gentle Aslan. Together they gazed upon a reality beyond human understanding. When Kirke was about to leave, Aslan presented him with a gift: an apple from one of the magical trees. Back home, the boy planted its seeds in the garden. Over time it grew. Then one day a storm hit the town and blew the tree down. In any other story, that would be the end. But Kirke used some of the fallen wood to make a wardrobe. Years later, Lucy stumbled through that doorway whilst visiting the professor during the Blitz. The story lived on, even though human hands wrote 'the end'.

My story should have ended at The Theatre. The decision to choose selfish ignorance had set the course for the rest of my days. And then Santiago happened. He sacrificed himself so that I could have another chance. The ultimate gift. Love's demand. Apple seeds.

Planted in my heart.

Was it possible? Could I really fashion a wardrobe to get back to The Theatre?

The only way to answer was through mystery.

*****

The intercom buzzed.

I pressed the door release and then waited for our guest. Even so, the knock on the apartment door made us both jump. Tshilaba walked in without even a greeting. She was here for one thing: my book, the one written in secret. It detailed everything about my journey in PARADOX and what this last year was about to lead to. It was Eki's idea to bring her into our plan. We needed someone to slip away with the book unnoticed. She would place it in The London Library, hidden with all the manuscripts in the room by the dial. There was no guarantee someone would see it, but that's what mystery was all about. Trust.

"Is this the one?"

With a single nod of the head, I broke my sacred tradition. She picked up the manuscript and letter, then carefully placed them in her bag. Any sense of a holy moment was rudely disrupted with the sound of Eki clambering to her feet.

"Wait. We'd better check you weren't followed."

"I wasn't."

The suggestion of carelessness annoyed Tshilaba. A nervous smile stretched across Eki's face, leaving with it a restless atmosphere in the room. She was hiding something, but it was too late to ask. Eki had already walked outside to check.

*****

Dora sat outside Abrahams' apartment block.

She reached into her bag and picked up a flask of homemade lemonade. There was nothing like the real thing. After offering some to her guest, She took a sip, all the time thinking through the upcoming moves on the board.

E2 to E4. Sit in an open space so that The Magician's spies would notice who was next to her.

Black's response, C7 to C5. The traders would then report back.

G1 to F3. Signal intent. Tshilaba will hide the book in the library.

D7 to D6. The penny drops for The Magician, realising that there are two books.

And then the invitation for weakness. D4 to D6. A move that supposedly puts her game on the back foot. Dora looks over to her guest.

"Are you ready for this?"

Pevensie stood up, making sure hidden eyes noted his presence.

Clever.

Theatrical.

And bloody imperious.

It was rare for The Magician to be a man of few words, but tonight was one of them. He couldn't decide if the moves provoked anger or admiration. Even with careful surveillance, his traders never picked up on the sleight-of-hand. It was impressive that Abrahams had kept up the pretence of writing the destined book. The detail the boy had gone into deserved an award. His selfish spending of money and deliberate ignorance of the pain of others had convinced The Magician all was fine. There wasn't even a visit to the graveyard, seeking forgiveness from the two he had sent there. But the boy couldn't have done all that on his own. Whether he realised or not, the hand behind those moves was Dora.

Bloody Dora.

And how did She get Tshilaba to turn on him? He had trusted that woman, giving her the one thing she desired above everything else. She wanted an end to the perpetual loop of being abused by people always wanting to open the Mystery Box. In return, her payment for freedom would be the messenger and his message. But she had played him. Pevensie was alive. Which meant his message was alive too.

The Twins.

He now needed to find those two kids. But wait. This was precisely what the old lady wanted him to do – respond without thinking. The Magician played through the moves again. Tshilaba would be at the apartment for one thing. The book written in secret. He smiled at the obvious choice of where she would take it. Flaw number one. The boy still believed in magic. That room was as outdated as the idea of trusting in the power of mystery. Nobody wants to stumble into their future anymore. The hip-thing is to be purpose-driven.

And what about the destined book? Knowing Abrahams, he would want to destroy it in a meaningful way. That was flaw number two. He should have destroyed it while he had a chance. Prolonging temptation meant one thing – there was still hope.

Flaw three from Abrahams was trusting in the wrong people. Eki was desperate to get back to PARADOX, no matter the cost.

CHAPTER 67
ALL GOOD PLANS

"I do not kill with my gun; he who kills with his gun has forgotten the face of his father.
I kill with my heart."
(Stephen King, The Gunslinger)

TSHILABA *couldn't wait any longer.*

Eki hadn't returned, and she had a feeling the woman was never going to. There were no goodbyes to Abrahams as she left the apartment. She wasn't doing this for him. Her phone rang just as she reached the lift. She recognised the number. The Magician. On the fourth ring, she answered.

"Thought you wouldn't pick up."

"And why would that be?"

"Because you would be afraid of what I would do to you."

"You can't do anything to me now."

There was a pause on the line. The chime of the lift rang out.

"Is that a bell I hear?"

The lift doors opened.

"What of it?"

Tshilaba stepped inside.

"Just saying. Whenever there are chimes, there is usually a lesson. You never know what it..."

The line cut off as the lift doors shut.

There was something in The Magician's tone that made her uncomfortable. She played out his conversation again as the lift indicators slowly blinked before her eyes. Floor Six. Five. He knew something. Sort of. An educated guess. What was she missing?

Four. Three.

Eki. It had to be. But she would never side with him. He ruined her life.

Unless.

The lift juddered as it stopped at Floor Two. She frantically kept pressing the Ground Floor button, but the doors opened. On the other side was a familiar face. Tshilaba looked down at the glistening knife.

"Give me the book."

"You?"

"Give me the book."

"Why are you doing this?"

There were many possible reasons, but only one mattered today.

*****

Dora had no idea how this move would play out.

It was a gamble drawing Eki into her plan. She was the one who had told her the apartment address, encouraging the woman to help Abrahams get back to PARADOX. Such a selfless act would always bring temptation. Eki's Path had long closed, but that wouldn't stop her from trying again. From the bench, Dora watched Eki rush out from the building, holding Tshilaba's bag. Another storyline had just been written. There were no guarantees where it would lead to. And the sense of the unknown was excruciating.

Even for her.

Dora found Tshilaba sitting on the wall outside the apartment block. Shaken, but OK. She didn't need prompting to talk about what had happened, but her detailed account wasn't detailed enough. Dora pressed for the minutest of information, wanting to hear about facial expressions, the look in the eyes, the shake of the hands. It was the last thing Tshilaba expected.

"You. Of all people. Why?"

Dora's face went ghostly white, resisting the urge to defend. Even the myth of a grand storyteller has its flaws. There was a reason why She had placed the unknown note in the Box all those years ago. The audience thought it was a clever trick or profound statement concerning humanity. But it was always something more. The Mystery Box was a reminder to Dora: no one is immune from the temptation. If She stopped believing in mystery, her stories would come to an end.

"I'm sorry."

But her words fell on deaf ears. Tshilaba was already walking away. Dora considered following, then held back. Their friendship demanded more than a few scrapped seconds to deliver rushed words. They had a lot to talk about.

A lot to cry over and find healing.

*****

I picked up the phone and called Eki.

Two attempts with no answer. As I tried for a third time, the apartment door slammed behind me. Under my arm, the box file. In my pocket, the apartment keys to hand back to the Estate Agents. It was my final day of the rental agreement. Tomorrow, everything would be in storage.

It felt disruptive to my safe world, leaving the apartment. This place had so much of my history wrapped up in it. There was a day when I considered it to be the marker of success and a way of proving my love to Terri. But behind those hopes was just selfish want. I exited the building via the back door; 'The Poor Door'. It seemed fitting walking out of this complex through the very thing I had always tried to avoid.

My walk took me via Doughty Street. There had been many times I had accidentally on purpose got lost at the home of Charles Dickens. Occasionally I would go inside the museum. Most times, I just stood outside and thought about the magic of imagination soaked into its bricks. It was here that Dickens had written *Oliver Twist*, a story that changed society's view of child labour. Those pages brought the horrors of the hidden workhouse system into every comfortable living room. Number 48 Doughty Street was a pilgrim's monument to how stories could change the world.

And tonight I needed to believe in that magic again.

The chime from a nearby church tower told me it was time to move on. My destination was a nearby cemetery.

A grave was waiting for me.

*****

Eki looked at her phone.

Three missed calls. Ignored calls. She wanted to speak to Abrahams but struggled to find any words. How could she adequately express the turmoil ravaging her soul? Ever since the first day of the plan, Eki knew she would steal the book. There was no way she would let such a story linger in some unseen, dusty room. That manuscript was her bargaining chip to The Magician, a way of getting back to PARADOX to save her family. "Let me in, or I tell the world about The Theatre." It sounded great in her head, but right now, the only thing she could hear was silence. What if He didn't care if the story got out?

Then what?

Her original intention was to head to The Seven Dials. The Magician would know where to find her. But three steps into her journey, Eki turned around. She needed a backup plan. Abrahams' box file. The Theatre had prophesied that book would bring enough riches to craft a new life. If Abrahams wasn't going to walk into that destiny, then she could. With the royalties, maybe she could buy her way back into PARADOX through good deeds and charitable donations.

Save the book, save her family.

A cemetery called.

CHAPTER 68
WITNESS

"Face your life, its pain, its pleasure, leave no path untaken."
(Neil Gaiman, The Graveyard Book)

"HE HASN'T ARRIVED."

The young girl walked out from the shadows to greet Pevensie.

"He will."

The messenger put his arm around the girl's shoulder and instantly felt the coldness of her skin. The disease of selfish ignorance had marched unmercifully through her weak body. Back in PARADOX, The Guide would have taken care of the children. But over the last twelve months, things had changed. Their carer had disappeared and The Twins were getting worse. It was now up to Pevensie to soothe their pain and it felt like a losing battle. The children were dying. He looked around for the boy.

"Behind the tree. He wants no one to see him."

She spoke softly about her brother. Each gentle word revealed her pain in seeing a loved one in such agony. It broke Pevensie's heart to hear her trembling voice. He hated that the children were here. Their bodies weren't up to facing the cold winds of emotional distress. Even though he assured the girl that Abrahams would come, there were no guarantees.

No guarantees.

That had been the story of the last twelve months.

When Abrahams tracked him down after returning from PARADOX, he didn't initially believe in the broken words and repentant heart. At that time, the traveller's plan was in the early stages of disjointed ideas and vague hope. But underneath it all lingered the possibility that the story wasn't over, just yet. One final twist. Before the end.

As the weeks turned into months, Pevensie shared his regular reports back to Dora who unsurprisingly already knew most of the details. But just like everyone else, mystery of the unknown still laid its claim to the final act. And it was the reason why he was protective over The Twins being here. Abrahams insisted they should be at the grave. But what if the traveller didn't go through with it? How would their fragile hearts cope? They wouldn't. And that's what Pevensie hated most of all.

The young girl turned her head towards the entrance.

"He's here."

A wave of relief hit Pevensie. The final act had begun.

But there were no guarantees.

*****

I placed my apple seeds on top of the entrance pillar.

A short prayer followed. Nothing profound. Just a reminder that all Paths lead back to the beginning. It had taken me a while to figure out what my mother eluded to when she gave me that scallop shell. Every journey starts with the same thing. And thanks to Santiago, I finally understood.

I took my time walking down the cobbled track of the cemetery. The flashlight on my phone guided the way. I took the second right, then counted the gravestones. They were the fourth and fifth on the left.

Terri. Natasha.

Finding their graves was one of the first things I had done after returning from PARADOX. Every Monday, for twelve months, I visited their plot, making sure no one saw me. In death's silence, I would clear the weeds and bring fresh flowers. My tears broke up the hard ground in my heart. I would tell Terri about how I had failed to live up to her hopes. In her peaceful oasis home, she believed in me. And yet, when it mattered, the only card I chose was the very image that had sentenced them to death. Through quivering lips, I promised her I could and would change. *'The chain I forged in life... I made it link by link, and yard by yard; I girded it on of my own free will, and of my own free will I wore it.'*

Chains could break and tonight was the night I would keep that promise.

I bent down and cleared the fallen leaves around their graves. A final act of respectful liturgy. The plot of ground next to their resting place was still untouched. It was by an old tree whose overstretched branches had made the spot feel forgotten. Maybe that's why no one ever used it to remember their loved ones. It had one of those unspoken titles over it. 'Paupers Grave.' A perfect spot for what I needed to do.

As my hands clawed into the dirt, I caught sight of a shadow, then two, three, next to the tree. Pevensie had kept his promise. He had brought The Twins.

The Magician stopped outside the cemetery.

A hunch brought him here. Seeing the apple seeds confirmed He was in the right place. His fingers crushed the magical pips, sending a tingle of satisfaction across his skin. Ironically, for someone who earned a living from illusion shows, He hated anything to do with magic. Particularly storytelling magic. It was the worst kind because it gave people hope. False hope. Sooner or later, Abrahams would come to his senses. He would never destroy the book. No one throws away a golden future for the sake of love – love for people they don't even know.

He was about to walk inside when the shadows caught his eye. Three by the tree. And one on the other side of the cemetery. Seeing Pevensie and The Twins there wasn't a surprise. It made sense, Abrahams wanting them to witness his feeble attempt at an apology. But Eki's presence was of great interest. Maybe He didn't need to save the book after all. Eki would do the dirty work for him.

Whatever the outcome, The Theatre's destiny for Abrahams was safe.

I stood over the empty grave.

Scrooge had The Ghost of Christmas Future to witness the end of his journey. For my journey's end, I had a crowd of witnesses. The neighbouring graves of Terri and Natasha were from my past; the present were the three shadows watching by the tree. As for my future, its welcoming gift was a layer of damp soil and broken roots. A fitting home for a man with broken feet.

In the Christmas tale, Scrooge begged for another chance. When the cruel businessman saw the emptiness of his death, it revealed his selfish heart on The Theatre's stage. Applauding the illusion brought him into the light. It was tempting to do the same. *'I will be a better man ... give to the poor ... buy a Christmas feast for every Bob Cratchit.'* But that would only cause more pain for The Twins. I had chosen selfish ignorance too many times. The only way to stop its evil curse hurting others was to place my life in its dirty grave.

Love's demand.

The start of every Path.

CHAPTER 69
FINAL ACT

"Love is our true destiny. We do not find the meaning of life by ourselves alone – we find it with another."
(Thomas Merton, Love and Living)

THE DEALER always wins.

That's what Trott once told me. I reached into my pocket and pulled out the card from The Theatre. With an outstretched arm, I dangled it over the grave then watched it gently float down onto the watery base. I expected the moment to be more dramatic than it was.

The book was harder to let go of. Laying this into the grave meant I was sealing up any chance of ever looking into the Mystery Box again. The golden future of success that was set before me would evaporate. In its place, a decision to walk the same Path Santiago demonstrated on *That* stage – selflessness. Love demanded that I gave up control of my life, not knowing what tomorrow would bring. It was the ultimate mystery.

The ultimate Mystery Box.

My book landed in the hole with a dull thud. Right on cue, the wind picked up, creating a little vortex inside the grave. Loose dirt and paper swirled around, and in the middle, my chosen card. I watched as it played out every bit of my future I was throwing away. It was as if The Theatre was giving me one last chance to change my mind. The card exploded with colour, a visual firework of every good thing this destiny would bring. Forget the book sales, the fancy apartment or the end to money worries – The Theatre's future did something nothing else could achieve. In front of my eyes the card revealed the true and raw brokenness of my life. If I destroyed the book, no matter how hard I tried to live for others, selfishness would always be a part of me. I could never defeat it. Neither would I ever want to. And in the years to come, living in a cold house with heating bills to pay, I would regret the night when I threw away my dream for the sake of an illusion. The card was right. I wasn't strong enough. My feet shuffled towards the edge. All the paper was still in the grave. My future could be salvaged.

"I'm sorry."

The cry wasn't for redemption, but forgiveness. My eyes of red shame focused on the two young children, shivering in the icy wind. The cancerous touch from my selfish heart had infected every part of their lives. I had brought them here to soothe their pain, thinking I was strong enough to turn my back on everything I had dreamed of. But I wasn't. Even though I knew my future was just an illusion, the price to applaud the show was too much.

Pevensie pulled The Twins towards him as they wailed the sounds of broken hearts. The young boy fell through the grip, collapsing into a heap of lost hope. In that crumpled body were the dreams of once more playing by the Magical Tree. The young girl followed, forming a protective shell over his shaking fleshy form. She too felt her world ripped apart by the only future coming their way. The Pillar would be their resting place, where the children would slowly die. On the bench, the echo of my selfish heart, watching from a distance.

The tug of the grave told me to jump in and save the book. With open arms I stretched out into the vortex. Loose papers banged against my skin. I could feel the warmth of my future drawing me into its safe embrace. The cover page landed on my hand, followed by the first chapter. It was all coming back to me.

"NO!"

I screamed out, my conscience twisting and turning in decision's grip. But the agony of knowing I wasn't able to do this on my own tore my heart in two. The chains of selfish ignorance would never be broken, no matter how hard I wanted them to.

"But we can break them together."

*****

Eki never questioned why she ran through the cemetery.

Pulling Abrahams back from the grave felt the most natural thing to do.

The sudden drop in the wind told her that the card's temptation had finally ended. Future's ink on every page had smudged into a messy blur of the unknown. She cradled Abrahams into her chest. Two pairs of hands joined in with the caring embrace. The young boy's skin looked different. A few less scabs. And the girl's face had a faint hint of colour. The Twins smiled at her. Eki had the strangest memory of taking care of them. It felt a long time ago.

She pulled away, leaving the three of them in their embrace. One more look into the grave. It wasn't just Abrahams' future that had smudged into an unknown blur. Why did she do it – throw away everything she had worked for, to help someone else? Out of nowhere, a gentle gust of wind picked up a water-soaked piece of paper and lifted it into the air. She watched it dance around the edge of the grave before soaring high into the night sky. Even when the wind dropped off, the paper continued to fly. Out of the cemetery. Over the streets. Heading for the Seven Dials.

Eki quietly walked back to where she had dropped the bag. She thought about her PARADOX journey many years ago when she tried to secure her family's future through profit and loss. The rewards were great, but only if the family agreed to clip their wings. Even when she tried to set them free, she fought that battle on her own. During this last year, planning to get back to PARADOX, she had repeated the same mistake that first caused her family pain. Selfishness can take many forms.

And yet.

She picked up the bag and checked Abrahams' book was OK. What just happened at the grave told a different story. Love's demand. She had laid down her own future to save another life, and now her journey to the Seven Dials felt different.

She would soar in the air once more.

Not alone.

With her family.

Maybe not today.

Soon.

The Magician looked down at the crushed apple seeds scattered across the ground.

Maybe the old lady was right about stories having more than two sides.

It surprised him that She hadn't come to watch the whole thing. But then again, no doubt her devious mind was already on the next move. Abrahams' story may have finished, but it hadn't come to an end. Another side of its tale would play out. It would take a lifetime for The Twins to heal. And there were no guarantees. Plenty of opportunities for that book to reappear in a different form.

Usually, the opportunity for a rematch would thrill his soul, but not tonight. His stretched out smile was as fake as a show on The Theatre's stage. He had witnessed a Change Agent on the board. And frustratingly, it had been there all the time. The Storyteller's and Magician's game didn't have many chess rules. And the ones they did agree on often adapted over time. But there was one rule that never changed. It was there at the start, and it would be there when the victor claimed their prize.

'The only hand that could move the pieces were the pieces themselves.'

That suited The Magician. The game leaned towards self-preservation; people would always put themselves before others. What He never considered was the board itself. Within those squares lay a storyline; a subtle, mundane tale about connection. It was an illusion for a person to think their solitary piece could win the game. The truth was that their futures were entwined together in the mysterious web of love's demand. Only when someone moves their piece for the sake of another, do they finally get to…

"See the whole board."

The fake smile disappeared, along with the seeds taken by the breeze. Above his head, a sheet of paper flew across the sky. He watched it weave gracefully towards a rendezvous with an old story. Caught within the whispers of the wind, another side to its tale could just be made out.

No longer did a solitary traveller walk along the Paths.

CHAPTER 70
ANOTHER CONFESSION

"Never say goodbye because goodbye means going away and going away means forgetting."
(J.M. Barrie, Peter Pan)

I USED TO THINK love was the loneliest Path to walk, because there were only one set of footprints in the dirt.

Mystery taught me otherwise.

The marks on the trail are not from my own feet, but the crowd of witnesses carrying me when I was weak.

It's hard to recount what happened at the cemetery. After Eki left, I sat at the edge of an empty grave, feeling invisible arms wrapped around my cold body. My heart felt their warmth, even though there was no sign of The Twins. Logic told me I had imagined the whole thing, but it never counted on the grave being by a tree. A magical tree, where the adult runs into the welcoming arms of a child and learns how to see the world again.

Words fell short to describe what it meant to destroy the book. My action wasn't about a determination to become poor or to live a saintly life that would have made Francis of Assisi humbly proud. A person can adjust the spreadsheet of life in a stranger's favour, even with a healthy bank balance. It was about loving one another with eyes wide open. And yet, even that description felt weak. At the grave I understood that the chains I forge during my days are connected to both stranger and friend. Every bit of my existence is not my own, including the decision to applaud the show. I needed help.

We all need help.

And that's why I packed my bags the following day.

I received a phone call. It was Eki, from a phone box. She didn't say where, and purposely avoided giving me the chance to ask. On a crackling line, she told me she was going on a journey, but wanted to let me know the book was safe. It wasn't at The London Library. Somewhere better. In keeping with the story. Before I could ask where she had left it, Eki hung up. I called back. No answer. I called again. A stranger answered. We chatted briefly. They told me that a storytelling busker had mentioned that they should answer the public phone. When stepping inside, they noticed someone had left a manuscript. I asked if there was a letter with it. Surprised that I knew, they read it out.

'Dear traveller,

I cannot begin to describe the journey about to take place. Its kaleidoscope of imagination will open your eyes to a world beyond sight. There will be days when you will be tempted not to believe, but in those fragile moments, look to your left and right. You are not alone.

There is no such thing as a stranger on these Paths.'

The person asked for my name. I ended the call. Questions would lead to answers. Spoilers. I flung the bag over my shoulder and headed out of the room. If Eki was here, I would have thanked her for leaving the book in the perfect spot – a place where a stranger becomes a friend. But I didn't mind. I would get a chance to share my thanks.

We had a rendezvous.

Somewhere. Somehow.

There was a family to find.

EPILOGUE

"Scrooge was better than his word. He did it all, and infinitely more; and to Tiny Tim, who did not die, he was a second father. He became as good a friend, as good a master, and as good a man, as the good old city knew, or any other good old city, town, or borough, in the good old world."
(Charles Dickens, A Christmas Carol)

DICKENS *stepped out of the theatre.*

The Twins at his side. Behind them, the sound of applause. The audience was on their feet. His reading of A Christmas Carol had surpassed all expectations. He felt a tug on his arm. The young girl suggested it was time to head home. She was aware that the cold weather wouldn't help his fragile state. Dickens gently smiled as he looked into her compassionate eyes. It was astounding that someone who had felt the cruelty of humanity's heart carried such love. He told them to wait back at his house. Dickens had one more place to visit, and he needed to do it alone.

Finding the cemetery was easy. But locating the spot where everything had changed for him, proved a challenge. The blanket of crooked headstones and overgrown weeds confused the memories. He had a vague recollection of a tree, somewhere near the back. What clouded his memory was the vibrant blossom of life stretched out like greeting arms. Wasn't the tree dead when he dug the grave all those years ago?

He counted out his steps then stood on the hard ground. Many years had passed since that day. The wounds hadn't closed, neither had the scars healed. But the illusion did end. Mercifully. He breathed in the cold air.

EPILOGUE

The lingering stench of the city's dark alleyways twisted his stomach with cramp. Although the pain was intense, he never begged for it to ease off. The odour of injustice convinced his fragile body he was still alive. Applauding. Willing to choose a card other than selfish want.

Scrooge was more than just a character that had arrived in his mind that night by the grave. His lost journal that the old lady had left for him had opened the door back into PARADOX. A Christmas Carol became a living story for him. Scrooge was Dickens. Dickens was Scrooge.

"Scrooge is each one of us. And each one of us is Scrooge."

He whispered the redemptive words. Everyone was a by-product of their decisions, and that's why The Theatre would never win. As long as Scrooge could become a loving parent to the stranger that was Tiny Tim, the dealer would always win with love.

"So God bless us, each and every one."

Dickens gingerly turned around. It was good to see The Storyteller again. She hooked her arm under his. He welcomed the support.

"I always love saying that line."

He nodded. It was his favourite too.

"Is it time?"

She shook her head.

"Soon."

Dickens was looking forward to seeing her cabin again. Every visit was special, but this approaching one carried the uniqueness of being his last. In the distance, the church bell chimed its hourly call. Within the fog and sulphur, the sound carried the tones of a teasing mystery. He didn't ask the question lingering on his lips; that would be like opening up the box. But he still wondered why the chime sounded so clear when his story was about to come to an end. The old lady's hand moved over his. He had felt this way before – thinking he had written his final chapter. But the end is the never the end. There is always another side to the story.

Maybe his final visit to her cabin would open up a new adventure.

He liked that thought as they headed out of the cemetery into the unknown.

THE END